D0642842

Veneer

Andrew Spencer

PublishAmerica
Baltimore

First printing

At the specific preference of the author, PublishAmerica allowed this work to remain exactly as the author intended, verbatim, without editorial input.

ISBN: 1-4137-7848-8
PUBLISHED BY PUBLISHAMERICA, LLLP
www.publishamerica.com
Baltimore

Printed in the United States of America

For Arnold Willcox,
who always said there was
something different about fourth babies.

ACKNOWLEDGEMENTS

As a graduate student, I was once mentioned as an acknowledgement in a book. It was quite possibly the single most anticlimactic experience of my life to that point.

I had put in several hundred hours of work to verify facts and piece together a jumbled mess of a manuscript—a biography of Elizabeth Barrett Browning—and I was merely one entry in a lengthy list of recipients of the author's gratitude. The only semblance of an ego boost I got from the whole thing was the fact that I was mentioned before the British Museum. It wasn't much, but I took some solace in that.

The reason for my tepid enthusiasm stemmed from the fact that words printed on a page didn't convey the thanks I thought I deserved. Names in a list didn't express the overwhelming sense of gratitude that I thought I was owed. That said, I hope these people know how truly grateful I am that they have been a part of my life. This project has been a lengthy labor and they all had a hand in it, whether they know it or not. Words on a page can't convey my level of gratitude.

My family has always supported me, no matter what damn-fool mission I set out on, this project being one at the forefront of my own mind. It's easy to brag about the kids when they're out taking the world by storm and bringing it to its knees. It's a little harder to brag about the one who packs it all in to move to an island in yet another seemingly random life choice. They still find a way, though. God—and I—love them for it.

Bill and Lucille Clarkson, my surrogate parents from the time I was at boarding school, have been everything from therapists to fishing guides. I think I owe you guys a real cake one of these days.

Former teachers—J.J. Connolly and John Allman from St. Mark's, Ted Blain and Richard Barnhardt from Woodberry Forest, Don Graham from the University of Texas. You were the teachers I wanted to be, but found myself sorely lacking. From now on, I'll leave the teaching to you.

Perhaps most importantly, the Nantucketers—natives, washashores, tourists, summer people, whatever. I owe you all. Most notably, Scott and Peter and Debba from the Rose and Crown; Phil and the gang at the Sunken Ship and P&P Salvage; Bill, Fifi, Jenny, Tom, Bruce, Biff and Lynda from N Magazine; Kirk from the Jared Coffin House. Nantucket, especially in the summer, is very much a community of transients who often remain anonymous. Seasonal workers, visitors and others—despite their anonymity—all contribute to the island's dynamic in one way or another. To the anonymous ones I say thank you and keep coming back.

Tops on the list of Nantucket folks are Jill and Jesse, who put up with me and support me more than anyone could expect, yet still manage to care about me. Hopefully they'll continue putting up with me and caring just as much for a long time to come.

If you're reading this and feel miffed that I left your name off, don't worry. I haven't forgotten. Words don't do justice to what I owe you. And trust me when I say that seeing your name here isn't all it's cracked up to be. Come find me and I'll tell you in person.

Andrew Spencer
Nantucket, Massachusetts

"If you ask me what I came into this world to do,
I will tell you that I came to live out loud."
—Emile Zola

CHAPTER ONE

Outside, the fog had unceremoniously announced its presence, not on little cat's feet, but rather with a dull sort of thud. It was as if a switch had been thrown and suddenly the entire island was shrouded in grey. Jack Carlisle hated the fog. It always made him feel uneasy for some reason and tonight was no exception. Perhaps it was the cold or perhaps it was just the fact that fog so often disrupted his travel plans when he came out to Nantucket. Getting here was always an adventure, as your flight might be cancelled or diverted due to fog, and the ferry might not run because of high winds. Over the years, Jack had found himself stranded overnight in Boston, New York and Hyannis, and more often than not that situation was due to fog-related problems. He stood at the bar nursing his beer. The bartender had announced last call, and the few remaining patrons were calling in their orders.

Glancing around the bar, Jack saw the regulars whom he knew by sight and with whom he spoke often but by whom he knew he would never truly be accepted. He was not one of them and they did not invite him in to their world. Jack was a member of that fraternity the natives called "Summer Scum," the wealthy summer residents who maintained second homes on the island, houses that were rarely occupied before June or after September. Jack, though, was different. He insisted on coming up to the island early in the summer just after school let out. He rebuffed, to a degree, the wealthy stereotypes and preferred instead the company of those men and women who lived and worked on the island, most of them year-round. Jack worked as a waiter every summer at the same restaurant—the Collins House Hotel— where he made fairly decent money from the tips left by the wealthy patrons. However, for Jack, money was not so much of an issue, because his parents owned a home on the island, so he was in the enviable position, from the perspective of other college students on the island for the season, of not having to worry about paying rent.

Looking at him, one was immediately struck by Jack's appearance. Standing almost six feet tall and fairly thin, he was the sort of person you always noticed, even in a crowded room. Tonight he was dressed in pleated khaki pants and a button-down oxford shirt, with a sweatshirt from his former prep school to ward off the early summer chill. He kept his blonde hair cut short and his face was strikingly attractive. He possessed the sort of Ralph Lauren-esque, rugged appearance women found attractive, slightly tanned, with just enough stubble on his chin to indicate the fact that he was older than he might appear at first glance. He had a sort of all-American appearance, with a distant look in his blue eyes; his mother used to joke with him as a child that he could have been a Norman Rockwell painting.

Jack sipped his beer, studying the amber liquid in the glass. It was local beer, more expensive than the standard bottles, but he liked the taste of it, and he usually ordered it with a lemon in it to give it a little more flavor. When asked why he put lemon in his beer, he usually sarcastically replied that it made him seem more eccentric and therefore that much more desirable. The truth of it, though, was that he simply preferred the way the beer tasted with lemon in it. As Jack looked around the bar, he again noticed the scattered groups of people who lived on Nantucket year-round. Though he was sociable enough with his parents' friends over at the Harbor Club, he would much rather share the company of the Nantucket locals. For some reason he envied them, as they seemed to be privy to a sort of existence that he could never have. In his own mind he saw these men and women as the soaring bald eagles of the world, while he was more like a canary in a very small cage. These people, though most of them would never be able to afford anything approaching the lifestyle to which Jack was accustomed, owned something his father's money couldn't buy. They owned a life in a place that he viewed as magical, a place he longed to live. Nantucket was the only place he felt truly comfortable; it was the only place where he could truly be himself. It was, he knew, a futile hope, but fantasies aren't supposed to be attainable.

The assorted drinkers at the bar that night were dressed in the same clothes they had spent the day working in—jeans stained with various elements of day labor. T-shirts were the garment of choice with these men, most displaying the company they worked for. Their conversations frequently crossed the bar, as people would shout back and forth across the bartender to tell stories or relive old times. The camaraderie these men shared with one another was amazing to Jack, and it further strengthened his feelings of envy of them. However he frequently had to remind himself that, again, he would never be one of them and would therefore never be initiated in to that camaraderie. That reminder filled Jack with a feeling of emptiness; *here is life in the margins,* Jack often told himself, *in the place where you want to be, but in the place where you aren't wanted.*

"I'm gone, Steph. I'm sure I'll see you tomorrow," Jack called to the bartender as he fished a ten dollar bill out of his wallet. He left the money on the bar for the bartender as he turned to leave.

"'Night, Jack. Thanks, honey," the bartender called to him as he walked out. "See you tomorrow." He exited the bar and turned right. Over his shoulder he could see the bar's sign. It was a replica of a British pub sign, rectangular and wooden, with the bar's name, The Jib and Jenny, painted in vibrant reds and greens. As he turned the corner, he saw the crowds gathering for late night ice cream at The Island Creamery. He thought about going in, but decided against it. The line was too long.

Christ, he thought to himself. *It's only May. I can't imagine what this place is going to look like come August.* He continued on through the fog and began to cross the street when he heard someone call out to him. The voice had a northeastern accent with a raspy quality. He didn't immediately recognize it as familiar, and Jack turned to see who it was. He couldn't make out the face in the fog, but he could see the figure of a man beckoning to him. He approached the veiled figure, walking down the alley, deeper into the fog. Then softly through the thickening mist came a muffled cry for help, but there was no one able to hear it. His cries were drowned out as the stranger put one of his huge hands over Jack's mouth and the other around his throat.

Shortly after the muffled cries were silenced, the sound of a truck's engine turning over thudded softly through the dark. Headlights cut through the cloud of fog that enveloped the area, and the rusty pickup rattled down the street past the steamship wharf. The driver turned right and headed past the Harbor Club and past the Ocean View Hotel, then stopped briefly at a stop sign before turning again. The stranger turned on to a side street and parked the truck in front of a children's swing set at the edge of a playground. He cut the engine, removed a duffel bag and Jack's lifeless body from the cab of the truck, then headed for the dock at the end of the street. As the stranger struggled with the dead body, one of Jack's limp arms hanging around his bulging neck, a young honeymooning couple laughed softly.

"Looks like someone had a little too much to drink tonight," the young man said jokingly, indicating the stranger's unconscious companion.

"Yeah," the stranger replied. "He got pretty lit up over at the Jenny. I'm gonna take him out to his boat. He's got an old junker out there in the basin. Lives on it during the summer."

"Nice of you," replied the young man, who immediately returned his attention to his new wife, ignoring the gruff response. The stranger labored to carry Jack's dead body, stepping lightly in to a small boat tied to the dock. Once he had gotten in and gathered his belongings into the boat, he started the motor, untied the rope from the piling to which it had been attached, and slowly motored away from the dock, glancing over his shoulder to see if the young man was going to watch the proceedings any further. He was relieved to see the newlyweds locked in a kiss, paying no attention to the stranger.

"Fuckin' tourists," he muttered aloud as he steered the boat through the maze of buoys that pocked the harbor. Once out of the harbor, he turned the boat to the north, passing Brant Point. "Nothin' to see here, folks," he said over his shoulder to the Coast Guard station. "Just me and my buddy going out for a little night air. Maybe do a little striper fishin' while we're out there." He cackled softly at what he deemed a magnificent joke.

The boat skimmed along the calm water, further into the fog. The fog was his ally; it would keep him safe from detection. He had made this trip a thousand times before and he didn't need his sight to know where he was going. He just followed the compass bearing he knew so well, following the rocks of the eastern stone jetty that marked the boundary of the ferry channel into the harbor. When he came to the end of the jetty, he cut the engine, allowing the boat to drift aimlessly. There was no wind, only the current to move the boat gently, and the tide was running in, so that the boat was pulled gently away from the rocks and toward the beach. The stranger then set to his task. He opened the duffel bag, removed its contents and began the grisly job of destroying the evidence in the murder of Jack Carlisle.

When he had finished his work, he wrapped a mesh belt loaded with seventy pounds of lead weight around the body. He dropped Jack's corpse over the side, watching it fall rapidly from sight, sinking to the sandy bottom, where the fish would feast tonight. He glanced quickly down to the bottom of the boat. Two bloody hands, two equally bloody feet, and Jack's severed head sat in mute testimony of the young life that had ended so abruptly. The stranger took two large plastic bags from his duffel bag and put the bloody remnants inside one, tying it shut. He then put that bag into the other and tied it again. Finally, he put the doubled-up bags inside his duffel bag and zipped it shut.

He looked at the interior of the boat, the white surface now stained red with blood. "Helluva night, boys," he said softly as if recalling a night's fishing with friends over a six-pack. "Didn't get a striper, but I caught me a big damn dogfish. Cut the bastard from head to tail and bled him out, then threw it back over the side. Hate those damn things, but that's what I get for fishin' with eels, right?" He lit a cigarette, the glow from the tip illuminating his face in the fog. He spat at the water, the very thought of catching a sand shark being such a hideous prospect to him.

The stranger reached down and picked up the bucket he kept in the boat, filled it with sea water, and doused the deck. The blood mixed with the green ocean water and then gradually collected in a macabre pool towards the rear of the boat. The stranger took a large brush and scoured the boat's deck, scratching the blood off the floor. He repeated the process until most of the blood had been collected by the water, and he then reached behind him to remove the plugs from the stern. He started the boat and gunned the engine, watching behind him as the water flowed out the openings. When the bloody water had run out of the back, the stranger idled the engine and replaced the plugs. He then pushed the throttle forward and turned back towards the harbor, again relying on his compass to get him back safely. Once back in the harbor, the stranger tied up the boat at its mooring, rowed his dinghy to the small beach adjacent to the harbor, and walked silently to his truck, carrying the duffel bag at his side.

When the stranger eventually returned home to the small cottage he had built himself on land that was immediately next to the airport, his only roommate, the Australian shepherd he had found at the local animal shelter, was there to greet him. "This island's a better place tonight, Mutt," he said to the dog with a playful scratch of his ragged and torn ears. "I got me one of them summer bastards. They want to take my island from me and make me live like an animal. Not gonna' happen. No sir. I'll make 'em sorry they ever heard of this fuckin' island." The dog wagged its tail in approval and the stranger chuckled softly. He went to the kitchen and found an open bottle of whiskey, some of which he poured into a dirty glass that was sitting on the counter. He took the glass of brown liquor and sat down on a dingy, stained, yellow sofa in the small living room.

Sitting atop the crate that served as a coffee table in the cramped room was a small mirror and a rusty razor blade. The stranger looked at the mirror, hoping for some sort of unexpected windfall on his part, some kind of Heaven-sent oversight, but found nothing. He glanced at his watch. It was just after four in the morning. His head began to throb—restless natives pounding out their drumbeats in his brain. He went to the bathroom and rifled through the medicine cabinet. A plastic bottle full of light blue pills fell out and he greedily ripped off the cap. He took two of the small tablets from the bottle and washed them down with the whiskey that was left in the glass. Shortly he drifted off to sleep, the drumbeats fading into the fog outside. Tonight had been easier and gone smoother than he'd ever thought possible. He smiled knowingly. The hard part of this was done. All the worry had been for nothing. He felt a new-found freedom. All he wanted to do now was sleep, letting his Vicadin-laced blood flow through his veins, carrying him away on a river of carelessness. He'd take care of the rest of the job tomorrow.

CHAPTER TWO

Nantucket Island was by no means a scuba diver's paradise, and Peter Oswald made no apologies to those brave souls who paid his exorbitant fee to go diving while vacationing on the island. The standard morning trip was billed, somewhat erroneously, as a lobster dive, during which divers were allowed to keep any legal lobsters they were able to catch within the caves and holes created by the large stones making up the jetty. More often than not, though, the diving party would return empty-handed. This morning found Peter piloting his dive boat out of the harbor with two paying clients aboard. An older couple, husband and wife, had gotten certified to dive on their last vacation in Grand Cayman, and thought that while they were vacationing on Nantucket it might be "fun," as one of them put it, to test out their newly-acquired skills. Not to be put off by Peter's assurances that diving in Nantucket was nothing at all like Grand Cayman because of currents, low visibility in the water, and cold temperatures, the couple plopped down their money and they were going diving.

Peter was what the locals called a "washashore," meaning he'd been born off-island but now lived here year-round. But he was a native Nantucketer for all intents and purposes. He had been born in small-town New Jersey, but had moved to the island when he was twenty-two, cashing in his entire life savings to buy a small building out of which he planned to run a business. Initially he saw it as a dive shop, but realized quickly that Nantucket would not support that sort of venture, so he instead opted to create something of a general store. Anything that one might need while on vacation—or while living on the island permanently for that matter—Peter sold. Dive gear, sporting goods, souvenirs, clothing, you name it, Peter sold it out of his store.

Davy Jones' Locker quickly became an island mainstay, serving the local population as well as the summer transients, and had been doing so for almost thirty years.

He stood about five feet-seven inches tall and had brown hair that was beginning to show the earliest sign of his age with a few grey streaks, and which was usually in some varying degree of disarray. His face looked like that of an old fisherman, as he'd spent the majority of his life working in and around the ocean. His skin was leathery and his hands were calloused, and the crow's feet around his eyes betrayed Oswald's having spent too much time in the bright sun. Though he wasn't tall, he was certainly strong enough, a by-product of years of working with his hands; he rarely used a wrench to loosen tight bolts, as his hands were usually more than strong enough to do the job. He had quit drinking long ago, and that decision had made him many friends on the island. When he was sober, Peter was very friendly and he possessed a wonderful sense of humor. Many people, though, remembered the days when Peter drank, and the stories of his fights were legendary. But he had cleaned up his life and found that sobriety paid dividends.

Though not wealthy by the standards set by the summer people, Peter did very well for himself financially. He owned his own shop, and business was booming. Every summer new records were set for monthly sales totals, and the profits went straight into his pocket. He had recently purchased a new home and gotten remarried to a wonderful woman, and Peter certainly felt that the prospects for his middle age were looking ever brighter.

The sun was rising lazily over the beach at Coatue as the boat passed the lighthouse at Brant Point. The morning was breaking clear and the previous night's fog had all but burned off. Peter guided the boat through the narrow cut in the stone jetty and idled the engine. He explained to the divers the morning's agenda. "What you want to do is head out along the rocks," he said mechanically, pointing towards the fog horn stationed at the end of the jetty, "and circle back around. The rocks go all the way to the bottom. Stay along the rocks the whole way. You'll come back down this way," he said, pointing away from the fog horn. "Surface when you get to about eight hundred pounds of air in your tank. Come up with the rocks. Make sure you are right next to the rocks when you surface—there's a lot of boat traffic through the channel there, and we don't want you to get run over. The tide's pretty high right now, so you'll be able to crawl back over the rocks and swim to the boat. I'll be right behind you the whole time, so if you need anything, just signal me. Do either of you need any help getting ready?" It was the same speech he gave at the beginning of every one of these trips, and every time he wondered to himself why he kept at it. He made enough money without doing these trips. He didn't need the added stress. Would this be the year?

Even though he had been diving here for as long as he'd lived on the island, it seemed that every time he went down with a group of divers on a trip such as this one, some new unplanned event would transpire. Once he had a student in one of his dive classes run out of air. Another time a diver had somehow managed to get himself stuck in the rocks. He had had more "experienced" divers than he cared to think about get sucked out by the current, only to find them surfaced in the middle of the ferry channel, directly in the middle of a procession of boats. These dives, though, offered him an excuse to get out of the shop for a little while and to be free of the tourists that seemed to grow in number every year. He realized that his disdain for the tourists on the island was nothing short of biting the hand that fed him, but he still couldn't escape the feeling that these people were invading his home, and he found himself, in his older years, resenting the summer visitors more and more for that fact. Returning his attention to the paying clients on board, Peter said, "First one in the water, follow the anchor line down and set the anchor in the sand. Bury it real good down there. Then come back up along the line, and we'll all go down together."

The husband was the first to complete his preparation, and he announced that he would go down and set the anchor. As he went over the side of the boat, Peter watched him descend, and when he was lost from sight, Peter returned his attention to helping the other diver get herself ready. Things were not going well, as the woman was struggling to get her gear on. Peter was becoming increasingly angry while continuing to help the woman, when there was a sudden burst of spray from the water in front of the boat and the woman's husband surfaced, retching violently as he floated in the glassy green water. He had spit his regulator out of his mouth and he began to vomit into the water around him.

Peter looked up, his eyes blazing with anger, and saw that the man was ghost white and terrified. He knew the signs of a panicked diver and it always worried him, especially when he didn't know the diver in question. He endlessly preached in his classes the importance of never panicking in the water, because that was how real trouble started. Peter reached down into the water and grabbed the man by one of his tank straps, pulling him to the side of the boat. "Are you okay?" he asked, trying to feign earnest concern as

17

opposed to exhibiting the incredible irritation and disdain he felt. He reminded himself that it would be worse to be at the shop.

The diver was clearly shaken. "There's...there's...a body...down there...on the bottom," he stammered. He was gasping for breath.

If Peter had known this man, he might have thought this was some sort of bizarre joke, some game that he was playing. But he didn't know him and Peter could tell by his face that this was no joke. He helped the man climb the small ladder at the rear of the boat and steadied him as he removed first his tank from his back and then the weight belt from around his waist. "Jesus," Peter said, shocked and suddenly very serious. "A human body?"

"Yes," the man replied. "Right down by the anchor line." He gulped for air. "No head, no hands, no feet," he stammered. He spat at the glassy surface of the water. "Oh my God," he moaned as he collapsed, leaning over the side of the boat.

Peter told his two passengers to try to relax, while he himself was anything but calm. He managed to keep up a façade of being in control, but inside his stomach was knotting up and his breathing was getting short. He couldn't even think. All the past craziness aside, nothing like this had ever happened to him before. Usually quick-thinking, Peter was suddenly stumped as to what to do. He thought for a moment and then finally did the only thing that seemed rational. He picked up the transmitter of his marine radio and issued a call to the Coast Guard. "Brant Point Coast Guard, Brant Point Coast Guard. This is the *Davy Jones*, channel sixteen, over."

After a brief moment of silence, the speaker on the boat crackled softly. "*Davy Jones*, Coast Guard Station Brant Point. Please switch and answer channel one-two, over. Channel twelve, skipper."

"Coast Guard, *Davy Jones*. Roger that. Davy Jones switching one-two." Peter fumbled with the dial, changing the channel on the radio, his hand shaking uncontrollably. When he had switched to the appropriate channel, he said again, "Brant Point Coast Guard, this is the *Davy Jones*, channel twelve, over."

"*Davy Jones*, Coast Guard Station Brant Point, channel twelve, over."

Peter continued in a shaky voice, "Brant Point, roger, this is Peter Oswald and I've got some divers out here at the east jetty out near the fog horn. We've got a little problem out here, and I think you need to check it out, over." His teeth began to chatter despite the relatively warm air temperature. His clients looked terrified as they huddled in the bow of the boat. Peter felt a vague responsibility to these people and he couldn't let them see him worried. He turned his back to them as he waited for the Coast Guard's reply.

"*Davy Jones*, Brant Point, roger that, skipper. Please state the nature of the problem, over." *They were always so business-like,* Peter thought to himself.

He swallowed hard and then uttered, "I've got a diver that says he saw a dead body on the bottom near the rocks, over." *That should get their attention,* he thought to himself.

There was a noticeable pause from the other end of the connection. Then, suddenly, "*Davy Jones*, Brant Point. Roger that, skipper. You say there's a dead body in the water, over."

"Roger that, Brant Point. That's affirmative." Another pause.

"*Davy Jones*, Brant Point. Roger, skipper. We're sending someone out there to investigate. Could you state your exact position and describe your vessel for me, over."

"I'm anchored outside of the east jetty, about a hundred yards south of the fog horn. It's a twenty-three foot red Sea Craft, dive flag flying, twin outboards. You can't miss us, over."

"*Davy Jones*, Brant Point. Roger that, skipper. We're on our way. Station Brant Point standing by channel one-two, over and out."

Peter replaced the transmitter on the top of the console and returned his attention to the two people in his boat. The husband was still dry heaving over the side and his wife was terrified. Peter told them to try to remain calm, assuring them that the Coast Guard would be there soon. He kept looking at his watch, trying to make the time pass more quickly. *Maybe,* he thought to himself, *that would get them there quicker.*

Looking back towards Brant Point, Peter could see the small Coast Guard boat streaking towards them. As the Coast Guard boat approached, Peter stood expectantly, with no idea how to handle the situation.

The small boat came near enough for one of the crew members to throw Peter a rope, which he secured to a cleat on the stern of his own boat. Peter explained to the Coast Guard officers what had happened, saying that he himself had not seen it. "He was the first one in the water," he said, indicating the man leaned over the side of the boat. "He went down to set the anchor. Next thing I know, he's flapping around the surface saying there's a body down there."

The assembled Coast Guard officers conferred briefly amongst themselves, and finally one stepped forward. He looked like he was about fifteen, Peter thought, and his appearance didn't instill Oswald with much confidence that this kid could actually handle the situation. But he recognized him from work he'd done for the Coast Guard, so he figured he'd turn over the position of authority to this young man. "Folks, I'm Executive Petty Officer Gregory Cope. We'd like to ask you all to step aboard our vessel. We'll be transporting you back to the station where some people back there are going to want to talk to you," the young officer said. He turned to Peter and said, "Okay, Peter. I'm going to come on board and we're going to figure out what's what down there."

Peter helped his passengers step in to the Coast Guard vessel, assuring them that everything would be fine. "Tell you what," he said, trying to smile. "I'll even waive the charge for the dive." The joke failed, but the husband managed a smile.

"Big of you," he replied. When the couple was safely aboard the Coast Guard vessel, Peter helped the officer step onto his boat and untied himself from the Coast Guard's boat. The boat that now carried his former clients began to move away, slowly at first, then with a sudden surge forward as the engines sprang to life. In minutes, the boat turned around Brant Point and was lost from sight.

For a moment, neither Peter nor the Coast Guard officer next to him spoke. Both seemed afraid to start a conversation; both seemed afraid of what they were about to have to do. Finally, the officer spoke. "Okay, Peter. I don't dive. That's your thing. I hate to ask you this, but will you go down there and find out what it is he saw?"

Peter took a deep breath, resigning himself. "Yeah. I'll do it. But God, it's gonna' cost you guys," he said, again trying to make a joke. "Just look around, right? I don't have to touch anything, do I?" He shuddered at the thought of having to move the body around, if in fact there was a body at all down there.

The officer shook his head. "Just go down and verify what it is that guy saw. I don't doubt he saw something, but I'm thinking—and hoping—it's just a dead shark or something. But I need your verification on this."

Peter slowly got into his dive gear and checked his equipment. He lingered over every detail, trying to postpone the inevitable. When he had finally satisfied himself that everything was in working order, he slid gently into the water. Immediately his stomach began to knot up and he started shaking. He swam slowly to the anchor line, took hold of it, and submerged into the green water.

Halfway down the line, he could see the ocean floor. It looked like an underwater desert—sand everywhere, as far as he could see, rippled by the current into miniature dunes. As he neared the anchor, he saw it. At first it was just a pale object in the distance clouded by the silt suspended in the water. His heart began to race as he neared it. He shut his eyes briefly and he paused in his descent. *Deep breaths, Peter,* he told himself. *Just stay calm.* His heart rate increased very noticeably. He inched closer and immediately stopped. Lying on the ocean floor, forty-five feet below the surface, was the decomposing remains of a human being. The body was completely nude, face down, and fish swarmed around what was left of the flesh on the skeleton. The head was gone, as were the feet and hands, but it was clearly the body of a human. Peter noticed a diver's weight belt attached to the body, the individual lead weights resting in the sand. He had seen what he came to see and immediately turned and surfaced, following the anchor line back to the boat.

At the surface, Peter spit the regulator out of his mouth and shouted to the waiting Coast Guard officer. "He's right. There's a body down there. No idea how long it's been there, but it's down there. Fish are eating what's left of it. Head, feet, and hands are gone." His heart was still pounding furiously in his chest and he struggled to get around to the stern of the boat. He climbed up the small ladder, removed the bulky tank from his back and collapsed into the chair behind the boat's steering wheel.

"Is it floating around down there or what?"

"No. There's a weight belt on it keeping it down. It's not moving at all," Peter stammered as he removed his dive gear. "It's a belt like this one," he said, indicating a blue nylon belt with lead weights that was sitting on the floor of the boat. "Divers use them to compensate for the buoyancy of their equipment. It's what keeps you down there when you're diving."

"You think it's a diver?" asked the officer.

"No idea, but I'm thinking not. No clothes. Nothing. Not a wetsuit, not a bathing suit, nothing. If it was a diver, he'd have other equipment on, but especially a wetsuit. Water's freezing down there this time of year." Peter unclipped his own weight belt, allowing it to fall noisily to the floor of the boat.

"My God," said the Coast Guard officer. He grabbed the portable radio he wore on his belt and radioed the station. "Brant Point, Cope here. I'm on Oswald's boat. He's on the surface. We're done out at the jetty. We'll be heading in shortly. Alert the OIC that we've got a confirmed dead body out here. Any orders from that end?" He looked doubtfully at Peter.

The radio was silent briefly, but then a voice came over the line, crackling through the static, "Cope, Point. Roger. We copy that. You're done there. Negative on any additional orders from here. Chief says he needs a little time to think this through. Says to leave the body. Says he'll take it up with the sheriff. Figure it out from there. Do you copy?"

"Roger that," the young officer said in to the radio. "Copy no orders, leave the body, over. Cope standing by, heading in soon, over and out." He replaced the radio on the plastic clip attached to his belt and turned to Peter. "You ever seen anything like this before?"

Peter looked at the officer, astonished at the question. "God, no. Only dead thing I've ever seen down there is a dead fish. Up until now, that is." He looked at the officer standing next to him. "What do we do now?"

"I have no idea," he replied. "First we gotta go back to the station, though, and get a statement from you. That much I do know. I'll turn it over to the chief from there."

Peter started the boat's motors and walked forward slowly. He loosened the anchor line from its cleat and began to pull the rope. He felt the anchor give way from its hold on the sandy bottom, and he pulled it into the boat. He shuddered briefly, knowing what the anchor had just passed by on its return to the boat. Once he'd stowed the anchor in its compartment at the bow, he returned to his position behind the wheel and slowly pushed the throttle forward. The engines began to roar and the boat sped north, around the end of the jetty, then circled back towards Brant Point. The sun was up now and the sky was crystal clear and bright blue. It promised to be a beautiful early summer day on Nantucket.

CHAPTER THREE

Back at Brant Point, Oswald tied his boat adjacent to the small boat that had just been on the scene of the aborted dive. He laboriously climbed out of his boat on to the dock, a task made more difficult by the bulky neoprene dry suit he was still wearing. Inside the Coast Guard station, Peter was escorted into a large conference room, where he found the couple he had taken diving that morning talking to the Officer in Charge of the United States Coast Guard Station at Brant Point, Senior Chief Albert Reynolds. As Peter entered, the assembled group looked up at him, both divers still visibly shaken from the earlier experience.

"Hi, Peter," said the chief. He was a large man, over six feet tall and weighing close to three hundred pounds, Peter guessed. His hair, what was left of it, was white, and his face showed the wrinkles of both his age and the stress of his job. He was sixty-three and was looking forward to retirement. "We're just finishing up here," he continued. "I've got the details of the initial encounter from Mr. Hunt here. Were you able to go back down and actually see it yourself?"

Peter looked at the wall over the chief's head. "Yeah. I saw it. Wish I hadn't, but I did."

The chief nodded grimly. He motioned for a man standing outside the door to escort the Hunts out, telling them that he would be in touch and that they should try to go about their vacation and enjoy themselves as best they could. "I know it's going to be tough, but try to have fun while you're here. But please don't talk to anyone about this until we can get to the bottom of it. We need to identify the body and notify the relatives. Until then, just act as if nothing happened." This request was followed by a wan smile attempting to convey empathy. The attempt failed.

"You're right," said Mr. Hunt. "It's going to be tough. It's going to be impossible. But trust me when I tell you that I'll be happy to keep quiet about it. I don't want to relive that experience. Ever." With that, he took his wife's hand, and the couple departed in stoic silence, venturing out to salvage what they could from their interrupted vacation.

The chief pointed to an empty chair next to the table in the room and told Peter to take a seat. He flipped through some pages on the yellow pad sitting on the table, reading back over the statements he had taken from the family. "Okay. He says he went down to bury the anchor in the sand and when he got to the bottom, he saw a dead body. Said it didn't have a head, hands, or feet. Didn't take too much time to look at it. Said he had to throw up and he wanted to get out of the water. So he surfaced immediately and that's about the end of his involvement."

Peter nodded as the chief read from his notes. "I was helping his wife get ready to go in the water. He went in, and the next thing I knew he was screaming at the surface."

"Hold on a second," the chief interrupted. "I need to go through the procedure here."

Peter wondered to himself what, exactly, the Coast Guard's procedure was when they had a middle-aged diver find a half-eaten dead body. "So he comes back to the surface and gets back in the boat and you called us. Sound right?"

Peter nodded again. "Yep. That's what happened."

"Okay. So tell me what happened after you went down there to see what it was." He shot an expectant glance at Peter, poised to begin recording the information.

Peter began to recount the sequence of events. He had gone down the anchor line, squinting through the water. When he got to the body, he looked at it for as long as he felt like he could, which, he admitted, wasn't very long. He described for the chief as best he could what he had seen.

"So what do you make of it?" asked the chief.

"What do you mean 'what do I make of it?' It's a dead person down there."

"That much I get," replied the chief. "I mean do you think it's a diver? A fisherman? Some drunk teenager that went swimming off Coatue? What?"

Peter shook his head. "I don't have any idea. I doubt it was a diver. The person wasn't wearing any dive gear. Wasn't wearing anything for that matter, except for a weight belt. No bathing suit, no underwear, nothing. I don't think you're getting out of this as easily as calling it a drunk teenager, either. No head, remember? Helluva party if some kid lost a few body parts at it." His hands shook nervously as he wiped his forehead of the sweat that had suddenly materialized there.

The chief looked at him, ignoring the evident sarcasm in Oswald's voice. "Could you tell the gender of the body?"

"I'd guess it's a man, just based on the size of it," Peter replied. "I didn't look that closely. It was lying face down, or what would have been face down if it had a ..." Peter looked awkwardly at the chief, who simply nodded and motioned for him to go on. "But it looked like a man," he continued finally. "Big body. Big frame, you know. Looked like a man, I guess." He shook his head. "I can't be sure, though. I didn't want to turn that thing over." He couldn't seem to put his ideas together in any sort of logical, coherent pattern. Peter found himself unable to concentrate, though his mind was completely focused—far too focused, he felt—on what he'd seen on the ocean floor just a few minutes earlier. The thought of it made him nauseous; the thought of how he would have reacted to actually touching it almost made him physically gag.

The chief nodded grimly. "So where were the head and the other parts?"

"If I knew, I'd tell you. All I know is that they weren't there. I didn't feel like looking around to find them, though." Peter wondered whether inquiries of this sort were really necessary, but he reminded himself that there was probably no "procedure" for this sort of thing, so he forgave the chief for what he saw as ridiculous questions.

The chief wrote down everything Peter said. "Can't say I blame you," he said as Peter finished. The chief looked up, his expression very serious. "Peter, what I'm going to tell you right now, you can tell nobody. Not your family, not your friends, not your employees, nobody." The chief took a deep breath and looked directly at Peter. "I'm really scared that we've got ourselves a murder here."

Peter felt that he should have looked shocked, but at the same time he knew that the chief's revelation shouldn't have surprised him at all. He didn't know the correct way to respond to the statement. He did know, though, that there was no other explanation for this. But a murder on Nantucket? Who would do it? He knew that some of the locals could be a little rough, but violence on Nantucket rarely exceeded a bar fight or some sort of domestic abuse.

After a long pause, Peter again wiped his forehead, willing his body to relax. He looked at the chief. "Why are you telling me this?"

The chief looked straight at him. "Because you're now going to be assisting in the investigation. You know that area better than anyone; you dive around there all the time. We're going to need your help on this."

Peter nodded slowly. Sighing, he said, "Okay. I'll do what I can. Anything else you need from me right now?"

"No," the chief said. "Go on back to your store, act like nothing happened. Don't tell anybody what you saw. I'm going to call the sheriff's office and see what to do next. This isn't really my department, you know. I don't know how they handle a situation like this. That's why I told you not to touch the body. I'm not sure how they want to go about recovering it." He stood and extended his hand. Peter took it in his, and the two shook hands silently. "Thanks, Peter. I really appreciate your help on this."

Peter nodded his head and turned to go. As he stood, a thought occurred to him. "Al, why is this not the police department's jurisdiction? Seems like if it's a murder, it would qualify as a crime for them to investigate."

Reynolds looked up from his notepad and said, "The dive rescue squad is housed at the fire department, and they're under the jurisdiction of the sheriff's office. Since the body's in the water and will require a diver to recover it, it's the sheriff's baby now."

Peter nodded. He knew the dive rescue operation. He'd done a lot of work for them before in terms of repairs, orders, and training. He turned again to leave, saying goodbye to the chief on his way out the door of the conference room and exited the building. Outside, the sun was bright and the air was pleasantly cool. He made his way back along the worn wooden planks of the dock and carefully stepped into his waiting boat. As soon as he was in the boat, the morning's events ran through his mind again. He closed his eyes and shook his head slightly, trying to banish the memory. He untied the boat and slowly pulled away from the dock, being careful to steer around the moorings in the harbor. Once he was clear of the moorings, he turned back towards the harbor where he kept the boat moored.

The small red dinghy was floating in the still water of the harbor, tied to the large pink ball that read "Davy Jones" in hand-painted blue lettering. As he approached, he cut the engines and allowed the boat's momentum to carry him to the mooring. He grabbed the algae-covered rope and pulled the line in, securing it on the bow cleat. Glancing around the boat, he thought briefly about retrieving the contents. A few tanks, some weight belts, a broken mask.

"The hell with it," he said aloud. He'd get it later. He didn't want to deal with it right now. He didn't want to deal with anything right now.

As he untied the dinghy and began to paddle towards the small beach, a group of tourists stood on the sidewalk watching him. One pulled out a camera and snapped a quick picture, remarking to the others that the man in the small boat was a diver. "See? He's wearing a scuba suit," he said to his companions. Peter paid them no mind as he walked past the group. He'd been so wrapped up in the events of the morning that he'd completely forgotten that he was still wearing his dry suit; truth be told, he often felt more comfortable wearing it than not. He quickly walked straight by them, continued on down the street and walked around the corner to Davy Jones' Locker.

As Peter walked in the door of the shop, he glanced around quickly. Hats lined one entire wall. His store was renowned for selling hats of all sizes, shapes, and styles. Many visitors referred to Davy Jones' Locker simply as "the hat store" or "that store with all the hats." He couldn't get them on the shelves fast enough it seemed. Every day he would have his employees restocking hats from the storage room. Hats even hung from the rafters, which helped to further reduce the already limited amount of light inside the store. The lighting inside was intentionally dim, as the shop had a way of becoming very dirty very quickly, and the low light made it harder to notice the dust. The effect, though, was of being in a sort of cave, or perhaps under water. In the middle of the shop was a rectangular area created by the joining of four separate glass and wooden counters, all of which displayed more items for sale, and the area behind the counter was accessible by an opening on one side. Inside this rectangle was the area Peter affectionately referred to as "the pit," the area that housed the cash register and the store's cashiers.

He walked slowly around the corner of the counter, passing boxes of children's beach toys and racks of coffee mugs, and said hello to the two employees working that morning. "How was the dive?" one of them asked. This from a thin, blonde manager who looked to be about thirty.

"Total bust, Jimmie" he said in reply to the manager. "One of them freaked out in the water and we didn't do a whole lot of diving. I swear I'm never doing another charter," he said. That was partially true. One of them had freaked out in the water. Peter just didn't say why.

"You say that every time you take a charter out, Peter," Jimmie replied laughing. "I'll believe it when I see it." He looked at Peter and said, "You look a little sick. Is something wrong?"

Peter shook his head, saying, "No. I'm just mad about that dive. It's such a waste of time to take those people out there and then have them be total idiots once they get in the water." He looked around the shop, noticing a few customers poking through the various T-shirts embossed with different logos of Nantucket. "Are you guys going to be okay by yourselves? I think I'm going to go home for a while."

"Yeah," the manager replied. "Take off. We're fine. You look like you could use some sleep."

Peter nodded in agreement. "Okay. I'm going to go change clothes, then I'll go. Call me at home if you need me." He went to the back of the shop to a small room reserved for the storage of dive gear. He stepped out of his dry suit and put on a shirt and a pair of jeans he had left there. He returned to the front of the store and walked silently out the door.

"Hey there, Pete," someone called. Peter looked to his left and saw a bartender from the Jib and Jenny next door. He was standing just outside the bar's door, smoking a cigarette before going inside to begin the process of opening the restaurant. "Whacha doin' this morning?"

"Can't handle this garbage today," he replied. "Took a charter out this morning to the jetty. Turned into a nightmare. I'm getting out of here." He was in no mood to talk, and he hoped the bartender would take the hint.

The bartender was oblivious to Peter's desire for solitude. "Don't blame you. You guys have been crankin' in there already this summer, huh?"

"Yeah. It's been busy," he replied, trying once again to end the conversation. Looking across the street, he noticed a Coast Guard truck parked next to the police station. He shuddered at the sight. Opting for the offensive side in the quest to end the conversation, he called over his shoulder, "I'll see you later." And with that he began to walk towards his truck.

"Bye, Pete. Be good," the bartender replied, stepping on the butt of his cigarette and walking back inside.

Peter walked slowly to his truck, trying to think of nothing. His mind kept going back to the vision of a small group of fish tugging at the flesh of a dead human body on the bottom of the ocean. He noticed a feeling of personal violation. It was the same feeling, he supposed, he would have had if he were to walk in to his house only to discover that he'd been robbed. The water around Nantucket—especially that stretch of the water—was almost like his home, and he was quite possessive of it. Somebody had violated what he deemed his personal territory. He noticed that his hands were still shaking slightly. He got to his truck and got in. The keys were still in the ignition—nobody would steal a truck on Nantucket. *Yeah,* he thought to himself. *Nobody would steal a truck, but apparently somebody would kill a person in cold blood.* He looked at his watch. Twenty minutes after ten. He could go home, go back to bed, and sleep for a few hours. *When I wake up,* he told himself, *things will be different. I'll feel better. My hands won't be shaking; I will have forgotten all about the whole morning.* He shook his head, knowing that would be impossible.

CHAPTER FOUR

Nantucket County Sheriff Andy O'Toole sat behind his desk, listening in disbelief to the story he was being told by the chief of the Brant Point Coast Guard Station. O'Toole had held the position of sheriff for over twenty years, and only once in his tenure had there been a murder on the island. The way he remembered it, some guy had come home from a night out drinking with the boys and caught his wife in bed with another man and he'd just lost it. He'd beat the other guy to death. But that was an anomaly; it had happened one February about fifteen years ago. The man in question—the murderer, if that was the correct term to apply to such a situation—admitted to it immediately, got a deal where he worked it down to involuntary manslaughter, and did his time. O'Toole remembered, in fact, that the guy had gotten out of prison recently and relocated to a suburb of Boston, opting for the anonymous setting a bigger city provided. That was during the winter, though, when there was snow on the ground and people were all a little on edge and sick of living on an island. And besides, it was more or less a crime of passion. It wasn't a premeditated murder, for God's sake. It wasn't during the summer. Those things didn't happen on Nantucket during the summer. The "Little Grey Lady" was a quaint, historic town built on the whaling industry. Modern problems didn't inject themselves into the lives of the summer crowds. But now there was a dead body, submerged in forty-five feet of water, just off the beach of this little sandbar thirty miles at sea. *So much for progress,* he thought to himself.

O'Toole was short and stocky, and despite his sixty-one years, he still had a full head of red hair. His Irish roots were only a generation removed, and he looked and acted the part. His voice was raspy, resulting from thirty-plus years of smoking unfiltered cigarettes. His face was hardened by years of work and strain. Life wasn't easy when you were the sheriff, but it wasn't without its rewards. He, like Chief Reynolds, was looking forward to the day he would retire, a time he saw in the not too distant future. O'Toole lived alone, his wife dead from cancer now three years.

When the chief had finished recounting all that he had been told about the situation, O'Toole cleared his throat and looked out the window. "This is dangerous, Al. We've got the season shifting into full gear right now. We need to get to the bottom of this. Quickly. We can't have this get out of control, because you know what that means to our economy here." He made eye contact briefly with the chief, and he could see in those eyes the fact that the chief knew exactly how important it was to have those tourist dollars flowing in.

"I know, Andy," replied the chief. "I want to get it done with as soon as we can. What's the plan, though? I deal with boats in distress, not dead bodies."

"Obviously we need to recover the body. That's our first move. Take it out to the hospital and let some doctors look at it. See what they can figure out. My God, Al. The summer's shaping up to be a real SOB."

"I hear ya'," said Albert. "But do we publicize this thing? I don't want to scare people, but if there's some kind of psycho out there, people need to know."

Andy weighed the chief's question briefly. He was right on one hand. They did need—perhaps had a duty—to keep the public informed if there was some sort of dangerous killer on the loose. But on the other hand, publicizing a murder could potentially destroy the summer business, and the island's economy lived and died by tourist dollars during the summer. He shook his head as he said, "No. Keep it quiet for right now. We don't know how this person died. We just know there's a dead body. For all we know, it could have washed here from the Cape." This idea he added as an afterthought of sorts, with a twinge of hope in his voice. *Maybe it isn't really our problem*, he wanted to suggest.

The chief shook his head. "No way, Andy. Peter Oswald said there's enough weight on that body to sink it fast and keep it there. Somebody planned this. Somebody here."

Andy looked at him and said, "Okay. Let's don't start trying to figure out who done it until we know what it is that's been done. I'll call Frankie down at the fire house and see if he can't get some people out there to look at it and see what's what."

31

Reynolds sat silently as Andy called Frank Hess, the deputy chief in charge of the dive rescue squad, at the fire department. "Frankie, it's Andy," he heard the sheriff say into the phone. "Need to talk to you about something in private. You alone?" A brief pause from O'Toole, followed by, "Okay, here's the deal. Seems we got a dead body that's sunk out at the end of the east jetty. Peter Oswald had a dive charter out there this morning and one of the divers found it." Another brief pause from the sheriff, then, "Relax, Frankie. Nobody did anything to it, we just need to know how you want us to proceed."

Al Reynolds could imagine the reaction from Frank, the burly, grey haired deputy chief with the demeanor of a bi-polar teddy bear. Hess was notorious for flying off the handle in specific situations and letting his temper get the better of him, but was usually known as a friendly, cheerful guy that people liked to be around and to be associated with. "Okay, Frank. I'm not sure where he is, but I'll get him on the horn as soon as I can. Thanks, Frankie. See you in a second." He hung up the phone and looked at Reynolds.

"Frankie wants Peter to recover it, given that he actually saw it. Says he's going to come down to investigate it himself. Wants to make sure first-hand that the job goes smoothly." In the back of his mind, O'Toole wondered briefly about the wisdom of letting in an "outsider" to assist in the investigation. After all, this was a police matter, not a civilian one, and the closest Peter had ever gotten to being a cop was being arrested back during his heyday. But he knew in his heart that it was a wise decision, because there was nobody on the island that was as experienced a diver—both in terms of diving in Nantucket's waters and in terms of actual years of diving—than Peter. So he silently gave his assent to allow Peter to accompany Hess.

Reynolds nodded. He wasn't terribly concerned about the actual recovery, as long as he didn't need to get in the water with it.

O'Toole lit a cigarette, spitting tobacco flecks onto his desk. He exhaled deeply, sending a cloud of smoke across the desk. "You know that's illegal, don't you?" asked Reynolds, indicating the lit cigarette in O'Toole's hand. "You can't smoke in any public building on this island any more."

Andy looked up at him, smiled, and replied, "They let me get away with it. They let me get away with all kinds of stuff around here. As long as I don't do it anywhere else, they let it slide." Then his face turned suddenly serious. "I need to get over to Davy Jones' Locker and talk to Peter about this right now. Frankie's on his way down here right now. So I guess you're done, but you know the drill. Keep it quiet down there at the station, business as usual.

I'll keep you posted." He extended his hand across the desk towards Reynolds. "Thanks, Al."

The chief stood and shook Andy's hand. "Just doing my job, Andy. Let me know what I can help you with. And thanks for keeping me posted." He turned to go, then turned back around to face the sheriff. "Good luck with this thing, Andy. I mean it. I don't envy you at all for having to deal with this, but I want you to know that I'm pulling for you to get this solved quickly."

"Thanks," replied the sheriff flatly. He didn't envy himself either, but this was his job, and he'd do it as best he could.

Reynolds turned and left the sheriff's office, closing the door behind him. He exited the large, red brick building that housed, among other official town offices, the sheriff's office, into the bright sunshine. Already cars were streaming along the street, carrying passengers to the beaches and the shops. People were walking along the sidewalks, paying no attention to the uniformed Coast Guard officer standing outside the Nantucket Town Building. He hurried to his truck parked next to the building, anxious to get back to the station and away from this whole mess. Like everyone else involved, he wanted to get as far away as possible as quickly as possible. He hoped to be able to forget about it, or at least to pretend that it had never happened in the first place.

Andy exited his office and ran across the street to Davy Jones' Locker. He thought to himself that every time he entered this store it seemed like there was more stuff—he couldn't think of a better term for the mish-mash of randomly assorted items for sale in the store. Brushing past the vintage Navy diver suit that hung just inside the entrance, O'Toole immediately found himself enveloped in the semi-darkness of the store's interior. He walked around the side of the counter and gestured to the manager. "Peter in today?" he asked, trying to keep his voice from betraying the information he had stored in the front of his mind.

"Not right now, he's not. He was here earlier, but he went home. Looked a little tired. We sent him home," replied the young manager. "He works too hard anyway," he added laughing. "It's about time for him to retire, if you ask me."

The kid sounds too happy to know anything about it, Andy thought to himself. *What a nice way to be. Totally naïve to all of this, no worries in the world, no thought of the fact that some person's life ended so abruptly and that there was a dead body sunk out there in the water.* "So he's at home right now?"

"Yeah. He lives out in Polpis. You want to call him from here?"

O'Toole considered the offer briefly, then declined. He didn't want to publicize this any more than he had to, and he figured that he'd be better off not having the conversation he had to have right there in the crowded store. "Just give me the number. I'll give him a call from my office. I've got some things I need to talk to him about." The young man jotted down Peter's number on a sheet of paper and handed it to O'Toole. "Thanks," he said, walking towards the door. He walked back across the street to the Town Building and went straight back to his office, closing the door behind him.

He sat down at his desk and picked up the phone. He dialed Peter's number and waited for him to answer.

"Hello," came the voice on the other end of the line, sounding frail and scared.

"Peter? It's Andy O'Toole here. I just got briefed on this whole situation you had this morning, and I've talked to Frank Hess. He's on his way to my office now—should be here soon, in fact. He wants you to help him out, if you can, in the recovery. He said that because you found it, you can be a big help to him."

No response from the other end was audible.

"Peter? You there?"

A long pause, followed by, "Yeah. I'm here. I was scared as hell you were going to ask me to do this."

"I'm sorry, Peter. I really am. I hate to put you in this position, but Frankie asked specifically that you do it. Also, and I hate to add any stress to your day, we're trying to keep a lid on this thing and get it solved quickly. How soon can you get here?"

"It'll take me about twenty minutes. Depends on the traffic."

The sheriff looked at his watch. Eleven-fifteen. O'Toole immediately began the process of delineating his estimates of how long this process would take, something he had done since his youngest days. In his mind, he wanted to have a timetable for any major sequence of events. His mother had always said that Andy was always two steps ahead of everyone because of his constant schedule-making. Andy began to figure the time in his head. Twenty minutes puts him here at a little after eleven-thirty, he thought. Give him twenty minutes to get his stuff together, twenty more minutes to get out there, that's almost twelve-fifteen. Just in time for the twelve-thirty boat to leave the dock, be passing the fog horn, and have all the passengers see a headless corpse coming out of the water. "Okay, Peter. We'll wait for you. Can you step on it, though? Like I said, we'd like to avoid any publicity, so the sooner the better."

Peter sighed heavily. "I'll leave right now," he said, and hung up the phone.

O'Toole turned towards the window in his office. It faced out onto the brick building that housed the Nantucket Whaling Museum across the street, which already had a line of eager patrons waiting to get in and see the exhibits, a line that extended to the street, with people craning their necks for a better view of the few exhibits visible from the front door. He glanced at his desk calendar, which was open to Thursday, May twenty-eighth. "My God," he said to the calendar. "Memorial Day Weekend. We don't need this. We can't have this. Not on Nantucket." He returned to his desk and began to fill out the paperwork on the morning's grisly discovery.

A few minutes later, he was startled by a knock at the door. His secretary stuck her head in the office and said that Frank Hess was waiting to see him. "Send him in," the sheriff replied as he got to his feet. Hess entered the office timidly. He was still in shock over what he had been told. When he closed the door behind him, the sheriff said, "Hey there, Frankie. Long time no see. Wish it was different circumstances." He paused a moment. "Peter's on his way down, but it doesn't sound like he's real excited to be involved with this."

Hess nodded, adding, "I can't say I'd be real excited either, if I were him. Hell, the guy's a store owner and a diver. He's not trained to do this stuff. I'm trained to do it, but I still don't want to go down there." The deputy fire chief took a seat in the office, and the two waited in silence. Ten minutes later, another knock on the office door, this time followed by the announcement that Peter Oswald had arrived. "You sure are popular today, Andy," his secretary remarked.

O'Toole said nothing in response other than, "Send him in, too. And just in case, no more visitors for the time being." Oswald entered the office and again the sheriff stood, this time walking to the door and locking it behind him. He wanted to ensure their privacy for this all-important meeting.

Frank Hess shook Peter's hand and thanked him for agreeing to come down and assist with the recovery. Peter couldn't help but notice that everyone seemed to be thanking him for his participation, albeit an unwilling participation, in the early phases of this investigation. He laughed inwardly, thinking that these same people used to curse his very existence when he was still drinking. But now they needed his help and were very grateful for it.

"Don't worry about it," replied Peter. "Let's just go and do it and be done with it." Despite the fact that he'd been diving for most of his life, and salvage diving for the better part of twenty-five years, Peter had never been involved in the recovery of a dead body before, though he had helped to salvage a doomed fishing boat once. The boat had sunk off the tip of Great Point in a nor'easter one December, and the crew, true to the sailor's code of ethics, had gone down with the ship. Though searchers combed the submerged wreckage of the boat, they found no sign of the crewmembers and the boat had been left on the ocean floor, the insurance companies citing the dangerous currents and rip tides as making it economically infeasible to raise the vessel. The bodies of the crewmen, though, had never been found.

"What all do you need in the way of equipment, Peter?" asked Hess.

"Just my suit," he replied. "Everything else is on my boat."

"Okay," replied Hess, "then we'll take your boat, if that's okay. I've got all my equipment in the truck, so I can grab it on the way out."

Peter nodded, indicating that it was fine that they take his boat. They walked out onto the street again and stopped at Hess's truck. They quickly grabbed the gear he needed, Peter telling him to leave his weight belt and tank, as there were plenty of both in the boat. Peter slipped in the door of Davy Jones' Locker, trying to seem invisible, and made his way to the back of the crowded store. He retrieved his dry suit from the equipment room located in the rear of the store, then slipped out the same door, remaining unseen by his staff members. Once back outside, he and Frank continued quickly to the harbor on Easy Street, ignoring the people they passed. They walked in complete silence, each man focusing on the task they were about to have to perform. At the wharf, they loaded the gear into Peter's dinghy and he rowed slowly out to the boat. He attached the dinghy to the mooring line and helped Hess get into the boat, then handed up the gear to him. He then hoisted himself up into the boat, started the engines, unclipped the mooring line and they slowly began to putter out of the harbor.

As they traveled towards their destination, Peter started to mentally prepare for the task at hand. He didn't want to do this; he wanted nothing more than to rewind the morning and start over by canceling the dive. But he knew that he was helping out an old friend by doing so, a friend that had helped him out in the past. That loyalty, paired with the civic duty he felt he had, helped him to put aside his own personal feelings about this mission. On the deck of the boat next to the fire chief's gear was a black nylon bag, about seven-feet-long that zipped from one end to the other. Oswald hadn't noticed it before when he was helping Frank to load the gear onto the boat. Peter looked at Hess, who had been watching him, and nervously asked, "What's that?"

"It's what you think it is," Frank replied nonchalantly. "Try not to think about it. Just try to do this whole thing without thinking." He talked as if this were old hat to him, though inside he was as nervous as Peter.

Peter wasn't quite capable of being so outwardly blasé about the recovery. *Plan the dive and dive the plan* was one of his mottos for teaching scuba classes, and that adage seemed especially pertinent to this specific dive. "What, exactly, do I do here?" asked Peter. "I've never done this before," he reminded Hess.

"All you need to do is take me down there and then help me if I need any help. I should be okay, but you never know. Regardless, though, the main thing is this: don't think about what it is, don't think about what's happened to it. Just show me where it is and watch me to signal you if I need any help. Simple as that."

"Simple as that, huh?" said Peter sarcastically. "Don't think about it. Sure thing. Sounds easy enough to me." He focused his attention forward, steering the boat towards its destination at the fog horn. The ferry horn bellowed behind them as they neared the end of the stone jetty, signaling its imminent departure.

"This is about right," Peter said, scanning the area around them. "This is right about where it was. I didn't think to save the location in my plotter. Guess I wasn't thinking straight at the time."

"Nobody would have expected you to, Peter. I'm sure it was a crazy time," Frank offered in reply. He scanned the water around him with a grim scowl, steeling his nerves.

Peter cut the engines and walked forward, carefully avoiding any contact with the black bag sitting near the bow. He threw the anchor over the side, let out the line, and pulled sharply to set the anchor in the sandy bottom. When he was satisfied that it was holding, he cleated it down on the bow and turned back to Hess.

"There's one thing we have to do here, Peter," he said, "before we begin this whole thing. You're going to be working for the sheriff's department as my deputy, so I have to officially deputize you before you can legally assist me."

Peter almost laughed. The whole situation seemed so outlandish to him—sitting there in a boat floating over a dead body—that the concept of "officially" making him a deputy of the sheriff's department sounded almost too ridiculous to be believable. But rules were rules, he figured, so he allowed himself to be deputized. He had to swear that he would perform his duties in an ethical and professional manner and act in accordance with all laws governing the Commonwealth of Massachusetts and the laws of the County and Town of Nantucket, and that he would serve the community to the best of his abilities. He heard himself say, "I will," in response to the questions regarding his oath, and it reminded him, in a strange way, of his wedding vows.

"Okay. Now you're officially a deputy sheriff of Nantucket County, Mr. Oswald, so let's get on with it." The two quickly assembled their gear and Frank gave Peter his last instructions. "Remember, now. Just take me down there to where it is and let me handle it. If I need your help, I'll signal you." With that, the two rolled backwards into the water and met up together at the bow of the boat. Peter signaled that he was ready to descend, and Hess, after returning the thumbs-up sign, followed him down into the blue-green ocean.

The water was still remarkably clear. The visibility was almost thirty feet despite the day's boat traffic through the area. Peter knew exactly where he was and he knew almost exactly where the body was lying. This was, after all, his personal turf and he prided himself on knowing it like the back of his own hand. He descended quickly, wanting to get in and out of the water as fast as possible. When he reached the bottom, he slowly began to pull himself along the ocean floor, digging his hands into the soft sand and pulling forward. He looked back periodically to check on Hess, who continued to give him the okay sign by making a circle with his thumb and index finger, allowing the other three fingers on his hand to extend upwards.

Ahead through the green lens of ocean water, he could see it. Despite his best wishes that it might have somehow disappeared, the body was still anchored in the same place he had last seen it, a horde of fish still nibbling away at the rotting flesh. He closed his eyes for a moment, then turned around to face Frank. He pointed at the body ahead of them, and Hess nodded, indicating that he saw it, then swam past Peter to retrieve the body. Oswald turned again to face the body, grimacing at the sight, and waited to see if his assistance would be needed.

Hess took three deep breaths, a relaxation technique he had learned during his scuba certification class which Peter himself had taught. It was supposed to help divers out when they felt panicked in the water. He'd always told Peter it didn't work for him during the course, and he was discovering that it didn't work now, either. Finally, he resigned himself to what he had to do, and, mustering all the inner strength he could find, he reached down to undo the weight belt that was keeping the body in place. The plastic buckle gave way, and the human remains lifted slightly. He slid the open bag around the body quickly, avoiding contact with it. When the bag completely covered the corpse, he zipped it shut, took another deep breath, and looked back at Peter. He pointed towards the weight belt that now rested heavily on the sand as a way of asking Peter if he wanted to retrieve it. *Always the pragmatist,* he thought to himself. Peter shook his head to tell Hess to leave it. Getting a free weight belt was the least of his concerns right now. Hess gave Peter the "okay" sign again and indicated that he was ready to surface. The two ascended slowly with Peter in the lead, refusing to look back at the mass that Hess towed in his right hand.

At the surface, they saw the boat about seventy-five yards from where they were. The tide was beginning to go out, and the ascending divers had been pushed away from the boat by the current. They swam, with some difficulty, back to the boat and when they had gotten there, they rested for a minute.

"Okay, Peter," Hess said, "here's what happens next. One of us has to get in the boat and lift this thing in, and the other has to stay in the water to help lift it. Got any preference?"

Peter couldn't help but notice the word "thing" in reference to the dead body. Maybe, he thought, that was some sort of mental trick Hess was employing, trying to dehumanize it. Make it seem like nothing more than a sack of rocks. "I don't care, really," he said. "I want as little to do with it as possible."

"Okay, then," Hess continued. "I'll get in the boat, and you can lift it up. It shouldn't be so bad from that end because it'll still float, more or less, in the water, so you won't have to do much." With that, Hess handed the end of the bag to Peter, who shuddered noticeably at the weight, and then he climbed up the ladder and got back in the boat and immediately removed his tank and his weight belt so as to better maintain his balance. He leaned over the stern of the boat and said to Peter, "Okay, just guide it over here."

Peter gently lifted the end of the bag up to Hess's waiting hands and backed away to let the chief hoist it onto the boat. The bag hit the deck of the boat with a solid thud as he let go of it, letting the corpse fall to the floor. As Peter climbed up the ladder, Hess looked over his shoulder. The ferry had not yet made it as far out as their position, and it would have been impossible for anyone on board to see what they had pulled out of the water. The two men sat in complete silence, staring at the recovered body, now safely zipped inside the black body bag. Peter took off his weight belt and tank, and put them quietly to one side of the boat.

"Let's get out of here," Peter said. "I need to get out of here."

"Sure thing," replied Frank. "You and me both." Frank stood in the bow of the boat pulling the anchor up as Peter started the boat's engines. When Hess had finished retrieving the anchor and had stowed it in its compartment, Peter pushed the throttle forward. The boat immediately sprang to life, sending out waves that crashed in to the rocks. They pulled through the cut in the jetty, passed the ferry and waved to the passengers on deck. "If they only knew," Hess said to Peter.

"I'd love to be one of them," Peter replied, "and have you say that about me."

CHAPTER FIVE

As they neared the lighthouse, Peter turned to Frank and said, "You know what we didn't think about?"

"How we're going to get this bag to my truck without getting caught," Hess replied, as if reading Peter's mind. "I just thought about that, too." He shook his head in disapproval of his own oversight resulting from his hurry to get the body recovered. "Let me think for a minute. Take it real slow here, give me some time." Peter slowed the engines further, hoping the passing boats wouldn't think they were in some sort of distress and attempt to offer them good-natured assistance. "I've got an idea," Frank said after a moment's thought. "Drop me off at the dock at Safe Harbor over there by Children's Beach. I'll run to the truck and meet you at the Coast Guard station. We should be able to get the bag in to my truck there without anyone noticing."

"Sounds good to me," Peter replied, thinking that it sounded anything but good, but he knew that there wasn't much choice in the matter. "What do you suggest I do while I'm waiting for you? Tell people that I'm just sitting there waiting for you to bring your truck up so we can take a dead body to the morgue?"

Frank shook his head. "No, you're going to go check on something. You need to go find a boat out in the basin somewhere, somebody thought they saw a boat that needed to be checked on, so you're going to go do that."

"You're the boss," Oswald replied doubtfully. He thought this idea was destined for disaster, but he thought better about arguing. "I'm just the deputy, and I have to do what I'm told, right?" He eased the boat into the dock at the harbor and Frank jumped out.

"Back in a flash," he said over his shoulder as he made his way quickly to his truck. Peter attempted to calculate the time it would take Hess to get to his truck and get back to the Coast Guard station. He figured fifteen minutes, which was a long time for him to spend with a body bag aboard his boat. Fifteen seconds was a long time for him, but he did as he had been asked.

He made his way out into the boat basin, acting as if he were looking for a specific boat. He saw the Harbor Master's boat making its rounds through the basin, and the Harbor Master waved to Peter, who returned his wave. He crossed his fingers in hopes that the Harbor Master wouldn't come over for a chat, which he was sometimes prone to do, and thankfully it worked. Peter continued on his course, heading in the direction of Wauwinet and the Harbor Master passed by without incident. He puttered around the large boats moored in the basin for what seemed like an eternity and looked at his watch. Exactly six minutes had elapsed since he left Hess at the dock, and he was paranoid that everyone was watching him. He felt like he couldn't keep up the charade of looking for a boat in need of assistance any longer, so he steered around towards the head of the harbor, figuring that people might think he was just going out for a boat ride.

He looked at the houses along the beach to his right as he passed, using the scenery as a distraction from the amorphous lump in his boat. Small sailboats dotted the landscape, colorful sails filling with wind and carrying passengers along their merry way. He began to think back to his own childhood, of weekends spent on the New Jersey shore with his parents and his younger brother. His father got two weeks vacation every year, so the family would spend one of those weeks in New Jersey, staying at a cheap motel and packing an entire summer's worth of fun into seven days. He envied greatly those kids here, those kids whose parents could afford to send them to Nantucket to play for three months out of the year. He looked again at his watch and noticed that it had been ten minutes. He turned the boat back around and aimed it directly at the Coast Guard station. He wasn't sure how fast he should go; he didn't want to attract attention, but at the same time he wanted to get the bag—and its contents—off his boat and out of his life. He decided it was better to go slower rather than faster, as large wakes were prohibited in the boat basin and he didn't need to have someone notice his speed. As he neared the station, he saw Hess pulling up in his truck. *Perfect timing,* he thought to himself. *Now let's get it over with.*

At the Coast Guard dock, Peter pulled the boat into an open berth. Hess had parked his truck alongside the pier and he looked down from the dock into

Peter's boat. "I'm thinking there's no better side to be on in this equation," Frank said, "so I guess let's just stay where we are and get it in the truck." Peter sighed in resignation and walked forward to where the bag lay. He took another deep breath and lifted the front end up slightly.

"You've got to get it higher than that, Peter," said Hess flatly. Peter closed his eyes and lifted the weight off the floor and, thankfully, he managed to lift it high enough to get it into the waiting hands of Frank Hess. Hess took the bag and deposited it rather noisily and unceremoniously in to the bed of the truck, then returned his attention to Peter.

"As far as I'm concerned, Peter, your job here is done. I can't thank you enough for your help," Hess said in a tone laced with genuine relief that he was finally able to grant Peter his freedom from this horrific task.

"You're welcome, Frank. I know you would have done the same for me, so let's just say it's a friendship thing. I'll take your gear off the boat and leave it in the shop if you want me to."

"That'll be fine, actually," replied Hess, "if you don't mind. I know I'm going to need to get a couple of tanks filled if nothing else, so I'll need to come by anyway. Thanks, Peter."

Oswald waved his farewell, reversed the boat out of the slip and turned towards his mooring, progressing slowly. Frank watched him turn the corner around the ferry dock, and then got into his own truck and started the engine. He picked up his cellular phone and dialed Andy O'Toole's number.

"O'Toole," the voice on the other end answered.

"Andy, it's Frank. I'm on my way to the hospital right now. Mission accomplished."

"Great, Frankie. You're one in a million, kid. I'll see you out there." He hung up without a further word and Frank slowly pulled back onto the street. He drove around one of the rotaries that served as something of a traffic control device and headed back towards town. He wanted to stay away from the business sector, though, so he opted instead to drive up the cobblestone hill that led up the cliff. As he drove, he couldn't help but notice the intensity of the early summer colors, the green of the grass beginning to show through the winter-induced browns, the vibrant colors of the late-spring wildflowers, with promises of more to come as the summer approached. The houses he passed, grey shingled with white trim for the most part, looked so inviting, so happy. His thoughts soon turned, though, to the juxtaposition created by the macabre cargo in the bed of his truck and these wonderfully idyllic scenes around him.

As he turned down New Lane and headed for the hospital, he passed by the old cemetery. It suddenly occurred to him that there seemed to be an inordinate number of cemeteries for an island as small as Nantucket, and he wondered why so many people chose the island as their final resting place. He mused briefly on the thought of a family friend, a longtime summer resident who wanted to be cremated and have his ashes strewn in the water when the bluefish were running close to shore. "I've eaten enough of them that I figure I owe them something," he used to joke. Andy's thoughts quickly returned, uncontrollably, to the lifeless body in the back of his pickup. There was no way to spin that into a humorous conversation.

When he arrived at the hospital, he pulled around to the emergency room parking area and he saw an older man wearing a long white coat wheeling a gurney out to meet him. Andy O'Toole was right behind him. Frank got out of the truck and looked at the sheriff, who remarked that he had gotten back pretty quickly. "Didn't get caught out there, did you?" he asked Frank.

"Nope," Frank replied. "Even waved to the ferry. Went real smooth."

"Good," the sheriff replied. "You know Doctor Tom Latkin, I'm sure. He serves as the town medical examiner in addition to fixing up those of us who need it," he said, indicating the tall man in round-rimmed glasses standing alongside the gurney. "I've told him everything about the situation, and he's going to examine the body." The men hoisted the body bag onto the gurney and Frank turned to the sheriff.

"So are you through with me here?" he asked the sheriff.

"Yeah. I know how difficult this was for you, and I can't imagine how difficult it was for Peter," said Andy. "But regardless, I'm really grateful. With any luck, we'll get to the bottom of this soon."

The two men shook hands and Frank Hess returned to his truck. He rolled the window down and said to the sheriff, "I'm heading back to the fire house. Let me know if you need anything more from me." Rather than speaking, O'Toole just waved his acknowledgement and Hess slowly made his way back to his own office.

Back in the hospital parking lot, Doctor Latkin wheeled the gurney back inside the hospital through sliding glass doors and walked quickly down a long corridor. At the end of the corridor was the morgue, a cold metal room with a wall of small cubicles and three bright silver metal tables in the middle. Latkin's office was directly across the hall from the morgue, a location he found very convenient, as his job duties, though primarily as a physician, did sometimes require his skills as a medical examiner. And being directly across from the morgue tended to keep away the average drop-in visitor.

Latkin had originally wanted to go into pathology, but found himself drawn to working on the living as opposed to the dead. When he'd been hired in Nantucket, though, one of the conditions had been his agreeing to serve as the town M.E. As they entered the room, Andy was overcome by the intensity of the smell of industrial strength antiseptic, and the sheriff winced. "It's awful the first time," said Latkin. "You'll get used to it." He hoisted the bag onto one of the tables and unzipped it. Neither man was prepared for the sight that met their eyes. Lying in the bag was exactly what they had been told to expect: a human body, minus a head, hands, and feet, with a great deal of flesh gone from the bones. But words did not do the picture before him justice. Despite every warning and despite all his training, Latkin was horrified at the sight that met his eyes.

The sheriff couldn't stand the sight and immediately looked away. He began to take deep, loud breaths through his mouth, gulping for air like a fish out of water. After some minutes, he regained his composure slightly. "Mind if I go outside and smoke?" he asked nervously.

"Go ahead," replied the doctor. "This will take me some time. If you want to go back to town and wait, I'll call you when I know something."

"Actually, if it's okay with you, I'll stick around for a little while. I feel like I need to be here, just in case," said the sheriff. "But I will be waiting outside." He quickly left the room and walked back down the hall. He exited the building through the sliding glass doors and took in a deep breath of fresh air. He fumbled in his shirt pocket for a cigarette, took it out and lit the end with a match. He sucked in the smoke deeply, closed his eyes and exhaled.

"Those things'll kill you, Sheriff," he heard a voice say. He opened his eyes to see a nurse that he'd known for many years. "But what better place to be when you drop dead, right?" She smiled at what she thought was a funny joke.

"Right," the sheriff said softly. "I know I gotta quit these things, but trust me. It's not the time." Then, recalling a joke he frequently made to people who suggested that he needed to quit smoking, "It could be more hazardous to my health to quit now than to keep it up. It's pretty busy down at the office, you know? Lots of stress down there."

"So what brings you out to our neck of the woods, Andy?" she asked. "Not hurt or anything, are you?"

Andy hadn't thought that far ahead. How could he explain his presence here? He said the first thing that came to his mind. "I think I might have Lyme disease."

The nurse looked suddenly concerned. "Lyme disease, Andy? That's dangerous stuff. Do you have a rash or anything?" she asked, referring to the tell-tale bulls-eye rash that was the most prominent symptom of the tick-borne illness that had reached almost epidemic proportions on the island.

Andy shook his head. "Nope, just joint pain and generally feel like hell. Figured it's better to get it checked out though."

The nurse nodded her approval. "Absolutely, honey. I better get back to work. Good luck with that. You take care of yourself, Andy O'Toole." She turned and walked into the hospital waiting room and Andy sighed in relief. That had been a close call. Too close for comfort, in fact. He dropped the cigarette to the ground and stepped on it to extinguish it, then returned to Latkin, who was beginning his examination of the body.

"I was thinking, Tom. I better get out of here. I don't need people to know that I'm up here, because they'll start asking me questions. Nurse outside just asked me what I was doing here and I told her I had to get a test for Lyme disease. So if anybody asks, you gave me the test and it came out negative, okay?"

"Sure thing, Andy. Like I said, though, you've got a few hours before you'll know anything from me, so head back to your office and do whatever it is you do over there." He winked at the sheriff, who had to smile despite the situation.

"I just do as little as possible, Tom. So you'll call me when you know something?"

"Of course, Andy. Now get out of here and let me work."

Andy left without further comment and exited the hospital building. He returned to his car and drove leisurely back to his office. After parking his car alongside the Town Building in his designated space, he walked around the corner to the police dispatch office to get a cup of coffee. The dispatcher was on the phone when he entered.

"You've tried to call him at home?" the dispatcher said into the receiver. She paused, while the voice on the other end explained that yes, he had tried to reach the person in question at home. "Somebody saw him at the Jib and Jenny, right?" Again, the voice on the other end explained that yes, somebody had seen him at the Jib and Jenny a few nights ago. "How long has he been absent from work?" she asked. She wrote down the information the voice on the other end was providing and said, "Okay. I've got the information. I'll pass it on to one of the officers on duty, and he'll be in touch soon. Let us know if he shows up." She returned the phone to its cradle on the desk.

"What's that all about?" asked the sheriff.

"Some kid that works at the Collins House didn't show up for work the last three days. They say it's not like him to just not come in without calling. He's some rich kid, family's got a house up on the cliff. Works out here because he doesn't want to deal with his life at home, I guess. I'm guessing he got smashed somewhere and shacked up with somebody. Probably'll turn up tonight, tail between his legs, talking about how sorry he is."

O'Toole's heart was pounding into his throat before she finished. Though he couldn't tell exactly why, he was immediately tense and worried. Worse than that. Scared. The police instinct he'd cultivated over his years on the force was telling him that something was very, very wrong. The last thing he'd heard the dispatcher say was "not like him." He turned to the dispatcher. His face, he was afraid, showed the tension that he was feeling. "Let me handle it. I'll walk up to the Collins House right now and see what's going on."

The dispatcher noticed a tremor in his voice that wasn't normal, but didn't think much about it. "Sure, Andy, if that's what you want to do. I figured I'd pass it off to one of the boys down here. You know, no big thing. Kid's fine, I'm sure."

"No," replied the sheriff, attempting to sound unconcerned. "I'll take it. I need some exercise anyway." He left the small room, exiting onto the sidewalk across from the Jib and Jenny. He turned to his left, walked to the corner and turned left again. He made his way quickly up Broad Street to the red-brick Collins House Hotel and climbed up the large, polished granite stairs. He entered the hotel and walked to the reception desk, explaining that he would like to talk to the manager. He was directed around the corner to the dining room.

He entered the dining room and was reminded of the last time he had been here. He and his wife had celebrated their twenty-fifth wedding anniversary here. They had spent a fortune on dinner, surrounded by the beauty and elegance of the old hotel. There were quite a few patrons eating lunch this afternoon, mostly older couples on vacation, enjoying their golden years. The manager saw him from across the room and beckoned him over to the bar. O'Toole sat in a high chair next to the manager, who seemed to be at his wit's end.

"I didn't expect to see you here," he said to the sheriff. "I figured it was going to be some summer cop who got assigned to the hungover waiter detail."

The sheriff tried to laugh, but ended up coughing. "We don't really have one of those," he said good-naturedly, then became suddenly serious. "This kid that's missing. How long has he been gone?"

"He was here on the twentieth. He had three days off. He was supposed to be back here for dinner on the twenty-fourth. He didn't show, so we called his house. His parents have a house up on the cliff. Summer people. Anyway, like I was saying, I call his house. No answer. I started to get a little pissed, you know, 'summer help and some are not.' So then somebody said he'd been at the Jib and Jenny the night before. Then I start to figure he's somewhere passed out. I was furious at that point."

The sheriff was calculating in his head the time that had elapsed. "So you're telling me that someone saw him at the Jib and Jenny on the night of the twenty-third?"

The manager nodded, seemingly more irritated than concerned. O'Toole continued his calculations. Today was the twenty-eighth. The kid had been seen on the night of the twenty-third. Four days had passed since he was supposed to have been at work. The math worked. The body at the morgue could very easily be that of the missing waiter. He interrupted the manager. "What's the kid's name?"

"Jack Carlisle," the manager replied.

The very name sent a shockwave through the sheriff's bones. "Oh, God. The senator's kid?"

"Yep. The same."

The implications began to grow increasingly ugly. The son of a United States Senator, working on Nantucket for the summer, was presumed missing, and if Andy's hunch was right, he wasn't missing at all, but rather lying dead in the Nantucket Cottage Hospital at this very moment. "Okay," Andy began. "I need to ask you a huge favor. Tell your staff that he got sick. Make something up. Food poisoning. He had some kind of reaction to shellfish or something. I don't care. Just make sure people know that he's not missing. He's just gone home for a little while because his father was worried about him."

The manager gave O'Toole a look of uncertainty, then said in a suspicious voice, "Sure thing. But why the story?"

Andy paused for a moment, weighing the options. He didn't know for a fact that it was the senator's son that was dead. For all he knew, the kid might have met some woman at the Jenny and gone off to the Vineyard with her. "We just don't want to create any kind of rumors," he said, opting for something close to the truth. "You know, his being a senator's son and all. No need to frighten his parents, because you know they'll find out if we tell anybody he's missing. We'll find him. I'm sure he just forgot what day it was. Or maybe he went over to the Cape. He might be sailing in the Figawi this weekend."

Figawi Race Weekend—or Figawi, as it was frequently called locally—was a long-standing Nantucket tradition, and nothing short of a nightmare for the police. Every Memorial Day Weekend, hundreds of sailors set out from Hyannis and raced to Nantucket. Along the way, they managed to drink themselves into a collective oblivion and then set themselves loose on Nantucket for the weekend. Public intoxication arrests spiked on this weekend, as the revelers frequently left the Figawi cocktail party in search of new venues. After the weekend, though, there was a moment's respite, as the sailors all left en masse for what had come to be known as the Reverse Figawi, a sort of purgatory for the various crew members to endure as they sailed across Nantucket Sound back to the Cape, most of them still suffering the after-effects of the night before. The sailors only added to the already swollen number of people that appeared on the island for the Memorial Day holiday simply for a vacation. Andy knew the kid wasn't sailing anywhere, but he didn't need to have stories circulating about a missing kid, a senator's kid at that, when all of these people were going to be on the island.

"Okay," replied the manager doubtfully. "I'll spread the word."

"I'd appreciate it," said O'Toole. "I'll keep you posted when I find anything out about where he is."

"Thanks," said the manager. "And tell him when you find him that I'm going to kill him when I finally see him," he added with a laugh.

Andy tried to force a smile. "Will do. Thanks again." He turned and left, his stomach doing cartwheels and his heart racing. Outside he lit a cigarette and sucked the smoke into his lungs with a noisy hiss. *Somebody already beat you to it, son,* he thought to himself as he exhaled slowly, trying to release the incredible tension that had been building up inside him during his conversation in the hotel. *Somebody already did kill him.*

Chapter Six

Sheriff O'Toole walked slowly back to the Town Building. His mind was already going in a multitude of different directions. The son of Senator Leonard Carlisle, he was sure, was the body that had been discovered that morning. He couldn't explain his certainty; he just knew somewhere in the dark recesses of his mind that he was sure. It was a feeling he had in the pit of his stomach, something that wouldn't go away and kept gnawing at him. He needed to be absolutely sure, though. He needed some kind of concrete proof before proceeding any further. Back at his office, he found a message from Doctor Latkin. He picked up the phone and dialed the number the doctor had left.

"Tom Latkin," the voice on the other end said.

"Tom, Andy O'Toole here. Whaddya find out?"

"Not a lot," the doctor replied. "No hands means no fingerprints. Of course, given the amount of time the body was in the water, I'm not sure the fingerprints would have been any good anyway. No head means no dental records. Whoever did this knew what they were doing and how to cover up the evidence of the crime."

Andy thought for a moment, then asked, "You mentioned the time it had been in the water. Any idea on how long, exactly, it's been in there?"

The doctor made a noise as if contemplating some great unknowable truth and said, "Andy, it's really hard to make that determination. I'd say less than a week, but certainly more than a day or two. So I'd say, as nothing more than an educated guess, that it's somewhere in the neighborhood of three to six days, probably about five."

The sheriff thought back to the conversation he'd had about the length of the Carlisle kid's absence. Again, the time frame he'd established worked out. "Okay. Did you find anything that might help us identify this person?"

The doctor replied, "Well, your corpse is that of a male. No doubt about that. I would guess he's between twenty and thirty-five, judging from what was left of his skin. No birthmarks or anything like that. There is something, though. I'm not sure if it'll help at all, but at this point it's all I've got to work with. It looks like whoever he was had a tattoo. It's mostly gone, so there's no telling what it was, but there is a splotch of what looks like blue ink. Given the color of it, I'm guessing it was a tattoo."

O'Toole was writing as the doctor spoke. "Thanks, Tom. Can you figure out the cause of death?"

"Yes," Latkin sighed. "It's what you were afraid of. The guy's been murdered. Strangled by somebody with huge hands. Whoever it was left what look like some fairly monstrous hand prints around the base of the throat and the upper torso, but he was wearing gloves of some type. No fingerprints. Again, though, even if they were present, I'm not sure the prints would be of any significant value at this point. I'm not like one of those TV pathologists that can find evidence after twenty years. Hell, my training only lasted a little over a year before I transferred to general medicine."

"No need to apologize," O'Toole replied. "And to be honest, I wasn't expecting any fingerprints. That would make it too easy for me. Are you done with him yet?"

"Not quite. Still got a few things to do. I'll let you know what else I turn up."

"Thanks again, Tom." He hung up the phone and immediately picked it back up. He rifled through the phone book on his desk and dialed the number for the Collins House Hotel.

"Good afternoon, Collins House Hotel."

Andy cleared his throat. "Yes, hi. This is Sheriff Andy O'Toole. Could I speak to the manager on duty? I think he's back in the restaurant." He was placed on hold, then the line rang again.

"Jethro's," the voice said. The restaurant had been named for Jethro Collins, the original proprietor of the hotel.

"Yeah, hi. Can I speak to the manager, please?"

"Speaking."

"Hi. This is Andy O'Toole. We spoke a little while ago about the Carlisle kid that was missing?"

51

"That was quick," said the manager. "Did you make any progress on finding him?"

"I'm not sure," the sheriff said. "I was wondering if I could come back to the restaurant and talk to you and maybe to a few of your staff members. I just need to fill in a few details for my report. You know, police procedure and all." He hoped with all of his might that he sounded convincing. "Are you free right now?"

The manager cleared his throat and lowered his voice. "Yes, sir, I'm free right now, but I would suggest we meet somewhere else, out of the range of hearing of the other staff. One of them saw you here and started talking. If you were to talk to any of them right now—even just for your report—I think it would set off an avalanche of rumors. Can I meet you somewhere?"

Again Andy wanted to hit himself for being so overtly visible. Twice in less than twelve hours he'd been places where it wasn't easy to explain his presence. In the case of his visit to the Collins House, his presence as the investigator no doubt lent a sense of urgency to the whole situation, and urgency was something he didn't need in the public sphere right now. "Sure," he said, "name the place."

"There's a coffee place down on Steamboat Wharf. Ratzo's is the name of it. I could use some coffee right about now. How's that work for you?"

"Fine," Andy said. "I'll be there in two minutes." He hung up the phone, grabbed his note pad and a pen, and headed out of his office and onto the street again. He knew the place the manager was talking about. It was a little café that used to be a fish market, Andy recalled. Now it served coffee and juice and breakfast sandwiches, along with burgers and that sort of thing. It was just down the street from the Town Building, so he was there before the Collins House manager. He ordered a cup of coffee and sat at a small table to wait.

When the manager arrived, Andy waved to him, and the young man came over to the table. "Let me just grab some coffee real quick," he said, "and I'll be right back." He went to the counter and got his coffee, then returned to the table. "So what questions can I answer for you?" he asked.

"We've already got a few leads on the kid, so like I said, it's no big deal. What we're basically doing now is trying to get as much description on him as we can. I've already seen a picture of him, so I know what he looks like," Andy continued, lying through his teeth. He'd never laid eyes on the kid that he knew of and he wouldn't know him if he'd walked through the door. "What we're wondering, though, is if he has any identifying marks. You know, scars, birthmarks." He hesitated for a moment. "Tattoos, perhaps?" The word hung in the air like a balloon waiting to pop.

"Um...Let me think. He doesn't have any moles or scars or anything. Really good looking guy. Guess it comes with the money, huh? But it's funny you mentioned tattoos, because I know that he has one. Something on his left leg. What is it? God, for the life of me I can't remember, but I do know he has a tattoo on his left leg. It was almost an issue with his working at the hotel. You know, we have standards for our wait staff, as our guests tend to not be in the tattoo crowd, so to speak. So he had to make sure it was covered up at all times while he was working. Any other questions?"

Andy was silent, writing quickly on his notepad. He had heard what he needed to hear, what he hadn't wanted to hear. He absent-mindedly asked a few other questions, just to make it seem more official. He was very careful to phrase all his questions, though, to make it seem as if Jack were still living. How long has he worked for you? Ever have any problems with him? Does he drink a lot? Does he do any drugs that you know of? None of the answers really mattered at this point, though, because in Andy's mind it was already more or less official. The son of a senator had been murdered on Nantucket. The press would love this. When he felt like he'd asked enough questions, he thanked the manager for his time and returned to his office. Once inside, he sat behind the desk. He picked up the phone and called the morgue. When Latkin answered, Andy asked him, "Is what you think is a tattoo on his left leg by any chance?" He crossed his fingers, hoping against hope that the doctor would say no.

"Sheriff? How did you know that? It's on his left calf, to be exact."

Andy was silent. He dropped his head as his stomach immediately dropped past his feet and fell through the floor below him. "Lucky guess," he muttered. "Look, Tom. You can cancel the search for the kid's identity. I know who it is. His name is Jack Carlisle, and he was a waiter at the Collins House. His father is Senator Leonard Carlisle."

"Oh my," the doctor said. "I can see that this is going to be a problem. How do you propose we handle it?" And then, after a brief cough, he added, "Or how do you propose *you* handle it?" O'Toole noticed the doctor's special emphasis in referring to this situation as Andy's problem. *Rats abandoning the sinking ship,* he thought to himself wryly.

"I haven't given it a first thought yet, Tom. I suppose I should notify his parents, though. At this point I would say the sooner the better, too. Need to get the ball rolling on an investigation."

"I'll leave that to you, Andy. I'll finish up here and let you know what else I can find out."

"Thanks, Tom. I'll talk to you." He hung up the phone again and began to chew on the end of his thumb, contemplating the situation. He didn't know the senator personally, but he knew of him. He was a very public figure on the island, giving generously to the local preservation society and other philanthropic causes. Leonard Carlisle was a Republican senator from Texas. His family lived in Waco, Andy seemed to remember, and he spent the majority of the year living in northern Virginia while the Senate was in session. His wife came out to the island in early June and stayed through to late September. They had four children; Jack was the youngest.

They had a house up on the cliff overlooking the ocean. O'Toole had been called up there once many years ago when he was still working as an officer on the Nantucket police force. Mrs. Carlisle had noticed a bonfire on the beach and had called to report it. He'd been sent up there to chase the kids off and put the fire out. Other than that, he had never had any dealings with the family at all. Until now, that was.

He had no idea how to reach the Carlisles, and what's more, he had no idea what he'd say to them once he did get in touch with them. On a whim, he called directory assistance, but learned, to no shock of his, that the family's home number was unlisted. Then it occurred to him that the family belonged to the Nantucket Harbor Club and that the club would surely have his home phone number. He looked up the number and dialed, and asked for the club manager. He explained to the manager that it was a potential police emergency and that he desperately needed the phone number. The manager gave it to him and Andy hung up.

He waited, staring at the phone. He lit a cigarette and sighed deeply. He had refused to allow his office to become a no-smoking area, despite the town's orders. He always kept a window open and nobody complained, so people turned a blind eye. He figured that he'd earned it. Twenty-three years as sheriff and eight before that as a local cop. His thoughts soon returned to the phone call he had to make. He asked himself how one notifies a parent that their child has been found murdered. He shook his head. *There's no easy way to do this, Andy,* he thought to himself. *Just do it. Pick up the damn phone and call them and tell them. It's your job.*

He picked up the phone and dialed the number. He swallowed hard when he heard the ring, and his breath stopped when he heard the voice.

"Hello?" It was Mrs. Carlisle.

"Mrs. Carlisle?" he said hesitantly.

"Who's this?" the voice asked.

"This is Andy O'Toole. I'm the sheriff on Nantucket Island. Is this Mrs. Carlisle?"

"Yes it is, Sheriff. Is something wrong? With the house?" The voice was noticeably worried now.

"Well, ma'am, we're not entirely sure, but..." His voice trailed off. "Ma'am, there's no easy way to say this, so I'm just going to say it. We have reason to believe that your son Jack was found dead this morning." There. He'd done it.

"Excuse me, but is this some kind of joke? I do not see any humor in this at all," the voice exclaimed, irritated.

"No, ma'am. This is not a joke. A body was found this morning by some divers. We think it's the body of your son," he replied, his voice almost calm now.

"What do you mean you 'think?' Is it or isn't it?" Irritation was mixing with panic in her voice.

"This is not a conversation I would like to have over the phone, but there's no other way I guess. A body was found this morning. The head and the feet and the hands were missing from it, though, so we have no way of identifying it through traditional means." It was apparent to Andy that the conversation had started off badly and spiraled downwards very fast. He needed to get out of this. A long-distance phone call was certainly not the way to inform a mother that her child had been found murdered. Before he could continue, though, he heard sobbing from the other end of the conversation. He started to say something about how sorry he was to have been forced to inform her this way when she cut him off.

"How can you guess it's Jack?" she asked, her voice pleading for some sort of flaw in the identification, some sort of evidence that would point to a different victim. She could barely speak and she was gasping for air between sobs.

"Your son was working as a waiter at the Collins House. He hasn't been to work in three days. The body was found this morning, partially decomposed. The medical examiner thinks that the victim had a tattoo on his leg, and I've been told by Jack's boss that he had a tattoo."

Momentary silence, then a rush of hysterical wailing. Though two thousand miles separated the sheriff from the distraught mother, from her reaction Andy now knew for certain that Jack Carlisle was dead. The mother's crying told him that she knew it, too. "Mrs. Carlisle, I know this is beyond difficult for you and I want you to know how sorry I am to be the bearer of such tragic news. We're starting an investigation immediately. Do you have plans to come up to the island any time soon?"

Mrs. Carlisle was sobbing into the phone. "Yes. I was planning to come up there with my husband for the Memorial Day Weekend. My husband is out playing golf right now. Oh, God. I'll call him. I'll tell him. We'll be there as soon as we can. Oh God." More sobbing. Andy couldn't imagine the pain she was feeling. He couldn't imagine what it would be like to get a phone call in the middle of the day informing you that your son had been murdered and decapitated on an island where he had spent every summer of his life.

"Mrs. Carlisle, let me leave you my phone number here. If you or your husband wants to call for any reason, please do. Like I said, we're already well underway with our investigation and we will find the person who is responsible for doing this to your son. I promise you that. You have my solemn word that we'll find the person." He gave her his direct office phone number and had her repeat it to him so he could make sure she had it right. "Please call me when you get here, Mrs. Carlisle. I'd like to meet with you all to discuss the investigation."

"Yes. I'll do that. I'll call you when we get there," she said, almost mechanically. "My husband will want to talk to you, too, I'm sure. He'll only be on island for a long weekend, then he's going back to work, but I'm sure he'll want to talk to you." Her voice had lost the initial hysteria and had taken on a quality of absolute and utter shock. "He's out on the golf course right now." Andy knew that, as she'd already told him, but he also knew that the woman was in a traumatized state right now. A bomb had literally just gone off in her life and she didn't know how to deal with it. "Goodbye, Sheriff. Thank you for calling. We'll be in touch."

Before O'Toole could say anything else, she had hung up the phone.

CHAPTER SEVEN

Andy sat at his desk, staring off into space. He didn't want to think about it. He couldn't believe there had been such a heinous crime committed on Nantucket. The picture of his wife sat on his desk, facing him. He thought of his own children, the children he and his wife had raised on Nantucket. They had long since moved away and made him a grandfather. How would he have reacted to this as a parent, he wondered to himself. How would he have taken the news that his youngest child was dead. Worse than dead, actually. A murder victim. The clock on the wall announced that it was four o'clock. He scanned the phone book, found what he was looking for, and picked up the phone and dialed Peter Oswald's number.

"Hello," Peter's voice said. Andy heard the exhaustion and dreamlike quality of his words. *Poor guy,* O'Toole thought to himself. *He thought he was just going out diving this morning. He's already gotten a lot more than he ever bargained for.*

"Peter, it's Andy O'Toole. Listen, thanks again for what you did for us today. I know it was hard on you and I'm sure you're still shook up about it, but I really do appreciate it."

"You're welcome, Andy." He paused. "I know you didn't call me to just thank me. What's up?"

Andy sighed heavily. "We've got a little problem, Peter. We're pretty sure that the body that was recovered was Senator Carlisle's kid. You know him?"

Peter's voice was immediately tense. "The senator's kid? My God, Andy. Yeah, I knew him. He took dive lessons here a few years ago. Didn't really dive much with us—just sort of hung around the shop some times."

Andy thought for a moment. *Good a place as any to start an investigation*, he told himself. He grabbed a legal pad from his desk drawer and took a pen from his pocket. "He did dive with you?"

"Yeah," replied Peter. "Not real often, though. Just once or twice a year at most."

"Did he ever talk to you about anything?"

Thoughtful silence met the question. "What do you mean?" asked Peter.

"Did he ever tell you anything about his life? People he knew, places he went, anything like that? We're just trying to figure out who would have wanted to do this and for what reason."

Peter thought for a moment, then replied, "No, not really. He didn't like to talk about his personal life. Everyone in the shop thought it was really amazing that his dad was a senator, but he wouldn't talk about it. Always said it was no big deal and changed the subject whenever it came up. I do know he was a regular at the Jib and Jenny, though. I've heard from a few of the bartenders that he spent a lot of time in there. And I can remember seeing him in there a few times when I'd go in there to eat lunch."

Andy scribbled the information down on the pad. He knew that Jack had last been seen alive at the Jib and Jenny. He made a note to stop by the bar. "So he didn't talk about anything personal at all?"

"Nope," Peter replied. "Like I said, he didn't like to talk about himself. It sounds kind of weird, but I think he was kind of embarrassed of it. It was almost like he felt like he didn't deserve the life he led just because of who his father was. He was especially embarrassed of him, I think. Sort of like he didn't want people to think about him being like his father."

This made no sense to O'Toole. Why would a child of privilege be embarrassed of his own life? Why would a kid not want to be like his father, a successful attorney-turned-senator? He knew some of these rich kids that preferred to have people not know much about them, but he didn't understand it. "Okay, Peter. I tell you what. You've had a bitch of a day already and I don't want to make it any worse. If you think of anything, anything at all, let me know."

"I'll do my best," said Peter. "I've got to relax now, though. I'll talk to you later."

"Thanks, Peter," he said as he hung up the phone. Andy turned to a new page on the pad and began to write notes to himself. He needed to talk to Jack's boss at the Collins House to see if he could shed any light on the kid's personality and who he might have come in contact with. He would also need to talk to the staff at the Jib and Jenny to see what they could tell him. His first instinct was that the murderer was somebody Jack had known. He remembered from his training that personal acquaintances were usually the prime suspects. But on Nantucket, where almost everyone had at least a passing acquaintance with everyone else, this instinct wasn't terribly helpful. As he was finishing up writing notes to himself, the phone on his desk rang.

"O'Toole," he answered.

"Andy, Tom Latkin again. Just wanted to let you know that I found something else on this kid. He broke his left arm. Not recently, but it's been broken before. I can see where the bone has fused back together. I'm not sure if that'll help at all, but it's something."

Andy scratched the new information down on his notepad. "Thanks, Tom," he said. "I guess we'll use that to confirm his identity. I'm sure I'll be getting a call from the senator soon. I'll ask him about it. If it turns out to confirm my guess that it's Carlisle, we'll have to call the newspaper."

"Okay," the doctor replied. "I'm about done here."

The two said goodbye, and Andy hung up the phone. He returned his attention to his notes. He had told Mrs. Carlisle that he had already started an investigation and all he had to this point was a page of random facts about the kid. Nothing was adding up. The chaotic jumble of information, he knew, wasn't from having dug too deeply. "You've got to go out and actually investigate," he said to himself out loud. "Then maybe things'll start to add up." He grabbed the notepad from the desk and tucked it under his arm. He exited his office and walked down the hall. He told his secretary that he'd be gone the rest of the day and waved goodbye.

He walked out the main door of the Town Building into the bright afternoon sunshine. The street was busy—the four o'clock boat was still unloading passengers. He dodged the traffic and crossed the street, heading for the Jib and Jenny. He looked at the pub sign hanging limply over the door.

It reminded him, on some level, of a tombstone.

He walked in the bar and looked around. He hadn't been in here since the summer before, but it hadn't changed at all in his absence. The bar was to his right and there were tables to his left—the bar served as a restaurant during the day and early evening, and became a nightclub after the dinner crowds had left. There was a DJ booth in an elevated platform up to his left, but it was currently empty, as there was piped-in music playing over the speakers during the day. He bypassed the hostess and walked straight to the bar. He walked up the two wooden steps and grabbed a chair.

The walls around him were covered with various signs and photographs—it was as if the decorator had not wanted to waste a single square inch of space. Wooden signs from old businesses hung everywhere—testaments to the changing face of the Nantucket economic system. Looking at them, he remembered his younger days when he was single. The Back Forty was a bar way out of town. They had closed down when the drinking age went up to twenty-one. The bar had burned down the next year under somewhat suspicious circumstances, and it was widely rumored that the owner had been losing money and needed the insurance payoff. O'Toole had met his wife at the Muffin Man, the sign hanging on the wall behind him now all that was left of the old bakery. They had lost their lease and been replaced by a clothing boutique, which had also gone out of business when the fad they endorsed had passed. Now, he thought, it was some sort of art gallery pedaling expensive antique artwork and furniture. There were signs from even before his day, one advertising Western Union telegram services and another one advertising a garage that specialized in "the greasing of cars," a message displayed prominently across the faded wood. All these signs made him nostalgic, thinking of the past on Nantucket, when things seemed quieter, calmer. When dead bodies didn't turn up at the end of the jetty.

"Sheriff O'Toole," said the bartender, smiling happily. "To what do we owe this pleasure?"

O'Toole turned his gaze toward the bartender. He knew her well. Stephanie Troppitz, an attractive woman, about thirty-two, with brown hair that she wore in a pony tail and big brown eyes. She was relatively tall and had the reputation of coming across as somewhat gruff if she didn't know you. Her regulars adored her, though, as she always remembered their names and their drinks. She had been working at the Jib and Jenny ever since she moved out to Nantucket ten years ago. All of her friends called her Steph. "Hey there, cutie," he said smiling. "Lemme have a beer."

She filled a glass from the tap and set it down in front of him. He reached for his wallet, but Steph said, "That's on me, honey."

She's always so friendly, Andy thought to himself. *I wonder how she manages to stay sane working in a place like this.* The Jib and Jenny could get crowded on a good night, and the bartenders were usually running around like mad on those nights, serving patrons that oftentimes were rude and demanding. The days were much slower, though, and he figured that was why Steph was willing to forsake the lucrative tips on the night shift, choosing instead to work primarily during the days. He reached into his shirt pocket and took out his cigarettes. He grabbed a matchbook from the bar in front of him, but before he could strike it, Steph looked at him and said, "Now Andy. You know better than that."

His brain had taken a momentary vacation; he had been about to violate the town's no-smoking ordinance. "It doesn't make sense to me, Steph," he lamented. "You guys give out matchbooks and you're a bar, but I can't smoke in here?"

She laughed. "Yep, honey, that's the facts. I don't make the laws, just enforce them." She winked at him and added, "Maybe you should start following those laws, Mr. Sheriff." He grudgingly returned the cigarette to his shirt pocket and thrust the matchbook in to his jacket. He thought for a moment, then his face took on a suddenly serious appearance. He looked at Steph gravely.

"Steph, I need to talk to you," he began. He looked around him. There were only a few people sitting around the bar, mostly tourists studying maps, mixed in with a few assorted locals on their lunch breaks. "Have you got time?"

She looked at him nervously. "What's wrong?" she asked.

He thought about how to answer that question. He wasn't sure how much information to divulge to her, but he knew he needed to start his investigation, so he figured it was worth the risk of telling her what was really going on. "We've got a little problem over across the street. Nothing to do with you or the bar. Don't worry."

A look of relief came over her face. Nothing spelled disaster for a bar on Nantucket faster than the suspension of a liquor license. In the last year, four separate restaurants had been discovered serving minors, and the amount of money they had lost during their suspensions had been nearly irrecoverable.

"Thank God," she said laughing, the good-natured and calm tone suddenly returning to her voice. "I can talk right now, if you don't mind me getting orders when I need to."

He sipped the beer in front of him and told her that would be fine. He looked around, afraid of being overheard. "You know Jack Carlisle, right?" he began.

"Yeah, sure I know him. Great kid. He and I have lunch once a year over at the Harbor Club. We dress up and go over there and have a great time. We go play the part of swank people, you know. Rich and famous and all that. It's our little tradition. We dress up, go drink white wine spritzers, eat great food, the whole deal." She stopped. "What's up with Jack?" she asked nervously.

61

O'Toole told her the story of the discovery of Jack's body at the end of the jetty. He left out the part about his hands, feet, and head missing, figuring the shock of the murder itself would be enough. He tried to buffer the information with the fact that he wasn't absolutely sure that it was Jack's body, that it was just a hunch. Despite his best efforts at softening the blow, his words hit her hard. She began to cry softly.

"Oh my God," she said. "I can't believe this. He was just in here the other night."

O'Toole nodded. "That's why I wanted to talk to you. This was the last place he was seen alive. But remember, too, Steph, we're not sure yet if it's him or not." He added this as an attempt at stopping her from crying. He flipped to a new page on the legal pad and scribbled "Jib and Jenny" across the top. "Do you know anyone that could have done this to him?"

She shook her head. "I don't know anyone who disliked that kid. He bought drinks for anybody that would talk to him, never got in fights, nothing. Everybody liked him." She took a napkin and wiped the tears off her face and went to refill a beer for a customer.

Andy wrote down what she had said, but figured there was no reason to. The more he thought about it, the more he felt like this murder might have been out of the norm in the sense that it came out of nowhere, like a bolt of lightning. In her absence, he mentally weighed the two conflicting basic premises about the murderer. When she returned, she leaned in closer to him. "There's one thing. I don't know if it means anything and I doubt he could do it, but there's a bouncer, Will Paterna. Everybody calls him 'Gowilla.' He's a big guy, got a temper. One night last summer, he and Jack got into it. We were closing, and I told Jack he could stay and have a drink with us after hours. Will got really pissed at him. He'd been drinking. Put him in a headlock and threw him out the back door. Said he didn't give a good Goddamn who his father was and that he lived on the cliff." She stopped suddenly, though, wondering if what she was saying was the right thing to do. "I don't want to get him in trouble, Andy. I can't believe anyone—not even Will—would do anything to hurt Jack. The poor kid," she said, trying to swallow a huge lump that was building in her throat.

Andy thought to himself as he copied down the information Steph was providing him. He knew the bouncer. Had known him all his life, in fact. Will had been in trouble for fighting on several occasions. Lived on the island year-round and hated the summer. Worked construction during the day and worked the door of the Jib and Jenny at night. And, O'Toole reminded himself, he was a personal acquaintance. A spark flared briefly in his brain as he looked at Steph.

"I know you don't want to point any fingers at anybody, Steph, but we've got nothing right now. Anything I can tell this kid's parents will help me out, so trust me when I tell you that it's important for you to tell me everything. Are you sure, in your heart and in your mind, that there's no way Will could have done this?"

She shook her head. "No way," she said in a voice remarkably self-assured for someone who moments before was doubting herself. "At least not that I could believe. He's one of those guys who gets pissed at nothing, then it's done with." She couldn't get her mouth to say the words her brain wanted her to. It was a jumbled mess.

Andy nodded. "I know Will. We've had to deal with him before." He thought about the last time he'd had to deal with him. It was two years ago at another popular nightspot, Shane's, a bar named for the owner of the place. Shane was a notorious character on the island because, as a younger man, he'd masterminded the planning of a massive beach party every year on the first weekend in August. Word of the party eventually spread so far and so many kids descended on the island every year for it that it finally became too much of a nuisance and the state police had to come in and shut it down.

The bar he now owned was almost as notorious for the fights that broke out there. Andy had been working late one night when a call came in that there was one such fight in progress. He went along, just to help out. When they walked in the door, Will was in the middle of five other men, all swinging fists at each other. The two bouncers on duty were trying their best to control them, but it had gotten out of hand. The officers jumped in, and O'Toole had grabbed Will. Will stood about six-three and weighed over two-fifty. O'Toole remembered that his wrists had been so large that the handcuffs barely fit him.

"One thing, Steph," O'Toole said. "And I need you to think really hard here and give me an honest answer. Was Will here that night you saw Jack?"

She looked away for a minute, as if in thought, then returned her gaze to Andy. "Yes, he was, Andy. He was sitting at the bar with some of the guys he works with during the day. They were drinking beer. But not too much," she interjected quickly. "And they were all laughing and having a good time. So it's not like he was drunk or acting mean or in a bad mood or anything like that. He was behaving, I guess I'm trying to say."

Andy wrote this new information down on his pad. "Thanks, Steph," he said. "I'll check him out and see what gives. Do me a favor, though, and don't talk to anybody about this. We're still not absolutely sure that the body is Jack's and we don't want to start any rumors before we're sure." He was still trying to make her feel better; he wanted to make her believe, at least temporarily, that it wasn't Jack Carlisle whose corpse had been found.

She nodded, trying desperately to hold back a flood of tears. Trying in vain. "I won't tell anybody. But Andy," she continued through now readily-flowing tears, "I don't believe Will could have done this, just between me and you. And if you do go check him out, please don't tell him I told you any of that."

"Of course I won't," he said. "And I hope you're right about him not doing it. Underneath all that skin, he's a good kid and his father was a good friend of mine. I hope you're right, honey." He stood and turned to leave. "Hey, Steph," he called over his shoulder. "If you think of anything, give me a call, will you?" He reached in his wallet and fished out a business card. He handed it to her. "We'll find whoever did this," he added.

"I'll call you," she said. And with that, she turned to check on her customers at the bar as Andy walked out the door.

CHAPTER EIGHT

Andy exited the Jib and Jenny and walked out into the late afternoon crowds. The sun was beginning to go down and the air had taken on a noticeable chill. He pulled his coat around him and sat on the bench outside the bar for a moment to smoke. He took out the book of matches he'd taken from the bar and lit a cigarette, then replaced the matchbook in his jacket pocket. Around him was the hustle and bustle of people walking and driving, the annual Memorial Day Weekend invasion. As he smoked, he watched the people he saw passing him. Many seemed tired, worn out from traveling all day. Some seemed overwhelmed by the crowds, while others seemed energized by the mass of humanity. Andy allowed himself the momentary pleasure of sitting back on the bench, relaxing and just taking it all in as it came to him. He dropped the finished cigarette still burning into the ashtray next to the bench and stood. He crossed the street and began to walk slowly to his car. As he was approaching his car, his cellular phone rang in his pocket.

"Sheriff, it's Claudia. You've got an urgent message here." His secretary had worked for him for fourteen years and she was trained to tell the difference between urgent and non-urgent calls, so he trusted her when she said that something was urgent.

"Yeah, Claudia. What's the message?"

"Someone by the name of Mr. Carlisle called. Said he had to speak with you immediately. Left me a number where he said you could reach him at any time." Andy mentally took down the number, hoping he'd remember it.

"Thanks," he said. "I'll call him back when I get to my car. Just about there, in fact." He hung up and opened the car door. Once inside his car, he started the engine and put the phone in its cradle on the dashboard. He dialed the number Claudia had given him. Senator Carlisle picked up after one ring.

"Leonard Carlisle," the voice said breathlessly.

"Senator Carlisle, Andy O'Toole," he said.

"Sheriff O'Toole, hi. I'm calling to find out about my son," the senator said in a tone laced with parental anxiety.

I know why you're calling, Andy thought to himself. *Wish I had something to tell you, though.* "Yes, sir. We've begun an investigation into the murder. There is one question that I need to ask you, though. Something regarding the investigation."

"Yes," replied the senator. "What is it?"

"Did your son ever break a bone?" He knew the question sounded out of place, but he needed to be sure.

The senator was silent for a moment. "Yes, he did. His arm, it was. A few years ago. We were skiing in Aspen and he took a pretty nasty fall. Why?"

Andy shook his head. "I just needed the information to confirm the identity. The coroner found evidence of a broken arm, and we wanted to be sure it was your son before we made any sort of public announcement."

"What do you mean you needed to confirm the identity? I was under the impression that you had already confirmed that it was my son." The senator's voice now sounded irritated.

"Sir, you'll understand that we're doing the best we can, but with no fingerprints—"

"What?" the senator shouted, cutting him off. "What do you mean no fingerprints?"

"Yes, sir. There were no fingerprints. Didn't your wife tell you?"

"No, she didn't," he replied in a tone of combined indignation and irritation. "Please inform me as to what's going on here."

Andy again relayed the story to yet another unwilling listener. When he had finished, the senator was silent. "Senator Carlisle?" he said in to the phone, fearing he'd lost the connection.

"Yes. I'm here. Sorry. This whole thing is unnerving," he said. "Two hours ago I was on the golf course. Now I'm talking to the sheriff on Nantucket about the murder of my youngest son."

"Yes, sir," Andy replied. "I know how horrible this must be for you, and you have my deepest sympathies. I assure you, though, sir, that we are giving this matter our highest level of attention and focus. I promise you that we will find who did this to your son."

"Well," said the senator, "what information do you have so far?"

Andy told him what Steph had said at the Jib and Jenny. He explained that the investigation was only a few hours old, so it was too early to say anything for sure, but he felt that the lead he had was a strong one. In fact, he planned to question Paterna at his first opportunity, he assured the senator. "And given that Nantucket's a pretty small, quiet place, sir, I promise you that this case will have my undivided attention. My case load is pretty minimal, so there won't be any distractions."

"My wife and I have chartered a plane from Boston," Carlisle said, seemingly ignoring Andy's pledge to give him his complete investigative focus. "We're flying out of here tomorrow morning. We couldn't get a charter all the way through, so we're having to take a commercial flight to Boston. We'll be in Nantucket by eight o'clock tomorrow night. Can you and I meet then?"

Andy thought to himself. *Friday night of Memorial Day Weekend. Figawi racers inundating the island the following morning. A murder investigation. Wonderful.* "Yes, sir," he said. "Tomorrow evening will be fine by me. It's going to be crowded downtown. Should I come to your house?"

"That'll be fine," the senator replied. "Why don't you give me a call some time after eight. You can come to the house and we can talk there." The senator gave Andy the phone number for the Carlisle's home on the island. "One more thing," the senator said. "I want this bastard caught, whoever he is. I don't care what you have to do, but find him."

"We're working on it, sir," O'Toole replied. "And again, sir, I can personally assure you that we will find the person responsible. And we'll do it quickly, sir," he added. But the senator hadn't heard this last comment, as he'd already hung up.

Andy pressed the button to end the call on his phone. He put his car in gear and made his way through the winding streets towards home. The traffic was heavy and it took him almost forty-five minutes to make the trip to his house. As he drove, his mind tried to wrap itself around all that had happened in the past few hours. His world that just this morning was so calm and predictable had now been turned upside-down by this completely random act of senseless violence. He managed to merge with the traffic at the rotary and turned right. He passed Shane's and thought about his last encounter with Will Paterna there, then turned left onto a winding side street that, he was glad to discover, was void of any of the town traffic he'd just endured. He pulled into his driveway, parked the car and got out. His heavy shoes crunched on the crushed clam shells that made up his driveway and O'Toole smiled. That sound, so much like the sound your feet make walking across new-fallen snow, always gave him a feeling of satisfaction inside.

He opened the front door, which he'd always kept unlocked, walked in and turned on the lights. The house was one-story and wooden, with windows looking out on the driveway and the few scattered bushes growing in the yard. It was a pretty simple layout: one bedroom, a living room, a kitchen that opened onto a dining room. It was not much more than a small apartment, but it was comfortable and had all the space he required. More importantly, though, it was someplace different from the old house. Since his wife had died, he had sold their old home and bought this one. He just couldn't live alone in the same house he had shared with his wife for thirty-three years. He went to the kitchen and poured himself a drink—Jameson's neat, just like his father.

He sat down in the living room and briefly sorted through the mail. The phone bill, a few catalogs, and an invitation to apply for a credit card were all the communication he had received today. His nightly mail ritual completed, he went immediately to his computer and turned it on. He wanted to find out all he could about the Carlisle family. Perhaps somewhere in that information was the lead he needed, the lead that would explain who might have done this, or at least what enemies the family might have. He needed to find something that would possibly help shed some light on the situation. He would check on the Will Paterna lead, but he didn't hold out much hope, despite his assurances to the senator. The more he thought about it, and the more he thought about what Steph had said at the bar, he just felt in his heart that Paterna, for all his faults, could never have murdered someone.

Andy searched the senator's name on his favorite Internet search engine and got several hits. On one site, he found the senator's biography, a web site dedicated to the United States Senate, and read Carlisle's life story.

Leonard Erskine Carlisle, born March 17, 1940, in Middletown, Delaware, the only son of a successful accountant. He had graduated from St. George's School in Newport, Rhode Island, in 1958 and gone on to Princeton. He graduated Princeton in 1962, receiving degrees in political science and economics. After graduation, he enlisted in the United States Marine Corps, did two tours of duty in Viet Nam and was highly decorated. He was honorably discharged from the service in the summer of 1968 and he went straight on to the University of Texas Law School, where he graduated in the spring of 1971. He had worked as an attorney in private practice in

Waco, Texas, for ten years before running for the Senate. He was a Republican and currently served on the Senate Finance Committee. He was in the fifth year of his current term and would be up for re-election in November of the following year. He and his wife Lorraine lived in Waco and had four sons—Geoffrey, age 37, Richard, age 34, Christopher, age 29, and Jonathon, age 22. As O'Toole read the last name on the list, he felt a twinge of guilt, thinking that Jonathon—Jack, to those who knew him—was no longer among the living.

The rest of the information the biography gave was contact information, so that interested parties could write the senator a letter expressing their personal feelings about specific issues. There was nothing, though, that offered any sort of insight into what might have prompted someone to kill his son. He searched for any matches on the senator's name and came up with several articles from various newspapers that detailed the senator's actions while in office, citing specific issues he had voted for and against. There was a website dedicated to the church he and his wife attended while he was in Waco—it featured a picture of the two of them at a church picnic. Another site showed the senator delivering the commencement address at his former prep school the year he'd been named alumnus of the year. And that was all. Nothing that seemed to tell O'Toole anything about why someone would want to murder young Jack Carlisle.

He decided to focus his investigation instead on Jack himself. It must have been something personal between Jack and the person who killed him. He brought his mind back to the idea that it could have been someone Jack knew personally, perhaps even well. O'Toole felt that Jack must have known his killer, or else—he cut the rest of the thought out of his mind. He realized that he was so obsessed with the personal acquaintance angle because it was the only way he could find to keep himself sane for the moment. Then it popped back in, as if out of O'Toole's own conscious control. *Or else it was just a random act,* he thought to himself. And that thought was too horrific for the sheriff to contemplate right now.

He looked at his watch and realized that he had been reading about the senator for over three hours now. He turned off the computer and returned to the kitchen. He opened the refrigerator, found the leftovers from last night's dinner and threw them in the microwave. While he was waiting for his dinner to heat up, the phone rang.

"O'Toole," he said instinctively into the mouthpiece.

"Andy, goddamnit, what's this about Senator Carlisle's kid getting murdered?" the voice on the other end screamed. He recognized it immediately as Tim Hawkins, Chairman of the Nantucket Board of Selectmen, the local governing body on the island.

Andy was dumbfounded. "What are you talking about, Tim?"

"Turn on the TV and tell me what in the hell *they're* talking about," Hawkins screamed.

He ran to the living room and turned on the television. The network was airing a special report interrupting regular programming. There was the senator, sitting in front of a bank of microphones, his wife crying next to him. He heard the senator talking about the murder of his son, saying that the body had been found by a diver in Nantucket this morning. He and his wife vacationed on the island, and Jack had been working there, as he did every summer, living in the family home alone. He and his wife would be traveling to the island tomorrow morning, and he would not rest until the person or people responsible for the act were found and punished severely. Andy's body tingled from head to toe. His body was racked with feelings of fear and uncertainty.

"It's true, Tim," O'Toole finally said into the phone. "Peter Oswald, from Davy Jones' Locker, found the kid's body this morning out near the fog horn. It was sitting on the bottom, weighted down so that it would sink." He sat down in the recliner that was in the small room as Hawkins began to speak in increasingly angry tones.

"Why did I find out about this from the news?" Tim asked, clearly irritated at being left in the dark regarding what was, arguably, the most important event to date during his tenure as selectman. "Given my position, I would think—at least I would like to think—that you would feel the need and the obligation to keep me abreast of a situation like this."

"Look, Tim. We just figured out it was the Carlisle kid. I was trying to keep it quiet until after Memorial Day. I didn't want a bunch of hysterical tourists running around talking about the bloodthirsty lunatic killing people on Nantucket."

"You've got some great instincts there, Andy," the Selectman said angrily. "I suggest you get on the phone and figure out how to spin this thing. We don't need this publicity right now and you know that. We can't afford it. They're already saying that Daffodil Festival this year was the worst in history in terms of money." Andy felt a sudden stab of anger bordering on hatred for Hawkins at that moment, especially because of his comment about the Daffodil Festival. Every year, the Chamber of Commerce together with the Nantucket Garden Club and a few other civic organizations worked together to put on a spectacular weekend show in April to commemorate the blooming of daffodils all over the island. They planned, among a host of other things, a huge antique car parade and tailgate picnic, as well as flower shows and gardening lectures. Like the Figawi race, the Nantucket Daffodil Festival brought in thousands and thousands of tourists, all of whom, it was hoped, would spend thousands and thousands of dollars each. This year, though, the numbers had been down, and prognosticators all over the island were predicting a slow summer economically. Hawkins, Andy realized, was just like any other businessman who was concerned only with the bottom line, and when that bottom line was too low, he didn't care about history or beauty or tradition. He just wanted the money.

"We've got a big goddamn mess here, Andy, and you better get it cleaned up quickly," Hawkins continued, shouting into the phone. "I want this to be a distant memory very, very soon. I'll be in my office tomorrow morning. I want you to come by and we'll talk about how to handle it. We need to end this right now." He paused, as if to catch his breath, and Andy seized the opportunity to speak and, hopefully, end the call.

"I'll see you in the morning, then," Andy said meekly. "I'll come by first thing."

"I'll see you then," he huffed. "Get to work on this."

"Starting right now, Tim," Andy said as he hung up the phone. He stared blankly at the television, where a news anchor was wrapping up the events and updating viewers as to the investigation. He heard the news anchor state that investigators were "sure they have a strong lead into the case." He shuddered. Had he told the senator that there was a strong lead? He recalled the conversation he had had with Carlisle. He had said something about a lead and had said that it was a strong one. Or had he? He couldn't think straight right now and he couldn't honestly remember what he'd said at the time. He was trying to save his own skin, trying to make it look like he had more information than he really did. He was trying to help the senator to feel better and more confident about everything, especially O'Toole's investigative skills.

The phone rang again. He picked it up.

"O'Toole."

"Sheriff O'Toole," a female voice said, "what details can you give us regarding the Carlisle murder?" It was a news reporter from a Boston television station seeking a statement from him. *Sharks smelling blood in the water,* O'Toole thought to himself.

"No comment," he said and hung up the phone. Before the phone could ring again, Andy unplugged it from the wall, thereby assuring himself of at least a peaceful night's rest, if not a restful night's sleep. The microwave beeped softly, which made Andy jump. *Just the microwave,* he told himself. He went to the kitchen and opened the microwave door. Taking out the container of leftovers, Andy studied it briefly. He realized that he'd suddenly lost his appetite. The thought of food at that moment did nothing for him and he left the plastic container on the counter in the kitchen. He returned to the living room, retrieved his drink and sat on the sofa, allowing the television to drone on in the background, providing, for the moment, a sort of relaxing white noise. If Andy had chosen to focus on what it was that the reporter was saying, he'd have realized that it was anything but relaxing, but given his current state of being—a state more surreal than real for him—he was incapable of focusing on anything, especially the television. Not tonight, anyway. Tomorrow he'd check out Will Paterna.

CHAPTER NINE

Early the next morning, Andy drove to his office and met his only full-time deputy, Lance Abbott. Lance was tall and built like a brick wall; he worked out religiously. He'd worked under Andy for two years now and had always been a good deputy as far as Andy was concerned. Lance had heard about all of the goings on from the previous day and was excited to finally be involved in what he referred to as "some real police work." O'Toole would have gladly relinquished control of the investigation to the kid if he could have, but he knew that was just wishful thinking on his part. Instead Andy told Lance that he'd be accompanying him to pursue a lead, namely a suspect in the case. The suspect's name, Andy told the deputy, was Will Paterna. Though there wasn't an overwhelming amount of evidence that implicated Paterna—O'Toole was careful to leave the details vague—he was a suspect that warranted questioning, at least in O'Toole's professional opinion. He also said, perhaps overplaying the father figure, that he thought it would be good experience for Lance to be involved. He tried his best to sound the part of cool and calm sheriff who did this sort of thing all the time. In truth, though, he was terrified, both of what he might find and of what might happen. The main reason he wanted Lance along, he had to admit to himself, was that he wanted the protection that the burly deputy's presence afforded him.

The two men were silent as they drove to Paterna's house, Lance eager and excited to be involved with such a major investigation, the sheriff alternately wondering what he'd do if Paterna did turn out to be the killer and what he'd do if he turned out to have nothing to do with it at all. On the one hand, if Paterna was guilty, O'Toole would be a hero who'd saved the island from a crazed murderer, but he'd also have to risk the confrontation with Will that would inevitably come before his hero status was conferred. On the other hand, if Paterna was innocent, Andy would have to explain to the senator, among others, that his "strong lead"—his only lead—had turned out to be a wild goose chase. He wondered to himself if detectives more accustomed to this sort of work felt the same way when beginning a case and pursuing preliminary leads.

As they neared the house, Andy was conscious of the sounds of planes flying close overhead, shuttling more and more people onto the island for the weekend. *Like lambs to the slaughter,* he thought to himself. *All these people following each other, coming out here to spend their money.* Then he cringed at the thought of the comparison he'd made. *Like lambs to the slaughter,* he thought to himself again. *So many targets coming out here, and a murderer waiting for them.*

Andy turned sharply onto a dirt road that served as a driveway to Paterna's house, which sprang out of a thorny patch of nondescript bushes, and the two got out of the car. Attempting to negotiate the path to the front door was something akin to walking through a tropical rainforest, the branches intertwining like a fence protecting the house on the other side. As Andy and Lance made their way through the dense foliage, O'Toole looked around. The house was built in a clearing in the brambles. It was small and squatty, grey shingles covering the exterior as required by the local building codes. There were few windows and the house felt cold from the outside. At the front door, O'Toole looked around on the ground near the door in a preliminary search for anything that might suggest this was his man. He was desperate to find support for being there, both to protect Steph's anonymity, but also to assist in eradicating his many doubts about the wisdom of being here. Empty scallop shells, bleached white by their lengthy exposure to the sun, sat in the dirt, but they were one of the only indications that anyone had ever been here before. O'Toole lifted a shaking hand and knocked on the door.

"Who is it?" a voice asked from the other side of the plain wooden door.

"Will, it's Andy O'Toole. Just want to talk to you about something."

"I didn't do anything, Andy," the voice said. "You're barkin' up the wrong tree, whatever it is you're thinkin'." Paterna still hadn't opened the door and the sheriff had to shout to be heard.

"I just want to talk to you about something, Will. No accusations. Just talking. Please open the door."

He heard a lock turn and the door opened slowly. Will stepped out onto the porch and closed the door quickly behind him. Andy thought he smelled marijuana smoke coming from inside, but that wasn't why he was here. He ignored it for the moment.

"What do you need?" Will asked impersonally.

Andy looked at him. The nickname of Gowilla suited him well. He was enormous, with very short dark hair and a wide, round face. His eyes were bloodshot and he was dressed only in a pair of oil-stained jeans. A tattoo of a snake wrapped around a dagger adorned his left arm, a nude female torso tattooed on the right arm. His stomach bulged out over the waistline of his jeans and his feet were filthy dirty.

"Can we come inside?" Andy asked.

"No," Will replied, looking first at Andy then at Lance. "I've got company."

Andy figured that was a lie but didn't want to push his luck right now. He had no warrant, no evidence. Just a suspicion that he didn't put much stock in himself.

"Okay. Then we'll talk out here," he said in a tone approaching congeniality. He had to remind himself that he was most likely taking an innocent man away from whatever it was he'd been doing. He was an imposition of sorts. "I wanted to ask you where you'd been on the night of May twenty-third, say between eleven and two o'clock."

Will looked at the sheriff with a blank expression. "No idea. I don't keep track of my days like that."

"Think," the sheriff said to him, "it could help me out here. Did you work that night? Like at the Jib and Jenny maybe?" Andy already knew the answer to this question; Steph had told him the day before that Will had been drinking at the Jib and Jenny on the night in question. He wanted Will to say it, though. Attempting to assist as best he could, Lance stood imposingly behind Andy, trying to play the part of street-smart cop, hoping to force the answer out of Paterna by looking at him with his most intimidating face. Will just smiled back at him. He knew Lance was nothing more than a glorified meter maid who was probably going to have to go home and change his pants after this conversation.

"Nope. I've been off from working the door for the last three weeks. Been workin' so much during the day that I didn't have the energy to work the Jenny. I've been hangin' around here mostly during the night."

"Think again, Will. Is it possible, just possible, that you were maybe drinking at the Jib and Jenny that night?" Because he'd been friends with Paterna's father, Andy wanted to see the kid do the right thing. Most of all, though, he wanted the kid to tell him the truth. He hoped he wasn't coming across to Will as confrontational. The last thing he wanted right now was to pick a fight with Will.

"Sure it's possible, Andy," Will sighed. "Like I said, though, I don't keep track of my days like that. It's not like I've got one of those hand-held computer things that tells me where I am and where I'm going and when I'm doing what. I just do what I do and go where I go." He cleared his throat and looked out at the bushes behind Lance, who continued to stand in statuesque motionlessness, arms still crossed, face still screwed up in the most serious-looking expression he could muster. "So yeah it's possible I was there. I just don't remember."

"So you've been working a lot, huh?" Andy asked, trying to change tacks. "Construction, right?"

"Construction, yeah," he said absent-mindedly. "Had a lot of contracting work over the winter, trying to finish it all before the summer rolls around and people start showing up. That's when it gets really busy for me. But you know how that goes, huh?" He coughed loudly. He seemed nervous to Andy, but the sheriff had questioned enough people—enough innocent people—in his lifetime to know that anyone who is confronted by the police is going to be nervous, regardless of whether or not that person is guilty.

Andy looked down at the scallop shells next to the front porch. "You do some scalloping last winter?" he asked.

"Yeah, but I got a license," Will replied with a tone of suspicion. "Not against the law, is it?"

"No," O'Toole replied, forcing a smile. "You go out and push for 'em?" he asked, trying to seem like he was on Will's side, trying to be his friend in this whole mess. O'Toole himself had never been scalloping, but he'd seen enough of it to know the basic idea. Either you took a long-handled net and pushed it along to pick them up or you dragged a sort of net behind a boat and caught them that way.

"Nah," said Will. "I dive for 'em. Usually have a few places scouted out by late October, wait until the commercial season opens in November, then hit it hard and fast. Lots of times by the middle of December, my secret places are all done, so I start following other people. Peter Oswald's one of 'em. He's always gettin' his limit every day."

At the mention of Peter Oswald's name, Andy's brain sparked briefly. "So you're a diver, huh?"

"Not really a diver," Will said. "I dive some. Most of the diving I do is for scallops. It's not like I can just take off and go diving, you know? I have to work it into my schedule."

Andy nodded. "I see," he said. "Been diving recently?"

"Nope," Will said. "Too much work, not enough time."

"Not at all? I mean, you haven't been diving at all?" asked the sheriff.

"Not at all," he said. Then the tone of his voice suddenly became much more defensive. "What the hell? Did some lobsterman report his pots gettin' picked? Talk to Oswald. He's the guy you want for that." He laughed. Then, shifting back to his previous tone of irritation, "Are we done yet? I'd like to get back inside."

Andy nodded. "Yeah, we're done here. I'm sorry to bother you." Andy felt like he'd gotten the information he wanted, and he could verify it with Peter. Anyone who went diving on the island would, if nothing else, have to get their air tanks filled at Davy Jones' Locker, so he'd ask Peter to find out if Will had been diving recently. He gestured to Lance, and the two turned back and started to pick their way through the thorn bushes covering the walkway. On the way to the car, Andy caught the smell of something that his brain processed as something out of place and, looking in the direction from where the smell came, O'Toole noticed a shed that was behind the house and a large plastic bag to one side on the ground next to it. On a hunch, he told Lance to stay where he was and returned to the front door. Again, hand shaking even more, he knocked.

The door opened again and Will thrust his head out. "What now?" he asked.

"You mind if I check your shed over there?" Andy said, indicating the shed with a slight shrug of his head.

"Jesus Christ," Will replied. "I told you I didn't rob any lobster pots. I really wish you'd just leave."

"Look, Will," O'Toole said. "I'm just asking you if you mind if I go over there and look at your shed." He thought this was pretty shaky ground, legally speaking, but if Will gave him permission, he wouldn't need a warrant. Probably nothing anyway, he reminded himself. But his pulse had quickened noticeably.

Will walked out, slammed the door behind him and accompanied the sheriff to the shed. He was mumbling to himself as they walked, clearly growing angry with the sheriff's repeated interruptions. At the shed, O'Toole noticed that flies were crawling on the plastic bag and the smell that he'd caught a moment earlier was that of something rotting inside the bag. He turned around and asked Will, "What's in there?"

"Striper guts," Will replied. "Caught a few yesterday afternoon out at Smith's Point. I'm gonna' take 'em to the dump tomorrow, don't worry." Andy lifted the bag.

"Pretty big fish, huh?" he asked, his heart beginning to beat even more rapidly. The bag, he thought, felt heavier than it should have if it contained only a few striped bass carcasses. ,

"Yeah," Will said. "I guess so." He yawned and stretched, trying to exaggerate the boredom he felt at being led through what he saw as a pointless waste of his time.

The sheriff reached down and untied the bag. The sun was now up in the sky and a sunbeam seemed to reach straight down into the top of the bag. As he opened it, Andy was overwhelmed by the stench of rotting fish. He let out a sigh of relief; his suspicions had been unfounded, just like he'd thought they were. He'd never been happier to smell day-old fish.

"See?" said Will. "It's just fish guts."

The sheriff peered in to the bag. Four large fish heads criss-crossed inside, eyes wide open in final death stares, the black lines showing darkly against the scaly white bodies. He closed the bag, his heartbeat returning to normal, and looked away to get a breath of fresh air. Then it hit him. He saw the whole thing in his mind, but it didn't look the same in his brain as it did sitting there on the ground. There was something beneath the carcasses. Something different. Something wrong. The sheriff opened the bag again and shook it. Below the dead fish was a bloody and tangled mass of blonde hair. The sheriff looked up at Will.

"Don't move," he commanded in a measured, even tone.

"What?" asked Will. His anger was still there in his voice, but now it shared its existence with confused fear.

"You heard me. Don't move. You're under arrest for the murder of Jack Carlisle." He reached into his pocket and took out his cellular phone. He dialed the police dispatcher and told her where he was and to send a cruiser immediately. He called for Lance to come over and assist, and the young deputy came at a run.

"Are you gonna tell me what's going on here, or do I have to guess?" asked Will as he complied with the sheriff's orders. Through his past run-ins with the law, he'd learned that it was always better to cooperate first and fight it later.

78

"Just shut up and stay right there," said O'Toole. "You're under arrest." Lance eyed Paterna suspiciously, hand poised to draw his gun if Will decided to run for freedom. Paterna, though, looked pretty content to allow himself to be taken into custody, not as if he were about to make a break for it.

The cruiser took only minutes to arrive at their location, and Will Paterna was taken into custody. The arresting officer read Paterna his rights and asked if he would be willing to answer questions. Paterna agreed in a confused voice, still proclaiming that he had no idea what it was he'd done wrong. "All the fish were legal size," he added, hoping his supposed offense was as minor as that.

But when O'Toole confronted him with the evidence in the bag, he denied ever seeing it. "Oh, shit," she said, unable to contain the emotional outburst. "I haven't got a clue what that's all about." O'Toole forced him to look at the unseeing eyes of Jack's head.

"Don't tell me you didn't know him either, Will, because I know you did," O'Toole said accusatorially.

"Yeah, I knew who he was," Paterna began, swallowing his gag reflex. "But I didn't really know him." He coughed loudly and spat. "He came in the Jib and Jenny all the time, so I knew him from workin' the door in there. He's some little rich summer kid; father was a senator, I think."

"Seems like you knew a lot about him, Will. Maybe you know so much because you planned his murder," he suggested.

"For Chrissake, Andy, everybody knew who he was. I said I didn't really know all that well. That's what I mean," he pleaded. Now he was sounding like a criminal caught red-handed, O'Toole thought. The story's changing as we go along. He decided to seize the advantage and stuck with the full-frontal assault.

"But you had words with him, right?" O'Toole prodded. "You threw him out the back door one night. Remember?"

"Yeah, I remember," he replied, turning away his gaze from the bag. "But that was a long time ago, Andy, and it was really no big deal. I swear." He looked straight at the sheriff, meeting his gaze. "It was just a little pushing and shoving, that's it." He looked back towards the bag, despite his best efforts to prevent himself from doing it. "But nothing like this," he added, wincing at the sight of the bag's grisly contents.

"So why'd you kill him?" asked the sheriff, not believing for a moment that Paterna was innocent. So much for his earlier doubts.

"I just told you. I didn't do a damn thing to that kid," said Will, still not comprehending the magnitude of what was happening to him in this surreal scene that was unfolding on his front lawn.

"It's not lookin' good for you, Will," said O'Toole with a tone of resignation. "Not good at all." He shook his head and clicked his tongue against his teeth.

"I'm done talkin'," said Will. "I listened to my rights and I know I don't have to talk, so do what you gotta do and let's get it over with. I didn't do anything. I want a lawyer." He fixed his gaze on a spot somewhere over O'Toole's right shoulder, willing his eyes to stay focused on some distant point.

"Innocent people don't need lawyers," said Andy. "Only guilty people do."

Will looked up at him and said, "I didn't do a damn thing, but I still want a lawyer."

With that, O'Toole stopped his interrogation and loaded Paterna into the back of the waiting cruiser. The drive back to the station was silent, Will, handcuffed, sitting in the back of the Nantucket police cruiser, O'Toole following in his own car. At the station, Will was fingerprinted and photographed and allowed to call his attorney. He knew who he wanted to call, but he didn't know the number. He asked for a phone book and he looked up the number. He called the attorney who had handled a charge of drug possession for him during the previous winter and told him where he was. The lawyer told him to stay quiet and just do what he was told. After he hung up, Will was locked into one of the three cells in the station. "This is a fuckin' joke," yelled Will at one of the officers. "I didn't do anything."

The officer on duty stayed silent.

"I don't believe this," he fumed. "I didn't do anything," he repeated, as if he believed that saying it again would somehow make the officers change their minds.

When the lawyer arrived at the police station, he found Andy O'Toole together with three other officers. They were talking about the arrest and filling out the paperwork required for the courts. "So what's the charge, gentlemen?" he asked nonchalantly.

"Murder. First Degree. He killed Senator Carlisle's kid," replied the sheriff.

The attorney was stunned. "Will? Murder? You've got to be kidding me. Worst thing that kid ever did was broke somebody's nose during a bar fight. He's no murderer, Andy, and you know it."

"Surprises me as much as it does you, counselor," Andy replied. "But here's the problem with feeling that way. We found the victim's head at his house," said O'Toole. "He had it buried in a trash bag of fish carcasses." And then, as if to add a tone of finality to the investigation, he said, "He's the one."

"I want to talk to him," said the lawyer, ignoring O'Toole's accusations. He was shown to Will's cell by one of the officers and he asked to be left alone with his client. When the officer had left them, he turned to Will.

"So what's up here, Will?" he asked.

"I don't know," he said. "All I know is I'm sittin' at home, O'Toole comes to the house, starts askin' me where I was on some night. I told him I didn't know, then he starts askin' me about divin' for scallops. He leaves, then comes back, tells me he wants to look at the shed out behind the house. I go out there, he opens a bag of striper guts, then tells me I'm under arrest."

"They found a kid's head in that bag, Will. You know that, right?"

"Hell yes, I know I that. I was standin' right there when he found the damn thing. I don't have any idea how it got there, though."

The lawyer looked at Will skeptically. He had long ago made it a point to never defend anyone whom he knew was lying to him about his innocence. If the client admitted his guilt, then he was willing to represent him in whatever sort of plea bargain he could arrange. But if a client wanted him to get up and argue in court that he was completely innocent of all charges, he needed to believe it in his heart. He looked at his new client, sitting there on the bed in his cell. He wanted to believe Will. He had to truly believe him if he was going to defend him, but it was pretty damning evidence, he had to admit. "So you didn't have anything to do with it?"

"Hell no, I didn't. Like I told them, I knew the kid, I'd had arguments with him, and I didn't like him. That was no secret to anybody. But I swear to God I didn't kill him."

"Are you absolutely positive, Will?" the attorney asked, trying to convince himself. "I need to know. I'm your lawyer, Will. You've got to tell me the truth."

"I told you I didn't do it, and I didn't do it. I swear to God I didn't do it," Will said pleadingly.

"Okay, Will. I'll see what I can do for you. I'll warn you, though, this won't be cheap for you."

"I don't care. Just figure out what happened, get me out of here, and I'll pay you whatever you want. I didn't do a damn thing and I shouldn't be here."

The lawyer called for the officer on duty to let him out of the cell and turned to Will. "Just keep your mouth shut. You hear me? Not a word to anybody."

Will nodded silently. The officer appeared, opened the cell door, and let the lawyer out. He approached the assembled officers in the main office of the police station. "He didn't do it," he told the officers. He knew that he was trying to convince himself of the fact as much as he was trying to convince the officers themselves.

"Of course he didn't," replied O'Toole. "Nobody in prison is actually guilty, counselor. You know that."

"I honestly don't think he did it," said the lawyer. He hoped he sounded convincing.

"Then explain the head we found at his house," said O'Toole.

"I'm working on that," said the lawyer as he walked out the door.

"Just keep working at it," shouted O'Toole. The sheriff turned to the other officers. "Get somebody out there right now. I want a uniformed officer watching that house at all times."

"Already been done, Andy," replied one of the officers. "We've got two guys out there."

"Good," replied Andy. He told Lance to hang around, assuring him that he'd call him when he needed him. Then he raced to Tim Hawkins' office upstairs and burst through the door, saying, "We got him, Tim. Will Paterna. He killed the Carlisle kid. Got him dead to rights."

The selectman looked up, shocked at the sudden interruption, and saw that it was Andy. His anger from the night before was still present, but it sounded as if Andy had some good news to share. "Slow down, Andy," said Tim. "Now tell me again what's happening."

So Andy told him everything, trying to highlight his own police intuition, saying he had had "a feeling" about Paterna all along, and that he'd found him through "good old fashioned police work."

"That's great news, Andy," said Hawkins, sighing heavily. "You realize, though, that this doesn't get you off the hook entirely, right? I'm still a little peeved about not being informed."

You bastard, thought Andy. *Here I tell you I caught the murderer, and all you can do is tell me you're mad I didn't tell me about something earlier?* "Yeah, Tim," he sighed, resigning himself to his position, "I'm sorry about that. I promise to keep you informed of all things pertaining to major investigations—especially this one—as they occur." He tried to look contrite.

Tim smiled, indicating that all, for the moment, was forgiven. He took the sheriff's hand and said, "That's great, though, Andy. Seriously. Great news and great work. Make sure, though, you do all this by the book. Make sure you've got this kid beyond any shred of any shadow of any doubt. I don't want this to backfire. You know the press is going to be all over this case, and everything has got to be sealed up tight."

"Not a problem, Tim," Andy replied confidently. "It's all taken care of."

He turned and walked out of the office, feeling very pleased with himself. In just over twenty-four hours, he had apprehended the murderer of Jack Carlisle and he was now, he guessed, as much of a celebrity as the senator himself. He walked up the stairs, carrying himself with an air of authority reminiscent of the ruler of a large country, and once inside the safe confines of his own office, he lit a cigarette and looked out the window. There was a momentary buzz in his brain, something unconscious that wasn't painful so much as it was disturbing. He dropped the cigarette out the window and sighed heavily because he was unsure as to why he couldn't shake the feeling that something wasn't right still. It was another one of his hunches that he couldn't quite pin down, but he felt confident in the fact that things were not necessarily what they seemed. He turned back to his desk and resumed filling out paperwork, hoping the feeling would pass.

CHAPTER TEN

By early the next morning, news of Paterna's arrest had spread quickly. News agencies from across the country were calling the sheriff's office, desperate for new information. The office had issued a press release, authored by Sheriff O'Toole, stating the name and details of the accused: William Thomas Paterna, aged twenty-nine years, resident of Nantucket, working for Coffin and Coffin Construction. The press release also explained how Sheriff Andy O'Toole had single-handedly discovered the murderer's identity, and praised him for his excellent investigative techniques. O'Toole had made sure the report contained that information, because he wanted to be damn sure he got the recognition he deserved here. Most importantly, though, Senator Carlisle had yet to learn of the report, as he was aboard a plane bound for Boston. O'Toole wanted to be the first one to tell him, so that he could see the senator's face when he learned that Andy was, in fact, a hero.

Andy spent much of the day fielding calls from reporters and granting interviews to television news crews. The island was also awash in visitors, with the ferries and planes continuing to unload their cargo of bodies, and more people were en route, as the first boats in the Figawi were beginning to arrive. The Massachusetts State Police had shipped in reinforcements, and O'Toole had used the extra men to work crowd control in and around the downtown area as more and more people descended on the island.

During a lull in the phone calls, Andy slipped across the street to Davy Jones' Locker, leaving Lance and Claudia at the office to deal with any more requests from interested parties. Inside, the store was crammed with people and the cash register was beeping like an alarm clock as it rang up sale after sale. Andy made his way to the far side of the counter. "Hey there, Peter," he said.

Peter Oswald looked up from the register. "Hey, Andy," he said smiling. "Heard you caught the guy that did it. Good job."

Andy smiled. "Yeah. We couldn't let that get in the way of Memorial Day, huh?" He looked at the display counter in front of him. "Not selling any more illegal knives, are you?"

Peter smiled. "Not since three years ago, Sheriff," he said smiling, playing along with O'Toole's joke. "And I swear we didn't know they were illegal." It was nice for Peter to able to now act lightheartedly about what had been, at the time, a very serious and tense situation. His store had been caught selling knives that, under state law, were considered illegal. Double-edged knives or knives with brass knuckle-style grips were illegal in Massachusetts. Peter had claimed that the knives were solely for diving purposes, as far as he knew, because they were excellent for disentangling ropes or other debris from boat propellers. The state, though, had disagreed, and had seized all the knives and fined the store.

"Bullshit," said Andy laughing. "Looks like you got enough customers in here, though, illegal knives or not."

Peter laughed. "Already sold seven thousand dollars worth of this garbage today, and it's only eleven. We're cranking in here."

"Peter, I wanted to talk to you about Will Paterna, if you've got the time."

He looked around the store and then looked at his employees. Not including Peter, there were four people behind the counter, and they were all busy. "We're pretty swamped right now, Andy," Peter said. "Could we do it later?"

"We can handle it," one of the employees said. Andy recognized the young man who'd spoken as the manager he'd met the day before. "We'll just make the bastards wait their turn," he added winking. Davy Jones' Locker had long been known as a place where the employees were at best rude, and often bordered on hostile in their behavior towards the customers. Peter encouraged the attitude. He thought it gave the store a sense of character.

"You sure, Jimmie?" Peter asked.

"Yeah, I'm sure. Get outta here, ya' big lug," the young man said laughing.

Peter left with Andy, and they walked next door to the Jib and Jenny. They walked up to the bar and sat down, and Peter asked for a menu. Steph smiled at him as she gave him the menu, saying, "Peter Oswald, you eat lunch at that same seat in here every day, and every day you ask for a menu. Do you think it's going to change from day to day or something?"

Peter laughed and replied, "Hey, you never know. I might have overlooked something in here."

"Yeah," Steph said snickering. "Like cheeseburgers and sodas, right?" She then turned to check on her other customers at the bar.

As Peter examined the menu, Andy began asking him questions about Will Paterna.

"So what do you know about Paterna?" Andy asked.

"Not much. He took dive lessons about five or six years ago. He's one of those guys that dives for scallops with us during the winter, but he's not really a diver. He's more of a pain in the ass."

"What do you mean?" asked O'Toole.

"He's always getting in the way. You'll go to pick up a scallop or whatever and he's right on top of you, kicking up sand and just being in the way. He doesn't watch where he's going. I remember one time I had him diving with me on a wreck over off the Cape. I saw the absolute biggest lobster I'd ever seen in my life and I was all set to catch it, when he stuck his big foot right in my face. I wanted to kill him. He's just a pain in the ass," he repeated as he put the menu down flat on the bar. Peter turned to Steph behind the bar. "I'll have a cheeseburger, please. And a soda."

She laughed and shook her head. "Something new, huh? Cheeseburger and a soda. Sure thing, Peter. Anything for you, Andy?" she asked.

"I'm good, thanks, Steph. I'll just have a glass of water." She entered the order into the cash register behind the bar, which was hooked up to a terminal in the kitchen so that the cooks could see what they needed to prepare.

"So he doesn't dive with you much?" continued Andy.

"No," replied Peter. "I told him I don't like diving with him. Aside from the fact that he's a pain to deal with underwater, he's got some other problems. He's doing coke, you know."

"So I've heard," said O'Toole. "You don't dive with him because he does cocaine?"

"Yeah," said Peter. "I don't like diving with those guys. Scare the hell out of me."

Though he wasn't necessarily surprised at this information, Andy was momentarily taken aback by Peter's response. He remembered all too well the years during which Peter had been drinking, before he'd joined Alcoholics Anonymous, and to see the change that had taken place in his attitude regarding such social issues was amazing, if not frightening. He was like a born-again religious zealot who had found God after years in prison. There was a time when Peter would have embraced the behavior of drug users doing things like risking their lives scuba diving while under the influence. Today it was a much different story.

As the two men continued their conversation about Will Paterna, Andy's cellular phone rang. He turned to Peter. "Hang on a sec." He pulled the phone from his pocket. "O'Toole."

As the voice on the other end of the line spoke, Andy's face gradually lost its expression of mission accomplished. "What do you mean an 'irregularity?'" he said. He was silent for a moment, listening to the voice. "Don't give me this police talk. Just tell me the story." He turned his back to Peter and began to speak in quiet, muffled tones.

"No way," he said finally. "Absolutely no way. He's the guy." He stared at the wall, listening. "I don't care what it looks like." Another long pause, punctuated by O'Toole alternately muttering and coughing.

"Don't touch anything. I'll be there as soon as I can," he finally said. He angrily stabbed his finger at one of the buttons on his phone and turned to Peter. "Son of a bitch," he muttered.

"Let me guess," Peter said. "Another body?" He immediately regretted saying it. He knew it was an inappropriate comment. But before he could apologize, O'Toole interjected as if it was perfectly apropos of the situation.

"Don't even joke," Andy said. "Seems we've got something out at the crime scene. Something not quite right. I gotta run," he said. He stood up. "I'll talk to you later, Peter. Thanks, Steph." He turned and walked out the door.

"Bye, Andy," Steph called behind him. "Thanks, sweetie."

Andy raced through the crowds to his car. He got in and started the engine. He pulled away from the curb and drove as quickly as he could through the strangled, narrow streets of downtown Nantucket. He pulled onto South Water Street and headed towards Paterna's house. His mind was racing. *This can't be happening,* he kept telling himself. *I know Paterna did it. There is nothing wrong. This can't be happening right now. Not today. Please, not today. He gripped the steering wheel tensely, then took a deep breath. Calm down, Andy,* he said to himself. At Main Street, traffic was at a standstill. A ferry had unloaded its passengers, and many of them were now wandering up the cobblestone street, trailing suitcases on wheels that were not designed for bumps, let alone large rocks. He lit a cigarette and cursed all of humanity at once.

When he finally crossed Main Street, the traffic thinned out somewhat and he pushed the accelerator. He paid no attention to the yield signs at the rotary, flipping on his sirens as he sped straight through. He passed the airport and turned left onto the dirt road that led to Paterna's house. When he finally got to the house, he ran through the bushes to the waiting officers.

"What gives," he said to the pair of officers assigned to watch the house.

"Well, Andy," one of the young officers began. "We were just looking around the shed over there when we saw a set of footprints in the dirt. Here. I'll show you." The officer led O'Toole around to the side of the shed and there, in the dirt, was a set of footprints, large footprints, leading to the shed and then leading away, back into the bushes. The bushes surrounding the yard had served as a sort of barricade against the wind, and the dirt had been moist from the recent fog, so the footprints were perfectly set into the soil. It was clear even to the most casual of observers that they led both to and from the shed. And it was equally clear that somebody—somebody other than Will Paterna— had been walking there.

"So what?" Andy said. "It's just somebody walking around over here. Probably Paterna's footprints," he added, in hopes of turning this problematic discovery into an irrelevant side issue.

The young officer shook his head. "They don't go to or from the house, Sheriff," he said meekly, as if he were afraid of upsetting O'Toole. "It doesn't make any sense. And if you look over there at those bushes," he continued, pointing at the large patch of blackberry brambles growing wildly in the yard, "you can see where somebody walked through there." O'Toole looked in the direction the officer indicated and saw that, in fact, the bushes had been broken off, as if someone had tried to blaze a trail through them.

"And that's not all, Sheriff," said the officer. "Look over here," he said, pointing to the opening in the bushes. O'Toole's stomach dropped as he contemplated the young officer's latest revelation. "There's something else back here. Something weird." The officer's description of the new evidence as "something weird" almost made O'Toole laugh, as he felt like nothing could be more weird than what he was living through right now. O'Toole followed the officer back into the bushes about fifteen feet and looked down at the ground where the officer was pointing.

"I found those sitting there and that's when I called you," he said. O'Toole bent down to look at what was before him on the ground. Six cigarette butts, Marlboro lights. Rather than touch them, O'Toole bent down and looked. On each butt, O'Toole could see a faint red stain that looked at first like lipstick, but which was too far up the cigarette itself to be from a person's lips. Rather, he determined, it was blood from someone's hand, someone who had been standing back here smoking. And the butts didn't look to him as if they'd been there a real long time. He'd smoked long enough to know when cigarette butts sat around for some time, but these looked as if they'd just been deposited. And though he wasn't any kind of forensic scientist, he recognized the value inherent in the butts.

"What do you think, Sheriff?" asked the officer.

Andy shook his head as the scene before him percolated through his over-taxed brain. "I'm not sure, son, but it looks like someone was back here smoking cigarettes while they were waiting for something." He knew this information sounded almost too obvious to point out, but there was nothing else really to say to the kid.

Andy didn't know what exactly to make of this new discovery, but he did notice that the trail through the bushes led in two directions: in one direction it led to the shed where O'Toole had found the trash bag containing Jack Carlisle's head, and in the other direction it led to the street. Andy surveyed the scene around him, noting that from where he stood, presumably the point where the person or people in question had deposited their cigarette butts, he could clearly see the shed outside Paterna's house, while at the same time being hidden from view of the house. Suddenly it dawned on him. "Somebody planted that head there," he said matter-of-factly.

The officer looked at O'Toole and said, "What do you mean, Sheriff? You mean like somebody's trying to pin the crime on Will?"

Andy nodded, thinking to himself that these summer cops—usually college kids who were interested in joining the police force after graduation who gained on-the-job training by working for the Nantucket Police Department during the summer—would one day say something so ridiculous that he would go certifiably insane. "That's exactly what I mean, son," he said as he swallowed his frustration. "I'm thinking that somebody, the same somebody who's our real killer, was back there smoking cigarettes, and he had blood on his hands. He was waiting for a chance to put that head in the garbage bag. That, son, is what I think." He led the officer back to the shed and took out his cellular phone. His fingers were shaking as he dialed the number for Tom Latkin.

When the doctor answered, Andy was very short and very to the point: "Tom, we've found some cigarette butts out here in the bushes behind Will Paterna's house. They've got what looks like blood on them, like somebody with bloody fingers had been smoking them. Is there any way to figure out what the blood type on there is?"

The doctor mumbled something on the other end of the line, then replied, "Yeah, Andy. There are all sorts of tests I can do on it. It's hard to say how much value the tests will be, given the fact that you found them outside and that there's no telling how long they've been there. What sort of information do you want?"

In all honesty, Andy wasn't entirely sure what information he wanted and he wasn't sure what to tell him. "I don't know, Tom. What kind of information can you give me? Realize, though, doc, that I just looked at them and I don't think they've been here for very long. I'm no expert, but they don't look real old to me."

"Well," the doctor began, "in that case, I can do a conventional serological analysis, just to tell you the blood type. I can also do what's called a Restriction Fragment Length Polymorphism analysis, which will tell you the DNA makeup of the blood. Or I can do a Polymerase Chain Reaction analysis, which also gives you a genetic makeup of the DNA. Whatever information you want, I can probably find it for you. Assuming, of course, that you're right about them not being out there too long." Latkin's voice sounded authoritative, as if he were addressing an assembled group of doctors at some sort of medical conference.

Andy looked at the other officers in a very confused way and said into the phone, "Doc, can you just tell me if it's Jack Carlisle's blood?" And then, with a short laugh, "And can you tell me in plain English?"

"Almost certainly, Andy," the doctor said. "I'm not sure how you want this to stand up in court, but if you're looking to convict someone on it, you'll need to do at least the RFLP test to prove the DNA matches."

"Okay," Andy sighed into the phone, "you know better than I do. Can you come down here and pick these things up and get started on testing them?"

"Be there in a flash," the doctor replied. "Day here is done here, so I'm free. Give me ten minutes." Andy gave the doctor directions to the house and told him he'd meet him in the front yard. He hung up the phone and replaced it in his pocket. He then turned to the other officers.

"Tom Latkin's on his way over here to collect those things," he said as he gestured towards the discarded cigarettes. "He's going to do some tests to see whose blood is on there." While they waited, O'Toole retrieved a camera from the car, as he wanted to document the location of the evidence the officers had discovered. He snapped several pictures, then returned the camera to the car. Several minutes later, the doctor's ancient Jeep pulled up to the house and he got out, carrying with him a brown briefcase. Andy met him in the yard and pointed out the path where they had located the cigarette butts.

The doctor set his bag down and opened it, removing several glass vials, each with different colored caps. Andy thought better of asking the differences between the various collection jars, fearing another scientific explanation from the well-meaning doctor. Latkin proceeded slowly into the bushes and began the recovery of the evidence there. He methodically picked up each butt with a pair of silver forceps and placed them carefully into different vials. When he'd completed the retrieval, he returned to where Andy was standing and told him, "Okay. All done here. I'll have the blood type in about fifteen minutes for you. I think the samples I've got should be sufficient for that test, and it requires the most blood. The DNA tests don't need as much, so I should be able to do all the tests with what I've got left over. DNA tests will take a few weeks, so don't get too antsy about your identification." Andy nodded silently. "Of course, if it's Jack's blood, I should know that by the type."

Andy looked puzzled. "What do you mean, Tom?"

"Ordinarily, blood types aren't very reliable ways of identifying people. But Jack's blood type is rare—AB-negative, the rarest type there is. Something like one person in every five hundred has it. So I can type the blood on these things and, if it's AB-negative, you can be relatively confident that it's Jack's. But again, you'll have to wait for the DNA test to confirm that fact."

"That's fine, Tom," Andy said. "Can you just get me the type as soon as possible? I'm afraid that if that blood is Jack's, then somebody planted that evidence there, and that means that our boy Will Paterna is innocent."

"I'll get on it right now, Andy," the doctor replied gravely. "I'll tell you what I know as soon as I know it." He replaced the vials in his briefcase and walked back to his car. From where they stood, the men assembled by the shed could hear the engine turn over and the car pull away, as Latkin went to make O'Toole's worst nightmare come true.

Andy looked at the officers on duty and said, "You two have been here all day, right? Nobody's been here besides you guys?"

"Nobody, Sheriff, and we've been making sure that nobody comes even close. One of us has been standing here for the last..." The officer paused and looked at his watch. "For the last fifteen hours," he announced proudly.

Personally he had a hard time believing he'd been there that long; the time had gone by surprisingly quickly, and he suddenly felt put-out by having been assigned to such a mundane task for so long. But he'd also been told to expect to be there for quite a long time, given the circumstances with the holiday weekend, and with that thought, his self-righteous irritation waned.

O'Toole chewed the end of his thumb as he thought about his next move. Finally he pulled out his phone and dialed his own office number. His secretary answered after three rings. "Claudia, it's Andy. How are things down at the office?"

"It's crazy here, Sheriff. Everybody wants to know what's going on, and between me and Lance, we're barely keeping up with all of them." *She sounds excited, like a kid on Christmas,* Andy thought. *She thinks everything is solved.*

O'Toole swallowed hard. "Claudia," he said quietly, "we might have a little problem here. Don't answer any more questions from anybody until I get there, okay? Just tell anybody who asks I'm not there and I'll get back to them as soon as I can, and that you're real sorry, but you just don't know anything about the investigation."

"Okay," she said, sounding somewhat surprised and concerned. "What's wrong, Andy?"

"Nothing," he said. "Nothing at all. Just don't answer any questions, okay? I'll handle it."

"Sure thing, Andy. Whatever you say," she said in a nervous tone. He hung up the phone without further comment and turned to the officers.

"Okay, boys. Let's figure this out," he said. "And let's make it snappy. We need this to look good by eight o'clock, because I'm meeting with Senator Carlisle tonight and I want to tell him that we've got the case solved." He pulled out a cigarette, thought about lighting it, but then remembered that this was officially a crime scene. He grudgingly replaced it in his shirt pocket and turned to one of the officers, saying, "Let's you and me go find out where those footprints go, son. You," he continued, indicating the other officer of the pair, "stay here until we get back. And remember, nobody gets on this property." The officer addressed nodded his head solemnly. O'Toole turned to the other officer and said simply, "Let's go find us a murderer."

CHAPTER ELEVEN

Before setting out along the trail left by whomever it was that had been walking through the bushes, O'Toole grabbed the camera from his car, as he wasn't sure what else he might find that would be pertinent to the investigation. Once he'd secured it, he, together with the other officer, followed the footprints in the soft dirt. They led back into the blackberry brambles. Multiple broken branches showed where the person had walked. The only question was where the footprints ended. They led toward the paved road that ran by the airport, and as they neared the pavement, they became progressively harder to identify. They ended at the side of the road, where Andy was able to see faintly the tire treads that had carried off the person. In the street, where the tire treads began, there was a pool of black, viscous liquid, which O'Toole presumed was oil leaking from the vehicle that had transported the mysterious person. Stuck in the oil was a piece of yellow paper, what looked like a receipt. O'Toole quickly snapped a few pictures of the oil patch and the tire treads, then bent down to retrieve the paper. Across the top, he could just make out the words "Brady's Local Seafood." Beneath that, in barely legible, faded writing was a person's name, only the letters h, l, and e distinguishable in the first name and the letters h and m in the last, with some sort of shorthand writing below that. The number thirty-one was also printed on the paper, with the word "paid" written directly below that. He had no idea what it was, but he kept it in his hand, thinking it might be of some sort of investigative value. He turned to the officer next to him, indicating the paper. "Any idea what that is?"

The officer shook his head. "Looks like a receipt, but beyond that, you got me," he replied.

Finally, O'Toole said, "Goddamnit. Looks like somebody's been prowling around back here. You guys are sure you've been watching that place?"

"Yes, sir," the officer said. "Like I said, we haven't taken our eyes off it since we got here, and we've been here all day. Even had floodlights on that shed when it wasn't really bright enough to see very well. Nobody's been there since we've been watching."

Andy didn't know what to do or what to think. He started pacing the side of the road as he tried to figure out his next move. This was definitely a new wrinkle, and it was definitely a wrinkle that could potentially ruin any possible case against Will Paterna. He motioned for the officer to follow him back to the shed, and when they'd arrived, he said, "Okay. You two stay here and keep watching the place. Make sure nobody, and I mean nobody, goes on this property. You don't let a reporter, you don't let a photographer, you don't let anybody near there. We clear on that?"

The two officers nodded. Andy walked back to his car and called Tim Hawkins. "Tim, we've got a problem here."

"What's wrong now, Andy?" asked Hawkins.

"Couple of officers out here at Paterna's house found a set of footprints and some bloody cigarette butts in the bushes. We're waiting to find out the results of the blood test—Doctor Latkin is working on that right now—but it's not good, Tim. Seems somebody might have put that head in that trash bag. It's starting to look like somebody might have framed Will."

The selectman was clearly not amused by this development. "What are you saying, Andy? We've still got some crazed murderer loose out there?"

"That's pretty much it, Tim," O'Toole replied. "Seems like Paterna might be innocent after all."

"Absolutely not," replied the selectman. "No way in hell am I letting that little scumbag out of jail during Memorial Day Weekend. People are talking about this thing all over the island. If we let that bum out now, we'll be dead in the water." Hawkins sounded scared, Andy thought, scared more about the loss of economic prosperity the island might be facing than about the potential of another murder taking place.

"We can't keep him in jail, Tim," Andy said. "Like I said, it's looking like he didn't do it."

"You find a way to keep him in there until after the weekend. Then we'll talk about it. Just keep your mouth shut. Pretend you didn't find it until Monday," Hawkins said flatly.

Andy hung up the phone, mortified by the selectman's suggestion. He couldn't believe what Hawkins had just said. A member of the Board of Selectmen—the Chairman of the Board of Selectmen—had asked him to cover up evidence. He couldn't do it. He drove his car back to town and went straight to his office. It was already four o'clock in the afternoon, and the Figawi racers had arrived and begun their annual tradition of excessive drinking. People were everywhere, and town looked like some sort of upscale bus terminal, with crowds walking en masse everywhere, but all seeming to get nowhere. He parked his car and walked into the police headquarters. He asked to see Paterna and was escorted back to the cell.

In the cell, he asked Will, "Remember how long I've known you, kid," he said sternly, "and level with me here. Did you do it or not? Look me in the eye, son."

Will looked him straight in the face. "I did not kill that kid, Andy. You know me. You know I've done some stuff in my time, but I have never done anything like this. You've got to know that's true."

Right then and there the sheriff was convinced, despite his earnest longing to have this case solved, that this wasn't his murderer. Andy had known him for a long time and he knew that Will had done some "stuff" in his time. Fighting, driving under the influence, drug possession. But those did not add up to first degree murder. "Then tell me, Will. How in the hell did that kid's head end up in a trash bag in your back yard?" Now he wanted and needed Will on his side, because obviously somebody had it in for Paterna, too.

Will continued to look at him in the eye. "I don't have any idea, Andy. I told you everything I know about it, and that's nothing." Andy closed his eyes and nodded, knowing that was as much as he was going to get from Paterna.

"I'm not sure, kid. I don't know what to believe right now." He thought briefly for a moment, then added, "I need to ask you two questions, son, and I need you to tell me the truth." Andy had no reason not to believe Paterna at this point, but he really didn't know what to believe anymore. "One, do you smoke? And realize that I can find out real quick if you're lying to me."

Paterna shook his head. "No sir," he said firmly. "I've got some bad habits, but smoking cigarettes isn't one of them. Why do you want to know that?" While ignoring the question, O'Toole noted the emphasis Will placed on the word "cigarettes," and thought he was a little too clever for his own good. *Still playing little games with the authorities,* he thought to himself. *Just teasing us.* It was irritating, but he held his feelings in check because he knew it was just a game for Will now.

"Okay, then, question two. Do you know your blood type?"

Will looked at him as if he'd asked him if he had three legs. "How in the hell would I know?" he asked. He sat in thoughtful silence for a minute. "I think it's O-something-other. Does that sound right?" he said finally.

Andy let it go at that, waving off the response as unimportant. Again, he didn't think Paterna would lie about something like this, because he wouldn't know why Andy was asking, and even if he did know, Andy didn't think Will was smart enough to cover it up that easily. He made a mental note to check on it anyway, though, just in case. "Okay, Will. Thanks for your help," he said. He turned to go.

"When am I getting out of here?" Will asked. "You know I'm innocent, right?"

"We'll see, Will," Andy replied meekly as he motioned for the officer on duty to come open the cell so that he could leave. He exited the cell and walked outside. The crowds were swelling, and there was already a line to get into the Jib and Jenny. He walked over to Davy Jones' Locker and found Peter fitting a young girl with a wetsuit.

"Peter, I need to talk to you," he said.

Peter looked up. "Can it wait a minute? I'm almost done with this."

"Yeah, it can wait," Andy said. He looked around the store. "Everything from soup to nuts," was how Peter described the store's contents. O'Toole looked around the area immediately surrounding him. Dive gear lined one part of a wall, then gave way to foam bodysurfing boards. On the back wall was fishing gear, bordered by skateboards on one side and foul weather gear and raincoats on the other. "God," he said aloud. "How do you find anything in this store?"

Peter laughed. "Lots of practice, Andy," he said. "How's that feel?" he asked the wetsuit-wearing customer.

"Kind of tight," she replied.

Peter laughed softly. "Yes," he said to one of the young men behind the counter. "Kind of tight. The best way." Laughter from both men. *Must be an inside joke,* Andy thought to himself.

When the customer was satisfied that it was supposed to fit that way, she unzipped the suit and walked toward the counter with her father to pay for the purchase. Peter turned to Andy. "Now. What can I do for you? You need a wetsuit?" he asked laughing.

"Nope. Not today," replied O'Toole. "Need to ask you something. You sell plaster here? You know, the stuff you use to make casts of stuff in the ground?"

Peter scratched his head. "You know? I think we do, actually." He disappeared behind a mound of soccer balls. All Andy could see of him was his jeans, which hung low on his hips, exposing more than Andy cared to see, and a pair of black rubber sandals held together with electrical tape. He emerged after a moment of digging, holding a small box covered in dust.

"Knew it was back there somewhere," he said, laughing. "Welcome to Davy Jones' Locker, folks," he announced. "We got it all. Professional dive headquarters and boxes of plaster, too. If we don't got it, folks, you don't need it." He turned to Andy. "What do you need this stuff for?"

Andy took the box from him. "Need to go make a cast of something. Nothing much." He scanned the directions on the back of the box. "How do I use this?"

Peter looked at him blankly. "Beats the hell out of me. I just sell it. I don't actually give directions, too." He laughed again. "I guess you need to mix it with water."

Andy looked around. "Got a bucket?"

"Yeah, sure," Peter said. "Come on," he said, gesturing for Andy to follow him. They went to the back of the store and down the narrow hallway to the dive room. Peter grabbed a bucket and dumped the contents out. A pair of rusty pliers and some fishing line clattered out onto the cement floor. "There ya' go," he said.

"Thanks," Andy said. Then he thought of the paper in his pocket and he showed it to Peter. "You ever seen something like this before?"

Peter studied the paper for a moment then replied, "Yeah. It's the receipt you get from the scallop shanty during the season. You bring in the scallops, they shuck them for you, then give you a receipt saying how many pounds you got and what price you got for the meat and how much the total check is for. Where'd you get this one? Looks like it's been through the washing machine," he said.

"Found it out on the street by Will Paterna's house. You recognize the name?" he added hopefully.

Peter looked at the paper again and shook his head. "I recognize the shanty. Brady's is out of town a ways. But I don't sell my scallops to him. Danny Newcomb's got a shanty in the alley out back, so I just use him. Pull up in the truck, drop off the scallops, and then come in to work. I can't really read the name on it, either, so I can't tell you. You know how it is, though, during the winter. So many people out there getting scallops, you'd be lucky to know who half of them were."

O'Toole nodded. Even though he himself wasn't a scalloper, he knew the number of those who were was relatively high. He made a mental note to call Brady's to see if they could help, but he didn't hold out much hope. Then, thinking that Oswald might be useful out at the crime scene, O'Toole suggested, "Want to come help me out on this?" He indicated the box of plaster and the bucket.

Peter looked at him. "What's up? You don't seem real happy."

Andy explained what was happening with the investigation, figuring that Peter already knew enough to where it wouldn't matter if he knew anything more. "Oh shit," Peter said softly. "That's a problem."

Andy nodded. "Yes, it is. So you want to come help me out? I'm still hoping this guy might be a diver that you know. Come with me and see if you can give me any information."

Peter grudgingly agreed and the two men left the store. As they were leaving, Peter called over his shoulder, "I'm leaving for a few hours. It's too crazy in here for me." He laughed. "I'll be back soon. Call Kristin if you get too busy to handle it without me." The two men then walked out the store and up the street to the sheriff's car.

As they drove to Will Paterna's house, Andy explained everything that had happened that day, starting with the phone call he had received at the Jib and Jenny and ending with the discovery of the footprints in the dirt. At the house, he guided Peter to the area where the footprints were. Peter looked at them. "Looks like Bigfoot to me," he said. He put his own foot next to one of the prints in the dirt. "Guy's gotta have at least a size thirteen foot," he said as he compared the size of his own foot next to the mammoth print in the dirt.

"Exactly," O'Toole said. "You know any divers with feet that big?"

"I don't know, Andy," Peter replied. "We keep track of dive gear purchases—it's our one real bookkeeping thing. We like to think of ourselves as a dive shop, so we keep track of it. But off the top of my head, no. I don't really go around checking out guys' feet, if you know what I mean."

"You don't say, Oswald," the sheriff replied sarcastically. "But you do keep track of the sales, huh? That's what I was hoping you'd say." He put the box of plaster down on the ground in front of him next to the bucket and said, "I'll keep that in mind. But first things first. Let's mix this stuff and see what it looks like." Andy opened the box and removed the plastic bag of powder from inside. He emptied it into the bucket and looked around for a water spigot. He found one attached to the house and turned it on, letting water run into the bucket. When the proportions looked to be about right, albeit to his very untrained eye, O'Toole turned off the water and began to look for a stick to stir with. Sensing his need, Peter took his hand, thrust it in to the white mixture, and began to churn it until it resembled wet oatmeal.

"Is there anything you don't do with your hands?" he asked with a grin.

Peter just laughed at the sheriff. "Nothing," he replied bluntly. And suddenly both men laughed nervously for a split-second, and then were awkwardly silent.

O'Toole cleared his throat to break the silence. He took the bucket of plaster and poured its contents in to the clearest and deepest footprint he could find. The box said to wait a minimum of an hour for the plaster to set, so the two sat together as they waited for it to dry. They filled the time with idle chit-chat, both men consciously avoiding the topic of the investigation. While they waited, O'Toole took a photograph of the wet plaster in the footprint and made a notation in his notebook regarding the location and time. When the requisite sixty minutes had elapsed, Andy stuck his fingers in one end of the dirt and pried it up. The plaster had dried and the now solid mass came up easily, revealing an enormous cast of a right foot. Whoever it was that had been walking back there was a large man who had been wearing some sort of tennis shoes.

"Looks good to me," remarked Peter. He looked at his watch. "Christ. It's already six-fifteen. I need to get back to town. We're about to get creamed by the dinner crowd."

"Okay," said Andy. "Let's head back. Remember to keep this between us. No need to frighten anybody more than we already have."

Peter smiled knowingly. "Yeah, yeah. I know. Keep my mouth shut and don't answer any questions."

"You're getting good at this police business, Peter," O'Toole said. "You ought to think about running for sheriff."

Peter laughed. "Hell no," he said. "This is as much crime fighting as I want to be involved in ever."

"You and me both," Andy said nervously. "I never bargained for this. They don't pay me enough." They made their way back to the sheriff's car in silence and drove back to town. As they sat in the car, Andy's phone rang. He answered it and was greeted by the voice of Tom Latkin.

"Andy," the doctor said. "I did the type test, and it looks like your theory might be right. It's AB-negative blood, same as Jack Carlisle. I'd be amazed if somebody else just happened to have that same blood type and, at the same time, happened to be in the vicinity where Jack's head was found. Too coincidental."

"I know what you mean, Tom," the sheriff said as he sighed deeply. "This is going to get messy, it looks like. I think I already know the answer to this, but I'd hate myself in the morning if I didn't ask it anyway. Were there any fingerprints on those butts?" he asked, his voice full of hope.

"Nope," replied the doctor plainly. "Not a one. Looks like whoever it was had on some gloves."

"I figured as much," O'Toole said, the tone of hope now completely vanished. "Thanks for the information." He hung up the phone and turned to Oswald. "Looks like we've got a big problem on our hands now, sir. Blood on those cigarette butts I told you about matched Jack's blood type, so it looks like somebody is planting evidence. My theory is that somebody had that head in their hands, got all the blood from it on their fingers, then was smoking a few cigarettes back there in the bushes, waiting until he could dump it in Will's trash there."

Peter just shook his head. "And to think," he said, "I keep my truck keys in the ignition with the door unlocked." He looked out the window of the car, watching the buildings they passed on their way back to town. "This place is changing," he sighed. "I think it might be time for me to ship out."

"Me, too," O'Toole replied absent-mindedly. "I'm going to Belize before it's all over."

CHAPTER TWELVE

As Peter and Andy drove slowly back to town, O'Toole was talking on his cellular phone and clutching the steering wheel and the receipt he'd found at Will Paterna's house with the same hand. "So that doesn't ring any bells at all?" he asked. He paused briefly, listening to the response. "Okay. Thanks anyway. I figured it was a shot in the dark." He pushed the button to end the call and replaced the phone in its cradle. "Brady's Seafood doesn't have a clue who it is," he said to Peter.

"I figured they wouldn't. You know, there's no number or anything you can read on the receipt. And you didn't hear this from me, but those shanties aren't necessarily what you might call the best record keeping places in town. They make my operation look organized," he added with a slight laugh.

"Yeah," O'Toole sighed, "but I was hoping that the letters in the name might jar somebody's memory. No luck, though." After that, it went silent in the car as they wound their way through the streets. It was after seven when Peter and Andy finally made it back to Davy Jones' Locker. Downtown was more crowded than ever, and police officers were stationed on major corners, directing people to their desired locations. The Figawi cocktail party was getting geared up in the tent by the wharf, and there was a sort of electric buzz in the air. Peter had to literally push his way to the counter, as there were more people in the small store than there was room to hold them all. People were shouting across the store at each other, telling friends about the discoveries they had made and the great things this store had. Peter managed to block them all out.

"How's the total?" he asked the employees.

"Haven't had time to check it," one replied. He turned the register key, pressed a few buttons on the register, and printed out the total sales amount for the day.

"Not bad," Peter said as he ripped off the register tape that had the hourly sales of the day printed on it. "Already up to twelve thousand. My God. We might break fifteen before the night's over," he said. "Good job, guys," he added smiling. He turned to the sheriff, who was standing next to the counter. "So what do you want to do now?"

"Let me see your records of dive gear sales. I need to know about anybody that bought either boots or flippers in a really big size," O'Toole said.

"Andy, let me ask you this," Peter began. "Why are you so sure it's a diver that committed this murder?" Peter was somewhat protective of local divers, as they didn't necessarily have the best reputation for being the most upstanding members of society, but they tended to be a tight-knit group, and Peter was sort of their unofficial leader.

"It's all I've got to go on right now, Peter," Andy replied. "This isn't some kind of witch hunt, you know. The kid's body had a diver's weight belt attached to it, and we found the body in an area that is frequented by local divers. It's the only thing I can cling to in terms of a lead right now," he said.

Peter sighed heavily, a look of resignation on his face. "Hang on a minute," he said finally. "It'll take me a while to find it. I know where it is, but it's buried." Andy followed Peter up the stairs to the storage room over the shop and watched Peter as he dug his way through the masses of inventory. Sweatshirt boxes stood in front of the filing cabinet, and he didn't want to get them out of order. "Need to keep everything organized," he said.

"Organized? My God," said Andy. "Looks like a hurricane blew through here." Peter finally managed to get to the filing cabinet and he opened the top drawer.

"Let's see," he said. "Masks, wetsuits, dry suits, flippers. Here you go," he said, handing the file folder to O'Toole. "Every pair of flippers we've sold in the last five years is on that list. At least it should be," he added hopefully. Then, with a more confident tone he added, "If he's a diver, he probably has turbo fins. So you'll want to find something that says T and at least XL."

"T and XL?" Andy asked, not understanding the importance of the letters.

Oswald nodded. "Yeah. Those are the abbreviations for extra-large turbo fins. While you're looking, I'll see if I can find the booties file, too." Peter returned to his search while Andy scanned the list of flipper sales. His finger stopped on one in particular.

"Here. This guy. He's got triple-XL flippers. That means he's got pretty big feet, right?" asked Andy.

"Yeah, Andy. That would be an indication of big feet," he said somewhat sarcastically. What's the name on it?" asked Peter over his shoulder.

"Jamie McKenzie. Who's—" Andy stopped himself. "Is that the Jamie McKenzie I think it is?"

Peter turned around, holding a file folder in his hands. "Yeah, I'm afraid so. He's kind of a strange one. I can remember when worked over there with you."

Andy nodded, remembering his past relationship with Mr. McKenzie, a relationship that had always been rocky. Some might even call it contentious at times.

"But I haven't seen him around for a few months," Peter continued. "Ever since scallop season ended. He had a bad year; didn't manage to cover his costs. Said something about giving it all up."

"What do you mean about covering his costs?" Andy asked, not understanding the intricacies related to the cost of harvesting scallops.

"You have to buy a commercial permit, then you have to pay for boat fuel and upkeep costs, then you have to pay the shucker, then you have to pay for your dive gear if you're diving for them." He had the tone of a football coach talking to a young player who was contemplating suiting up for his first game. "I talked Jamie into diving with us last year and he just had a bad run. It happens to all of us eventually. But he didn't want to hear about. He had trouble paying for everything he needed, let alone making any kind of profit on top of that. He ended up losing some pretty serious money, from what he told me." Peter almost fell backwards over a box on the floor while he was talking. He regained his balance and added, "He was pretty bitter about it, too."

Andy nodded, understanding the frustration that must come with being in that position. Peter turned back to face Andy and handed him another file folder. "There's the bootie folder. If he bought boots for those flippers, they'll be in there," he said.

Andy took the folder from him and scanned down the names. He found McKenzie's name and slid his finger across. "Here we go," he said. "Size twelve to fourteen neoprene boots." Andy's cellular phone rang in his pocket. "O'Toole," he said, still gripping both folders tightly.

"I assume, Sheriff, that my client will be released shortly, pending all paperwork?"

"Who is this?" he asked the caller.

"This is Franklin Marshall, attorney for one Mr. Will Paterna. I understand that you have discovered evidence indicating that my client was framed. Am I correct in that understanding?"

Andy was shocked. How had he found out about that so quickly? "We have reason to believe that your client might not be as guilty as we'd first imagined. That much is true. It does not mean he is innocent, though, and I have no plans to release him at this time." *Selling out to the town,* Andy thought to himself. *Giving the selectmen what they want. Keeping the image safe and sound.*

"On what grounds are you holding him, then?" asked the voice on the phone.

"We still have reason to believe that he was involved in the murder and we're not releasing him at this point."

"Andy," the voice continued, now suddenly informal and almost friendly, "you know that's ridiculous. Let the kid out of jail. He didn't do it. He couldn't have done it. I've got three people that swear up and down that, on the night in question, Will was face-down drunk at Shane's until one in the morning, and that one of them had to take him home. He couldn't even walk he was so drunk. There's no way in hell he could have done it."

The anger began to swell inside the sheriff. *Why didn't the little bastard tell me that before,* thought Andy to himself. "Why is it that all of a sudden you have this information?" he asked the attorney.

"He blacked out. He didn't remember anything. The last thing he remembers is going to Shane's at nine. He'd had a bad day at work and he went in there to get absolutely blotto drunk. That's just what he did, too. At one point he was apparently so drunk that he was dancing on the bar, if you can believe that. There's no way he was physically capable of killing that kid, Andy. So, you'll be releasing him shortly, I'm sure?"

Andy sighed. "I'll see what I can do, counselor. You realize, though, that this doesn't close our investigation into him as a suspect."

"Of course not," the voice responded confidently. "You can investigate him up one side and down the other for all I care. He's innocent and you know it."

Andy started to say goodbye, but then stopped himself. "Tell me something. How did you find out about any evidence that we supposedly found today?"

A chuckle from the attorney. "Ah, Andy, you should know better than to ask that. It's like asking a reporter to name his confidential source." Another quiet laugh. "I'd suggest, just between you and me, that you might want to look in to hiring more tight-lipped summer cops in the future. Just in case you were trying to hide exculpatory evidence, of course." Now the attorney was in his element and he sneered into the phone. "Kids these days can't keep a secret to save their own lives. Just took a phone call or two. I'll be down at the station in ten minutes. I'll look forward to seeing you there." And with that, Mr. Marshall hung up.

"Goddamnit," Andy muttered aloud. He turned to Peter. "We have to release Paterna. His attorney found out about the evidence we found out at the house."

Peter looked at him. "Pretty good security you've got over there, huh?"

Andy scowled. "Can I take these with me?" he asked, indicating the files.

Oswald hesitated for a moment before answering. "Yeah," he finally said. "Just please make sure to bring them back. I know it doesn't look like it to you, but I really have an organizational pattern here that I use to track these sales, and I need to keep all the files together." His eyes looked worried, like he was sending his baby off to college for the first day of classes.

"Don't worry," Andy reassured him. "I'll get it back to you." Andy tucked the files under his arm and walked back down the stairs with Peter following him. The store was still filled with customers and Andy pushed his way out the door into yet more crowds. Outside, the line to get into the Jib and Jenny extended almost to the door of Davy Jones' Locker. He crossed the street to the Town Building and went up to his office. Once inside, he shut the door behind him and sat at his desk. He picked up the phone and called Tim Hawkins.

"I wanted to tell you before you heard it somewhere else, Tim. We're releasing Paterna." O'Toole braced himself for the onslaught.

He could almost hear the selectman, sitting in his own office in the same building, shout from down the hall and up the stairs. "Don't go anywhere. I'll be right down."

Thirty seconds later, a breathless Tim Hawkins burst through the door to Andy's office. "What are you saying to me? We're going to let a murderer out?"

"He's not the one," Andy replied, trying to maintain his composure in the face of this adversity.

"What do you mean he's not the one? He had the kid's head sitting in his yard for God's sake. What else do you need?" Hawkins was screaming.

"Tim, relax. We found some footprints leading up to the shed. They stopped right where the bag was. We also found a whole pile of cigarette butts with blood on them, and Tom Latkin determined that the blood on them was the same type as Jack Carlisle's. We're not for sure whose blood it is, but he's pretty confident it's Jack's." He hated having to watch what he said, but he was verbally dancing around stating anything that he wasn't sure was a fact. "Anyway, it's not Paterna's," he continued. "He doesn't even smoke. So it looks like somebody framed him and planted that kid's head in his yard." He explained to the incredulous selectman his theory regarding the planting of the head in Paterna's yard.

"Who cares if it was planted there by someone else?" fumed Hawkins. "Let me explain the situation to you. Just in case you give a damn about this town."

O'Toole tried to interject a defensive reply, but the selectman put his hand up to silence him. "Pay attention for a minute, Andy. Economics apparently isn't your strongest subject, so I'll give you a little lesson. We've got tens of thousands of people, tourists, on this island for the weekend. They are here on vacation. That means that they are trying to get away from real life. Away from murders and rapes and all that." His voice took on a slight twinge of greed, O'Toole thought, as he said, "And they're all going to spend money. Gobs of it." He paused for a breath, but O'Toole stayed quiet. He didn't want to get another lecture. "So now, right in the middle of that spending spree— our lifeblood, for God's sake— we're going to release the guy you told me not twenty-four hours ago was the murderer of a senator's kid? What are you doing to me here?"

Andy was quiet for a moment, waiting to be sure the selectman was done with his diatribe. "Look, Tim," he finally asserted, "we can't hold Paterna. His attorney found out about the evidence and he's ordering him released. If you think letting him go will be bad publicity, just try holding him. Then you'll see some bad publicity," O'Toole said. "His lawyer will have every reporter in the country banging down your door wanting to know why you're keeping an innocent man in jail."

Hawkins was growing more and more irate with every passing second. "The only way he could have found out about this supposedly new evidence was if you told him, Andy." He pointed his finger straight at the sheriff. "I am sure you don't want that sort of albatross hanging around your neck, do you?"

The selectman's face told Andy that he wasn't kidding about the potential ramifications to his own future.

The sheriff flinched. He didn't appreciate Hawkins' insinuations. "It was one of the damn summer specials out there. The ones you're responsible for hiring," he added out of spite. "Those kids aren't more than twenty-two years old. Somehow Will's lawyer found out we were out there, made some calls, and figured out what it was. My guess is that he lied to the summers about it and got it from them." *So don't blame me you self-righteous bastard,* O'Toole said to himself.

"You don't understand, Andy," Tim yelled as he slammed his fist on the desk. "I can't have him released. I've already told his father we've got him in custody." Hawkins' face now reflected fear, genuine fear, at the prospect of having to explain Paterna's release to the senator.

Andy closed his eyes and took a deep breath. Now the selectman's anger and his suggestion that O'Toole illegally keep a man in jail for a crime he clearly didn't commit made sense. At least the motivation was clear. He looked at the clock on the wall. It said it was seven-thirty. "I'm meeting with the Carlisles at some time around eight. I'll explain it to them." He looked up at Hawkins. His white hair stood out all the more on top of his face that was now red with rage. O'Toole couldn't believe he was willing to take the fall for Hawkins, but that was what he had to do. He needed Hawkins' support, because without it, his job, now and in the future, would be impossible.

"So you're going to let this kid go. Right out there. Right in front of the goddamn Jib and Jenny, where people are lined up to go in and eat. Lined up to go pay their money to enjoy themselves. And you're going to let this kid out of jail so he can walk out in front of them? Just like that?"

"I have no choice in the matter," said O'Toole calmly yet with a firmness he'd found somewhere in his inner psyche. "The law is the law and there's nothing I can do." The phone on Andy's desk rang. "O'Toole."

"Andy, it's Greg downstairs. Will Paterna's lawyer is here to see you."

"Thanks," he said as he hung up the phone. He turned to Tim. "His lawyer's here. We've got to release him."

"Please, Andy. I'm begging you. Find a way to keep him here," the selectman pleaded.

"Tim, I've told you. There's nothing I can do. He's free to go." O'Toole stood and walked out of the office, leaving Tim Hawkins writhing in anger. Andy walked calmly down the stairs to the police station and entered the office. Marshall was waiting for him, beaming.

"Glad to see you, Sheriff," he said mockingly.

"Right," replied Andy. He grabbed a few papers from behind the desk in the office and turned to the attorney. "Come on," he said, motioning for the attorney to follow him. They walked through a door and down the hall to the cell where Will sat.

"Good news, my boy," called the lawyer. "You're a free man."

Will stood. "Seriously?"

"Seriously," replied his attorney. "Free to go. Your lawyer got you out."

Will yelled in excitement. "I told you I didn't do anything. Lemme outta here, damnit."

The sheriff motioned for the officer on duty to come and open the cell. As the door slid open, Will raced out. "I'll come back and get my stuff later," he said over his shoulder. "I've got places to go right now." He started to run for the door.

"Not so fast, son. I've got some paperwork you have to sign first." O'Toole indicated a room off the hallway, and the group entered. They sat at a large conference table and O'Toole began to fill out the requisite forms for Paterna's release. He gave the pen to Will and indicated the lines on which he would need to sign. "All this says is that you're acknowledging we're letting you out, but that you're still considered a suspect until we formally clear you. Also says something about us not beating you up or anything."

Paterna eyed the sheriff suspiciously, then turned to his attorney, who nodded. Will scratched the pen across the indicated lines, then passed the signed forms back to the sheriff. "Okay, son," O'Toole said. "You're a free man."

With his attorney following behind him, Will ran out the door, shouting. Across the street, a group of local contractors were eyeing the women in line at the Jib and Jenny.

"Will," one of them shouted across the street. "You bustin' out, you murderer?"

"You know it, brother man," Will shouted back, running down the sidewalk.

One of the contractors turned to the assembled line outside the Jib and Jenny. "Look out, folks," he said laughing. "There's a murderer loose on the streets of Nantucket. Any of you lovely ladies looking for a safe place to spend the night?"

CHAPTER THIRTEEN

Andy sat in his office until five minutes after eight. The crowds outside had swelled to massive proportions, and he had been getting constant phone calls from reporters regarding the release of Will Paterna. He had told all of them that he was unable to comment on the matter, beyond saying that Paterna had been released due to new developments. At five minutes past eight, he picked up the phone and dialed the number of Senator Leonard Carlisle. After three rings, a male voice answered.

"Senator Carlisle?" asked O'Toole into the phone.

"Yes, this is Leonard Carlisle," he responded.

"Senator, this is Andy O'Toole down at the sheriff's office."

"Sheriff," Carlisle said, "thanks for calling. Can you tell me what is going on here? I got a message earlier that you had the suspect in custody, and now I hear that he's been released. What exactly is happening with this so-called investigation of yours?" His voice sounded anxious. He was clearly not happy with Paterna's release.

"Sir, with all due respect, I would rather not have this conversation over the phone. You'd mentioned to me yesterday that you'd like to meet up at your house. Is that offer still good?"

A brief pause, followed by a sigh. "Yes. That'll be fine. We've just arrived, but we can talk here. I have to warn you ahead of time, though, Sheriff, it's a madhouse out there. We've got reporters and camera crews attached to the street like barnacles to the bottom of a boat. But come on ahead up here. Do you know where we are?"

Andy looked down at the address for the senator's house, which he'd written down on a piece of paper on his desk. The house was on Lincoln

Circle, up on the cliff. He knew where it was. "Yes, sir. I know the address. Town's a little crowded right now, so it might take a few minutes, but I'll be there as quickly as I can." He hung up the phone and walked outside to his car. He pulled out into the traffic and made a quick left onto a cobblestone back street. He headed up Cliff Road and turned right onto Sherburne Turnpike. He wound his way up the Turnpike, remarking to himself that it wasn't much of a turnpike at all, but rather just a normal street like any other on Nantucket. He turned sharply to the left, and then around to the right, following the directional arrows dictating traffic flow around Lincoln Circle.

As he made the right turn, he could already see a mass of vans and people milling around outside the Carlisles' home. He parked his car on the far side of the circle in the hopes of keeping a low profile. He walked a circuitous route towards the house and did his best to look like a tourist out for some night air and a little sightseeing around the senator's house. As he meandered around the parked cars, he thought about what to say to the senator. Before he could develop any ideas, though, he was suddenly confronted by a woman carrying a microphone. She had recognized him as the sheriff and began asking him about the murder. As soon as the other groups realized who he was, they came at a run and blocked his progress towards the house.

"No comment," he said to the assembled mass of lights and reporters. "I don't have anything to say. There is nothing new to report." He detached himself from the news crews, pushed his way to the safer confines of the Carlisles' front lawn and rang the doorbell. The senator met him at the door.

"My God," he said over the sheriff's shoulder. "This is supposed to be a vacation home. Reminds me more of Washington than Washington itself does." He motioned for the sheriff to enter and shut the door behind him. Leonard Carlisle had aged gracefully. His hair still retained most of its original brown, though he was graying somewhat. He was of average height and build, and his face looked strong. His eyes were dark brown and didn't reveal the pain he must have felt. He was a veteran of fights both in the field of battle and in the Senate, and he wasn't going to let this one get the better of him. He was dressed casually, wearing jeans and an oxford button-down shirt, a blue nylon belt embossed with the Harbor Club burgee, and brown, expensive looking tasseled loafers without socks.

Once inside, the sheriff looked around him. The house was very tastefully decorated, especially by Nantucket standards. There were a few paintings by local artists, and a large antique ship model dominated one wall. A huge bay window looked out over the cliff to the ocean below. The sun had set and the sky outside was illuminated a brilliant red.

"Red sky at night, sailor's delight," he said to the senator.

"So they say," replied the senator. "Guess that means I'm not a sailor." He wasn't in the mood for small talk. He wanted answers. "Let's sit down, Sheriff. I'd like to talk to you about the situation at hand." He indicated a high back chair for the sheriff to sit in, and the senator sat directly across from him. He looked at the sheriff. "Well?"

Andy didn't know how to begin. "Mr. Carlisle, the man we arrested wasn't the guy. I know he wasn't. I'm sure of it." He began to tap his foot nervously.

"I was told that it was an open and shut case. I was told that you had found my son's head," he shuddered momentarily, "in a bag at this monster's house. I was told in no uncertain terms that you were sure. Positive. Do they teach you the meaning of that word, Sheriff?" he asked angrily. He shook his head, stood and paced the floor. "I'm sorry," he conceded. "I'm just feeling totally lost here. I thought you had this, this...barbarian," he said as he picked his words with deliberation. "And now you're here telling me it wasn't him?"

Andy could hear Mrs. Carlisle crying in a back bedroom. "That's true, sir. We did find evidence that implicated this man. However, one of the officers that was investigating the crime scene discovered some footprints that led to the location where we found the bag. The same footprints led away from the location. There was also a small pile of cigarette butts, stained with blood, inside the bushes leading away from the shed." He continued his explanation, telling the senator how the blood was the same type as Jack's and that it seemed as if the evidence—he was careful not to use the word "head"—had perhaps been planted by someone else, someone trying to implicate Will Paterna in the murder. He also explained that Paterna had an alibi.

"And why were you unable to figure this out before telling me that you had the suspect in custody, Sheriff?" asked Carlisle, growing angrier. "When you told me you had him caught, I was relieved. You have no idea how much it hurt me to hear that he was let go. I don't see how you can call this bumbling around an investigation," he said scornfully. "I have to say it sounds more like the goddamn Keystone Cops."

Andy looked at Carlisle, unable to defend himself because he knew the senator was right. "Senator," he offered, "I was not the one who told you we'd solved the case. While it's true that I had told people I was sure Paterna was the murderer, Tim Hawkins was the one who told you it was solved." He was trying to pass the buck, trying to get the heat off of himself for a change, and he couldn't think of a more deserving recipient of that heat than the selectman himself. Noticing the senator's pained expression, he added, "I'm terribly sorry. I can assure you, though, that we're moving ahead with our investigation."

The senator was silent, looking out the window at the vast expanse of water in front of the house. The view was majestic. There really was no other word for it. People paid millions and millions of dollars for a view like this, and properties like this came up for sale once in a lifetime, if that often. The fog horn's green light blinked on and off in the distance, and O'Toole was suddenly, painfully reminded of the fact that these people had to look out on the place where their son's body had been discovered. Money couldn't do anything to change that, he thought. There wasn't a real estate agent in the universe who could move that crime scene. The senator looked outside towards the blinking light. He stretched his arm out slightly, resting a hand lightly on the window. "Do you have children, Mr. O'Toole?"

"Please, sir, call me Andy," O'Toole replied casually. "Yes, sir, I've got two, a son and a daughter. They're both grown and moved away, though."

"Then you can understand, perhaps," the senator began, still staring at the light in the distance, "how your kids represent all that you hope for in the world. All I wanted was for Jack to be successful and happy, and I worked my entire life to ensure that for him, as well as for all of my family. Now Jack's gone," he said in a saddened voice. His eyes were still fixated on the light in the distance. It pulsed on and off methodically. It was almost hypnotic. For a brief instant, O'Toole found himself following the senator's gaze out the window and fixating on the light.

"I can only imagine what you must be going through, sir," Andy consoled him. But his voice sounded hollow. He could hear it. He snapped back to the moment, breaking his gaze from the light. "I wish I could say something more," he added.

Suddenly whatever force it was that had held the senator's attention freed him, and he turned his head to face Andy. Still standing, he said in a much sterner sounding voice, "So where do we go from here?" he asked. "You've got to understand what this is doing to my family. We want this solved. Quickly."

Andy nodded. "Yes, sir," he said. "I know you do. We want it solved just as quickly as you." He looked at the table behind the senator. On it were family pictures, many of which showed the now deceased Jack Carlisle enjoying himself. "We do have a new lead, though," he added, trying to offer some gem of hope for the senator. "I've got men following it up right now." That was a lie. He hadn't even thought about beginning to follow it up yet, but he certainly planned to.

"Who's your new suspect?" Carlisle asked.

Andy paused in thought before offering an explanation. He didn't want to provide any sense of false hope, because he was afraid of going through the whole process again of the arrest and then subsequent release of a new suspect. "I'm not really at liberty to say, sir," he said cautiously. He knew that the senator would want details, but he wasn't prepared to give them.

"Sheriff, don't give me that. I have a right to know what's going on in the investigation of my own son's murder." His voice was growing angrier and more impatient. "And you have a responsibility to tell me, I should think," he added.

Andy sighed heavily. The senator was right and Andy knew it. The sheriff, though, continued to remain cautious and only told as much as he was sure of. He was a little gun shy when it came to giving the senator any information he wasn't absolutely positive about. "Okay," Andy began hesitantly, "we are pretty sure that your son was murdered by someone who knew scuba diving. We have reason to believe that the murderer was a local diver. Your son's body was found with a weight belt wrapped around him. The kind of weight belt divers use. We're focusing our investigation on local divers that fit the profile of what we believe the killer looks like."

Carlisle crossed to the bar. He took down a crystal glass and poured himself a drink. "Single malt, Sheriff. Nectar of the gods," he said off-handedly, indicating a bottle of expensive looking Scotch on the bar as if O'Toole had never seen Scotch before in his life. He took a sip of the drink and set the glass down on the bar. "Can I offer you a drink?"

Andy shook his head. "No thank you. I'm on duty. Don't want to be drinking." That was also a lie. He did, in fact, want to be drinking, and heavily at that. He wanted to be sitting at home, nursing a Jameson's, and not thinking about a murder investigation. "Besides," he added, "I'm an Irish whiskey man myself." He smiled.

"Ah," the senator replied. "So we're at odds on our country of origin." The senator winked at O'Toole. "Not to worry, Sheriff. I won't hold it against you."

Carlisle retrieved his glass from the bar and returned to his seat. He sat down heavily in the chair. It had been a long day for him and he wanted it to end. His tone turned suddenly serious again. "You said you were basing your investigation on what you think this animal looks like. What sort of description do you have of the killer?" he asked.

"We don't have any eye-witnesses," Andy began, "but we think he's a pretty big guy. The evidence we've collected indicates that he's a big man. He's got big feet, at least." As soon as he'd said it, Andy wished he hadn't. He knew this sounded ridiculous. He could see it now. Headlines reading, "Nantucket Sheriff Seeking Yeti in Murder Case." He winced in expectation of the verbal assault he knew was forthcoming. "And we think he smokes, sir," he added hopefully. Again, as soon as he'd said it, he wished he were anywhere but sitting in front of the senator. The thought of sitting on a beach in Belize suddenly popped into his mind, and that, he decided, was where he wanted to be.

Carlisle coughed loudly on the Scotch he had swallowed while Andy was speaking. "All you know is that he has big feet and you think he's a smoker? Oh, and let's don't forget that you have a suspicion that he's a scuba diver. What kind of investigation is this?" he asked in a loud voice, tinted heavily with a tone of incredulous disbelief.

"You've got to understand, Mr. Carlisle," Andy said. "We're a small force. We're not set up for this kind of major investigation; we don't even have a staff of detectives to help us out. But I assure you, sir, we're going to find the killer." O'Toole looked at the senator expectantly, hoping for some sort of validation of his predicament, but got none. He continued, "Nobody saw anything, at least nobody that we've been able to find to this point. All we have is footprints. And cigarette butts," he added.

The senator looked straight at O'Toole. "Look," he barked, "I want this son of a bitch found. I want him punished. I want him to pay for this. If I need to call in the goddamn FBI, I'll do it," he said as he pounded his fist on the arm of the chair. "I'll do whatever I need to do to get this solved. I don't care how it makes you look and I don't care how it makes your department look. I want this bastard caught." He slammed his glass down on the table in front of him.

The force in Carlisle's tone had taken Andy by surprise. He felt small and intimidated. He wanted to be in charge here. He was the sheriff. He didn't need the FBI. He would solve it himself. "Mr. Carlisle, it's like I told you. We've got another suspect that we're investigating. We will find this person. We will make him pay for what he's done. I promise you that."

"Do you have any idea how much I pay in property taxes for this house?" Carlisle asked in an egotistical tone. "I'd guess it's more than you make in a year, if you can believe that." He paused briefly to sip his Scotch. "This is my tax dollars hard at work, I'm glad to see," he said as he shrugged his head in the sheriff's direction. The senator shook his head. Finally he seemed to shrink into the chair. "I just wish I had more faith in you, Sheriff. No offense, but it seems like you haven't made much progress in finding any useful information so far." He lifted his glass and took another sip. "Information that turns out to be true, at least."

This last comment stung O'Toole. He felt as if he'd done some pretty damn good investigative work. This was a murder, after all. It wasn't like some guy had beaten his wife. This was homicide. And, he reminded himself, this was Nantucket, where this sort of thing didn't happen, and in the unlikely event it did, they didn't have the resources to investigate it like bigger, more urban, departments had. "Mr. Carlisle," he said, "I feel like we're getting away from the real goal here. Can we focus on the investigation itself?" he asked pleadingly.

Carlisle sighed in resignation. "What do you need from me?" he asked.

Andy was momentarily relieved. He was once again the one in charge, at least for right now. "Well," he began, "can you think of anyone that might want to do this? Anybody you know? Anybody your son might have known?"

"Nobody," the senator replied immediately. "I don't know of anyone. My son was always private about his life up here. He had a lot of friends that we didn't necessarily like—you know, the local people he liked to pal around with. He had friends down at the Harbor Club, but he lived another life. When he was up here, he would go out to the bars and do his thing. We let him go. We figured he's an adult, and he was making his own decisions."

Carlisle paused, contemplating how to proceed with what he wanted to tell O'Toole. "Don't take this the wrong way," he began, "but Jack had some interesting ideas about how he wanted to live his life." He shifted uncomfortably in his chair. "He had a sort of blue-collar fantasy. He wanted to be a 'working man of the people.' But he still wanted to live this lifestyle," he added with an all-encompassing sweep of his arm around the room.

Carlisle looked around suspiciously. "And honestly? We always thought he might have a drinking problem." He punctuated this statement by draining the remaining Scotch in his glass. "And I happen to think he had some depression issues." And then, as if he wished he hadn't said it, he added, "That's off the record, Sheriff. Strictly between you and me." He gave O'Toole a stern look to further make the point.

O'Toole took the overt hint and didn't scribble that information down with his other notes. This wasn't about whether or not the kid drank too much. This was about a murder. In hopes of securing the senator's confidence, O'Toole replied, "There's certainly more than a few alcoholics on this island." He waited a moment before testing the waters of another theory he'd secretly been developing. "What about any political enemies of yours? Would any of your opponents be capable of doing something like this? To see you suffer or to hurt your political standing?"

The senator scoffed loudly at the suggestion. "I assure you, Andy, I have enemies, but the United States Senate is not made up of killers. We're a civilized bunch, if you can believe that."

"Okay," O'Toole said. Then, returning to the senator's original statement about his son, he said, "So you didn't know anything about what Jack was doing up here?" Surely, he thought, a senator would keep tabs on his youngest son, especially on an island where gossip spread like an epidemic.

"He didn't talk about it," Carlisle said bluntly, leaving it at that. In other words, it was of none Andy's business.

O'Toole scribbled a few notes on his legal pad. If the kid hung around with the locals, somebody would be talking. Somebody in town would know. He had a suspect, but he didn't want to race into anything. He'd learned that lesson already. He decided he would start talking to some locals. See if they could shed any light on the kid.

"I'm only going to be here until Monday," the senator announced suddenly. "The Senate is back in session on Tuesday, and I need to be there for it. I've got commitments, you know." As if in defense of his own statement, he shrugged his shoulders and took a sip of his Scotch.

Andy stopped writing and looked at the senator. He nodded, indicating he understood, but in his mind he couldn't fathom how a man could seem so callous regarding the death of his son. He asked in a meek voice, "Sir, are you sure that's the best thing to do?"

"I've got my obligations, Andy," he replied firmly. "The Marines taught me the importance of that, and my duty as a senator is one I take a great deal of pride and responsibility in, so yes, I'm sure it's the best thing to do." He cleared his throat loudly. "Let me explain it to you like this, Andy," he began in a more didactic tone. "I'm a very vain person, to be quite frank with you," he said. "In case you haven't already drawn that conclusion," he added with a slight laugh. "I wear custom made suits, shirts I buy from a tailor in London, ties made by Hermes, a Breitling chronograph wristwatch. My wedding ring is hand-hammered platinum. I only write with a Mont Blanc fountain pen. But there is one piece of clothing I put on every day that is more important than anything else." He looked at the sheriff expectantly.

O'Toole returned the gaze, staring silently. When he realized the senator was waiting for an acknowledgement from him, he said meekly, "And what's that, Mr. Carlisle?"

The senator smiled briefly. "Clean shoes," he replied curtly. "I always make sure I'm wearing clean shoes, because I know that the ass I kick today might be the ass I have to kiss tomorrow. And I damn sure want to be wearing clean shoes when I'm kicking it. You get my drift?"

He didn't, but he nodded anyway. All he could tell from this speech was that Carlisle had enough money to dress well. The senator interpreted his silence, though, as confusion.

"To put it real short and sweet," he said with a touch of good-ole-boy twang, "I'm not a big fan of kissing a dirty ass." He laughed roughly. "Or any ass for that matter," he added. "And if I miss a day of work—even for the death of a family member—I'll have some ass kissing to do."

Andy's face betrayed his reaction to the senator's words. He couldn't remember a more callous defense from a human being in his life. Even Eichmann defended himself more eloquently for his war crimes at Auschwitz, he thought. The senator sensed his distaste for his work ethic.

"That's why my kids call me '*jefe*,'" he countered. "It's Spanish for 'boss.' I'm the boss and I can't take a day off, if you know what I mean."

Andy nodded again, attempting to feign if not appreciation for the senator's sacrifice, at least understanding of his situation. *It must be some sort of political thing,* he told himself. *Some sort of issue with missing work. Maybe it's a Marine thing. Machismo keeps him going back to work, no matter the circumstances. Might even be a psychological defense to the murder,* he mused. He grabbed his pad off the table and said, "Senator, I know this has been a horrible day for you and I am sure you want to get to bed. I'll go so you can get settled. We'll work from here and see what we can dig up. I'll keep you posted. You've got my number and you know where to find me. If you think of anything, please let me know. Don't worry. We'll catch this guy." He stood and extended his hand. "Thanks for your help, and I'm terribly sorry you're having to go through this."

Carlisle remained seated. He took the sheriff's hand in his and shook it briefly. "Thanks, Sheriff. Sorry to have attacked you. It's just this whole thing is like a nightmare. The only problem is, as hard as I try and as much as I want to, I can't seem to wake up."

Andy looked down at the senator. "I know," he said. "Goodbye, and thanks again." He walked to the door and out into the darkening night. As he stepped out of the door, as if on cue, flashbulbs went off and the night was lit up by spotlights from the television crews. He walked quickly to his car, looking straight ahead and remaining silent as he walked. He got in and slammed the door, closing out the world. He started the engine, put the car in gear and drove quickly home.

CHAPTER FOURTEEN

By late Sunday morning, downtown Nantucket resembled a third-world country on the brink of revolution. It was reminiscent of *Life Magazine* photos from the evacuation of Saigon, with people climbing over one another and fighting for a place on the last plane out. Given the proximity of O'Toole's office to the ferry dock, he could hear the masses of people trying to get to the boat. People heading back to their everyday lives, having spent a glorious long weekend on Nantucket. It was Sunday, a day of rest. *No rest for the weary,* O'Toole thought to himself.

He had pulled the police record on Jamie McKenzie and he was scouring over it now. He knew Jamie; he had worked with him before. Jamie had been an officer with the Nantucket Police Department several years earlier, but had left the force for personal reasons. O'Toole knew it was because of a cocaine habit. It had become increasingly apparent that McKenzie wasn't enforcing the law, and repeated reprimands led to his choice to resign from the force. Since his resignation, McKenzie had worked at various jobs for several years. His drug problem and subsequent resignation had begun a downward spiral in McKenzie's personal and professional life. Initially he'd owned a construction business, but soon lost that as addiction got the better of him. In an ironic twist, he'd ended up working for the first man he'd hired for his own company. That job, too, had proved too difficult, and Jamie had begun to bounce around from job to job. He finally found himself working as a diver doing odd jobs in the Nantucket boat basin. It was seasonal work at best, but apparently he made enough money to survive on. His wife, Andy recalled, worked as a secretary somewhere, but he couldn't remember where.

119

McKenzie's police record was limited to petty crimes, for the most part. He'd been busted twice for drug possession and had received suspended sentences both times. He had a few speeding tickets, a few disorderly conduct charges, and one charge of public intoxication. Most of the activity detailed in the report seemed to be from the last few years. Despite the increase in semi-criminal activity recently, Andy wondered if Jamie McKenzie—the same Jamie McKenzie he'd worked with many years ago—was capable of such a horrific act as murder.

O'Toole looked at his watch. It was almost eleven-thirty, and he had scheduled a meeting with Jack Carlisle's boss at the Collins House for eleven-thirty, so he grabbed his legal pad and headed out the door and up the street to the hotel. He found the manager in the restaurant, where he was showing a new waiter the procedure for ordering food from the kitchen. When O'Toole entered, the manager looked up. "Hey, Sheriff," he said. "Give me a second here. Trying to show him the ropes. Had to hire a new waiter." He shrugged, as if to say that he wasn't the one dead and he still had a business to run here.

Andy nodded grimly. He took a seat at the bar and waited for the manager to finish his instruction. When he joined O'Toole at the bar, Andy put his notepad down in front of him. He turned to the manager. "What can you tell me about Jack?" he asked. "What piece of this puzzle am I missing here? What kind of guy was he, what was he like to work with, anything you can think of. Is there anything you can tell me?"

"Nothing more than I've already told you, Sheriff," the manager replied. "He was friends with all of the staff here. He didn't have any enemies to speak of. None that I knew of, at least. Not that that's saying much. I don't really hang around with these guys, you know. Once the work day is done, it's done, and we go our own separate ways," he said, almost apologetically. Andy knew the manager wanted to help out, but couldn't give information he didn't have. "I just don't know who would have done this to Jack," he said awkwardly.

Andy nodded his acknowledgement. "That seems to be the sentiment of everyone I talk to," he said. "Nobody can think of anyone who'd want to do this or who would have been capable of doing it." O'Toole, as he spoke, watched the manager, looking for any sort of clue he might be able to garner from his facial expressions. The manager didn't seem like he was trying to lie, Andy thought. He seemed more like he was trying to appear like he wasn't lying, and at times he was doing a bad job of that. O'Toole decided the manager was harmless and that he was telling the truth.

"He just seemed like a friendly kid all around," the manager finally concluded. "I mean, he was a friendly kid all around from what I knew of him," he added, trying to add an air of credibility to his character interpretation.

That didn't help Andy's investigation. He asked about other waiters. "Were there any other people here that he hung around with? People he might have gone out drinking with or something?"

The manager looked around and hailed one of the waiters. The young man approached the two, dressed in the standard uniform of the Collins House waiters—white button down shirt, black slacks and a floor-length black apron tied around his waist. "This is Byron. He and Jack were pretty good friends. Maybe he can help you out," he said, indicating the young man standing next to them.

Andy looked at him. His hair was cut short, bleached blonde, and combed very neatly. He had bright blue eyes and wire frame glasses. He was skinny— too skinny, Andy thought—and tall. Both ears were pierced, and small diamond studs were implanted in the holes.

"Hi," Andy said. "I'm Andy O'Toole. I'm the sheriff here on Nantucket. I'm investigating the murder of Jack Carlisle. Do you have a minute to talk to me about him?"

The young man looked almost sick, as if he were on the verge of collapse. He looked to the manager, who nodded his head and stood to leave. The young waiter sat down next to the sheriff in the seat vacated by the manager and turned to face O'Toole.

"I don't know what I can tell you," he began in a soft voice. "The whole thing is just terrible." His voice cracked as he recalled his dead friend.

"I know," Andy said soothingly. "But anything you can tell me would help. Can you think of anyone that would want to do this to him?"

The waiter shook his head. "This whole island is getting so unfriendly. People aren't the same," he said, almost as if he wasn't responding to the sheriff's direct question. "It used to be you could live your life and nobody bothered you. Now, though, it's like you can't even go out and enjoy yourself. You always have to be looking over your shoulder. You have to wonder what the people around you are thinking about doing to you." The waiter had tears in his eyes as he looked past O'Toole, out into the expanse of the dining room.

121

Andy looked at the young man, perplexed. "What do you mean? Did somebody threaten him?"

"What do you think?" replied the waiter bluntly, suddenly sitting up straight in the chair, his voice tense and his eyes focused now directly on O'Toole.

"I don't know. That's why I'm asking you. Did somebody threaten him?"

The waiter looked around, as if he were convinced that the very room they were sitting in was bugged by some kind of enemy intent on hearing this clandestine conversation. He was clearly breaking confidentiality, though Andy had no idea as to what the secret was. "It's hard enough to live on this island, you know, with rent costing you your entire paycheck. You'd think they'd let us just live our lives. But no, they want to talk about you and tell jokes and screw with you."

Andy's face was blank. He looked the waiter in the eye. "What do you mean by 'us?'" he asked. "What's going on?"

The waiter looked back at the sheriff and laughed sarcastically. "You don't have any idea, do you?" The waiter shook his head in disbelief. "Not the first clue. My God. You're just like the rest of them. Don't ever open your eyes, do you?"

Andy was perched on the edge of his seat, waiting for the information. The waiter wasn't offering, so Andy forced the issue. "Please tell me what you're talking about. It could really help me out here." He noticed that the kid was wringing his hands. "I'm on your side here, son," he said soothingly.

The waiter laughed softly to himself. He looked straight at Andy, straight in his eyes, and said, "It's impossible to be gay on this island. That's what I'm talking about. It's impossible to be a gay man and live in peace on Nantucket."

Andy dropped the pen from his hand. "Are you saying that Jack Carlisle was gay?" he croaked, almost inaudibly, unable to comprehend it.

The waiter nodded. "Kind of a surprise to you? It's my guess you're not the only one. He was way in the closet. Didn't want to come out to anybody. His parents didn't even know. We were the only ones he really felt comfortable coming out to," he said, indicating the waiters in the dining room. "Us and a few close friends. We were the only ones who knew."

Here was a bombshell dropped right in the sheriff's lap. He'd never consciously thought about any sort of gay lifestyle on Nantucket. It hadn't ever been an issue to him. But here it was, staring him in the face, in the person of the young waiter talking to him. "So do you think it might have been something related to the fact that Jack was gay?" O'Toole finally managed to ask the waiter.

The waiter rolled his eyes. "How clever of you, Sherlock," he said sarcastically. "Of course it was because he was gay. Some of these guys get their jollies by beating up us 'fags.' That's what they call us when they're being nice. They can get ugly when they want to."

The sheriff was writing constantly on his notepad. At last he had a motive, of sorts. But this was going to be hard to keep quiet. A young gay man, the victim of a hate crime, is killed on the enchanted island of Nantucket.

"Everything I've heard, though, says that he was kind of a ladies' man," the sheriff offered. "You're sure he was gay?"

The waiter laughed. "Oh, yes. Quite sure." Andy didn't ask the source of his assurance. He wasn't sure he wanted to go down that road, especially not now. "He kept up appearances, though. That's the way he always talked about it. He was always going on about the 'importance of keeping up appearances.' You know, for the sake of the family." The waiter let out a scornful laugh. "It's like people who stay married for the sake of the kids, you know? They're just concerned with appearances. That's how his family is. Very into appearances, and he respected that enough to keep his little secret. Though I'm not sure he respected himself enough, and that might have been the source of the real problem." The waiter was beginning to sound something like Jack's therapist, but Andy wrote down everything the young man said.

He looked at the waiter sitting in the chair next to him. Byron had the faintest hint of a smile laced with smug self-righteousness curling across his lips. It was as if he had won some game he was playing with the sheriff. Andy said to him, "I need to know if you can think of anybody, anybody in particular, that had threatened him or that knew he was gay and harassed him for it." He sat in his chair, poised to receive the tip that would solve this case.

The waiter's face turned suddenly serious. "Go out some night. Go to the Jib and Jenny. Go to Shane's. Go anywhere that the locals go. You'll see the people that harass us. Or fuck with us, in a manner of speaking," he added with a half-hearted smile. "I don't know any of them by name and they all start to look the same to me after a while." He laughed momentarily. "Now I sound like one of them," he said almost accusatorily. "But as I was saying, I couldn't tell you who specifically said what. I just know that some of those guys didn't agree with what you'd call our lifestyle and they expressed their disagreement openly. Very openly." And then, wiping a tear from his eye, added, "And sometimes violently, too."

"I see," said O'Toole. "I didn't realize it was so hostile out there."

"Hostile isn't the word for it, Sheriff. It's a fucking war zone out there for us," the waiter replied bluntly. "Pardon my French, sir," he added with a smirk.

Andy found himself unable to look the young man in the eye. He had been completely naïve to the existence of homosexuals on the island, so it had never occurred to him that there might be any sort of anti-gay feelings amongst the residents, especially feelings so strong that they could lead to murder. He himself had never agreed with homosexuality and he certainly didn't endorse it. But he would never have thought to openly harass a gay man. "His parents didn't know?" he asked.

"Nope. He was terrified to tell them."

This was going to be difficult for O'Toole. How to explain to Senator Carlisle that his son, his gay son, had been murdered because of the fact that he had been gay. And on Nantucket of all places. This was *Moby Dick* land. Even the high school teams were the Whalers, for God's sake. Nantucket was historical and nautical. There just weren't these kinds of problems here. And just to make the whole problem that much more vivid for O'Toole, he reminded himself, the fact that the kid had been gay was unknown to the man to whom he was supposed to explain it. Where was Herman Melville when you really needed him?

So the job of publicizing Jack's post-mortem confession regarding his sexual orientation would fall to him. But the sheriff wasn't ready to assume that job. At the same time, he felt that he owed it to the parents to tell them everything. He had promised to keep the family updated on the progress of the investigation. He'd find a way to get around it, he hoped. He would come up with an explanation that would make everyone happy, but still preserve the image that Jack had worked so hard to perpetuate. He had no idea, however, what that explanation might be. He would somehow cover for the young deceased man, killed in an act of hatred; of that much he was confident. He would protect Jack's image and at the same time protect the Carlisle family image. He began to feel a strange sort of camaraderie with the dead young man.

"You mentioned," O'Toole said to the waiter, "that a lot of people here knew that he was gay. Was there some reason he felt so comfortable telling you all and not others?"

The waiter nodded, almost the way he would to a small child who had asked if two and two really equaled four. "Yes, there's a reason," he said. "Most of us could relate to what he was going through. Brace yourself, Sheriff," the waiter said with a smile, "but you're surrounded by gay men."

O'Toole looked around at the wait staff in the room. All were clean-cut men, all thin, all attractive. But he didn't think any of them looked gay, not that he considered himself any sort of authority on what a gay man "really" looked like. He gave the waiter a quizzical look.

"Yep," he said, "we're all gay. All the waiters here, except for one or two that I know of, are. It's almost like our own little fraternity here at the Collins House."

"I had no idea," was all that Andy could come up with to say. He was immediately embarrassed. He felt out of place.

"I'm surprised to hear that," the waiter replied. "Most people that live here know that this place has that reputation. I'm almost shocked that you hadn't heard all the rumors."

Andy shook his head. He hadn't heard the rumors. He didn't go out that much, and when he did, it was rarely to a place as expensive as this. But slowly, in the back of his mind, the story he'd tell the Carlisles was beginning to take shape. If the Collins House had that reputation, then it was possible that Jack could have been confused for someone else. *It might just work,* he thought to himself.

He thanked the waiter for his time and his help and then asked him to let him know if he thought of anybody in particular. He stood and turned to go.

"Sheriff," somebody called from behind him. He turned around and saw the hotel manager coming towards him. "Was Byron any help?" he asked.

O'Toole took a deep breath. "Yes," he said flatly. "He gave me some information that might be helpful. But then again, if you or anyone else can think of anyone or anything—"

"I'll call you," the manager said, cutting him off. "Don't worry. I'll call you."

Andy smiled, said thanks to the manager, grabbed his legal pad and headed out the door. Once outside the hotel, he lit a cigarette. He walked slowly to his office, trying to delay the inevitable. He didn't want to go inside and make the phone call he had to make. He had to think first. He had to decide how to explain this to the Carlisles, had to get the story straight in his own mind before he tried to pass it off on somebody else, especially the family members. He paused briefly outside the door to the Town Building, finishing the cigarette. He stamped it out on the ground and walked in. He needed to talk to Tim Hawkins before any of this got out.

CHAPTER FIFTEEN

O'Toole walked into Tim's office without knocking and closed the door behind him. Hawkins looked up, startled by the abrupt entrance. "Andy. Good to see you. What's the good word on the Carlisle investigation?" The selectman was eating a sandwich and drinking a can of soda.

"He was gay," Andy blurted out.

Hawkins was noticeably shocked. He put the sandwich down on the desk. "What are you talking about?"

"Jack Carlisle," the sheriff said. "He was gay. I just talked to one of the waiters at the Collins House. He swears the Carlisle kid was gay. Says he's sure of it." Andy sat down in one of the chairs in front of Hawkins' desk. The selectman kept his desk immaculately clean. It was completely empty, except for a phone, a fountain pen set that had been a gift from the Town of Nantucket and a picture of his family in an austere metal frame. On the wall behind him was a picture of Tim in his United States Navy uniform; Hawkins had served in the Navy for ten years.

"That's a big one, Andy," Tim said. He exhaled heavily. "You're sure the kid's not just blowing smoke?"

Andy shook his head, saying that he was as sure as he could be that the waiter was telling him the truth.

"That's a new one on me, Andy," the selectman said. "I have to admit, the thought never occurred to me. Seems like from all the things you'd told me about him, he had his choice of the ladies."

Andy nodded his head in agreement. "I know, Tim," he said. "Kid I talked to at the Collins House just now told me that it was a cover. Said Jack was trying to keep up appearances for his family's sake. It's kind of odd, too, because the whole idea of a gay population on this island was something that I never thought about. But from what this kid at the Collins House told me, there is definitely a population of them, and they're not treated too well by some of our local boys." Andy told Tim everything that the young waiter had told him about his experiences as a gay man on Nantucket. "The kid said they always get harassed when they go out."

The selectman looked out the window. "Then why in hell do they go out? Why don't they just stay home and not bother anybody?"

O'Toole was stunned. "Whoa now, Tim. I'm not saying I agree with him, but the kid's got a point. Shouldn't they be allowed to go anywhere they want to go?"

"Not at the expense of their own safety, they shouldn't," Hawkins replied bluntly. "And also not at the expense of this island's prosperity and image."

There he goes again, thought O'Toole to himself. *Businessman's thinking. Only concerned about the bottom line, and he knows that the bottom line is based on an image. You have to keep the image safe to keep the money rolling in, and there's no place in that image for gay men.* Andy could see this conversation was not going to help, so he decided to change tacks. "Regardless, Tim. The kid was murdered, the kid was gay. You can do the math here as well as anybody. He was murdered because he was gay." Andy paused momentarily, then continued. "What I'm saying is that this murder was a hate crime."

Tim rubbed his temples. He could feel a massive headache brewing in the back of his brain, and this new information wasn't helping to ease the pain. He took off his glasses and placed them on the desk in front of him. "A hate crime, Andy?" Hawkins asked, almost frightened by the very words themselves. "That's not something that happens around here." He looked at the sheriff expectantly, hoping the sheriff would agree and somehow realize the error of his ways in terms of his labeling of the crime. Or maybe he'd come through with the punch line to this twisted and sick joke he'd begun so ineloquently.

"I know what you're saying, Tim," O'Toole responded, "but the facts are the facts. This is definitely looking like a hate crime, Tim, an honest-to-God, big-city-style hate crime. I'm thinking that the Carlisle kid either did something or said something to someone, someone who didn't take too kindly to it. But it gets worse."

Hawkins shook his head. "That doesn't surprise me at this point. It's been all downhill from the start with this. We began with a random murder, which was bad enough for starters, but now you tell me it's a hate crime. What else is there?"

"Nobody, or almost nobody, knew he was gay. Not even his parents," Andy said. Another heavy load for the selectman to deal with. "Nobody except some people he worked with and a few other close friends of his."

"Oh, Christ," he muttered. "So not only do we have a dead kid, but now we have a dead, gay kid whose father is a senator and didn't know the kid was gay?" Tim ran his hand through his hair. The situation was getting worse by the minute. Now he had to deal with a murder, coupled with having to tell a United States Senator that his now-dead son was actually an in-the-closet homosexual.

Andy looked out the window at the crowds making their way to the ferry. "What do you suggest we do next, Tim?"

Tim laughed, unable to actually believe the question. "My God, Andy. You're the sheriff here. You should be telling me what we do next."

"You told me you wanted to be included in this investigation, so I'm including you," Andy said, feeling suddenly empowered as a result of what he saw as his own moral superiority to Hawkins. The truth was, though, he didn't want the responsibility anymore. He wanted someone else to take the lead in this investigation.

"I'll tell you what I think you should do. You can take it for what it's worth." Hawkins took a deep breath and exhaled before continuing. "If I were you, I'd get my ass in gear and start trying to find a way to explain this to the senator. And make it look good," he said.

Andy nodded, adding, "That's exactly what I was planning." He was glad to see that, at least for now, he and Hawkins were seeing eye-to-eye. "I've been trying to think up a story that won't be a total lie, but which will still protect the family." Andy mentioned briefly his plans about telling the family that Jack was mistaken for someone gay, while still being very careful to assure them that he had no reason to believe Jack himself was gay.

"Sounds good to me, Sheriff," Tim said. "Make it snappy, though. You know as well as I do that we need to get this little incident done and behind us before the summer kicks into high gear. Memorial Day was bad enough. We don't need this hanging over our heads like some dark cloud all summer," he said, signaling to Andy that the conversation was over and that the sheriff should resume his sheriff-related duties quickly.

Andy turned and left the office, returning to his own desk downstairs. In his mind he was going over possible stories to tell the Carlisle family. He wrote out his plan on a legal pad sitting on his desk. Jack, he would tell them, was working at a hotel where many of the waiters were gay, information he'd gotten from various sources. It was common knowledge around the island, he'd tell the family. So naturally when someone saw Jack—a good-looking, clean-cut man, a stereotype he hated to use, but one which he figured would lend credence to the story—walking out of the hotel after work, they'd assume he, too, was gay. Throw in a little local color just to make the story sound more believable, something like locals angry at the summer people or just out to get their kicks by beating up a gay man. *A man they thought was gay,* he reminded himself. He had to emphasize that part of the story. It was all about perception here. He retold the story to himself several times until he was sure he had it down and could relate it in a believable manner. He rehearsed it once, out loud, as he sat in his chair, pretending to talk to the senator. Then he took a deep breath, picked up the phone and called Senator Carlisle's house.

When Mr. Carlisle answered, Andy cleared his throat. "Senator," he began, "I think I've found something that might help our investigation, and I wanted you to know so you could advise me on how you want me to proceed."

"Go ahead," said Carlisle. "I'm listening."

"We have reason to believe that your son was murdered as a result of a gay-bashing incident. He was—." The senator stopped him short.

"What are you talking about, Sheriff? Are you suggesting that my son was out beating up homosexuals?" he asked in a tone laced with defensiveness.

"No, sir. We have reason to believe that your son was murdered by a gay-basher, if that's the correct term to use here. In other words, sir, your son was the victim of a gay-bashing, not the perpetrator."

"Sheriff," the voice said, "that's patently ludicrous. My son wasn't gay, for God's sake. Honestly, this is ridiculous."

"I know how it must sound to you, Senator," he said. So it was true. The parents didn't have any idea. Either that, or the kid at the Collins House was lying. He suspected in his gut that the kid wasn't lying. "But try to bear with me here. I'm not saying that he was gay. All I'm saying is that we have reason to believe that someone might have suspected he was gay."

"On what information do you base this absolutely inane theory, Sheriff?" This wasn't going to be easy for either party to deal with, but Andy did his best to remain calm. He kept telling himself that he knew his story and he knew that he could tell it so that it sounded true. At least he hoped he could.

130

"He worked at the Collins House Hotel, Mr. Carlisle. Many of the employees there are homosexual. We believe that someone saw him leaving the hotel one night, and, because of where he worked and how he looked, assumed that he was gay." O'Toole held his breath, hoping Carlisle wouldn't see through the story. He couldn't tell this man that his youngest son was everything he thought he wasn't.

"That's insane, Sheriff," the Senator replied. "Absolutely and positively insane. He'd had the same girlfriend for three years. There's no way anyone that knew him could think he was gay."

The conversation continued back and forth, Andy digging himself deeper with each passing minute. He wouldn't tell Carlisle the truth about his son, though, no matter what. He promised himself that. He wouldn't betray Jack's wishes. The kid hadn't wanted his parents to know, and it wasn't Andy's place to tell them now.

Finally, Leonard Carlisle conceded. "Okay, Sheriff. If that's what your take on this is right now, that's fine. At this point, I don't care what you think, just so long as you get to the bottom of this. Who else knows about this little pet theory of yours?"

"Only Tim Hawkins, Mr. Carlisle," he said.

"Make sure that neither of you breathes a word of this to anyone. Do I make myself perfectly clear?" he asked.

"Yes, sir," Andy said. "Crystal clear. We don't want this to get out any more than you do, sir. Tim and I have already talked about that very idea, in fact. Neither of us plans to utter a word about it to anybody, sir." *We'll be sure to keep your family's precious image safe and sound, Senator,* O'Toole thought to himself. *And Nantucket's precious little image, too,* he added scornfully.

The senator asked to be kept up-to-date on the investigation, thanked O'Toole for calling, and then added, "And remember, Sheriff. I'm leaving for Washington this evening. I'd prefer it if you called me directly as opposed to calling my wife. She's already a complete wreck as a result of this whole thing, and there's no reason to upset her further." He gave Andy the phone numbers for both his direct office line in Washington and for his townhouse in Alexandria, Virginia, and then said goodbye. Andy hung up the phone and heaved a sigh of relief. He sat for a moment and thought about what to do next. He recalled that Jack Carlisle had frequented the Jib and Jenny and that he and Steph were good friends. He'd try again to talk to her about him. Maybe she could shed some light on Jack's life and what might have happened that night. He looked again at his notes relating to the investigation and circled Jamie McKenzie's name. He needed to talk to her about McKenzie, too.

He walked out the door of the Town Building and crossed the street to the Jib and Jenny. The bar was mostly empty, as the two o'clock lull set in around the restaurants in town. It struck him as almost impossible to believe that, only a few days before, the island had been teeming with people, but had now settled down momentarily. *The calm before the summer storm,* he thought to himself. As O'Toole entered, he saw Peter Oswald sitting at the bar reading the day's newspaper and eating his lunch. Tim walked up and sat next to him.

Peter looked up from his paper. "Hey, Andy. Any news?"

Andy shook his head. "None good, I'm afraid," he said. He motioned for Steph to meet him at the end of the bar and excused himself from Peter. Steph leaned her head down to hear him, and Andy asked her softly, "Did you ever see Jack Carlisle leaving here with any women?"

Steph laughed. "Jack? God, no, Andy. He was gay. Why would he want to be in here picking up women?"

Andy looked up at her with an expression of disbelief. "You knew he was gay?"

Steph laughed again. "Of course I knew he was gay, Andy. It's not like it was real hard to tell." She grabbed a rag from behind the bar and began to wipe down the bar in front of him. "I knew Jack when he was fifteen. He used to come in here and buy a soda every afternoon. He and I would talk for hours. Hell, I watched that kid grow up practically. I knew everything about him."

"Why didn't you tell me any of this before, Steph?" he asked. He couldn't believe that a piece of information like that would have gone unmentioned in their earlier conversations.

"I didn't think anything about it," she said. "It never even crossed my mind that you'd be interested." Andy understood. When he really thought about it, he wasn't sure he'd have considered it important had he been in her shoes. Steph always said what was on her mind, and he knew she wouldn't intentionally hide anything from him, especially in a case like this.

He continued. "Okay. So you knew he was gay. Did he ever say anything about people harassing him because of it?"

She looked at Andy and smiled. "Andy, honey," she said, "you really need to get out of the house more. You've got to realize that there are a lot of gay men on this island. A lot of people don't like to deal with that fact. Personally, I don't care one way or the other. But yes, to answer your question, he said that a lot of people harassed him. He felt safe in here because he knew it wasn't an issue with me. It was just something we both knew, but neither of us talked about. It just wasn't something that we ever brought up when we were talking together. You know?"

Andy was writing mechanically as she spoke and he didn't realize that she had stopped until he noticed a pause in his own writing. "You were working in here the night he disappeared, right?" he asked. He already knew the answer, but he wanted to create a segue into the questions he wanted to ask her about McKenzie.

"Yep. Sure was. Pretty slow night. Few of my regulars, a few people out early for the weekend. Nothing much."

He nodded. "Did you see him leave with anyone?" He was hoping she had, given that it had been a slow night.

"Nope," she said, shaking her head. "He left alone. I always make it a point to say goodbye to my regulars, and I saw him walk out the door by himself." She turned to refill a beer for a customer at the other end of the bar. When she'd returned, Andy looked up at her from where he stood.

"Is Jamie McKenzie one of your regulars?" he asked her.

Steph looked at him suspiciously, eyeing the sheriff. "Yep," she replied off-handedly. "He's usually in here every night right after work. Why do you want to know about Jamie now?"

O'Toole ignored the question, assuming that she'd figure out his motive soon enough. "Steph, I need you to think really hard here. Do you remember Jamie being in here that night? The night Jack disappeared?"

She looked out the window, thinking, trying to clear her thoughts before she spoke. She, as Andy had expected, knew what information the sheriff wanted. She must have suspected that Jamie was involved. But Steph, like Andy, didn't want to start falsely accusing anybody. She already felt guilty enough as it was for her role in implicating Will Paterna, and she didn't want to do it to anybody else. She looked down at Andy, who was standing there like a large dog expecting a treat. "Yeah," she said finally in a soft tone, "he was in here. He was sitting with a group down at the end of the bar over there," she said, pointing towards the back of the building.

Finally, O'Toole thought to himself. *Maybe, just maybe, things were starting to work out.* "Thanks, honey. You're the best," he said, smiling.

Andy turned and walked back to where Peter was sitting, now finished with his lunch.

"How's the weekend?" Andy asked.

"Oh Christ," Peter sighed. "We got slammed. But it's pretty much over now, thank God." He folded the newspaper and laid it down on the bar.

"I need you to tell me everything you know about Jamie McKenzie," Andy said, suddenly changing the subject.

Peter laughed. "What do you want to know? I don't know much, and what I do know isn't all that good. And besides," he added, "you probably know him better than I do." Peter told Andy how he and Jamie had once been drinking buddies. Peter had taught Jamie how to scuba dive several years ago. The two had lost touch, though, when Peter had quit drinking. Jamie still came around occasionally, usually to fill air tanks when he was working on boats in the harbor. Just last winter Peter had suggested that Jamie go out and dive for scallops with him, and Jamie had taken him up on the offer. Peter had told him it was easy money, and good money, too. So Jamie had agreed, but had not done as well as he'd expected to do. "And like I told you yesterday. He said he's giving it up."

Andy jotted down notes on the legal pad. "Yeah, I remember you told me that. Let me ask you something weird," he said, "and this falls under the whole don't tell thing. What is his opinion of," he cleared his throat and lowered his voice, "his opinion of gays. Is he really violent about the subject of gay men?" Andy gave Peter an awkward look. O'Toole knew the question sounded bizarre, but he didn't want to elaborate on the subject just yet.

Peter looked up at the sheriff. "I don't have any idea, Andy. He's got a temper, no question about it. But I have no idea what he thinks about gays. I don't really know what he thinks about anything, for that matter. We don't sit around and talk, you know? We didn't when we drank together, and we sure as hell don't now." And then, changing his tone to one of incredulity, he asked, "Why is that important?"

Andy looked at him. He was still bound to the promise he had made to the senator. "Just curious," he said. "We're trying to figure out every aspect of this thing, and we're wondering if our suspect might have had some kind of weird fetish." He looked away. Even he had trouble believing that one.

"You think Jamie raped the kid?" Peter laughed. "Oh, God. Now I've heard it all."

"Like I said, Peter," the sheriff said. "Just a theory. And there's no need to go around talking about it, remember."

Peter nodded in response. "No worries there," he said. "You can bet I won't be saying a word about that. They'd lock me up over there across the street if I said Jamie McKenzie was gay, Andy," he said as he smiled at the sheriff, still not able to believe the craziness of the suggestion about Jamie raping Jack Carlisle. "He's got a wife and two kids. He's not gay. Not even when he's drunk," he added laughing.

O'Toole felt a wave of relief go through his body the moment he was sure that Peter hadn't figured out where Andy was headed with his questioning. He still needed to keep the wraps on this theory of his. Andy patted Oswald on the back as he stood to leave. "Thanks, Peter. We'll be in touch, I'm sure."

"Yeah. I'm sure of it, too," said Peter as he reached into his back pocket to retrieve his wallet to pay for lunch.

"You're all set, Peter," Steph said to him. "Get out of here and get back to work." She winked at him and returned to her other customers at the bar.

Peter and Andy walked out of the bar together, and Steph told them to behave and to work hard. O'Toole looked back and offered her a slight smile, reminding himself again that it was Sunday, a day of rest. But he had things on his mind and a lot of work to do. He couldn't afford to rest, not yet. "Miles to go before I sleep," he mused to himself in a quiet voice. "Miles to go before I sleep."

CHAPTER SIXTEEN

On Monday, Memorial Day, Andy O'Toole wasn't sitting at his house cooking out with friends. Rather he was sitting in his office in the Town Building, working on gathering papers together. He'd had to work hard to secure the things he needed before proceeding with his investigation, but he'd finally managed to get everything together. He put the papers he needed in his jacket pocket, walked slowly to his car and drove out to Jamie McKenzie's house. It was just after three o'clock in the afternoon when the sheriff pulled into the driveway. The front yard was littered with stray boards and rocks, and a swing set sat rusting in one corner of the yard to the side of the house. Andy walked up the front porch steps and knocked on the door. The door opened slowly and Sylvia McKenzie, Jamie's wife, stood in the open doorway.

She was a short woman, though relatively large for her frame. She had long dark hair that she pulled back in a ponytail, and her face was pale. Andy didn't know a lot about her, beyond the fact that she was married to Jamie. She stood there in a pair of jeans and a T-shirt, and her bare feet were calloused.

"Hi, Sylvia," Andy said to her, trying to sound friendly. "Is Jamie home by any chance?"

She opened the door further and silently motioned for the sheriff to come in. "Jamie," she yelled over her shoulder, "Sheriff's here to talk to you." She led the sheriff into the kitchen and indicated an empty chair at the kitchen table. "Have a seat, Sheriff. He's in back watchin' TV I think." He looked off in the direction she had motioned with her head and heard someone walking down the hallway. Jamie walked in to the kitchen.

"Hey, Andy," he said. He sounded as if he hadn't slept in a week and he looked the part, as well. His face showed a few days' worth of stubble and his dirty-blonde hair was a mess. He was wearing a T-shirt, one from the Jib and Jenny, O'Toole noticed, but it was not sufficiently large to fully cover his bulging stomach. He shuffled his feet when he walked and the sheriff noticed their enormous size.

"Jamie," he said, "how you doing?"

Jamie scratched the back of his head and said, "Been better, Andy. Tied one on last night over at Shane's. Figured I had to get in early to beat the crowds and once I got in there..." He gestured with his hands as if to say, "It was totally out of my control," and laughed, allowing the sheriff to fill in the blank for himself.

"We need to talk, Jamie," the sheriff said, suddenly serious.

Jamie looked at his wife, who took the silent hint and left the two men alone in the kitchen. Jamie sat down in the chair opposite the sheriff. He put his huge arms on the table, crossing them, and coughed heavily. He leaned back and reached into the pocket of his T-shirt, producing a crumpled pack of cigarettes. O'Toole noticed that they were Marlboro lights and his skin tingled slightly at the recognition. Jamie took one out, lit it and looked at the sheriff. "What's up?" he asked.

"You've heard, I'm sure, about the Carlisle murder," the sheriff began.

"Yeah, I heard about it," said Jamie. "Was actually drinkin' last night with Will Paterna. He was a sight, lemme tell ya' what."

So Will had picked up right where he left off, thought Andy. *Wonder who took him home last night.*

"I bet," said O'Toole. "What I'm wondering, though, is anything you might know about it." He paused, allowing the question to hang there in the open for a second. He looked at Jamie, hoping for some sort of clue from his reaction. He got none.

Jamie smiled, revealing yellow and crooked teeth. "I know Will didn't do it," he laughed.

"Then who did, Jamie?" the sheriff asked, not missing a beat. He knew if it had been someone local, and he was convinced that it had been, then the person would talk. Somebody knew something. Andy was sure of that. Nantucket was a small community, and people that lived here knew each other. Frequently people knew more about their friends and neighbors than one might want them to know, in fact, so Andy was sure that the murderer had been talking to someone.

"No idea, Andy," said Jamie.

"You haven't heard anybody talking about anything? Come on, Jamie. You get around. You have to have heard somebody talking. You were a cop, for God's sake. Surely you still have that insight into people. I'm sure you've picked up on something from somebody, haven't you?" He kept plugging away with his questioning, hoping to get something useful from him.

"Honest to God, Andy. Haven't heard a thing." His face was stone. His expression remained blank, like a gambler holding four aces and trying to milk the others at the table for all their money.

Andy diverted his gaze from Jamie's face and glanced around the kitchen, but found nothing suspicious. He decided it was time to cut to the chase. "Look, Jamie. Here's the deal. We got a dead kid and we got some pretty big footprints near where we found the kid's—." He stopped short. "We've got some pretty big footprints near where we found evidence relating to the murder."

"You mean where you found the kid's head?" Jamie asked mockingly. "Will was tellin' the whole bar about it last night. Don't worry, Andy. I know what's goin' on."

Son of a bitch, Andy thought to himself. *That little bastard was at Shane's last night blabbering to the whole bar about the details of the investigation.* He pulled out a cigarette of his own. "You don't mind if I smoke, do you?" he asked.

Jamie shook his head and the sheriff lit the cigarette. "Gotta quit these damn things before they kill me," he said as he exhaled, trying to sound friendly. Bad cop had gotten nowhere, so he figured that good cop might get inside McKenzie's brain. "So like I was saying. We got these footprints, Jamie. Big damn feet. Somebody with some big feet was over at Paterna's house the other night, and we think that person had something to do with the murder." Jamie looked down at his own feet, curling his toes under to make them appear smaller.

"So you think I did it because I've got big feet?" he asked suspiciously.

The sheriff looked straight ahead. "I've got an idea or two," he said. "Were you at Will Paterna's house in the last, say, week?"

"Nope," replied Jamie. "Haven't been over there since—." He thought about it briefly. "Been at least two years," he concluded. "It's not like we're best friends or anything, you know. We see each other at a bar, we drink together. That's about it." Andy looked at Jamie's hands, which were sitting crossed on the table in front of him. He noticed a gauze bandage wrapped around Jamie's right index finger.

"What happened there?" O'Toole asked, pointing to the injured finger.

Jamie looked at his hand. "Oh, that," he said absently rubbing the bandage. "Cut my finger the other day. Out workin' in the yard," he offered. Andy knew that wasn't true. He'd seen the yard and it was obvious that no work had been done out there any time recently. Certainly not as recently as the other day.

The sheriff paused for a moment before continuing. "Jamie," he began, "I've known you for a long time, and that fact makes what I have to say tough for me." He took a deep breath. "Don't take this the wrong way, but I need to look around your house for a little while. I'm looking for some pretty specific things. Is it okay with you if I search your house?"

Jamie took a drag off his cigarette. "Got a warrant?" he asked confidently. He'd never been in the position of using a search warrant when he'd been a cop, but he'd watched enough TV shows in his time. He knew the right questions to ask.

Andy slid his hand into his jacket pocket and produced a folded sheet of blue paper. He was certainly going to be official here, given how much work he'd had to do in order to find a judge on Nantucket on Memorial Day who was both available and willing to sign a warrant based on flimsy evidence. "Signed, sealed and now delivered," he said, pushing the folded piece of paper across the table to McKenzie.

Jamie picked up the warrant without any idea of what it should look like or say, and his earlier confidence all but disappeared completely. He wasn't sure what he hoped he'd figure out by looking at it, but that just seemed like the right thing for him to do at that moment. He scanned over the warrant and waved his hand, indicating that the sheriff could look to his heart's content. Andy stood. "Where's your bedroom, Jamie?" he asked.

Jamie pointed down the hall that went off the kitchen. "Last door on the right," he said in something of a dazed voice, his attention still focused on the warrant. Andy walked slowly back to the bedroom, unsure of what he might find. The warrant explicitly stated that Andy was searching for a pair of tennis shoes that matched a plaster cast he had in the evidence room. He thought that if he could match the plaster cast of the footprint he'd made, then he'd have his man. He walked into the bedroom and opened the closet door. Shoes were piled on the floor in no particular pattern of arrangement. In the middle of the pile was a pair of worn out tennis shoes. Andy looked at them;

they were covered in dried mud. On closer examination, he saw something that stuck out worse than Jamie's cut finger. A dark brown splotch, darker than the caked-on mud and shaped like a jagged circle, splattered on the right shoe had caught his eye. Suddenly it all clicked in his mind and he could see it as if it had been shown to him in slow motion. He quickly grabbed the shoes and returned to the kitchen.

"I need to take these with me," he said to Jamie, who still sat motionless at the table staring out the open window over the sink. He didn't wait for approval. "I'll be in touch," he said as he walked out the door. When he got back to his car, he phoned the police department. "Get a cruiser over to Jamie McKenzie's house right now. I want that guy under surveillance. Twenty-four, seven," he said to the dispatcher. "He's at twenty-three Red Barn Road. Get somebody over here now. And for the love of God," he added sternly, "don't send any summer cops out here. Real deal only." He reached in the back of the car and got a clear plastic bag, then placed the shoes carefully inside. He sat in the car, watching the front door. There was no movement.

Several minutes later, a police cruiser pulled up behind him. He looked in the rearview mirror and saw two officers seated in the car. He heaved a sigh of relief when he saw the officers, as they were veterans of the force and not kids on island for the summer. He got out and approached the car. "Hey, guys," he said to the officers. "Don't let Jamie out of your sight. And please, whatever you do, do not answer any questions from anybody. I don't care who calls you and I don't care what they say. Do not answer any questions and don't let anybody in that house. And if McKenzie leaves, I mean so much as walks out his front door, you let me know immediately, okay?"

The officers were initially shocked by the forceful tone of his voice, and both nodded in a stunned silence. He returned to his car and drove back to the police station. When he got to the station, he found only the dispatcher and one other officer at the station. "I need to get in to the storage room," he announced in an official voice to the dispatcher.

She looked up from the magazine she had been reading. "Go ahead," she said flatly. She returned her attention to the magazine. Andy entered the small room the department used as the evidence storage facility. He took the plaster cast of the right foot that he had taken from Will Paterna's yard from the shelf in the small room and placed the corresponding shoe he'd taken from McKenzie's closet on top of it. The shoe fit perfectly. "I've got you now," he said confidently. "I caught you, you son of a bitch." He ran out of the room

140

and yelled to the dispatcher. "Get those two guys watching McKenzie on the radio for me. Now."

The dispatcher radioed the two officers, who responded immediately. "Sheriff wants you," she said without emotion into the microphone.

Andy glared at her and grabbed the microphone. "Is McKenzie still at home?"

"Hasn't left, Andy," one of the officers responded.

"Good," Andy said in reply. "Make sure he doesn't go anywhere. If he does, radio me immediately. I'm on my way." He ran out the door to his car and sped off towards Jamie McKenzie's house. He was grateful that the crowds had dispersed almost as suddenly as they'd arrived, because there was no traffic to speak of to hinder his progress towards Jamie's house. He had the volume on his police radio turned all the way up, afraid of missing a call from the officers on watch duty. He pulled into McKenzie's driveway, leapt from his car and knocked on the front door. Jamie opened the door. His appearance and his demeanor were just like they'd been when O'Toole had last seen him. He looked sheepishly at the sheriff.

"Jamie," he said cautiously, "I need you to step outside for me."

Jamie gave the sheriff a look of irritation mixed with disbelief, but did as he was told. As soon as he'd cleared the threshold of the door and was outside, O'Toole reached in his back pocket and grabbed his handcuffs. He looked at Jamie and ordered, "Don't do anything stupid here. You're under arrest for the murder of Jack Carlisle."

Jamie looked stunned. "What are you talking about, Andy? I didn't do anything." Andy didn't answer him. He put the handcuffs around his wrists and led him to the waiting patrol car as he read the accused his Miranda rights. The officers had gotten out of the car, waiting to be of any service O'Toole might need.

"Get back in the car," he said. He put Jamie in the back seat of the squad car. "Take him to the station," he said. "I'll follow you. No sirens," he added. He went back to his car and started it as the officers pulled away. He followed them back through the narrow streets to the police station downtown. As he drove, he found himself again congratulating himself on his investigative skills. He was sure this time. He'd found the shoes, Jamie had denied having been there, and he suspected that the stain on that shoe would turn out to be blood. And he went so far as to convince himself that the blood would, no doubt, be AB-negative, the same as Jack Carlisle's. Again he thought it was done. But again he feared it had been too easy.

"So what?" he asked himself aloud. "So what if it was easy? Maybe that's just because I'm a damn good cop who's damn good at what he does," he said. He smiled confidently, proud of the work he had done. As soon as he got back to town, he'd call Senator Carlisle and tell him the good news. He pushed the voices of doubt out of his head and allowed himself to bask in the moment, confident and sure in his own mind that this time he had his man. This time there would be nothing to get in the way to change that fact.

CHAPTER SEVENTEEN

By the time the officers had processed Jamie McKenzie into the jail and Andy had gotten back to his office, it was after nine. He kicked back in the chair behind his desk, the size of his own self-worth growing by leaps and bounds. He knew he'd done it this time, and no footprints or blood or anything else was going to screw it up for him. He'd done it, damnit, and he was going to enjoy it. He picked up the phone and dialed Leonard Carlisle's number at the senator's townhouse in Alexandria.

"Senator Carlisle," Andy said into the phone. "Andy O'Toole. I apologize for calling so late, sir, but I thought you might want to hear the good news." *Just like old friends,* he told himself. *Buddies just shooting the breeze.* "Game over, sir," he said with an air of officiousness. "Suspect is in custody. It's all over but the crying on this end, sir. We'll have a confession out of him before the sun sets tomorrow." He felt like a movie star.

"Hold on, Sheriff. Before you turn into Dick Tracy on me, why don't you back up and slow down a little. Are you saying that you've got somebody else in jail now?"

The news hadn't reached that far yet, Andy thought. *He would be the harbinger of good news for the first time in quite a while.* "You remember that lead I told you about, Senator? Turns out my own hunch was right." He went on to describe the sequence of events leading up to his arrest of Jamie McKenzie a few hours earlier. He made himself out to be the hero of the day. It sounded vaguely familiar to his previous premature celebration in the arrest of Will Paterna, but he was sure this time. He knew it in his heart; he had hit the bulls-eye with McKenzie. His aim was dead-on this time. When Andy had finished with the embellished story, the senator was momentarily silent.

Andy thought he might not have totally understood what he'd just told him. "Senator?" he said.

"Yes, Andy. I'm thinking here. Forgive me for asking you this, but past circumstances seem to me to deem it necessary. Are you absolutely positive about your new suspect? This Jamie McKenzie person?"

Andy's voice, seconds earlier jovial and celebratory, now turned defensive. "Yes, sir, I'm absolutely positive. One hundred percent." He resented the senator for asking him, but he, too, understood his hesitance in accepting Andy's findings immediately. As a way of reassuring him, O'Toole recounted all the evidence that they'd found linking McKenzie to the murder. He desperately wanted the senator to believe that this time there was no mistake whatsoever.

There was another brief pause on the other end. "Sheriff," Carlisle said, now suddenly quite serious, "if you're sure and he really is the one, then you have my deepest thanks." His voice, Andy thought, was beginning to sound more animated and less suspicious of the sheriff. "In fact, Sheriff, that's the best news I've had all day." Andy was glad to be of service and could only imagine the happiness the senator must be feeling, knowing that the man responsible for the murder of his son was now safely ensconced in the Nantucket jail and would be severely punished for his crimes. "Sheriff," the senator's voice continued, now sounding almost friendly it seemed to Andy.

"Yes, sir," Andy replied. He was still all business. He was the master investigator here and he wanted Senator Carlisle to know it.

"We've scheduled Jack's funeral for Friday afternoon. The service will be at four at Rock of Ages Baptist Church up on Centre Street. The burial will be at the cemetery out on Vesper Lane. Do you think you can make it? It would mean a lot to the family," he said. The sheriff noticed the change in the senator's tone, glad that he had, at least for the moment, convinced him that he'd done his job this time.

Andy glanced down at his desk, looking at the blank calendar page. He, the master investigator, had been invited to the funeral of a senator's child. It was a public display of the family's gratitude for all of his hard work. They wanted to show him off to their friends as the savior that fixed everything for them. "I think I can make it, sir," he said smiling. "I'll shuffle some things around here. I want to be there. It's a personal thing," he said. *It was a white lie,* he told himself. He wanted to make himself look busy. He needed to seem important here. *He was important,* he told himself. It was just a matter of showing the rest of the world how truly busy and important he was. But of course he was never too busy to attend to his friends. Like Senator Carlisle. His face melted into a broad smile.

"Great," said Carlisle. "Jack's brothers are all flying in and they'll be there. I know they'll want to thank you for all your work, and I certainly do, too. Thank you, Andy. You've turned into a real hero for us. Have a great night, Sheriff. Go out and get yourself a drink. Irish whiskey, right? Go get one and send me the bill," he added with a gentle laugh. "I need to call the rest of the family now, though, and tell them the good news."

I might just do that, thought Andy to himself. *I might just go across to the Jib and Jenny and get myself a drink. In fact, that sounds like a damn fine idea.* "Thanks, Mr. Carlisle," he said. "I'll see you at Rock of Ages at four on Friday." He hung up the phone and swiveled around in his chair so he could look out the window. The streets were nearly empty and town was, for the most part, peaceful and quiet. He looked across the street at the Whaling Museum. A young couple sat in one of the benches outside the museum, holding hands, looking at each other romantically. It was a clear night, Andy noticed, and the fog was staying away. The young couple in front of the museum was locked in a passionate kiss when Andy returned his glance to them, and he quickly looked away. His eyes came to rest on the picture of his wife sitting on his desk.

"What?" he asked the photograph guiltily. "I didn't do anything," he said smiling. He held two fingers to his lips and kissed them, then placed the two fingers on his wife's picture. "I miss you, old girl," he said. "I miss you like hell." He was conscious of a feeling of sentimentality and longing welling up inside his chest and he knew that he needed to get out of the office. Whenever he felt this way, and it seemed that he felt it more often recently, he made it a point to never cry. *Real men,* he told himself, *don't cry, especially not master investigator sheriffs.* He walked out of the office and locked the door behind him. He went down the stairs and out the door. The air outside was chilly, but O'Toole felt invigorated. He had solved—he was completely sure this time, he kept reminding himself—the murder of young Jack Carlisle. With every passing moment he gained confidence in the fact that he had solved the case. He had never in his life felt as truly alive as he did right now. He crossed over to the other side of the street and looked in one of the windows of the Jib and Jenny. It was still too early for the real nightlife crowd to be in yet, and the place wasn't very crowded. He decided to take the senator up on his offer and he walked in.

At the bar, he ordered a Jameson's neat. "Startin' early tonight," the bartender joked to the sheriff.

"Nah," Andy replied. "Just havin' a little nightcap, Adam." Andy knew most of the bartenders on Nantucket, especially those that had worked on the island for many years. Adam had begun working at the Jib and Jenny while still a student at Andover, and he had come back to work at the Jib and Jenny every year since. He'd started out as a dish washer, but worked his way up to the coveted position of bartender, making up to several hundred dollars a night in tips at the height of the tourist season. He had a Master's degree in theology, and Andy had always thought it was such a waste of a great mind for him to work in a bar, but Adam constantly defended his choice, saying that he wouldn't change it for the world.

"Have you seen Steph tonight?" Andy asked him. He wanted to tell her about the news regarding Jack's murder.

"She's off tonight. Worked the day shift. She told me something about going out with some friends. Said she planned to come in here early—I think she said something about going out to Shane's later tonight, but she always tries to stop by here first," the bartender told him in a friendly voice that lacked any concern about the evils that lurked in the world, even here on Nantucket.

Andy nodded as he removed a cigarette from his shirt pocket. He grabbed a matchbook from the end of the bar and, leaving his drink sitting where the bartender had placed it, walked out into the cool night air to smoke. He sat at a bench outside, smoking and contemplating, when he heard a loud laugh from inside, a laugh that he recognized. He threw his still-lit cigarette into the ash tray next to the bench and walked back into the bar, scanning the assembled groups. At the far end of the bar, O'Toole saw the source of the laughter he'd heard outside. On a stool, sitting with a group of friends, was Will Paterna. Andy retrieved his drink from the bar where he had just left it and began to walk towards him. He wanted to make amends.

"Hey there, skipper," Will said as Andy approached. "You plannin' to take me to jail for sittin' at a bar now?" A few members of the group around Will laughed sarcastically at the sheriff.

"Not just yet, Will," the sheriff said. "I think it's still legal." He winked as he said it. "Whacha drinkin' there?" he asked.

"Depends on who's buyin'," Will said with a sideways snicker intended for the audience of friends sitting around him.

"Let's say it's on me. Whacha drinkin'?"

Will tapped the rim of his glass. He looked at the sheriff and smiled. "Slap-Happy-Smash," he said.

Andy looked at him, not entirely sure what he had just said. "A what?" he asked.

"A Slap-Happy-Smash," Will repeated. "It's good. You need to try one." He laughed again. "Slaps you in the face, then makes you happy, then you're smashed." He grinned widely at the sheriff.

"I'll pass, thanks, but let me get you one," Andy said. He turned to the bar and called to Adam. "Lemme have a Slap-Happy-Smash for my friend William over here, Adam, if you don't mind good sir."

"On the way," replied the bartender. He took a large Mason jar from a shelf above the bar and placed it ceremoniously in front of Will, and then filled it with ice. He reached down and grabbed two different liquor bottles, but Andy couldn't tell what they contained. He poured streams from both bottles into the jar, then replaced the bottles back in the metal well at his knees. He grabbed two other bottles and repeated the process. He then took a plastic container containing a mixture of fruit juice and filled the glass. He dropped in a cherry and an orange slice and then handed the drink to Will. "Six-fifty," he said to the sheriff, who was still staring at the jar.

"Good Lord," replied O'Toole, his concentration broken upon hearing the high price. "I can remember when you couldn't walk away from six dollars worth of liquor." Andy put a twenty dollar bill on the bar. "That's for both his and mine," he said. As the bartender grabbed the bill and rang the sale into the register, Andy turned to Will. "I'm sorry about everything that's happened to you in the past couple of days, Will. I am truly sorry for putting you through that," he said. "I was wrong and I admit it. I apologize, kid," he said solemnly as he placed his hand on Will's shoulder. "Can we put all that behind us and just start over?"

Will looked at the sheriff as if he were seeing him for the first time in his life. "Andy, you know me. You knew my dad and you still know me. I know I'm not a model citizen. I've screwed up a few times in my life. And I admit it," he added mockingly. "I'm sorry for my screw-ups. But I have never in my life done anything like what you tried to say I did, and when I told you I didn't, you didn't believe me. I can forgive you for what you did, Andy, but it's gonna' be hard to ever forget you not believing me."

Andy nodded his head. "I know, Will. I knew your father. He was one helluva man, let me tell you what. He was a good man and a good friend. That made all this that much harder for me, and I'm sorry again. That's all I can say." He'd played the ball into Will's court. It was now Paterna's choice to either accept or reject the apology.

Will turned in his chair so that he was facing the sheriff. He extended his hand and took Andy's hand in his. The two shook and Andy knew that he was forgiven. "I probably would've thrown my ass in jail, too," Will finally said laughing, breaking the thick tension that had hung between them. "And I wouldn't have bought me a drink after I did it, either," he added with a smile.

Andy looked down at his own drink and noticed that he'd finished it. "Hey, Adam," he called down the bar. "When you get a chance," he said, pointing to his empty glass. Meanwhile O'Toole glanced down the bar and then turned back to Will. "Thanks, Will. I owe you one," he said. He gave Paterna a good-natured pat on the back. "Be good, mister. I got some business to attend to," he said. The bartender put Andy's refilled glass down on the bar in front of him next to the change that O'Toole had left sitting on the bar. Andy left the money where it was, pointing it out to the bartender as he walked away. He didn't want to put out the image that he was expecting to drink for free. He slolwy began to make his way down to the end of the bar. He'd noticed that Steph had come in the door and she was standing near the door. Next to her stood the young waiter Andy had met at the Collins House who had broken the news about Jack being gay. He walked down to where they were standing.

"Steph," he said smiling. "Good to see you dear."

"Andy O'Toole? What in God's name are you doing in a place like this after five o'clock?" she said laughing.

Andy gave Steph a friendly hug and said, "Taking care of some unfinished business." He turned to the waiter. "You work at the Collins House. Friend of Jack Carlisle's. Name's Byron, right?" he asked.

"Yes," the young man said nodding. "Guilty, I guess you'd say, on all counts." He smiled weakly at O'Toole.

Andy suddenly said to the two of them, "We got him. We got the guy who killed Jack. Got him over there in the jail right now. No doubt about it this time," he said, giddy with excitement. And then, in a more subdued and secretive voice, "It turns out it was Jamie."

Steph looked hurt and then surprised. "You're serious? I mean, you're really serious? And you're sure?" She was swaying slightly. The news hit her hard, and her emotions were clearly mixed on the subject. On the one hand, her friend's murderer had been found. On the other, though, the murderer was also a friend.

The sheriff nodded. "Completely serious," he said. "Found evidence linking Jamie McKenzie to planting the evidence at Will Paterna's house. Got him stone cold," Andy said. "It's locked up and shut tight," he said.

"Don't get cocky on us now," Steph said with a voice infected by O'Toole's excitement. Her ambivalence had gone. Now she was just happy it was done. Assuming O'Toole was right, anyway. "Don't get my hopes up just to trash 'em when you have to let him go," she said jokingly.

"Excuse me," said Byron suddenly. "I'm off to the little boys' room. Be back in two and two," he said as he kissed Steph on the cheek.

As he walked down the length of the bar to the men's room, Steph turned to the sheriff. "He's a riot," she said. "He's so much fun to go out with. He and Jack and I, we used to have a time together." She looked off, realizing the sadness and misery that were now forever linked to the comment she'd just made.

As Byron neared the men's room, he walked past Will Paterna.

"What's up, faggot?" whispered Will under his breath. "You're next," he said. "Watch your back, motherfucker, 'cause you're next."

Byron ignored the comments. He was used to it by now, but he decided after all that he could wait until they got to Shane's to go to the bathroom. He turned back and returned to Steph, smiling and attempting to feign happiness at the news regarding the investigation into Jack's murder. He silently wished to himself that he had the sheriff's confidence.

CHAPTER EIGHTEEN

The next day found Andy O'Toole, accompanied by four Nantucket police officers, thoroughly searching the house of Jamie McKenzie. McKenzie's wife and children had gone to live with some friends while her husband was incarcerated; O'Toole had told her that he couldn't guarantee a time frame. He could come home today, he told her, but he might not come home ever again. In her absence, the crime scene was empty and the officers had the entire house to themselves. Yellow crime scene tape had been spread around the yard, and officers who would otherwise have been working bicycle patrol duties were assigned to guard the property. They were under absolute orders to let no person, regardless of who that person might be or claim to be, anywhere near the crime scene area. O'Toole had sent the shoe that he'd taken from Jamie McKenzie's closet, the one with what appeared to be blood on it, off to be tested and he was anxiously awaiting the results. He hoped those results would confirm his suspicions. If they did, this case was as good as closed.

The officers dug through the closets and drawers in Jamie's bedroom, but found nothing that indicated any participation in a murder. No bloody clothes, no bloody knives, nothing. It looked like an average bedroom with average clothes. Andy took one of the officers with him and said, "Let's go check the garage. Maybe there's something out there."

The pair walked out the back door to the garage, a small building detached from the rest of the house. It, like the house, was covered in grey shingles. An old pickup truck was parked in front of the door. O'Toole instinctively looked below the truck, hoping to find a puddle of oil that would confirm his suspicions and hopefully remove any doubt, as he remembered the oil he'd

150

found in the street at Paterna's house, but it looked as if the truck hadn't moved in ages and regardless, there was no oil puddle beneath it. Andy reached down and grabbed the small metal handle to the garage door and found that he had to pull quite hard to open it. As the door slid up, light filled the small interior of the garage, illuminating a sort of den, complete with a sofa and television set to one side. On the wall directly opposite the door was a long table that extended the entire length of the structure. Scattered across it were various pieces of diving equipment, as well as a few rusty wrenches and screwdrivers. *Tools of the trade,* O'Toole thought to himself. In talking to people about Jamie, Andy had learned that he was willing to do just about anything that involved his getting paid, from examining damaged propellers to cleaning boat bottoms. Andy had learned that the benefit to having a diver do these jobs, from the boat owner's perspective, was that it didn't require taking the boat out of the water. It didn't require taking the boat off its mooring, for that matter, because Jamie could get to them and do the job while the boat was still floating in the harbor.

He walked to the table and looked at the equipment strewn haphazardly around the rough wooden surface. Again, nothing seemed out of the ordinary. There was nothing to indicate that Jamie had murdered Jack Carlisle. Andy didn't know what he had expected to find, but in his heart he had hoped to find something that would serve to further link Jamie to the crime. Then he noticed a rectangular blue box on a shelf and took it down. Showing it to the other officer, he remarked, "Latex gloves. Why in hell would a guy that's a diver need latex gloves?" He smiled confidently, knowing exactly what Jamie had been doing with latex gloves. The cellular phone in his jacket pocket rang.

"Andy, we've got a huge crowd of people down here." It was Claudia, calling to update him as to the situation downtown. "Reporters, mostly. They all want to know what's going on in the Carlisle case," the voice on the other end said. Apparently the senator had phoned a few networks to let them know that the murderer had been captured.

"Tell them you don't have any comment right now," he said. "Let's take this one step at a time. I know we've got the right guy, but I would like to come back with a smoking gun to show them all." He hung up the phone and began to think about the evidence he'd procured. He still longed to find what he had told Claudia he needed. Some sort of positive evidence, some sort of smoking gun, would cement this whole thing shut and make his case air-tight. He turned to the officer. "I'm going to head back to town," he said. "I want to see if we've got any information on those shoes yet. Can you guys handle it here?"

"Sure thing, Sheriff," the officer replied. "We'll let you know what we turn up."

Andy turned and went back outside and walked to his car. Driving back to town, he kept thinking about where he might find the piece of evidence he so desperately sought. He knew it was out there, somewhere. The only question was where it was. He needed to have it. He needed to get rid of the voice in his head telling him he was still basically just chasing his own tail. The voice had no credibility to O'Toole, but he couldn't seem to shut it up no matter how hard he tried. And his greatest fear was that the voice's refusal to stop making its presence known would, somehow, begin to lend credence to what it was saying to the sheriff.

When he neared the Town Building, he could see the crowd of reporters and news crews massing in front of the door. A few onlookers walked by, gawking at the cameras, asking what they were doing. Reporters desperate for filler stopped passers-by to ask if they had any reaction to the murder. The locals turned the other direction and walked away without so much as a word, but the tourists were easier targets, fueled by a combination of fascination and vanity; being quoted in the newspaper was apparently better than a postcard for the friends back home. One reporter from *People* magazine had a line of six such visitors anxiously awaiting their chance to offer their reactions regarding the tragedy to the world. Andy pulled his car into his parking space and was immediately surrounded. He opened the car door and was bombarded with questions.

"Sheriff, who's the new suspect you've got?" one asked.

"Why'd he do it, Sheriff?" another asked.

"Has he confessed to the murder yet, Sheriff?"

He looked out at the sea of reporters and sighed heavily. "We've got a suspect in custody," he said. "His name is Jamie McKenzie. He's a local contractor who makes his living primarily by diving in the boat basin, working underneath boats. We're working on sorting through all of the evidence that we currently have and we're also working on finding more evidence to support the case. You'll be the first to know when we have a definite answer for you," he said. He began to push his way through the crowd, ignoring the questions being fired at him from different directions.

He walked up the stairs into his office, saying to Claudia as he passed her desk, "No calls, Claudia." She nodded to him, the phone already at her ear, with four calls on hold. He closed his office door behind him and sat at his desk. *Who'd have ever thought we'd be dealing with this kind of thing,* he asked himself silently. That was the sticking point in this entire situation. It just didn't make sense that a murder could happen here. He constantly found his thoughts circling around that concept, the idea that Nantucket was a quaint whaling village that had been stricken with this ghastly crime. This is something that happens in New York or Los Angeles. It doesn't happen on Nantucket, for God's sake. The phone on his desk rang.

It occurred to him that he'd told Claudia that he didn't want any calls, so he thought this must be something important. "O'Toole," he said into the phone, anticipating the notification of some grand discovery.

"Andy, it's Tom Latkin here. Got the results on that shoe you wanted tested."

O'Toole grabbed the notepad in front of him. "Shoot," he said.

The doctor cleared his throat. "The stain on the shoe is blood and it is human," he said slowly, reading the results off a sheet of paper. Andy wished he'd get to the point. He was waiting breathlessly for the answer he so wanted to hear.

"What was the blood type?" he asked solemnly.

"Andy," the doctor said, "are you sitting down?"

The suspense was killing him. "Yes, damnit, just tell me."

"AB-negative," the doctor said. Andy knew the doctor was smiling on the other line.

"Latkin, you're my hero, kid," he said beaming. "That's the best news I've heard in a long time." He was already envisioning the speech he would deliver to the assembled press.

"Hold on, Andy. Don't get too carried away. It's like I told you earlier," he said. "Just because it's the same blood type as the kid's, it doesn't mean anything for sure, because there's no genetic match yet. I've already started that process, but it's pretty lengthy. I had to send all the samples to Boston to be tested, and they won't have an answer for me for a couple of weeks at the earliest." He paused. "I don't want to rain on your parade, Sheriff, but be careful how much stock you put in just the matching blood types. Remember that it's not impossible for two people to have the same blood type." The doctor seemed to have lost the tone of assurance he'd had when last the two had spoken about how rare Jack's blood type was. "I just don't want to see you go through what you've already been through for a second time," he added cautiously.

Andy shook his head. "Nope, Doc, this is it. I know it. I can feel it in my bones. That bastard's the one." He hung up the phone and walked down to the dispatcher's desk. "Need to see McKenzie," he said, trying to sound official.

He was escorted back to the cell holding Jamie McKenzie. The prisoner didn't look up as the sheriff entered the cell. "Jamie," he said slowly. "We've got you. We've got the Carlisle kid's blood type both at Paterna's house and on your shoe. We've got other evidence, too, Jamie, and we know it was you. We know you planted that kid's head at Paterna's house, so we know you were in possession of it. That fact leads me to believe that you killed him. We've got two choices here, as far as I can tell. We can do this the hard way or we can do it the easy way."

Jamie snickered under his breath. "What's the easy way?" he asked.

"Well," began the sheriff, "you can confess to the murder, and that's that." Andy crossed his fingers, hoping Jamie wouldn't ask about the hard way.

"And the hard way?"

O'Toole sighed. "We can send the blood off to have it tested, send a sample of your blood in, too. We could have the DNA matched to prove that the blood we found on your shoes was Jack's, and that those cigarette butts had your DNA and his on them, if you want us to do that." He wasn't even sure if it were possible to find DNA on the cigarette butts, but he figured it sounded good, anyway, and he hoped Jamie wouldn't call his bluff. "It would take a lot of time, money, and effort, but we'll do it." He was also careful not to let on to the fact that Latkin had already sent the blood off. If McKenzie would just confess, he could cancel the tests, maybe. For the first time since the sheriff had entered the cell, Jamie looked up at O'Toole.

"I didn't kill that kid, Andy. I swear to you I didn't kill him." He had lost the tough edge to his voice. He sounded scared now.

"Let me see your hands, Jamie," O'Toole said to him. Jamie held his hands out, palm up, for the sheriff to inspect. His hands were large, callused, and dirty. They shook slightly from what Andy presumed was a life of hard drinking. He didn't want to judge McKenzie's habits, but he'd heard stories about how much the man drank, and by his standards it qualified as a major amount. The index finger of his left hand had a long cut, almost like a paper cut. *Almost like the sort of cut you'd get if you got your finger stuck on a blackberry bush while you were walking past it,* O'Toole thought to himself. "What's that?" he asked, indicating the cut.

"No idea," Jamie said. "Get lots of dings and scrapes and cuts in my line of work. I work with my hands," he added.

"Yeah, I know," Andy said. "You don't remember how you got this one?" he asked. He remembered the first time he'd noticed it, and reminded Jamie of their conversation. "You told me before that it was from working in the yard."

"That's right," Jamie said nervously, as if suddenly recovering a long forgotten memory. "I had been working in the yard. Wife was giving me grief about how it looked so bad. But you know, with my job I'm always cutting my hands, so it's possible I didn't get it from that." His eyes darted around the inside of the cell. "To tell you the truth, Andy, the honest truth, I really have no idea how it happened and I have no idea when it happened." He turned his face back to the wall.

O'Toole doubted the story, but he let McKenzie sit in silence for a moment, trying to add a sense of drama and finality to the situation. "Jamie, we've got you on this one," the sheriff said finally. "Now what do you say. You want to confess to it?"

McKenzie didn't turn his gaze from the wall. "Hell no," he said flatly. "Get me my lawyer. Hector Cornell's the guy. I don't know his number, but he's in the phone book."

That's it, Andy thought to himself with a sense of self-congratulation. *He wants to confess to his lawyer and tell him everything.* He mentally patted himself on the back. "So you want me to call Hector for you?" he asked. Jamie, as if lost in thought, merely nodded his affirmation that the sheriff was correct. O'Toole called for the officer on duty to let him out and he walked back up the stairs to his office. The two flights of stairs seemed to disappear beneath him and Andy felt like he was walking on air. He had done it. It was almost official. Ninety-nine and forty-four one-hundredths, he said to himself. Just like Ivory soap. It's a done deal. He walked into his office, looked up Hector Cornell's phone number and dialed the phone. "Your client," he said when Cornell answered, "Jamie McKenzie, has requested a meeting with you down at the jail."

He left it at that and hung up the phone without waiting for a response. No need to tell the attorney why Jamie wanted him. Just let the facts come out as they came. Maybe even let Cornell squirm a little. There was no reason to hurry now. He had won this little game of cat and mouse. He leaned back in his chair, lit a cigarette and smiled at the picture of his wife on his desk.

"Looks like we're chalking one up for the good guys," he said to her face. She smiled back at him. He turned his chair to face out the window. The sun was high in the late morning sky. It was going to be a great day.

CHAPTER NINETEEN

The next few days were filled with further searching of McKenzie's house and the gathering of evidence from the premises. With every new discovery, regardless of how seemingly mundane, O'Toole's spirits were buoyed. He grew increasingly confident that McKenzie was the murderer, and the voice of doubt gradually quieted down. Although the accused had yet to confess as Andy had predicted, he was sure that any minute now he'd come to his senses and start singing like a choir boy. After all, he couldn't run from the facts, and those facts were pretty damning. McKenzie's situation was hopeless; O'Toole was sure he'd eventually come to see that and would start working to save himself by confessing. On Friday afternoon, Andy sat in the back row of the Rock of Ages Baptist Church, staring up at the stained glass windows. He wasn't a regular church-goer, though he had been raised by devout Irish Catholics. At the pulpit in the front of the church stood a man dressed in a dark grey business suit who was delivering a eulogy for Jack Carlisle. The program identified him as Richard Carlisle, older brother of the deceased.

"My brother was so special to so many people," the speaker was saying. "He marched to the beat of a different drummer from the rest of the family, but he was always his own man. He never let people tell him what he should do with his life, and for that I will always admire him. He did what he thought was best for him, and he wasn't concerned about what others might think." As the speaker continued, Andy glanced around the church at the assembled mourners. A few of Carlisle's fellow senators had made the trip, perhaps sensing a publicity opportunity. The family members were all seated together in the front of the church, the senator and his wife sitting close together, the brothers sitting with their wives next to the parents. They seemed the picture of a perfect family. *Almost too perfect,* Andy thought to himself. And then he was reminded of the words Byron, the waiter from the Collins House, had said regarding appearances in the family. It occurred to O'Toole that it wasn't just Senator Carlisle who was the one in the spotlight; the entire family served as a collective ambassador for the senator himself. Like it or not, his life was their life, and vice-versa.

"I'm sure Jack is up there right now, smiling down at this," the speaker said. "He's probably laughing at all of us, wondering why we're making such a big deal out of him. Jack had that modesty we all want to have," he said. "He was my brother; he was my friend. We will all miss him and we'll never forget him." He looked towards the ceiling of the church. "We miss you, buddy," he said. "But you're still with all of us," he concluded, tapping his chest lightly with his hand. As he did so, the light from a window caught one of his cufflinks and reflected off in a brilliant display of colors. O'Toole couldn't help but notice the massive watch he wore strapped to his wrist. And he was momentarily focused on the crisply starched cuffs of his shirt where they cut a sharp line across his wrists.

Richard descended from the podium, drying a tear from his eye with a handkerchief he had in his jacket pocket. He returned to his seat slowly, patting his father lightly on the back as he passed. The organist began to play the closing hymn—"Joyful, Joyful We Adore Thee." The program said it had been Jack's favorite hymn.

Andy's wife had used to say that his voice wasn't ever made for singing, but he sang the words as best he could, albeit somewhat timidly and softly. The family began to process out during the song, following the grey metal coffin covered in white roses. By the beginning of the third verse of the hymn, Andy had lost his timid voice and was belting out the words. As the procession passed by him exiting the church, Andy was nearly shrieking the words: "Teach us how to love each other, lift us to Thy joy divine." At that moment, Andy caught the senator's eye as he was walking past, and Carlisle silently mouthed "thank you" to him. Andy smiled sympathetically. As the song ended, people began to make their way out the back doors and Andy merged with the crowds. Outside the church, the casket was loaded into the waiting hearse, and the mourners made their respective ways to their cars. As he walked, Andy felt as if all eyes were on him. People whispered to each other, occasionally pointing subtly in his direction. *That's right,* he said silently, almost egotistically. *I'm the one who caught him. I'm the good guy here.*

The funeral procession made its way slowly through town, up Main Street, winding through the narrow tree-lined streets, accompanied by a police escort. They inched their way along and finally came to Vesper Lane, where one of Nantucket's many cemeteries was located in a large field, and where Jack's family had prematurely, they had once thought, purchased a family plot. The preacher had said during the funeral service that it was only appropriate that Jack be buried on the island, given his love for the special place. The mourners parked some distance from the family plot and Andy walked slowly to the designated spot. American flags were interspersed among the grounds at the headstones marking the graves of deceased veterans. As he passed the headstones, he couldn't help but look at them. Many simply said "Mother" and "Father," while others had names, dates, and epitaphs. He noticed one small headstone in the shape of a teddy bear that read, "Martyn Drew, born December 3, 1988, departed this Earth December 4, 1988. With love always from Mom and Dad."

Poor kid, Andy thought to himself. *Died so young.* Then it occurred to him that Jack Carlisle was like young Martyn. He, too, had departed long before it was his time. Nearby, in the same section of the cemetery, was O'Toole's own future resting spot, alongside the remains of his wife.

The burial was followed by a brief prayer. The family members embraced one another, crying softly. The sons gathered around their mother to comfort her, while the senator himself stared at the horizon with moist eyes. Mourners gathered around them to bid their sympathies. The senator had arranged for a small gathering at the Carlisle's house immediately following the ceremony, and many of the assembled mourners departed, bound for the house.

Andy stayed behind briefly. He wanted to do a few things before he left. He walked across the graveyard, being careful to stick to the paths, and found his wife's headstone. He bent down and picked a few stray blades of grass that had grown up along the stone and then knelt down in front of it. Quietly, he spoke to her.

"Hey there, good looking," he said, choking back an emotional outburst. "Just stopped by to say hi to you." He never knew exactly what to say to her, because he felt awkward about the whole scene he created. He was sure that drivers passing on the road adjacent to the cemetery would look at him as if he were a homeless man mumbling about the end of the world. But he felt compelled to say something, even if he was speaking to nothing more than a piece of granite. "I'm still plugging away at it down here," he continued. "We found the guy that killed the Carlisle kid. It's pretty scary to think it could happen here, but we found him." He started to stand up, then paused and looked back at the smooth surface of the headstone. "Do me a favor, honey," he said. "Find that Carlisle kid up there. Tell him he's okay by me and make sure he doesn't get pushed around too much. I love you," he said. "I'll see you later. And remember to behave yourself until I get there. I don't want to hear any wild and crazy stories about how you've been carrying on up there when I see you again." He stood and turned around. Senator Carlisle and his wife were standing behind him.

The senator looked embarrassed. "Sorry, Andy. Didn't mean to eavesdrop," he said. "I just wanted to tell you thanks again for all of your hard work in solving this case." His hands were in his pockets and his wife looked embarrassed standing alongside him..

Andy blushed briefly, embarrassed himself for having been overheard. "Don't worry about it," he said, trying to laugh. "Just talking to my best friend in the world," he said, indicating the grave. The senator tentatively approached to see the stone. "She died three years ago," O'Toole offered as an explanation. "Cancer. Hell of a mess. She's in a better place now, though. Told her to look out for Jack up there. Make sure he doesn't get into any trouble," he said smiling.

The senator laughed softly, his eyes still damp from the tears he was fighting to hold back. "Thanks, Andy," he said in a wavering voice as he tried to conceal the pain he was feeling. "I appreciate it. That kid sure could get into trouble when he wanted to," he said as he winked at the sheriff. "Will you join us up at the house?"

Andy looked around somewhat nervously. He thought for a second, then replied, "Yes, sir. I'd be happy to. Thanks for the invitation. I'll see you at the house, sir."

The senator smiled and said to Andy, "Andy, please call me Leonard. All my friends do," and gave the sheriff a friendly nod. He then turned to leave with his wife. Andy followed them, leaving a space between them and himself. He slowed his pace as he passed Jack's grave and whispered, "You're okay, kid. Nobody's going to find out. You're safe. Rest in peace."

He suddenly felt like a weight had been lifted from his shoulders, as if he had just confessed all of his sins to a priest and been given absolution. He quickened his pace and exited the cemetery.

When he arrived at the Carlisle's house, there was a large group of people assembled in the main living room, the same room where O'Toole had, very recently, met with Senator Carlisle regarding his investigation into Jack's murder. People were simultaneously admiring the grand view of the Atlantic out the bay window and offering their deepest sympathies for the family's loss. As O'Toole entered, one of Jack's brothers, the one who had delivered the eulogy at the funeral, approached. He extended his hand to shake Andy's.

"Hi, Sheriff. I'm Richard Carlisle. Jack's brother."

Andy shook his hand. "How are you, Richard? Aside from the obvious, that is. Nice to meet you." Richard was a well-built young man, with slightly receding brown hair and brown eyes. His round face looked friendly—he looked like the kind of guy you'd want your daughter to marry. He was wearing a pair of tortoise-shell glasses and his smile revealed perfectly white teeth. Andy knew Richard worked as an attorney in Waco, a fact he'd learned from his research. *Following in the old man's footsteps,* Andy thought to himself. *Might even take over the old man's Senate seat one day.*

"I'm sure you've heard this quite a bit recently, but you'll no doubt hear it some more, too. Thanks for everything you've done, Sheriff," Richard said. "As I'm sure you can imagine, it's been hell on my parents. *Jefe*—I mean my father—has been a mess." Andy nodded in indication of understanding of the children's nickname for their father. "And Mom's been worse," he continued. "Knowing you have the guy who did it gives them, not to mention the rest of us, a huge sense of relief." His voice was deep, but still maintained the friendly timbre his face suggested. Andy felt like the kid must be great in front of a jury. *Might make a hell of a politician one day,* he thought to himself.

"Just doing my job, Richard," he said, "but you're certainly welcome and I thank you for saying that. It's nice to know I've been able to help. It's gratifying when this sort of thing works out the way it's supposed to, with the bad guy in jail."

Richard nodded in agreement. "Sheriff," he continued, now in a more inquisitive tone, "what was this guy's motive? I mean, why would he want to kill my brother?" He figured Richard would have heard it from his father, but after considering it briefly he decided that the senator probably kept O'Toole's theory from the family as a way of ensuring his own privacy. Although he hadn't expected the question from any family members, he had foreseen the reality that this question would come up at some point and he'd practiced the answer repeatedly. He reeled it off for Richard as if it were second-nature. And more importantly, he hoped, as if it were the honest truth.

"Your brother worked at the Collins House Hotel. The waiters there, many of them, are homosexual." Richard looked surprised at the mention of the word "homosexual," another reaction for which Andy had diligently prepared. "Now I'm not suggesting your brother himself was homosexual, just some of the people he worked with." Richard looked reassured, though his face maintained an expression of doubt. "Anyway, our suspicion is that the suspect saw him leave the hotel, figured he was gay, and decided he'd take out some aggression." He waved a hand in the air to suggest that Richard knew how this story would end.

Richard shook his head slowly. "I can't even fathom it," he said. "What's happening to this world? People are getting killed for everything nowadays. It's insane. You've got people getting killed because they're gay, because they're black, because they're Jewish. My God," he said. "And on Nantucket of all places," he added in tone of utter surprise.

Andy's face took on a grim expression. "Yeah, I know. I've been thinking about that a lot recently. This is the last place you'd think of when you think of gay-bashing. And this wasn't even gay-bashing in the true sense," he added. He mentally chided himself for losing track of his story. He needed to stick to the party line in order to pull this off. "You know, with Jack not even being gay," he said to recover his footing. "Just a horrendous case of mistaken identity." There was an awkward silence. "So I guess your life has been turned upside-down by this whole mess," Andy said, trying to change the subject.

"Incredibly so," replied Richard. "My parents called me and told me what had happened, and I was obviously distraught over it. Then I had to make arrangements to get up to Nantucket on short notice, which you know is never easy. It's been a nightmare. That's another reason I'm so glad this is wrapping up. Little stuff you don't even think of," he said, "like finding a house sitter on the spur of the moment. My wife convinced one of the neighbor kids to come by and check on the house, pick up the mail, deal with the burglar alarm, all that. She even got him to go by my parents' house, too. He's doing both houses for ten bucks a day. Kid needs a better lawyer to negotiate his contracts." He smiled. "I just hope he can manage. My wife left him a pretty detailed note with instructions, but he's only thirteen, so you never know," he added.

A large golden retriever walked up to Richard, tail wagging furiously. Richard scratched the dog on the head. "Hey there, Tucker," he said to the dog. He turned to the sheriff. "This is Tucker. He's my only child, and I think he's the only one who's glad to be here. He loves it when we bring him up here. He absolutely adores the beach," Richard said, pointing down to the beach in front of the house.

Andy stood there silently and offered his hand to the dog to smell. Satisfied that the sheriff was okay, the dog consented to let O'Toole pat him on the head.

"Well, Sheriff," said Richard, "I better get going. I need to mingle here. Thanks again," he said, shaking the sheriff's hand. "Why don't you get yourself some food?" he added, gesturing toward the dining room table.

"I'll do that," O'Toole said. "Thank you." The two men smiled at each other, and Richard left him standing there and went to accept the condolences of the assembled mourners. Andy made his way to the food table and looked over the offerings. The Harbor Club had catered the gathering, and it seemed that the senator had spared no expense in showing his appreciation to those who came to mourn his son's death. Cold lobster meat, boiled shrimp, clams on the half-shell and fresh vegetables lined the table, which was covered with a white linen cloth. O'Toole took a plate and began to pick up bits of food when he felt a hand on his shoulder. He turned to see Senator Carlisle standing behind him.

"You've got to quit sneaking up on me," the sheriff said smiling.

Carlisle laughed softly. "Yeah, I'm sorry about that. Bad habit of mine. Have you got a minute?" He led Andy down a hall to an unoccupied room that was something of a smaller version of the main living room. In it were two small sofas, a coffee table with a few magazines on it, and a bookshelf lined with paperbacks. The window in the room, like the grand bay window in the living room, looked out on the ocean beneath the cliff. The senator turned to Andy and asked, "So what's the story on this guy you've got down in the jail?"

Andy updated the senator on the progress they'd made so far in securing evidence that further implicated Jamie McKenzie, and added the information about the blood on McKenzie's shoes. "We're sure this time, Senator," he said. "No question about it. He hasn't confessed yet," O'Toole added with a note of anticipation, as if one were forthcoming any moment, "but he has been talking to his lawyer a lot these past days, so I think we're getting very close to wrapping it up."

"That's fantastic," said Carlisle with a tone of genuine relief. It was as if he'd doubted the validity of O'Toole's findings until this exact moment.

"That's absolutely fantastic. I haven't been able to focus at all on my work," he said. "This tragedy has been such a distraction for me, and I'm afraid I've been taking it out on my staff. And my poor wife has been nothing short of a basket case. The entire family has been completely torn apart inside by this. It's such a relief to know that the man responsible for this act is going to be punished." He thanked the sheriff again, adding, "You'll keep me posted?"

Andy nodded. "Absolutely, Mr. Carlisle." The senator raised an eyebrow. "I mean Leonard," O'Toole said awkwardly, smiling like a teenager asking a girl out on a first date. "You'll know as soon as we do when he confesses," he said, his voice turning suddenly serious again. Andy looked at his watch. It was almost eight. "Speaking of, I should get back to the office. I turned my phone off during the service, so there's no telling what new developments have come up. I'll call you when I know anything." He extended his hand to shake the senator's. Carlisle took the sheriff's hand and pulled him closer, embracing him briefly.

"Thank you, Andy. You've done well," he said. He patted the sheriff on the back and the two walked back into the living room. O'Toole felt a wave of pride sweep through his body as they entered the living room and guests turned from each other to watch this pair of friends walking towards them. Andy said his goodbyes and condolences to the family, then turned and walked out of the door, the feeling of pride carrying him all the way to his car.

CHAPTER TWENTY

Early the next morning, Andy O'Toole waited at the airport as a small plane circled then landed. A middle aged man in a dark suit descended the stairs of the plane and, seeing Andy, waved slightly. O'Toole was there to pick him up, the prosecuting attorney assigned to the Carlisle murder case. Andy had called the office of the prosecutor on the Cape, the office that handled such cases on Nantucket, and they had sent over an Assistant District Attorney to oversee the early arraignment and proceedings against McKenzie.

"Hello, counselor, I'm Andy O'Toole, Nantucket Sheriff," he said.

"Vincent Graves," the attorney said, "Assistant DA. Pleasure to meet you." As the two men exited the airport and headed for O'Toole's car, Andy asked the prosecutor about his knowledge of the case, which Graves assured him was adequate. "As long as you've got the evidence, Sheriff, it sounds like it should be no problem," he added. "I assume, though, that your office is still pursuing the DNA testing, just to make sure, correct?"

Andy nodded. "Yep. Expecting results back here in a couple of weeks, the medical examiner tells me." They drove back to O'Toole's office, the silence in the car only periodically broken by Andy's attempts at being a tour guide as he pointed out places of interest to the attorney. They got to town and O'Toole parked his car. He led the way into the police dispatcher's office, where Graves would need to sign in as a formal guest of the sheriff's on official business.

"Congratulations, Sheriff," Jamie McKenzie's attorney said as they walked into the police headquarters. "You've done it again."

Andy was shocked by the suddenness of the statement, and was equally shocked to see Hector Cornell sitting in a seat inside the headquarters. O'Toole looked at McKenzie's attorney with a confused look. "What do you mean?" he asked.

The attorney shook his head. "You arrested the wrong guy, Andy. He's not your murderer." Andy stared in disbelief.

"No way," he said. "I know he did it. He lied about being at Paterna's house, he had the shoes, and Jack's blood was on one of them. He's the one, damnit, no two ways about it."

The attorney looked around the room, and then at the sheriff and the prosecutor. "Can we have this conversation in private?" he asked. Andy nodded grimly and had the prosecutor sign in on the register. He then led the men out the door of the police station and up to his office. Once inside the relatively safe confines of his office, O'Toole indicated chairs for the two men to sit in and closed the door behind them. He went around to his own chair and sat, facing the lawyers across the desk.

"Now what's this all about, counselor?" he asked.

The lawyer fidgeted in his seat. Something was up, and Andy knew it. "First, let's get a few things settled. I'll swear to you right now he didn't murder Jack Carlisle. You can take that for what you will. If you want to pursue the charges against him, you'll lose, and I promise you that. I can prove he didn't do it. He's got an iron-clad alibi and it's not going to change. And you know him, Andy. He's trouble, I'll give you that. But he's no murderer. He doesn't have it in him." He then turned his attention to the prosecutor. "Now if you want to listen to me, we can talk about a deal here."

Andy stared straight ahead in absolute disbelief. Just when it seemed that he had the whole thing figured out, something else popped up. Alibis surfaced after he'd thought the case was solved, people weren't being straight with him, the world seemed to be against him. The voice in his head was no longer whispering doubts into O'Toole's ear. It was shouting now. Shouting and laughing at Andy's failures. Finally, O'Toole said, "If he didn't do anything, then what deal are you suggesting?"

"My client," the lawyer said, "was involved. He'll admit to that. But he didn't do the act itself. He will tell you who did it, though, in exchange for full immunity." The last words hung in the air like a bad odor. Andy pushed back from his desk and stood, looking out the window. Outside, life seemed so simple, so enjoyable. None of this existed out there. He lit a cigarette and spit a bit of tobacco at the window in front of him. It stuck to the window, black against the bright daylight through the glass. He turned to face the prosecutor, ashamed that he'd dragged this poor man into the quicksand of this case.

"This is Vincent Graves, Assistant District Attorney," O'Toole began. McKenzie's lawyer nodded in acknowledgement, as he knew exactly who it was. "He's the one you'll have to deal with." He shook his head again in disbelief. "What do you think, Mr. Graves?" he asked.

"I'd like to hear a little more before we start talking about any kind of deal, counselor," the prosecutor said, clearly interested, but at the same time wanting to prosecute somebody for this heinous crime.

The defense attorney shook his head. "You know me better than that, Vincent," he said, as if the two were best friends. "I don't give you anything until you tell me he's got immunity."

Andy sighed heavily in response to the defense's statement and said bluntly, "I've already told the senator that McKenzie did it. I can't go back and change that." It was starting to dawn on him that he'd acted too hastily once again. *Way too hastily,* he thought. He shouldn't have told Carlisle anything. Now he'd have to go back yet again and apologize like a child who'd broken a window. *Maybe there was a way to keep McKenzie in jail for just a little longer? Or at least to release him without any publicity?* He recognized immediately that he was beginning to think like Tim Hawkins, and the similarity scared him more than facing the senator.

"That's your own personal problem, Sheriff," the attorney said. "With all due respect, of course," he added. "And perhaps the fact that he's a senator's kid would suggest how badly you really need to make a deal here. You've got to get the real killer because Carlisle's a senator," he said. "Just something you might want to consider," the attorney concluded as he crossed his hands in his lap and smiled broadly straight at O'Toole.

You smug little bastard, Andy thought to himself. *You cocky little shit. You've got me by the short hairs and now you want to pull. Whatever happened to respecting your elders?* He set his eyes into a stern glare directed right at McKenzie's lawyer. "Let me get this straight. Your client, Jamie McKenzie, knows who did it. He himself was involved in it. He'll tell me exactly who did it, but I have to let him go Scot-free?"

"That's precisely what I'm telling you, Sheriff, and I'm not telling you any more until you agree to drop the charges." Andy returned to his seat and plopped down heavily.

He turned to the prosecutor, who looked back at him and said, "Let's talk in the hall, Sheriff." The two men exited O'Toole's office and the prosecutor began. "Look," he began in a low voice, "I'm not supposed to tell you this, but you're really under the gun here. People, important people, are starting to get really pissed off about the way you've handled this case so far and there's a lot of talk going on. I'm not privy to everything that's being said, but I'm sure you can imagine," he said as he arched his eyebrows as a way of indicating that there were no words capable of adequately describing the punishment awaiting O'Toole. His face seemed to warn the sheriff of some Dante-esque pit of fire, with Andy on a spit spinning slowly above it.

"This is crazy," O'Toole finally managed to say, ignoring the young prosecutor's implied threat. "So what do we do?"

The attorney shook his head slightly and said, "I'd suggest that we go in there and you try to get him to say what he knows. If he doesn't budge, then I'll step in." O'Toole nodded in understanding, then led the prosecutor back into the office. Andy thought back to what Cornell had said about Jack's being the son of a senator. The lawyer was right, though Andy didn't want to admit it. He needed to do whatever it took to find the real killer. It was that cut and dried. And if that meant making a deal, he'd have to do it. He was backed into a corner and there wasn't much fight left in him to get out of it. He'd make the deal and suffer the consequences. And he knew there were sure to be consequences. He just hoped somebody in power would, in hindsight, see the wisdom of what he was about to do.

He sat at his desk, faced the defense attorney and waited briefly before speaking. "How was McKenzie involved?" he asked.

The lawyer shook his said and smiled. "No ticket, no laundry, Andy," he said. "I don't tell you until you tell me he's free to go."

Andy had a passionate hatred for lawyers, especially those who made a living by defending the scum of the Earth, and this one wasn't helping to change his opinion. He looked out the side of his field of vision, trying to break the interminable gaze of the lawyer sitting across from him. He sighed heavily. He turned back to the prosecutor and looked helpless.

"We're willing to deal, Mr. Cornell, if your client is willing to be very specific in terms of who the murderer is."

Andy let out a groan. "Okay, fine. He's innocent," he muttered. "I'll fill out the papers to get him out of jail. I'll drop the charges. Goddamnit," he muttered. "You got what you wanted, counselor, so now it's your turn. Tell me who it was that killed that kid."

The lawyer looked across the table at him. His face said to Andy that he, the sheriff, had failed miserably in his duties, and that it had taken a lawyer only a few days to find the truth. The lawyer looked as if he had won the lottery. "Your murderer is a guy named Charlie Bordham. He lives out by the airport. His house is pretty much right next to a runway. I only met him once. I defended him on a DUI charge last winter. He's a strange one, I'll warn you, and when you see him, you'll know immediately he's the murderer. He's almost a caricature of the stereotype."

"Charlie Bordham? The name isn't familiar," the sheriff said. He thought about the receipt he'd found from Brady's Fish Market, mentally trying to piece together the letters he'd found written on it. He wondered to himself if the name would fit into the letters he could decipher on it. He returned his attention to Cornell. "Who is he?"

"Weird guy. Lives like a hermit out there on the south shore. Smells like all hell. Big guy, too. Scary. Looks like something out of a horror movie. Works around town doing whatever he can find. Last I heard he was mixing cement for some contractor," Cornell said. "And he also washes dishes part-time at the Collins House Hotel," he added. "You know the place, I believe. It's where Jack Carlisle worked?" He shook his head in disgust at O'Toole. "Come on, Sheriff. I thought they taught you guys to always check on the people who knew the victim in a case like this."

Ignoring the snide comments, Andy wrote down the information. "Do you know this guy's address?" he asked. He was too irritated to ask Cornell about the personal acquaintance angle. He'd had that thought at the beginning, the voice in his head reminded him, but he'd been too stubborn—or too stupid—to follow it.

"He's got a post office box in town. At least that's the only place I ever mailed him anything. The bum still owes me a hundred and fifty dollars for services, too. I do know where his house is, though." He gave the sheriff directions to the house, explaining that he would have to work to find it, because the house was literally built in the middle of a forest of bushes. "When you see it, you'll know why it's not worth going to for a hundred-fifty," he added with a sardonic laugh.

"You said your client was involved," the prosecutor interjected from the chair he'd been quietly occupying. "How so?" He had been copying the information Cornell was providing, but now he focused his attention on the specifics of what he'd given up in order to get the actual murderer.

The lawyer coughed. "All I can tell you is that he told Bordham to do it. He didn't tell me why he told him to do it, just told me that he had told

Bordham to kill the Carlisle kid. At this point, that's all I know and that's the honest truth."

The prosecutor stared at the attorney doubtfully, trying to force him to say more than he had already. He wanted something juicy for his report.

"Honestly, that's it," Cornell said, as if the prosecutor's look told him that he wasn't buying the story. "You know, honor among thieves," he added with a wry smile. Andy, unlike the prosecutor, didn't have the luxury of deciding whether or not he believed McKenzie's story. He had to believe it because he really couldn't afford to screw up again. At least if this one turned out to be a lie he could blame it on somebody else.

"Okay," sighed O'Toole. "I'll get the paperwork going for Jamie's release. That son of a bitch is going to cost me dearly," he added.

"Investigation one-oh-one, Sheriff. It's always safer to make sure you've got all the facts before you go spouting off like that," the lawyer responded. "I like to play it conservative myself. I recommend that attitude for the future."

"Thanks for the advice, Professor," he replied sarcastically.

"I assume, Mr. Graves," Cornell said as he turned his attention to the DA, "that you'll get started on the paperwork guaranteeing Jamie McKenzie's immunity from prosecution? It's not that I don't trust you, it's just that my client feels a little nervous about these sort of things."

The prosecutor nodded. "Yes, sir, I'll get in touch with my office as soon as we're done here."

"I think we're done here now," O'Toole said. Then he turned to McKenzie's lawyer and said, "You can show yourself out. I'll get the paperwork started for his release here. I've just got to make a few calls." Cornell stood and walked out of the office and O'Toole pardoned himself from the prosecutor for a moment. He then turned his attention to the phone on his desk. He dialed the number, pressing the phone buttons with shaking fingers. The phone rang twice before it was answered.

"Tim Hawkins," the voice said. It sounded as if Hawkins were sitting in a long tunnel, sound reverberating around him.

"Tim, it's Andy O'Toole," the sheriff said.

"Andy, it's great to hear from you. Congratulations—." Andy stopped him mid-sentence.

"Don't say it, Tim. We've got to talk." There was a click on the other end of the line as Tim took the phone off of the speaker and picked up the handset.

"What's the matter, Andy," he said, suddenly serious.

"Before you go off, let me explain here. McKenzie is involved in this crime; he's admitted to that much," he began.

"I don't like the way this is sounding, Andy. If you're telling me that—." Andy cut him off again.

"I told you to let me finish. Now look. McKenzie's lawyer got the information out of him. McKenzie was involved in it, but he didn't actually kill the kid. We've got the name of the guy McKenzie fingered, though, and I'm going to go pick him up right now." He took a deep breath. "Fire away," he said.

There was a long pause. Hawkins was trying to distill this newly discovered information through his brain, but it wasn't quite working. "Okay, Andy. So you got one of the two guys involved, right? You keep him in jail while you go get the other guy."

Andy braced himself. "Not exactly," he said meekly.

"What do you mean by that?" the selectman asked, clearly irritated at O'Toole's failure to accurately explain the situation.

"We had to let McKenzie out to get the information."

There was another pause. Andy could sense anger brewing, as he could hear the selectman's breathing getting faster. "Andy O'Toole, you hang up the phone this instant and get your ass in to my office. Right now, goddamnit." Andy heard a click as Hawkins slammed the phone down.

"I need to go see my boss," O'Toole said to Graves.

"Okay," said the prosecutor. "I've got to call my office anyway, so that we can get to work filling out the papers for McKenzie's immunity." O'Toole stood and told the prosecutor he'd be back shortly, he hoped, then walked slowly out of the office, up the stairs, and across the hall to Tim Hawkins' office. Gone was the celebrity-like swagger he'd enjoyed only hours earlier. Gone was the pride he'd felt at being the master investigator. All that was left was the voice in his head, laughing in carnival-like amusement at his continuing failure. He knocked on the door.

"Get in here," the voice on the other side shouted.

He opened the door slowly. Tim Hawkins was sitting at his desk. He had loosened his tie and his jacket lay in a heap on a nearby chair. When Andy entered, Hawkins looked up at him. "Care to explain just what in the hell is going on now?"

Andy remained standing, feeling more comfortable that way. He explained the situation to the selectman, who listened intently, shaking his head at intervals, expressing his intense frustration at the new developments.

When Andy had finished explaining, Hawkins stood up and faced him directly. He put his hands flat on the desk in front of him and leaned forward.

"Andy, you listen to me, and you listen real close. I'm only going to say this once. This whole investigation has been an embarrassment to this town, to the police department, and most of all to you as the sheriff and to me as a selectman. This isn't over yet, I guarantee you that. You get your ass out there, you arrest that little bastard and you bring him in here. You do it quietly and you don't tell a goddamn person anything about it. Do I make myself clear?"

Andy nodded. He didn't want to speak. He couldn't speak. He was frozen in place and his body refused to move, no matter how much his brain willed it. He was scared to utter a word, to take a breath. Tim Hawkins was right. This whole investigation had been an embarrassment. It was the first time he'd been involved in any kind of major police investigation and he'd botched it completely. There was no hiding from the fact. The press was going to have a field day with this. Earlier this morning, he'd been planning his award acceptance speech for excellence in the line of duty. Now he was contemplating how he'd spend his years once the voters heard about what a disaster he'd created and removed him from office in the next election. He'd be the laughing stock of the island.

Hawkins was so angry he was quivering. "I would suggest first, though, that you call the senator and inform him of the news. I'm sure he'll be happy to know that you're 'sure' this time. Now get out of here and go get that guy." He slumped down in his chair. Andy turned without saying a word and left the office.

He returned to his office to find Vincent Graves talking on his cellular phone to the prosecutor's office on the Cape, he presumed. O'Toole picked up the phone on his desk and dialed the Carlisle's number. When the senator answered, O'Toole realized he hadn't yet planned his story, so he had to think fast. "Senator, Andy O'Toole again. Just wanted to update you, sir. We've learned that there was a second person involved in the murder, a man by the name of Charlie Bordham. We're off to arrest him right now, sir." He said it as fast as he could and hoped the senator wouldn't ask anything about it. He consciously left out the fact that McKenzie was going free; he just hoped it wouldn't come up in this conversation. In an effort to end the call, he added quickly, "Sir, I'll be happy to inform you about this new information when I get back, but I need to get over to Bordham's house now so we can get him in custody as soon as possible."

The senator's voice came over the line, sounding somewhat shocked: "Okay, Andy, please do call when you get a chance. Right now isn't a good time; we've got some off-island guests that came in for the funeral here. But I would like to hear more about this. Bordham you say is the man's name?"

"That's correct, sir. I'll keep you posted." He spoke quickly, trying to convey to Carlisle that he wanted to get off the phone.

"Is he friends with this McKenzie person you've got in jail already?"

"Yes, Mr. Carlisle. They worked together. But I'll be happy to tell you all about it tomorrow, sir. Time is of the essence right now."

"Sorry to keep you, Andy. Thanks for the update and I'll be looking forward to getting the rest of the story from you tomorrow."

O'Toole heard a click on the other end. *Wow,* he thought to himself. *That was easy enough.* He'd been so worried about how the senator would react that it hadn't occurred to him he might just be able to gloss it all over for him. *Tomorrow it won't matter, because Bordham would will be in jail and the crime would be solved. So there were a few hiccups along the way. The end result is what matters.* He sighed in relief and slowly began to relax a little. *No sweat.*

O'Toole turned to the prosecutor and told him that he was going to get Bordham, and that he'd be back as soon as he could. He then left the attorney in the office, still talking to his own boss about McKenzie's conditional confession and the immunity deal his lawyer had wrangled out of him.

He walked down to the dispatcher's desk and asked for the duty officer.

When the officer appeared, Andy said to him, very quietly, "Let McKenzie go. Get the paperwork started. I'll sign off on it. His attorney cut a deal for him. He's free."

"But Sheriff," the officer began in a shocked voice.

"No buts," Andy said. "Just get the paperwork started." He looked around the office and saw his deputy Lance Abbot and another officer standing to one side. "You two," he said to them in a stern tone. "Lance, you come with me. You," he pointed to the officer next to him, "get in a cruiser and follow us." He turned and left the station, Lance following behind like a small dog, and walked around the corner to his car. Early season tourists were meandering along the sidewalk, many with cameras, and Andy realized that it was already June.

These vacationers were completely oblivious to what was happening. They knew, of course, that Senator Carlisle's son had been brutally murdered, but they also knew, of course, that the murderer was safely incarcerated in the Nantucket jail, and would no doubt soon be on his way to the state penitentiary for a long time. They felt completely safe and completely at peace as they strolled the historic streets of this lovely island. And why should they feel any differently? This was Nantucket, after all. It was like going back in time to a world where everything was peace and harmony. This was a fantasy land for these people.

For O'Toole, though, the reality was not nearly as rosy as the fantasy. He pulled out a cigarette and lit it as he walked to his car. He got into the car, started the engine and pulled around the corner, screeching to a halt just outside the police station. The other officer was waiting for him and signaled that he was ready to follow. O'Toole drove down the street, past the shops opening up for the day's business, heading for the home of Charlie Bordham.

"Third time's a charm," he said to Lance. "Let's hope so, anyway."

CHAPTER TWENTY-ONE

Andy and Lance drove silently, following the directions the attorney had provided, and eventually found themselves parked alongside a huge wall of bushes. He cut the engine and walked back to the patrol car parked behind him. He, Lance and the accompanying officer got together in a brief huddle between the two parked cars.

"Okay. Here's the story. There's a guy in there," he said. "His name is Charlie Bordham. He's the person McKenzie named as the murderer. We go in there assuming he's armed and dangerous. Don't do anything fast, don't do anything stupid. There's no telling what this guy might do." Andy led the way through an overgrown path towards the house, Lance immediately behind him. The sandy trail curved to the left, then back to the right before opening up into a small clearing, where a small ramshackle house stood. Andy's first impression was that it must have been a condemned building. It didn't look fit for human habitation, but he saw a light on through a broken window.

The three men approached the small house and O'Toole noticed a rusting pickup truck parked nearby. Before proceeding further, he wanted to verify, in his own mind, that Bordham could be linked to the crime. He walked over to the truck and looked beneath the front end, and was relieved to see a large pool of oil under the truck's hood. This, he assumed, was the same vehicle that had been at Will Paterna's house that day, the vehicle that had dripped the oil onto the street. The three men walked to the front door and Andy knocked loudly, announcing himself as the sheriff. There was no answer. He motioned for Lance to stay put and for the other officer to go around to the back of the house to make sure there wasn't a back door. He knocked again, louder this time, pounding his fist on the door. Still there was no answer, but Andy heard a dog bark inside. He listened intently, but heard nothing save for the dog. There didn't appear to be any movement inside the house and no noise to indicate any activity. He yelled at the closed door that he would break it down if nobody answered. There was still no sign of movement, so he reared back and kicked the door with the bottom of his shoe.

His foot went through the rotted wooden door and he almost fell backwards. He braced himself by putting his hands on the door and grabbed the doorknob to keep himself upright. He pulled his leg out of the hole it had made and paused, listening for any sounds. The dog's nose appeared at the hole and Andy could see his fangs through the small opening. He stepped back and heaved his shoulder into the door, which gave way. The dog ran in terror and Andy pulled his gun from its holster.

"Charlie Bordham, this is Andy O'Toole, Nantucket Sheriff's Department," he announced in a loud voice. "You're under arrest for the murder of Jack Carlisle." Nothing. No sounds, no movement. He turned to Lance, whose body was tensed and ready for action. He motioned for the deputy to enter the house. The other officer came around the corner, telling Andy that there was no other exit. "Okay," said Andy. "Let's search the house. First priority is securing Bordham." Lance entered the house and began to walk slowly forward, gun drawn, hand shaking feverishly. The door opened onto a small living room, which was cluttered with garbage. A small wooden crate sat in front of a decrepit yellow sofa, and an ancient television sat on a rickety stand in the corner of the room. On the coffee table was a piece of a broken mirror, a double-edged razor blade, and the white barrel from a cheap ball point pen.

The officer proceeded slowly into the house, alternating glances between the floor under his feet and the room in front of him. Off to the right of the living room was what appeared to be a kitchen and Andy motioned for Lance to check it out while he covered him from the rear. As Andy watched from his vantage point, Lance slid along the wall slowly, his back flat and his gun pointed towards the ceiling. As he got to the corner of the room, he took a deep breath and closed his eyes to calm himself. He opened them and turned sharply, facing the kitchen, gun pointed straight ahead. A split-second later he screamed, "Freeze!"

Andy moved as quickly as he could to where his young deputy stood, making sure to move along the wall so as to protect himself in the event of a gunshot from the kitchen. Lance was anchored in the same place, gun still pointed at the kitchen, his hands still shaking uncontrollably. Andy peered around the corner into the kitchen. Sitting at the kitchen table, slumped over and face down, was a large man with long, tangled brown hair. He didn't need to look any more. He knew the man was dead.

Charlie Bordham lay face down in a pool of his own blood with a single gunshot to the side of his head. "Guess that solves that," said the sheriff. "Son of a bitch. Don't touch anything. Don't touch a thing," he said sternly. "You guys come with me," he said to the officers. He led them out the door and stationed them in front of the house. "Stay here," he commanded and went back through the bushes to his car. He dialed the police department's number and said loudly into the phone, "Keep McKenzie locked up. This is a dud. And send somebody up to my office, please, to tell Vincent Graves to cancel that immunity deal."

He hung up the phone and immediately dialed the number for Tom Latkin, his fingers shaking from the adrenaline coursing through his body. When Latkin answered the phone, Andy told him where he was. "I need you over here. Pronto," he added. "We've got another body over here, and I need you to tell me how long he's been dead." Latkin said he would hurry to the location and hung up.

Andy put the phone in his jacket pocket and returned to the house. He told Lance and the other officer to stay put, adding that Tom Latkin would be arriving shortly. "Tell him to come in when he gets here," he said to them, "but don't let anybody else even close to that door." He walked back into the house and entered the kitchen. He was no expert, but this didn't look very old. The blood was still oozing out of the side of Bordham's skull and a large caliber revolver sat on the floor where it had fallen, and the faintly acrid-sweet smell of gunpowder lingered in the air. He didn't want to touch anything before Latkin arrived, so he kept a safe distance from the body.

"Couldn't face the music, huh?" he said to the corpse. "Too scared to face up to what you did?" He shook his head. "I can't believe this," he finally said, his voice dripping with disgust. He almost spat the words out of his mouth like they were a vile tasting liquid. Several minutes later he heard Tom Latkin's voice outside.

"I'm in here, Doc," he shouted towards the open door. Latkin made his way into the kitchen, looking around with a mixture of horror and disgust.

"This guy needed a maid more than anything else," he said. He looked at the body on the table. He bent down to look at the body. "Suicide, huh?"

Andy nodded. "Looks that way. This was our murderer, too, according to Jamie McKenzie."

Latkin looked up at the sheriff. "What are you talking about?" he asked in disbelief. "I thought you had him already. I thought McKenzie was the murderer."

"I'm getting really sick of telling people this, but here goes," he began, and he told the doctor of McKenzie's confession and implication of Bordham. "So that's why we're here. We were going to arrest this guy," he said.

The doctor stood up. "You couldn't pay me to be in your shoes right now, Andy. You really couldn't."

Andy laughed as best he could at the doctor's comment. "I know what you mean, Doc." Then he returned his attention to the body slumped over the table and asked in a serious voice, "But tell me. How long's he been dead, you think?"

The doctor bent over again and looked at the body. "Doesn't look like he's been dead all that long, Sheriff," he said. He moved around the body, looking closely. Without touching the body itself, he examined various parts of the corpse, occasionally pursing his lips and uttering low-pitched noises at things that apparently interested him. He looked at Andy after a moment and said, "Looks almost like he just did it, in fact." The doctor returned his attention to the body, not waiting for a response from O'Toole. After looking at it for what seemed to Andy like an eternity, the doctor finally said, "And you know what? From what I see here, it actually doesn't look like he did it to himself."

Andy's heart skipped a beat. Once again, just when he thought he had some answers. Every time it seemed like there was an end in sight to this whole mess, some new complication decided to rear its ugly head. "What do you mean, Tom?" he asked, scared of what the answer might be.

"Look at his wrists," the doctor said, pointing down to the dead man's hands. They hung limply by his side, dangling in the air. "I tell you, Andy, I'm pretty proud of myself. It's been a long time since I did any kind of real forensic work, but it looks like I've still got the touch." Latkin then pointed to Bordham's wrists as he said, "Those red marks there. You see them?"

Andy looked closely. He had to squint slightly to see them, but there, faintly, around Charlie's lifeless wrists, were two pink circular indentations, one on each wrist, circling around them like matching bracelets. He looked at the doctor. "Yeah. So what?" he asked.

"He didn't shoot himself," the doctor concluded. "It would have been pretty damn hard for him to get the gun around and up to the side of his head with handcuffs around his wrists, don't you think?" He raised his eyebrows in emphasis of the bizarre nature of the scene.

"Handcuffs?" Andy asked.

"That's what it looks like to me, Sheriff," Latkin replied. "Looks like somebody put 'em on pretty tight, too. Tight enough to make those marks anyway."

The doctor was kneeling by the body, looking at the wound itself, and Andy bent down to face him directly. "Are you sure about this, or is this another theory that's going to go bust in my face?"

The doctor stood and Andy straightened up. "As far as I can tell from a preliminary look," Latkin said, "that's what it is. It looks like he was handcuffed, or otherwise bound up, and then somebody else shot him. Not too long ago, either. I won't know for sure, though, until I run some tests on the body. I'll test for gun shot residue on his hand, too. If he shot himself, it'll show up. If somebody else did the deed, then it won't. I'd suggest dusting that gun for fingerprints while you're at it, too," he said, pointing at the revolver on the floor. Andy took a pen from his pocket and picked up the gun by putting the pen inside the trigger guard, and slid it gently into a clear plastic bag.

"This is turning into one hell of a mystery," Andy said to the doctor. "Now we've got somebody murdering murderers. This whole investigation is out of control," he said.

"You're right, Andy. Absolutely right. It's frightening," said Latkin. "I'll get the body to the hospital where I can do an autopsy. See if we can figure out what exactly happened here."

"Sounds good," said Andy. "Let me know when you find out," he said. "I'm going to head back into town and see if I can't do some damage control." He left the doctor to the grim task of collecting the body for transport to the morgue and returned to the waiting officers outside the house. "You guys are going to stay here. Nobody goes in, you got me? And get some crime scene tape up around this place. I want it completely secure." He turned to Lance. "Help the doctor with photographs and whatever else he needs in there," he said, tilting his head in the direction of the kitchen. "Let me know if he turns up anything."

They both nodded. Andy returned to his car and drove back to the Town Building. This was going to be a doozie trying to explain a murdered murderer to Hawkins. He slammed his palm onto the car's steering wheel. "Damnit," he yelled out loud. He felt his world rapidly spiraling in to disarray and he had to do something to regain control. His mind began to focus on McKenzie, sitting in the Nantucket jail, thinking he was going to go free. *Not on your life,* O'Toole thought to himself. He only had one living suspect now and McKenzie was it. He'd pay for it, whether he'd done the crime or not. Andy would prove he'd done it, somehow. He was now willing to lie if he had to. He had gotten to the point where he was willing to do whatever it took— legal or not—to protect his own job. *And,* he thought to himself, *to protect the island's image.*

He rolled down the window and let the breeze wash over him. What had he become, he wondered. He knew that he resented McKenzie because Andy had needed his help to solve this crime. He'd been unable to do it on his own, and he needed the accomplice of the murderer to come in and save his skin. And now all he wanted to do was take that accomplice and beat him to death. And that desire was driven by rage fueled by the need for revenge. He hated himself at that moment. He looked out the window and spat in disgust.

CHAPTER TWENTY-TWO

When Andy reached his office, the sun had set and evening had descended on the town of Nantucket. Groups of people were walking the street, many of them heading to dinner. Outside the Town Building, a crowd of reporters had gathered again. *They can sense something in the air, something not quite right,* Andy thought to himself. He parked his car and hurried up to his office, entering before any of the reporters were able to identify him. He walked into his office and was startled to find Leonard Carlisle and Tim Hawkins sitting there. Neither of them stood when he entered. They both looked irate.

"Andy," the selectman said, "you know Senator Carlisle and I'm confident that you know why we are here, so I'll dispense with any formalities." Andy didn't say a word; he had suspected that this meeting was coming, he just hadn't known it would come so quickly. He walked silently to his chair behind the desk and sat facing the two men across the desk. His face betrayed no emotion; he felt exhausted and spent.

"Mr. Carlisle is here—we're both here—to have you tell us the specifics of this so-called investigation of yours," Hawkins began. "Mr. Carlisle called me to ask me what I knew about a second murderer in this case, and I took it upon myself to inform him that you had been coerced into a deal that set Jamie McKenzie free so that you could obtain the identity of the true murderer. Now I am told that the suspect you went to arrest resulted in…" He looked down at a pad he held in his lap. "A 'dud,' as you told the dispatcher. Now, knowing that our patience is wearing painfully thin, Andy, tell us what exactly is going on." Hawkins and Carlisle sat in rapt silence, staring at the sheriff, waiting for an answer to the demand for information.

O'Toole fidgeted slightly in his chair as he tried to put his thoughts together. He sighed loudly and began to tell the story of his meeting with McKenzie's attorney, but Hawkins suddenly cut him off. "Get to the point, Andy. There's no point in rehashing your obvious failures."

Andy winced noticeably, but recovered enough to tell the story. He told the two men how he had discovered the body of Charlie Bordham, dead, in his home, the victim of a gunshot that both he and the medical examiner felt was inflicted a short time before the sheriff had arrived on the scene. He said that the death looked like a suicide, but the medical examiner had found evidence to the contrary, so he wasn't making any iron-clad statements about the cause of death or what, exactly, had happened before the officers arrived on the scene.

"What is that evidence, Sheriff?" asked the senator skeptically; he was unsure as to how to take the news of a suicidal murderer, a dead suicidal murderer who apparently hadn't actually committed suicide. The whole collection of thoughts made his head swim in an ocean of confusion, and it further served to irritate him. This seemed pretty simple to him. His kid had been murdered, the sheriff had the name of the man who'd done it. But he'd committed suicide. But he hadn't. He closed his eyes and shook his head, running his fingers through his hair. "I'm really not following your line of reasoning here. Forgive me."

O'Toole offered a sympathetic smile. He wasn't sure he understood it, either, so explaining it wouldn't be easy. But he gave it a shot. "It appears, sir, that the victim was handcuffed. Doctor Latkin is doing some tests to determine whether or not there is gunshot residue on the victim's hand. If there's no evidence of the deceased's having a fired a shot, then he didn't shoot himself," the sheriff said.

"I don't understand, Sheriff," said the senator. "Was he wearing handcuffs when you found him?" Confusion continued to reign in the senator's brain as he mentally pieced together the crime scene, trying to picture a handcuffed man holding a gun to his own head.

Andy shook his head. "No, sir, he wasn't."

"Then how," began the senator, now sounding furious and losing his last remaining shreds of patience, "did you concoct this cockamamie theory that he was handcuffed?" The senator shot a glance at Hawkins, his eyes showing his growing anger. Hawkins deflected the scowl by shifting his eyes to take in the sheriff, as if to say to the senator that O'Toole was the scapegoat here.

Andy began his explanation. "There were indentations around his wrists, sir, that the medical examiner felt resembled marks left by handcuffs." He emphasized the "sir" when he spoke, thinking now was not the best time to test the perceived friendship between himself and the senator; referring to him as Leonard at this moment would be a breach of the penitential code for O'Toole. Andy felt slightly guilty about telling them it was Latkin's idea that the body had been handcuffed. But the feeling passed quickly enough, as he thought that if this theory didn't pan out, he didn't want to be the guy left holding the rope. He'd let Latkin take the blame on this one. *Whatever it takes,* he thought to himself. *No holds barred when you're trying to save your own skin.*

Carlisle turned to Tim Hawkins. "You've got to be kidding me here, Tim. This has got to be a joke. This is more like a circus spoof than anything else," he said, laughing spitefully at the sheriff's failed attempts to offer any substantive proof of his own progress toward solving the crime. "First my son is supposedly gay, which is preposterous on its own, but now you throw this monkey wrench into the works?" He laughed scornfully. "Two great theories, Sheriff," he hissed at O'Toole. "Ever thought about taking up teaching for a living? You've definitely got some unique insight to offer."

Before Hawkins could respond, Andy stepped in to defend himself, because underneath the pride he took in his job, O'Toole knew that Carlisle was right on at least one level. No matter how he sliced it, O'Toole had failed miserably. "Senator, this is on my shoulders and I accept full responsibility for it," he said in his most pitiful voice. "I am the one who arrested both Will Paterna and Jamie McKenzie, and I was wrong on both counts. I understand completely if you want to take me off the investigation. I wouldn't blame you at all for having no faith whatsoever in me as an investigator at this point." He had hoped it wouldn't come to this, but he knew the time had come to admit that he was a small town sheriff who wasn't prepared, or qualified for that matter, to handle an investigation of this sort. He'd tried and he knew he'd tried his best, but that just wasn't cutting it. And he knew that, too.

"Admirable of you, Sheriff," the senator said, "falling on your sword like this. I have to admit that I've wanted to bring in my own people for some time now, but I thought you were handling it well. But now you're back at square one, with a dead man that you say killed my son, and some bum down in the jail who implicated him in it." Carlisle shifted in his seat. "If you wouldn't mind," he said, turning to Hawkins, "I'd like to bring in my own people here. I don't mean any disrespect to you or your town officials, you understand, but

I just want this whole mess cleared up and I truly believe that they'd be better able to get it done quickly." Andy couldn't help but notice that he was now being referred to in the third person, as if he weren't present in the room. He had officially been cut out of the loop.

Tim turned to the sheriff. "Andy? Any objections?" he asked. Hawkins and the senator had discussed this idea at some length before Andy's return, so it was no surprise to Tim that the senator had suggested it.

Andy shook his head in resignation. "Not a one. I've fought the good fight, but this is Nantucket. Our usual day consists of somebody losing their wallet at the beach and maybe a stolen bike or two. We're out of our league here, I'm afraid," he said. He turned his back to the two men and looked out the window. "Call in your people, Senator," he said. "My office and the police department will offer them any assistance we can provide. We're happy to help." The defensive and apologetic tone of his voice gradually dissipated and gave way instead to a tone more of resignation to the inevitable. He had been sure that this decision was coming; he'd just avoided admitting it to himself. But it was now staring him straight in the face and ignoring it was impossible. Carlisle sighed heavily. "Thanks, Andy," he said, his own vocal tone changing to one of relief as he seemed to slowly relax slightly. "And again, I mean what I said. I really do appreciate your help, and I'm also grateful to you for your willingness to allow outsiders to solve this crime." It sounded to O'Toole that he was being patted on the head like a child who'd tried his best but still came in third at the school science fair. Carlisle stood and Andy turned his chair back to face him. O'Toole stood and extended his hand across the desk. He and the senator shook hands.

"Glad to help, Mr. Carlisle. I'm just sorry I couldn't be of any more useful assistance," he said with a tone of sadness. He was giving up, and forfeit was not one his of favorite moves.

"Thanks, Andy," said Hawkins. "We'll be in touch about the investigative team. The senator's got some people lined up already, I think, and I'll give them your approval to do what they need to do and tell them that you'll offer any help you can." He and Carlisle left the office, leaving Andy sitting at his desk, staring into the empty space vacated by the two men. He was contemplating the comment Hawkins had made about the senator already having a team lined up when the phone on his desk rang.

"O'Toole," he said.

"Sheriff? Why is my client still in jail?" the caller asked.

Andy scoffed under his breath. *You snake,* he thought to himself. *Your client is guilty of planning a murder. Even if he didn't do it, he's just as guilty as if he had killed the kid. That is precisely why he's still in jail.* "The evidence your client provided," began the sheriff, "didn't quite materialize like we'd expected. I've relinquished control of the investigation over to Senator Carlisle. He will be bringing in his own investigative team and they will be handling all aspects of the case from now on. If you have a problem with your client's imprisonment, I suggest you either call Tim Hawkins or the senator himself. Thanks for calling," he added sarcastically as he hung up the phone. "There you go, boys," he said to his desk. "You all can handle it now. Let's see how your hot shit investigative team does with that."

"I think the senator's got some people lined up," he said to the empty chair across the desk, mocking Hawkins' voice. "I really appreciate you giving up and letting them take over." He grimaced. I bet he's got some people lined up. It didn't feel right, letting these people take over his job. It hurt. He hit his palm on his desk.

He stood and walked out of his office, turning off the light as he left. He locked the door behind him and went downstairs, out into the night air. It was brisk and a slight breeze was blowing, but the stars were shining brightly and the sky was clear. The sight lifted his spirits slightly. He looked up at the stars and said softly, "I must go down to the seas again, to the lonely sea and the sky, and all I ask is a tall ship and a star to steer her by." A voice behind him coughed to indicate the presence of someone.

He turned and saw Peter Oswald. "Hey there, Peter. Had no idea you were behind me," he said laughing.

"Sorry to interrupt you, Andy. That sounded nice, what you were saying. Poetry?" he asked.

"Yeah," O'Toole said. "Mom was an English teacher. High school. She drilled that stuff into my head and I've just never quite gotten it out," he said smiling.

"Nice night, huh?" Peter asked as he looked towards the sky.

"Sure is," Andy replied. "Looks almost like it was painted." He sighed heavily. "Day after day, day after day, we stuck, nor breath nor motion; as idle as a painted ship upon a painted ocean. Water, water everywhere, and all the boards did shrink; water, water everywhere, nor any drop to drink." He looked at Peter, who was eyeing him suspiciously. "Coleridge," he said. *"Rime of the Ancient Mariner."*

Peter's look of utter surprise didn't leave his face, but he put his arm around the sheriff's shoulder. "You're getting all soft on me now, Andy. Bad idea. Let's go over to the Jenny and get a drink."

Andy turned to him. "Thought you gave up drinking, Peter."

"I did," said Peter. "I'll have a soda with you, though. Let's go." The two walked across the street without speaking further and entered the Jib and Jenny. They found two seats together at the bar.

"Oh, no. Look what the cat dragged in tonight," said Steph as she smiled at the pair.

O'Toole looked up at her and asked, "What gives, Steph? You're working nights now, too?"

She nodded, adding, "Yeah, honey. I work one night a week in here." And then, as if she'd seen a ghost, she said, "Actually it was a week ago when…" Her voice trailed off.

Andy silently nodded, then changed the subject. "So you've got a pair of go-getters here, Steph. We need some fuel, you know?"

Steph managed a smile, which gradually grew in size until all traces of her momentary sadness seemed to vanish. "What's it gonna be, Peter?" she said to Oswald with a smile. "Cheeseburger and a soda?"

"Nah, just the soda, Steph," he said rubbing his stomach. "I'm on a diet."

Steph laughed, grateful to be feeling happy again. "Oh, right," she said. "I'll believe that one when I see it." She turned to Andy. "Jameson's neat, honey?"

"Yeah, Steph," Andy said. "Thanks." He paused for a moment then said, "Actually, Steph, no. Let me have one of those slap in the face things."

She looked at him. "What?" she asked laughing.

"You know, one of those slap your happy ass, or whatever you call them."

"Oh. You want a Slap-Happy-Smash? My, my, Andy, you're serious tonight, huh?"

"Serious isn't the word for it, Steph. I'm having a bad night," he said grimly. Steph knew from years of experience behind the bar that any customer who wanted to unload problems would tell her what it was when the time was right, so she went about making the drink for him and left O'Toole to vent to Peter.

"What's up?" Peter asked.

"Jesus, Peter," began the sheriff, "if I told you, I doubt you'd believe me anyway. Let's just say I've been taken off the Carlisle case."

"What happened?" Peter asked, his interest primed.

"Like I said. You wouldn't believe me if I told you. The senator's bringing in his own people to investigate it. Turns out McKenzie didn't do it, or so his lawyer says, and he's supposedly got an alibi. I don't honestly care anymore. I'm sick of the whole thing and I'm glad to be off it." Steph returned with the drinks. Andy looked suspiciously at the Mason jar in front of him. The drink was the color of pink grapefruit juice and he could smell the distinct aroma of rum emanating from it. He lifted the drink to his mouth, but stopped short. "Cheers, Peter," he said, clicking the rim of the jar on Peter's soda. He turned to Steph. "Here's to swimmin' with bow-legged women," he said as he winked at her.

Steph laughed. "You're too much, Andy O'Toole." She moved down the bar to wait on other customers, and Andy took a sip of the drink. It was incredibly sweet, tasted of coconut, and the previous odor of rum had now taken on a power more akin to that of a rum distillery. The liquor slid down the back of his throat and he could feel a warming sensation growing up his legs as it sank down into his stomach. "That's not bad," he remarked, looking at the jar in his hand like he'd just discovered a very rare and valuable ancient artifact.

Peter smiled. "Yeah, but it'll hit you in the morning," he said jokingly. "I'll come by and see you around nine. See how you're doing then. See if you still think it's 'not bad.'"

Andy laughed, knowing Peter was probably right. He had always been a fan of Irish whiskey because it didn't induce a vicious and vengeful hangover the morning after. Something about the refined nature of it, his father had told him. Triple refining process eliminates the impurities. The Irish filter their whiskey through so many different stages that nothing's left but the purest of the pure when you get to the end. Not like bourbon, which left him all but dead the next morning. *No,* he thought to himself, *the Irish got it right. You get all the sludge and the garbage out of it and there's nothing to make you sick the next day. Just get it down to the essence. Get it down to what's pure and right. Get rid of the things you don't want, the things that hold you back.*

He turned his attention back to Peter. "You want to hear one hell of a story, Peter?" he asked.

Peter looked at Andy, and saw that the sheriff looked very serious. "Yeah, Andy. What's going on over there across the street?"

Andy took a deep breath and proceeded to tell Peter everything that had transpired, ending with his voluntarily removing himself from the investigation and offering to help the senator's investigators. When he'd finished, he said in response to Peter's startled look, "Told you that you wouldn't believe me."

"That's wild," Peter said with a shake of his head to punctuate his amazement. "What are you going to do?" He knew that Andy wasn't one to give up on anything, whether it be a card game or a crime investigation, and he assumed that the sheriff had no intentions of breaking from his traditional character.

"I'm going to find the son of a bitch that did these things and string him up by his jockey shorts. I'm going to find that bastard and I'm going to get an apology from Carlisle and Hawkins. Then I'm going to accept an award for my service and I'm going to get the hell out of here and retire to Belize." He smiled a toothy grin.

"Sounds like a pretty good plan to me, you old pirate" Peter said, happy to hear that Andy wasn't really giving up.

"Why don't you come with me?" Andy asked jokingly. "I hear the diving's great." Both men laughed and Andy ordered another drink.

CHAPTER TWENTY-THREE

Andy awoke late the next morning with a pounding headache. "Slap-Happy-Smash," he said out loud. "They got that name wrong. Nothing happy about this. But that's what I get for drinking what Will Paterna suggests." He struggled painfully to pull himself out of the bed and shuffled to the bathroom. He showered and dressed, then drove into town. As he drove, it occurred to him that he had a sense of inner peace, almost a feeling of complete well-being, that resulted from his being taken off the Carlisle investigation. As he pulled up to his parking space, though, that feeling disappeared, for he knew something was different. Parked along the street next to the Town Building were three large, dark colored Suburbans, the windows of which were tinted almost completely black. They looked like something you would expect to see Secret Service officers in charge of the president driving. He walked in the door of the Town Building and entered the office of Tim Hawkins. Tim was seated at his desk, talking on the phone when Andy entered, and he motioned for the sheriff to sit.

"That's fine," said Tim. "Do whatever needs to be done. Whatever resources I or my staff can offer, consider it yours." A brief pause, followed by, in a much more secretive tone, "I'll suggest that to him, Senator. Thank you, sir. We'll be in touch. Let me know if I can help." He hung up the phone. He turned to O'Toole and said, "Damn, Andy. We're playing in the big leagues now. Senator Carlisle brought in a bunch of retired FBI agents."

Andy tried to seem unimpressed and unaware that Hawkins had just been talking about him. "That's good," he said slowly and quietly. "I hope they can figure out what happened," he added. In the back of his mind, though, he was secretly hoping they'd all fall flat on their faces, proving to everyone that he, in fact, had done his job. He was feeling as if he no longer had any sort of authority whatsoever, and any chance to watch these hotshots fail was a welcome opportunity to O'Toole. "What's new so far?" he asked.

"Not a whole lot," replied Hawkins. "Apparently Carlisle had these guys on red alert to be ready to get over here, though. He had 'em here first thing this morning and they took charge as soon as they got here. From the looks of it, I think he even had a few of those guys already on the island, just in case." He gestured out the window with his finger. "I guess you saw the trucks out there. They've got a crime lab on wheels in those things."

O'Toole tried to ignore the comment Hawkins had made about the senator's having investigators already on Nantucket, before the subject of his being taken off the case had even been suggested. "Have they managed to learn anything new?" Andy asked.

"Not much yet," Hawkins replied. "They're keeping McKenzie here for questioning. They seem to think he had more to do with it than he's letting on." Andy doubted that McKenzie knew anything more, but he didn't say anything. "They also have concluded that Charlie Bordham did kill himself. They apparently found gun shot residue on his right hand and arm, and his fingerprints were on the gun. Looks like your medical examiner went off half-cocked again. No pun intended, I suppose," he added in what O'Toole thought sounded like a little too friendly of a voice.

"I see," he said nonchalantly. "What did they say about those red marks around his wrists? The ones that Latkin thought were made by handcuffs?" he asked, suddenly more interested in the team's findings.

"They're working on that right now," the selectman replied. "They're thinking they were old marks, and not related to the suicide itself. Bordham, it seems, was a scuba diver, and they're thinking right now that the marks were left by a wetsuit cuff. They're trying to match them to a wetsuit they found in his house." Looking down at a stack of notes on his desk in front of him, he added, "They're also looking at the idea that the marks were made by latex gloves."

O'Toole gave the selectman a confused look. "Latex gloves?"

"He worked as a dishwasher. Remember? He wore gloves to work every night, kept them on for several hours at a time."

That made sense, Andy thought. Both theories seemed plausible on one level. Because he hadn't really had much time to think about it, he hadn't happened on the idea that the marks could be job-related. And he hadn't known that Bordham was a scuba diver, for that matter. He remembered watching Peter Oswald sell a wetsuit; he'd said that it was supposed to fit tight. He supposed the cuffs could create marks, but it seemed to him that someone would have to all but live in a wetsuit to leave marks for that long. He wondered if his doubts arose from jealousy or honesty. The whole idea still seemed a little far-fetched to him, but he decided in the end that he'd have to give credit to Carlisle's guys. Maybe they did know what they were doing after all. He paused, shuffling his feet uncomfortably. "So I guess I just go back to my everyday routine now?" he eventually asked.

"That's what I'd suggest, Andy." He paused for a moment, thinking of how best to carefully word his next thought. It wasn't coming from him so much as it was from the senator, but Tim didn't want O'Toole to think that the selectman had lost all trust in Andy and wanted him out of the way. Carlisle had not been so political about the matter. He'd told Hawkins in no uncertain terms that O'Toole's presence would do nothing but create unnecessary distractions. He suggested—mandated was more like it—that Hawkins convince the sheriff to get out of the way so that his team could investigate without any interference from him. If O'Toole resisted the suggestion, Hawkins was to force him to leave the island for an indefinite period.

"Andy," he began in a therapeutic voice, "I was thinking you might want to take some time off. This whole investigation has really kicked you around some. Maybe take a few days. Maybe take a week. Whatever you want, Andy. Go somewhere off-island. Relax a little." He tried to sound paternal, to sound like he was genuinely concerned. In truth, he was just repeating what the senator had told him to say.

O'Toole didn't know how to interpret the offer. "I'll think about it," he said after a moment's contemplation. "I've got a few rats to kill around here. Loose ends to tie up, you know. I'll see after that," he said. "I'm going to go down to my office. I'll be around if you need me," he said as he stood to leave.

"Andy," said the selectman gravely, "I want you to know I'm not trying to question your abilities here. I know how much work you did on this with pretty limited resources and I know it's not easy for you to give this up. We are all very grateful to you. Don't forget that," he said. O'Toole thought he heard a tone of artificiality from the selectman, like something you might hear from a puppet. But he wasn't in the mood to analyze speech patterns right now. He'd just been told, in no uncertain terms, that his presence wasn't needed, nor was it appreciated.

Andy nodded his own mock appreciation for the kind words and left the office. He had lied to the selectman when he'd said that he had some work to do. This investigation had consumed his life, and everything else had been delegated out since it started. He started to go down the stairs to his office, but then decided against it. He walked out into the morning sunshine and crossed the street. He made his way around the corner to the Island Creamery. He opened the rickety screen door and entered the small store, climbing gingerly up the single wooden step into the shop.

The Island Creamery had been around for as long as he could remember. They were well-known for their homemade ice cream, and anxious customers lined up every night to get huge hand-rolled cones filled with their favorite flavors. The counter ran the length of the store, with a glass partition to one side through which customers could watch the monstrous ice cream cones being made. "Can I help you, sir?" asked a young Jamaican woman behind the counter.

Andy looked at her and smiled. "Give me a minute here. I've gotta think about this," he said. He scanned the menu board hanging behind the young woman. It was all hand-painted and reminded him of simple times, like so many of the old places on the island. The Creamery reminded him of what it was like to live on Nantucket before the island had achieved the status of celebrity destination in the world of vacation locales. "Let me have a large orange juice," he decided.

The young woman turned and opened a small refrigerator situated below the sink on the back wall. She removed a clear plastic container filled with orange halves and began squeezing the juice into a measuring cup. He heard the door behind him open, squeaking loudly on the rusty hinges, and he looked over his shoulder. Richard Carlisle came in wearing expensive looking sunglasses, a knit shirt with a small blue flag on the left breast, and Nantucket Red shorts. O'Toole had never understood the fashion appeal of the Nantucket Red clothing line. The brick red clothes faded to a light pink over time through exposure to salt air and repeated washings. O'Toole thought they looked ridiculous, but the store that had created them had made a fortune. Richard was wearing leather boat shoes, one of which had green gaffing tape wrapped around it. Andy looked him up and down. *Tastefully rugged,* he thought to himself. *Rich guy trying to look poor, and spending a ton of money to dress the part.*

"Sheriff," Richard said. "Good to see you." Richard seemed almost embarrassed to be in the presence of the sheriff.

"Hi," Andy replied. "Richard, right?"

Richard nodded. "It's hard to tell us apart some times, but you're pretty good. How are things with you?" he asked, trying to be polite. He knew things weren't good at all. In fact, he knew that his father had taken over the investigation and had brought in his own personal team of retired Secret Service guys because, as his father had told him, the sheriff wasn't fit to find his own ass with both hands.

"Things are going," Andy replied and left it that. His eyes were drawn to Richard's wrist, where he noticed a small black bracelet. He'd not noticed it when he'd been so focused on Richard's wrists at the funeral. Andy assumed it had been hidden by his shirt when he'd seen him last. He searched his memory, trying to recall if he'd seen it. The watch was the same, he remembered. In his mental picture, though, there was no bracelet. O'Toole saw that Richard was absent-mindedly rubbing the bracelet with his other hand as he looked over the offerings painted on the sign above the counter.

"That's an interesting bracelet," O'Toole remarked nonchalantly, pointing towards Richard's wrist.

Richard looked down and flinched slightly but still noticeably. "Oh, that," he said in a quiet voice laced with melancholy. Or was it something else? O'Toole couldn't tell; his brain was still working to clear the fog from last night's revelry. "It's an elephant hair bracelet. It belonged to my brother. He loved it. Never took it off. I decided to wear it as kind of a tribute to him. Dad just got it back from the medical examiner. His guys," he said, then paused, realizing that O'Toole was the one Carlisle's team had replaced. "The guys my father brought in got it this morning from him." He looked away, again seemingly embarrassed at being in the same room as the sheriff. Andy looked closer at the bracelet. It was jet black, made of several strands of what looked like thin wire, and had two small coils sitting on top of it. Richard was playing with the coils, sliding them back and forth across the strands of hair. The coils served to enlarge the bracelet size, and slid back to tighten it.

"There's your orange juice, sir," said the young woman behind the counter. "Anything else I can get you?"

Andy looked into the glass counter in front of him. "Um," he said, "how about one of these strawberry muffins." The girl moved around to the display case, reached in with a small piece of wax paper, and removed a muffin.

"Do you want a bag?" she asked without much enthusiasm.

"No," Andy replied. "Don't worry about it. I'm going to go eat it right now." She handed him the muffin and the orange juice. He gave the young woman a five-dollar bill and told her to put the change in her tip jar.

"Thanks," he said. He turned to Richard. "Tell your parents again how sorry I am that I couldn't catch the guy," Andy said softly, looking down at the ground. "We're just not set up for that kind of investigation here," he said apologetically.

Richard nodded. "I know, Sheriff. We appreciate all you did for us, though. Really, we do. I'm sure I'll see you around," he said in a much more gracious, good-natured tone. "I'm going to be here for another week or so, taking care of some details and serving as a sort of on-scene director for my dad, so I'll be around."

Andy was again amazed at how seriously this family seemed to take its obligations. Mr. Carlisle was focused on getting back to work while his son acted as a deputy in Nantucket.

"Goodbye," Richard finally said as he stepped forward to the counter to place his order. Andy walked out the door and turned to his left. He entered Davy Jones' Locker and walked up to one side of the counter.

Peter Oswald looked up from the nautical chart he was studying on the counter in front of him and saw Andy. "I'm sorry, sir," he said jokingly. "You can't have any food or drinks in here."

Andy laughed. "Tell you what," he said. "You let me eat this in here and I won't run you in for ripping off lobster pots." He winked at Oswald.

Peter feigned an innocent look. "Lobster pots, Sheriff? I don't have any idea what you're talking about."

O'Toole looked at him. "I'm sure, Oswald," he muttered as he laughed. "Seriously, though. I wanted to ask you something."

Peter stopped looking at the chart and turned his full attention to Andy. "What's up now?" he asked. "Tell me you didn't find a car full of dead people that drove off the dock somewhere."

O'Toole shook his head. "No, I'm serious this time. When you picked the Carlisle kid up, I mean out there at the fog horn, was he wearing a bracelet?"

Peter studied O'Toole's face, waiting for the rest of whatever it was that Andy was going to say that would suddenly make this question sound as important as the sheriff seemed to make it sound. When he realized that any further information wouldn't be coming forth and the sheriff was waiting for his response, Peter asked, "A bracelet? I don't know. What kind of bracelet?"

"It's not important, really," O'Toole said. "Any kind of bracelet."

Peter thought for a moment. "Not that I remember," he said finally. "I didn't really have a lot to do with it, you know. I was just there as a helper, basically, so I didn't get real close to the actual body. But from what I remember seeing, I don't think he had anything on at all except that weight belt."

Andy was silent for a moment. "You sure?" he asked.

"Like I told you, Andy," Peter said, "I didn't look real close. I wanted as little to do with that thing as possible, so I just did what I was told to do, which wasn't very much. I'm not sure I would have noticed it anyway. But if you really want a totally honest answer, I'd have to say that no, I didn't see a bracelet on the kid." He kept his gaze fixated on Andy, trying to decipher his motive for asking.

O'Toole didn't notice; he kept on the same track. "Who else was with you out there when you recovered the body?" Andy asked. "Was it just Frankie Hess?"

Peter nodded. "Yeah. Frank and I were the only ones to go down and get it."

O'Toole was thinking out loud, speaking to no single person, just speaking out loud to the space around him. "Okay. Peter and Frankie are the only two people diving down there to recover the body. Tom Latkin's the only other guy who had contact with the body. That's strange, isn't it?"

Peter looked at the sheriff like he were changing into some sort of alien life form right before his eyes. "What are you talking about, Andy?" he asked.

"Oh, just wondering about some things. Like I said, it's nothing real important," he said absent-mindedly.

Peter knew there was more to the story than O'Toole was letting on. He couldn't crack it, though. He cocked his head to one side. "You don't look so well, Andy. Those drinks from last night getting to you?"

O'Toole shook his head. "No, it's something with the Carlisle case."

"I thought they took you off the case," Peter responded, now wondering what exactly his friend was up to.

O'Toole grunted softly. "They did. But something weird just happened. I was over next door at the Creamery. Saw one of the Carlisle kids. He had on a bracelet that he said was his brother's. Said his brother never took it off. Said his father got it from the medical examiner."

"So what?" Peter replied. "He's got on a bracelet. You know," he added smiling, "a lot of men wear bracelets nowadays."

Andy shook his head. "That's not what I mean, Peter. He said his brother never took it off. He made it a point to say that. And he made damn sure to tell me that his father had gotten it from Doctor Latkin."

Peter's face looked blank and Andy sighed. "Peter. Think about it. His brother never took that bracelet off, plus this kid's telling me that Tom Latkin found it on the kid. If that's the case, and Jack wasn't wearing it when you found him, then how in the hell did his brother get it?"

A look of understanding slowly crept across Peter's face. "Don't get crazy on me now, Andy," Peter said. "I told you I didn't see if the kid was wearing a bracelet. For all I know, he might have been wearing diamonds. I didn't want to even look at him."

"I know, Peter," Andy said. "It's just weird. Probably nothing," he said. He ate his muffin slowly, standing at the counter. He threw the wax paper into the large cardboard garbage box at the side of the counter. "Thanks, Peter," he said. "I'm going to go run some errands. I'll see you later."

He walked out the door of the store and began thinking. Something wasn't right here and he was sure of that. But what was it? That was the question that kept popping into his mind and he had no way of answering it. Latkin hadn't said anything to him about a bracelet. Andy thought he remembered him saying the exact opposite, in fact, that there was nothing on the kid. No clothes, nothing. His mind began racing in several different directions and he had to stop himself. Conspiracy theories weren't going to help him, not at this moment. But then the voice again. He had to silence it and he knew there was only one way to do that. The first step was to go out to the fire department and talk to Frankie Hess. He had to find out if Frank had seen a bracelet on the kid, but he was also officially off the investigation. He'd have to do it covertly, he thought. He looked across the street at the fleet of black trucks. He coughed loudly and made up his mind that he had to do it. He had to figure out what was going on here. If it turned out to be nothing, which he thought it most likely would, then he'd be free of the voice. But if it turned out to be something important, he needed to know. He quickly crossed the street and went to his car.

What he needed right now was to talk to Frank Hess.

CHAPTER TWENTY-FOUR

When Andy walked in the door of the building that housed the Nantucket Fire Department, he was greeted by a young firefighter who was sitting at the front desk, a huge street map of Nantucket behind him. "Sheriff O'Toole," the young man said in what was an attempt at a professional tone. "What can we do for you today, sir?" The kid was clearly trying to take his assignment as receptionist—the job that fell to the lowest ranking fireman on duty at a given time—very seriously.

"I'd like to talk to Frank. Is he around by any chance?"

The young man said that he was and told Andy to go back down the hall to Frank's office. Rather than call him on the phone to announce the arrival of his visitor, the young fire fighter simply yelled, as the fire house wasn't all that big. O'Toole made his way down the narrow corridor and knocked on Frank's door. "Come on in," a friendly voice said from the other side. O'Toole walked in the office and greeted the deputy chief. Hess smiled at the sheriff. He'd already been notified about the troubles with the Carlisle investigation, and he wanted to be sympathetic and supportive to the sheriff.

"Hey, Frankie," he said. "I wanted to ask you a question or two. You got a minute?"

Hess looked at Andy, who appeared crestfallen. *Poor guy,* Frank thought to himself. *He doesn't even know what's going on here.* "For you, always," Hess said graciously. He asked the sheriff to sit down in a large chair next to his desk and then asked him if he wanted any coffee.

"No thanks," O'Toole replied.

"I need some, so give me one minute," Frank said. He walked out of the office and returned a short time later carrying a steaming cup of coffee. As he entered, Hess shut the door behind him. He returned to his chair behind his desk, sat down and looked directly across the desk at Andy, his demeanor suddenly changing quite noticeably. The air in the small office was suddenly thick and Frank's normally friendly face looked stern and anxious.

"Before you say anything Andy, I've got to tell you something," Hess began. "I'm going to tell you this because you're my friend and because I've known you a long time." He looked gravely serious. "I don't know what questions you want to ask me, but I can imagine what they're about. And I have to tell you, Andy, I was ordered not to give you any information relating to the Carlisle case."

Andy was shocked. "Who told you that?" he asked.

"Some guy came by about an hour ago. Flashed some federal credentials and told me he was part of Carlisle's investigation crew. He said that you had been taken off the case, and that any information I had to offer the investigation should be given to him or to one of his fellow investigators. He gave me a phone number and said I should call with any information. But they said specifically that I was not to tell you anything. And he sounded pretty serious about that command."

O'Toole felt as if his knees were going to buckle beneath him. Had he not been sitting, he was sure this information would have caused him to lose his ability to remain upright. He couldn't believe he'd been completely shut out of the investigation. They were trying to keep him from doing his job. Didn't want to be upstaged, it seemed. He felt his sense of authority, his sense of power as the sheriff, disappearing rapidly. He fought the urge to yell at Hess, knowing it wasn't his decision. *Don't shoot the messenger,* he thought to himself. He paused for a long time, trying to regain some semblance of his former composure. He finally managed to slow his pulse down and relax a little. He took a few deep breaths and relaxed his tense fists.

"Okay," Andy sighed. "I understand and I don't want to put you in a bind." Like Frankie had said, they'd been friends for a long time and O'Toole knew it wasn't fair to put his friend in a situation where he'd be forced to compromise his own integrity and violate specific orders. "But please let me ask you one thing," he said, almost pleading with Hess.

"I'll do my best to answer," Hess responded, a tone of hesitation cracking through in his voice.

"When you brought that kid up from the bottom, was he wearing any jewelry at all?" O'Toole looked to the deputy chief's face for any sign of reaction. He was disappointed, though, as Hess looked more confused than anything else.

Frank looked at Andy, his eyebrow cocked. "I didn't see any jewelry, I don't think," he began. Then his tone became much more reserved. "But I have a habit of trying to not look too closely when I'm doing something like that, so it's entirely possible. What sort of jewelry were you thinking about?"

"Oh, you know, anything that might have been on him. A necklace or a bracelet, for instance" he said, adding a little emphasis to the latter item on the list.

Frankie shook his head. "Nope, I don't remember seeing any of that, but I wasn't looking for anything, so I can't be sure. I wasn't real excited about the prospect of touching the body, if you know what I mean." Hess looked and sounded a little nervous in the face of these seemingly pointed questions. He paused for a moment, then asked, "Why?"

Andy started to answer, then thought better of it. He didn't want to elaborate on his theory any more than he had to. After all, if Hess was as nervous as he seemed to Andy, there must be good reason to be so. "Just curious," Andy said. "I thought it might be nice to return it to his parents if you'd found anything. You know. Sentimental value and all," he said. He looked straight ahead, holding his eyes in the same place, waiting to see if Hess would be able to read the lie that was so apparent on his face.

"That's thoughtful of you, Andy," he replied. "But I don't remember seeing anything, so it looks like you're off the hook there." Andy heaved a silent sigh of relief that he'd pulled it off, then thanked Hess for his time and suggested they go fishing some day when they both had some free time. "I'd love to, Andy," he said. "Just promise me that we can go soon and that you won't catch all the fish" the chief said, slapping Andy on the back and smiling jovially, as if there were no secrets, nor any need for secrets, between them.

O'Toole drove back to the Town Building slowly. He wasn't in a rush to get back to his office and he wasn't really sure what he'd do once he got back there. He was turning over in his mind the information he'd managed to cull so far from the various people with whom he'd spoken. Richard Carlisle had on a bracelet that had been his brother's, and neither Peter nor Frank could recall definitely seeing it on the body. But the element that really stuck in his mind was the fact that this investigation team was trying to stymie his attempts at helping to solve this case. That was certainly a new and interesting wrinkle to what was rapidly becoming a situation approaching ever increasingly new levels of bizarre. He thought they'd be glad to have the extra hand.

Pompous bastards, he thought to himself. *They're terrified of a little town sheriff showing them that he actually knows what he's doing in an investigation like this, and realizing that they can't do anything better than he'd already done.* He had to smile at this realization. It made sense to him; big federal G-men can't stand being upstaged by a little sheriff on a little island. He shook his head. The facts he'd discovered so far were still jumbling around in his brain when he hit on a possible solution to the indecisiveness he'd seen in the two people involved with the recovery of the body. He thought about the only other person that would have seen the body on that day. He hoped they hadn't gotten to him yet and told him not to keep mum regarding giving details to the sheriff. O'Toole still needed to find out if there really had been a bracelet found on the kid's body.

Fifteen minutes later, Andy was parking his car in his spot on Broad Street and walking slowly in the side door of the Town Building. Walking up the stairs to his office, O'Toole noticed that there was a flurry of activity around the building. It was hard to miss, in fact, as the building had been converted in to a command central for the investigation. Men who O'Toole assumed were Carlisle's agents were walking in every direction like ants scurrying around a newly-toppled ant hill, carrying papers, asking questions, talking on cellular phones. Andy walked into his office. As he passed his receptionist, she gave him a sympathetic smile, knowing how hard it must have been for O'Toole to be taken off the case. He smiled back and entered his office, locking the door behind him. He sat at his desk and lit a cigarette, then picked up the phone and dialed the number for Tom Latkin.

"Tom Latkin here," said the doctor.

"Doc, it's Andy O'Toole. I needed to ask you a question. It won't take more than a minute, I promise." There was an uncomfortable pause on the other end of the phone.

"Uh, sure Andy," Latkin said hesitantly. "I'll tell you what I can. What was it you wanted to know?"

Latkin sounded like he was facing a loaded gun and his every word was chosen carefully so as not to set off the trigger. That noticeable tremor in the doctor's voice told O'Toole that there was something going on with the situation. *Bet they've already told him not to say anything to me,* he thought to himself.

"Tom," he said, "I was wondering if you'd found any jewelry on the Carlisle kid's body."

"Jewelry?" asked Latkin. "What do you mean?"

"You know," Andy said, feeling like he'd already been through this whole conversation before. "Jewelry. Watch, necklace, bracelet, anything like that. I'm especially interested to know if you found an elephant hair bracelet." He knew that sounded completely ludicrous, but he figured what the hell, he'd go for the jugular from the start on this one. He waited for the answer.

There was a kind of nervous laugh from the other end. "No, Andy. No jewelry. Why do you ask?" the doctor asked. Truthfully, Latkin had found no jewelry, and O'Toole's question struck him as strange, especially the specific mention of an elephant hair bracelet, of all things.

"Thanks, Tom," O'Toole replied hastily. "I've gotta run. I'll catch up with you later." He hung up the phone quickly without giving Latkin a chance to ask any questions of his own. His hands were sweaty and his breathing was fast. His heart pounded in his chest. He nervously sucked on the cigarette that he held between shaking fingers, blowing smoke out the open window. In his mind, he could see a vision of Richard Carlisle. Arrogant, stylish, wealthy, good-looking. *The kid had it all. Rich parents, successful law career, vacation home on Nantucket. He couldn't have done it,* thought O'Toole. *There's no way he could have done it.* He shook his head as he tried to clear his thoughts. *There's no way. First of all, there's no reason for him to have done it; there's no motive. And all defense attorneys will tell you that where there's no motive, there's probably no crime. People aren't always so purely evil. But maybe this is an exception.*

He had to stop himself. *This is crazy talk, Andy,* he said to himself. He crushed out the cigarette in the ashtray on the desk. He exited his office and walked slowly up the stairs to Tim Hawkins' office. As he went, he tried to calm himself, to keep his mind focused on acting naturally. He schemed as he walked, an idea rapidly taking shape in the form of a plan. He'd turn the tables on these guys and start pulling the strings himself and manipulating them.

He knocked on the door and then entered Hawkins' office. "Tim," O'Toole said gravely. "I've been thinking about what you said earlier. About me taking some time off."

Hawkins nodded, smiling. "I think it would be good for you, Andy. Get out of here," he said encouragingly. "Go on a vacation. Leave all this behind you for a few days. Give yourself some space from this. By the time you get back, it'll all be over with and we can go back to our normal lives."

"That's exactly what I was thinking," Andy said, trying now to feign a sense of relief in his voice. He wanted the selectman to think that he'd had to wrestle with this decision and had come to it only after hours of soul-searching. "I was thinking I'd take off for a while. Like you said. Clear my head and let this thing get solved. Let the experts do their work. It would be best for everyone, I think."

"Good," Hawkins said, relieved that the sheriff was finally going to be one more distraction that was out of the way. "Where do you think you might be headed?"

Texas, thought O'Toole silently to himself. "I hear Belize is nice," he said to Hawkins. He laughed. "I'm going to retire down there one day. Or so I keep saying anyway."

Hawkins smiled broadly. "I like the sound of that, Sheriff. Get out of here and enjoy yourself. No hurry. Take as much time as you need. We can handle things here while you're gone. Just give me some idea as to when you think you might be back, and I'll arrange to have somebody cover for you."

Andy thanked the selectman for his generosity and left the office. He went to his car and drove home. His mind was now racing forward. He was trying to figure out how he was going to investigate Richard Carlisle, who was sitting at his parents' house in Nantucket, from Waco, Texas, a place where he knew nobody. But that's where he was headed, there was no doubt about it. That's where he was now convinced the truthful answers to this mystery sat hidden.

Once he got to his house, he immediately sprang into action. He packed a small suitcase with a few changes of clothes and a toothbrush. He gathered together his notes and information on the Carlisle family and put them, together with a few other things, in a small duffel bag. When he had finished packing, he picked up the phone book and found the number for American Airlines. He dialed the number quickly and was immediately put on hold.

When the operator finally answered, he blurted out that he needed a round-trip ticket to Waco, Texas, flying out of Boston Logan. He wanted to depart today, sometime in the late afternoon, if possible. The operator told him that the best she could do tonight was a one-way to Dallas, which would put him close. He told her to issue the ticket and said that he'd pick it up at the counter in Boston. He hung up the phone, grabbed his two bags and rushed out the door. The clock had officially started ticking and he didn't know how long it would be until time ran out. He drove like mad through the winding streets to the airport. As he neared, his mind returned to the last time he'd been down this road, when he'd discovered the dead body of Charlie Bordham; he shuddered involuntarily. He turned into the airport and parked the car in the long-term parking lot. He took his keys and his cellular phone, and ran inside the terminal.

The Nantucket airport was built, as the old timers told the story, by the United States Navy. They had been trying to find a place to practice take-offs and landings in a foggy location, and Nantucket had fit the bill. From those inauspicious beginnings, the airport had blossomed into a sprawling conglomeration of buildings, due to the enormous increase in travel to and from the island. He walked quickly to the ticket counter for Cape Air, a local airline offering service between Boston and Nantucket. He placed his bags on the scale next to the counter.

As he did so, he removed an old baggage claim tag from the handle, the letters ACK black on the white tag. He'd long wondered about the designation letters for Nantucket Memorial Airport. ACK just didn't make him think of Nantucket. He had heard multiple explanations for the choice of abbreviations, ranging from a story that the airport was once named Ackerly Field to the use of letters in the name of Nantucket to everything imaginable in between. He'd never gotten a definitive answer. Or rather he'd gotten many definitive answers from so-called "experts," none of whom could agree on the actual origin. But for whatever reason, the Nantucket airport was abbreviated as ACK, and O'Toole just accepted it at that.

He pulled out his wallet and presented the clerk with his commuter book of tickets, and removed one of the white slips that enabled him to fly one-way ten times whenever he chose, space permitting. He'd only used two of the tickets out of the existing book. The agent looked at her computer monitor and told him that there was one seat left on the next section to Boston, and he quickly told her to put him on it. He presented his driver's license and she entered the information. "Weight?" she asked him.

"One-seventy," he said doubtfully. He wasn't sure he'd seen one-hundred-seventy pounds in a few years, but it sounded good.

"How many bags?" she asked.

"One checked, one carry on," he said. "I want the checked one to go straight through to Dallas, if you can do it for me." She told him that he'd have to reclaim his bag in Boston. "That's fine," he said. "I'll just have to hurry." She handed O'Toole a yellow strip of plastic with a number 9 printed in black on one side. He took a seat in the waiting area and glanced around at the other few travelers in his immediate vicinity. He nervously tapped his foot as he waited, anxious to get underway. Finally the announcement came over the loudspeaker that O'Toole's section was departing, and Andy headed towards the glass partition separating the security screening area from the rest of the airport.

After passing through the detectors, O'Toole sat and looked at the rows of Cessnas lined up on the runway. It amazed him that such a little thing could actually transport so many people such a long distance. When the young ramp agent entered the security area and called for the Boston passengers, Andy hopped up, presented the yellow boarding pass and followed the people in front of him out the door and out to the plane. As he climbed aboard the small twin-engine plane, he handed his duffel bag to the ramp agent who was now standing just outside the plane. The young man stuffed it into the wing compartment, and O'Toole, satisfied that it wasn't going to fall out, climbed in and took his seat. When all of the passengers were safely on board the plane, the pilot, who looked to be about twenty-five, introduced himself and said that the flying time to Boston would be about forty minutes. He asked the passengers to sit back, relax and just enjoy the flight. As the propellers started, the noise grew increasingly louder. Andy tried to relax, knowing he had a long day ahead of him. But it was no use; his body was as tightly wound as he could remember it ever having been. He couldn't clear his mind of what he was thinking and he knew he wouldn't be able to purge it until he had found what he was looking for.

An hour later, O'Toole was claiming his suitcase downstairs at the Cape Air baggage claim area. He ran back up the stairs with his luggage and found the American Airlines ticket desk, which he was glad to find in the same terminal. He didn't think he'd have the patience to ride the bus to another terminal. The line was not too long and he quickly moved to the front. When he presented himself at the desk, he said that he would like to pick up his ticket. The agent printed the ticket out for him and handed it over. He was early; the plane wouldn't be taking off for another hour, but he preferred to be early. It gave him a chance to smoke a few cigarettes before departure. The agent scanned his credit card and had him sign the slip. After he'd passed it back to her, she smiled and told him to have a nice flight. Andy smiled back and thanked her.

He headed out the exit to the street and sat on a large cement bench just outside the sliding glass doors. He lit a cigarette and sucked in heavily. A large woman next to him asked him where he was headed. "Dallas," he replied, exhaling a large cloud of smoke as he said it.

"Oh, Dallas," she said. "I'm from Nebraska myself. Omaha. Never been to Dallas," she said. She looked at the sheriff. "You don't look like a cowboy to me," she added laughing.

Andy smiled. "Looks can be deceiving," he said. Then he winked and added, "Ma'am."

CHAPTER TWENTY-FIVE

The flight to Dallas was uneventful, except for the small child that had screamed for the final two hours of the flight. The parents looked helpless to do anything and gave the passengers around them a look that said, "Hey, folks, we deal with this all the time." Andy was glad to be off the plane when they finally landed; his knees had begun to cramp while he sat wedged into a middle seat near the back of the plane. He collected his bag in Dallas and found the nearest rental car agency. He looked at his watch. It said it was almost eight o'clock. He looked out the door next to the rental car desk and noticed there was still a little daylight. He asked the clerk behind the desk what time it was.

"Ten minutes 'til seven," the young woman replied, smiling with bleached-white teeth, her face framed by equally bleached hair that been teased and sprayed into what could best be described as an unruly lion's mane.

Time change, he thought to himself. *Forgot to set my watch back for the time zone.* He fiddled with the dial of his watch, turning it first the wrong direction, then turning it back the other way until it read seven o'clock. Close enough, he said to himself.

"What can we do for you today, sir?" the young woman behind the desk asked him.

"I need a car. Cheapest thing you've got." She punched a few keys on the computer in front of her.

"I've got a sub-economy class. It's not much. Not much room. It's got an air conditioner, though," she said laughing, "and you're gonna' want that today, I can guarantee you that. I can get you in it for thirty-seven-fifty a day, unlimited mileage." Andy told her that would be fine and no, he didn't want supplemental coverage in case of an accident. Yes, he was sure. No, he'd take his chances, thank you very much. He filled out the paperwork and was directed to wait outside for the courtesy bus to take him to the rental lot.

As he walked through the sliding glass doors, the heat hit him full in the face like some kind of solid mass. He hadn't been prepared for that. "My God," he said out loud. An older man seated on a bench smoking outside laughed.

"Hot enough for ya today?" he asked. "I'm guessin' you're not from around here."

Andy looked over at the man, wondering silently what it was that caused people to be so congenial with complete strangers when they were together at an airport. Maybe it was the shared stress of traveling, a brothers-in-arms sort of relationship. "Yeah," he said. "Pretty much hot enough, I'd say. It sure isn't like this up in Nantucket. That's where I'm from." He sat next to the man and pulled out a cigarette. The older man offered O'Toole a light.

"Whereabouts is that?" he asked.

"Off the coast of Massachusetts. Way north of here," he added. "And much, much cooler temperatures."

He nodded, as if to say that he understood that Massachusetts was north of Texas. "Yeah," he said, "it gets pretty damn hot down here. I live down in Beaumont. Little town east of Houston. You should see it down there, boy, I tell you what. You think this is hot, you ain't seen nothin' partner. Down there it gets hotter'n a monk's face in a whorehouse." His eyes crinkled when he smiled, highlighting white creases along the man's sunburned face.

Andy laughed. He was definitely in Texas, just in case he'd doubted it. The speech was yet another difference he was discovering between his home and this new place. A large white bus pulled up in front of where the men were sitting, and Andy stood. "This one's mine," he said. "See you later."

The old man smiled. "We'll talk to you later, now," he said. Andy climbed aboard the bus, thankful to be rid of the older man. He wasn't in the mood for small talk. He wanted to focus on what he had to do. The bus lurched forward, spewing black fumes of exhaust. The driver made several stops along the way to allow passengers to get off at their respective airline gates and to allow new passengers to embark. The bus driver wound his way expertly in and out of traffic, exited the airport and headed towards the rental lot. When they arrived at the company's parking lot, O'Toole climbed down, walking sluggishly through the stifling heat that drained him of all his energy. He slogged through the heat to the small building that housed the company's dispatcher. After examining the papers the rental agent had given him, the dispatcher gave Andy a set of keys and escorted him to the back of the lot to a small maroon car. Sweat was running down the back of O'Toole's neck and his clothes were sticking to his body, and he began to wish he'd left the jacket at home.

He inspected the car for damage with the young man from the rental car agency, initialed the paperwork to say that there was no damage to the car and was told how to get out of the airport and then on to Waco. "What you want to do," the young man said, "is head west on Highway 183. You'll be going towards Fort Worth. That's the city west of here. You'll take I-35 south when you get to Fort Worth. Take the highway all the way to Waco. It'll run smack-dab into the middle of the city. You can't miss it." Andy thanked him and put his bags into the trunk of the car. He got in and immediately slammed his bent knees into the steering wheel.

He cursed the pigmy that had last driven the car as he carefully slid the seat back. He started the engine and slowly pulled out of the lot. As he merged with the traffic heading west, he turned on the radio, which was already tuned to a country music station. A male voice was crooning something in a very Southern accent about a rose and a yellow moon. *How Texan,* he thought to himself without a trace of irony. He turned the dial until he found a classical music station. Soothing, he thought. That's what I need. The traffic was heavy, and it took him almost an hour to reach the exit for Interstate 35 in Fort Worth. He turned south, like the young man had told him, and tried to calculate the time. It looked on the map like it would take him about two hours to get to Waco. It was now seven-forty-five. That would put him in Waco around ten o'clock. It was getting dark and he turned on the headlights. Through the dying light, he could see that he wasn't missing much. The drive was, he'd been told, through a very flat part of the state, and there wasn't much scenery to admire. He didn't care. A lack of distractions made it easier for him to keep his mind on his investigation. He was anxious to get to Waco so that he could get the ball rolling on it.

As he drove, he continued to mull over the facts of this new case as he'd managed to sort them out in his own mind. He was convinced that Richard had somehow been involved with the murder, but he had no way of proving it. He was beginning to convince himself, too, that Richard had, perhaps, actually participated in the actual act. The thought horrified him. His mind unconsciously returned to his childhood, to his Sunday school teachers drilling Bible stories into his head. He thought about the story of Cain and Abel. He remembered the story well. Cain slew his brother Abel, then denied to God that he was his brother's keeper. The first case of fratricide in history. He thought that this case, too, was another example of that horrid occurrence. Perhaps Richard didn't think that he was his brother's keeper either. His mind was still an unwilling participant in this mental debate. Was it possible that Richard had orchestrated the murder of his own brother?

At nine-twenty, he entered the Waco city limits. He hadn't been speeding, in fact just the opposite. People had been passing him all the way from the airport. He supposed it was just closer in reality than it looked on the map. He crossed over the Brazos River and saw a small motel on the right hand side of the interstate. He exited the highway and pulled up in front of the motel. The sign on the front door advertised, in garish red neon lights, "Vacancy, Y'all." He laughed and shook his head at the kitschy sign. At least it was a roof over his head, he reasoned, and he walked in the door, relieved to be in the relative comfort of the air conditioned lobby.

Andy told the clerk he'd need a room for a few nights, preferably a smoking room. He wasn't sure how long he'd be in town, but he'd like to reserve the room for at least five nights. The young man behind the counter entered the information into the computer and handed him the key to his room. He was shown a map of the motel, and the clerk told him how to get to his room in relation to where he currently was. "That's fine," he said. "I'll be fine." He walked back to his car and drove around the side of the motel to where the clerk had indicated. Once he'd located the correct number on the wall outside, he opened the door and turned on the light. *Standard motel room,* he thought. Two beds, neither of them comfortable, a television bolted to the table against the wall, a remote control bolted to the table between the two beds. Brown carpet, two prints of desert scenes on the walls above the bed, an open closet at one end.

O'Toole sat on one of the beds, almost collapsing from exhaustion. It hadn't occurred to him until now that he was absolutely worn out from the day's travel. He put his feet on the bed and lit a cigarette. Tomorrow would be equally long, he was afraid, and he needed to get some sleep tonight. He kicked his shoes off, letting them fall to the floor. He turned on the television and sighed heavily.

When his watch said it was ten o'clock, O'Toole found a news broadcast, and he watched the reporter delivering the day's offerings of newsworthy events. The lead story was of an elderly couple being carjacked while leaving the local shopping mall. The next story, though, caught Andy's attention. The reporter was talking about the investigation of the murder of Jack Carlisle, son of Waco's own United States Senator Leonard Carlisle. He turned up the volume on the television.

"We have learned from sources close to the investigation that Senator Carlisle has called in a team of highly-trained forensic investigators, a group that he himself has put together culled from former Secret Service officers and other federal officers. The team, we are told, has discovered that one of the primary suspects in the murder committed suicide at his home in Nantucket, and that the other suspect in the case is in custody."

Andy shook his head in disbelief. *They're calling it a confirmed suicide, are they? They're reporting that now,* he thought, *so it must be official. They couldn't say it on TV if it wasn't true,* he silently joked. *Guess they'll be saying next that it's all over and that they're the ones who caught the bad guys.* He laughed softly.

He absent-mindedly let his hand hang off the side of the bed, where it encountered the drawer to the table between the beds. He pulled it open and found a Gideon Bible sitting in the drawer. He looked down at the Bible. "At least you can always count on some things," he said. "Thank God for that." He opened the Bible at random and scrolled down the words.

He had opened, by chance, to the book of Leviticus, and as he read the words, he shuddered. Chapter twenty, verse thirteen read, "If a man also lie with mankind, as he lieth with a woman, both of them have committed an abomination: they shall surely be put to death; their blood shall be upon them." *Poor kid,* he said to himself. *Maybe it was God's will after all.*

He shut the book as if he were afraid of what else it might say and replaced it in its original position inside the bedside table. He closed the drawer, turned out the lights and fell asleep in his clothes.

Chapter Twenty-Six

O'Toole awoke late the next morning and got ready to begin his work. He didn't have any kind of plan as of yet, and he wasn't exactly sure what he was looking for. He had the addresses of both Richard Carlisle and Leonard Carlisle, but he didn't have any legal support for being at either house. He didn't even have a key for that matter. But with a wry smile he acknowledged that he didn't foresee that as being as much of a problem as it might seem on the surface. Getting in was the one thing he was certain he could do. But the fact remained that he would most certainly be breaking the law by entering, so he would have to do so in secret. He was more worried about making public any information he found inside the houses. That would be the sticky point. He mapped out his plan, which included searching Richard's house first. He'd gleaned enough details, he hoped, to make that the easier target. Depending on what he found there, and he had a mental inventory of what he hoped to recover, he'd decide on how wise it was to venture into the senior Carlisle's house.

But before he could get into Richard's house, he'd need to look at it from the outside as a way of cementing his strategy for breaking in. He also wanted information on the two men, and the thought of a relatively relaxing morning of research sounded more appealing to his weary brain than a reconnaissance mission. So he decided to start his day at the local university library. He wanted to read as much as he could about the family. Maybe the elusive motive would surface if he could get inside these peoples' heads.

The librarian he spoke with was very helpful, and she showed him how to access the university's own computer system, indicating that they were fortunate enough to have search engines that were dedicated to political articles in various periodicals, most of which were housed in one form or another at the library. On the offhand chance that he needed something not available, she assured him that she could facilitate the transfer of whatever document it was from other libraries. O'Toole took a seat at a corner table and began the arduous task of wading his way through newspaper articles, most of them about the senator's doings in Washington. As he read, he was reminded how much he'd despised this sort of work as a student. Research had never been his favorite element of higher education; his creative spirit longed to spout forth original thoughts, not rehash previously published facts. He found occasional references to Richard in a few articles, but wasn't able to uncover anything incriminating or even remotely suggestive of a reason for either man to commit murder. Regardless, though, as he read, he constantly wrote notes on his pad. Experience had taught him that details, no matter how seemingly inconsequential they might appear at first, frequently added up to some sort of relevant proof. And sometimes they even added up to a motive, if you were lucky.

He learned that Richard had earned his law degree from the University of Texas, just as his father had. He had returned to Waco to live, where he'd married his high school sweetheart, Heather Littleton. The two had no children. Andy remembered that Richard had referred to their dog as the only child, and smiled a strange grin at the recollection. Heather was actively involved in the community, volunteering her time with both the Junior League of Waco and the local historical preservation society. Richard had used his father's name to establish a private law practice in town, a practice which catered to the more upscale population of the city. He and his wife lived in a large, two-story house on Austin Avenue, just down the street, in fact, from his father's house, and O'Toole made a note to get a city map so that he could find out exactly where that was.

He worked slowly and methodically, as he was in no hurry and under no outside pressures. For all anyone knew, he was sitting on a beach in Belize, due to return to Nantucket whenever he saw fit. Ironically, it seemed to him that this cloak and dagger sort of existence that he was currently living was the most relaxing time he'd spent in the past few weeks. With no officials or outsiders pressuring him to hurry up and solve the case, he was able to go at his own relaxed pace, and he found the experience to be very satisfying and soothing.

He looked at his watch and found to his surprise that it was already six o'clock in the evening. He had spent the better part of seven hours researching in the library, and it dawned on him that he hadn't eaten anything all day. He packed up his notes and headed out in search of something to eat. He found a hamburger joint across the street, which he assumed was a local hangout for the college kids, and ordered a double cheeseburger and a beer. He ate quickly and silently, not looking around him; he was nervous about what the rest of the evening had in store for him.

When he had finished eating, he stopped off at a gas station, filled up the tank and bought a city map. He located Austin Avenue, and then he drove by the home of Richard Carlisle. The house was nestled behind a small hedge, with large trees dotting the manicured yard. The house was set back from the street and overshadowed the houses on either side of it in terms of its grandeur and elegance. It was an older looking, two-story brick home, with black shutters and large white columns in front. O'Toole noticed a small sign in front of the house, notifying any would-be intruders that the house was protected by a security system. He'd known the house had an alarm system; Richard himself had told him that much during their first encounter at the family home in Nantucket. He just hoped that he'd be able to get around it. He smiled to himself knowingly, though. The plan he'd been formulating started to come together in a more concrete way. It was going to work.

He drove by the house a few times, looking for the best vantage point from which to implement his plan; he sought out a spot hidden from the view of any nosy neighbors who might be watching, but close enough to the road so he wouldn't have to troop across the lawn more than was absolutely necessary. After four passes by the house, he located a suitable spot and mentally mapped it onto his brain, then returned to the motel. On the way, he stopped at a hardware store and bought a hammer and a chisel, along with a flashlight and some wire cutters. He also found a pair of canvas coveralls that he knew would come in handy, so he purchased them, too.

Back at the motel, he spent a couple of hours watching TV and, just before ten o'clock, decided that the time had come. He emptied the contents of the duffel bag onto the floor of the motel room and then packed his new tools in the empty bag, stepped into the coveralls and went out to the car. He drove slowly through the dark streets, not wanting to bring any attention to himself.

When he reached the house, he drove past it and parked two blocks away. He walked in the shadows back to Richard's house, pausing often to look over his shoulder. He felt like floodlights would be on him at any moment, and there would be men with guns coming to arrest him. He made it to the house safely and without incident, though, and he paused a moment to relax. Once he was in front of the house, he walked quickly to the side and waited, holding his breath, listening for any sounds. His breathing was shallow, though his heart was pounding furiously, and he continued to wait. He heard nothing and, figuring he had avoided detection to this point, crept up to the edge of the house. He located the vent cover for the foundation that he'd fixated on earlier. It was situated on one side of the house at ground level. This was to be his access point. Shining the flashlight on it, he mentally reviewed the steps he'd been over so many times that he knew them by heart. The wire mesh was embedded in the bricks around it, so he would use the chisel to remove the mortar holding it in, thereby exposing the mesh.

He delicately placed the chisel against the edge of the wire where it joined the cement of the foundation and tapped lightly with his hammer. He kept tapping until he felt the chisel meet the mesh of the wire grate. He continued in this way all the way around the rectangular opening, casting backwards glances every so often to be sure his work wasn't attracting attention.

The house had been built in the late thirties or early forties, Andy figured, and he was glad for the age of the house, as well as the humidity of the region, because both conditions had conspired to soften the mortar, making it relatively easy to chip away. When he'd exposed the entire frame, he put the hammer and chisel back in the bag and removed the wire cutters. The wire proved a more difficult opponent, but the strands slowly gave way to the force of the jaws of the cutter with a satisfying plink. He snipped every other diamond, loosening the tense grate but still leaving it intact for the most part. After cutting every other wire, he replaced the cutters and sat on the ground, his feet towards the vent. He bent his knees and brought his feet back towards his shoulders, then thrust his feet forward with a quick motion into the wire cover. When his large, heavy-soled shoes hit it, the mesh gave way and fell in to the crawl space under the house, taking with it the pieces of mortar that had held it in place. The plan had worked perfectly so far. By leaving the mesh partially intact, he'd assumed, the remaining strength would help to pull out any remaining loose mortar. Briefly shining his flashlight in to the newly made hole to illuminate the grate now lying on the ground, he found that he'd been correct.

His next task was to enlarge the existing hole as best he could. He began to chip away at the jagged remains of the old mortar that the wire had failed to rip out upon its untimely departure. Andy worked meticulously and methodically, trying to avoid making any noise. He worked at the hole for quite some time until he had managed to create an opening large enough, he hoped, to allow his stocky frame to fit through. He threw his duffel bag into the opening he'd created and heard it hit the earthen floor of the crawl space. He looked at his watch, almost instinctively, as if he were under the gun to get through with this operation by a certain time. The watch told him it was now two in the morning. It had taken him just about four hours to do this much, and the worst was yet to come.

Andy turned over on his stomach, pulling his shoulders in as far as he could, and wriggled slowly into the hole he had made in the foundation. He struggled to slide in, as the opening was not much bigger than a few feet across. He was halfway in when he thought he heard something behind him. He immediately froze. He knew that now there was nowhere to hide and anyone who saw him would certainly know he was breaking in. He could hear his own heart beating as blood rushed to his head. He waited breathlessly, sure that at any moment he would be caught. He tried to imagine how Hawkins and Carlisle would react to this news.

The sound, whatever it had been, did not come again, and O'Toole reached down, grabbing the hard dirt floor of the crawl space. He dug his hands in as far as he possibly could, held his breath, and pulled for all he was worth. He could feel the cement edge of the vent opening cutting into his body, scraping his skin below his clothing and, resisting the overwhelming urge to scream out in pain, he finally managed to pull himself in past his hips. From there, it was relatively easy for him to pull his legs in behind him, and he lay flat on his back, trying desperately to catch his breath. He knew he couldn't wait long. He had work to do, and it wasn't getting done while he was lying there. After he had managed to calm his breathing somewhat, he again turned on the flashlight and shined it at the floor of the house , which was now situated above his head. The piers of the foundation were spaced evenly throughout the crawl space and Andy had to squirm his way around them. He guessed that the opening for the crawl space would be towards the back of the house, so he began to move in that direction. He only hoped he'd be able to find it, wherever it was, and once he found it that he'd be able to open it.

He grabbed his duffel bag and made his way slowly back towards the rear of the house, pausing every few feet to shine the light above his head. In front of him, he could see the rear boundary of the house's foundation and he moved towards the corner. He would start there and work his way over. He moved the light slowly over the wooden floor above him and stopped when he found the tell-tale crack that he was looking for.

The opening, he guessed, was about three-and-a-half feet on each side of the square, and he could see the small crevice where the cover sat atop the opening. The crawl space was only about three feet tall, so he wouldn't be able to stand up to force it open. He hoped it wouldn't be too heavy.

He gently reached up and pushed on the square cover, which didn't move. He pushed harder, but the cover wouldn't budge. He lay down flat on his back again and bent his knees up to his chest. He put his feet flat against the cover and pushed as hard as he could. He could feel the muscles in his stomach tightening, and finally he felt the cover give way. He pushed it up with his feet and allowed the wooden cover to fall to one side. *Not bad for an old timer,* he thought to himself with an air of pride in his own strength. The crawl space cover fell noisily on the wood floor in the house, and O'Toole stuck his head up through the opening. He figured the crawl space opening would be in a closet, and his guess had been right. He found himself in a coat closet, with the door standing wide open. Apparently the Carlisles had packed in a hurry, and one of them had thought to grab a coat from the closet before leaving.

He first lifted his bag up through the opening and into the closet, then pulled himself slowly up into the house, sliding like a snake on his stomach, inching his way into the house itself, and shined the light through the open closet door. A stroke of good fortune already, because having to open the door would have created another set of problems, though he thought he might have managed to defuse those, too. *Best to keep it simple,* he thought to himself. *Just be glad that it was open.* The closet opened onto a large room that Richard apparently used as an office when he was at home. There was a computer on a large wooden desk in one corner, and bookshelves lined two walls. There was an ornate Oriental rug on the floor and in the corner of the room, near the ceiling, O'Toole noticed the small white plastic box that housed the motion sensor for the room. He put the flashlight in his mouth and gripped it with his teeth. He crawled on all fours, very slowly, through the room. The door leading to the rest of the house was open, and he continued to crawl, making his way slowly to the kitchen. *Thank God for big dogs,* he thought to himself. He knew that Richard would have his motion detectors set above the level of the dog so as to prevent false alarms.

The office opened onto a long hallway, and O'Toole continued to crawl along it. Rooms went off in either direction from the hall, and Andy could see on the far wall in front of him another motion detector. He looked up at it with a smile and softly said, "Woof." *Just the dog,* he thought to himself. *Nothing suspicious. Just the dog.*

At the end of the hallway he turned to his right into the main entryway to the house. To his left was the living room, or so it seemed, with a sofa and a few upholstered chairs. To his right was the room he was looking for: the kitchen.

He inched his way into the kitchen and looked around. He looked all over the walls before standing up, making sure that there were no detectors in the kitchen. He assumed that the detector covering the hall he'd just exited covered the kitchen, as well, and there was no door that led from the kitchen to the outside, so apparently the Carlisles figured any thief would have to cross the beam covering the hallway to get into or out of the kitchen. More good fortune. He wondered how long his luck would hold out. He still needed quite a bit if he was going to get done all that he wanted to do.

He stood up slowly and moved his light around the kitchen. It was large, with a circular table at one end, a stainless steel stove along the back wall and a large wooden butcher's block in the middle of the floor. He started at the table, looking for a paper that he knew would be there. He shined the light over stacks of mail, neatly piled on the table. *Popular people,* O'Toole thought to himself. *Or at least they just spend too much money on catalog shopping.* He moved the light past the mail stacks and found what he was looking for. A yellow notepad sat in the middle of the table, and on it was written in what appeared to be a woman's handwriting a detailed list of instructions for the house sitter. *Just like my own mother,* O'Toole thought. *Always planning for everything.* The thought made him smile.

Andy read the note carefully. It gave the burglar alarm code, in the event that the house sitter had forgotten it, and gave the family's secret password in case the alarm accidentally went off and the company called. The password, he noted with amusement, was "jefe." She'd also reminded the sitter to check on the senator's house. Richard's wife had been so kind as to leave the senator's alarm code, too, in case the sitter forgot that, too. She apparently didn't trust the kid to remember anything, but O'Toole guessed it wasn't easy to find someone to do such a job on such short notice. She left a list of phone numbers where the various family members could be reached in the event of emergency and a final note telling him she'd settle up with him when she got back. Andy's face broke in to an enormous smile. *Stupid people,* he thought to himself as he shook his head. *Stupid, stupid people.*

He dropped back to his knees and made his way towards the front door of the house. He saw the door in front of him, large and heavy looking. Just inside the door, to the right, was the keypad for the alarm system. He slowly inched his way up the wall, being careful to avoid the infrared beam of the detector on the wall in front of him and to his right, and entered the number sequence carefully. The indicator light went from red to green, and he heaved a huge sigh of relief. For the first time since beginning this project, he felt that he was safe. He turned around, now able to move freely, and saw that directly behind him was a flight of stairs leading to the second floor of the house. He walked deliberately up the stairs, shining the light ahead of him as he went. The wall along the stairs was decorated with family photographs, and Andy noticed that there was one of Jack and Richard, arms around one another, standing in front of Sankaty Lighthouse on Nantucket, the red stripe of the lighthouse showing brightly against the blue sky background. *And Cain rose up and slew Abel,* he thought to himself grimly.

At the top of the stairs, he turned to his left. Bedrooms lined the upstairs hallway and he assumed that the master bedroom was at the end of the hall. He walked to the bedroom door and opened it slowly. He entered and was struck immediately by the grandeur with which these people lived. A huge four-poster bed sat against the wall, the antique wooden posts almost black. The bed was covered in an expensive looking quilt of blue and white diamonds. An antique tall boy sat in one corner, containing Heather's clothes, he supposed. A shorter, but equally decorative dresser sat against the opposite wall, and he guessed it was Richard's. Cufflinks littered the top of it and there was a small mirror attached to the dresser. Next to the mirror he caught sight of a manila folder that was crammed with papers, and he opened it.

The documents inside, for the most part, made no sense to him. They were papers relating to various legal activities that Richard was currently engaged in and written in the legalese that he despised. He'd left in a hurry, so this was most likely work he'd brought home the day he'd left for Nantucket. O'Toole rifled through the papers, looking for anything that might refer to Jack. He stopped at a sheet of computer paper that had a brief message printed on it. "Price is right, *jefe*," the message read. "Talked to my man in Havana and he told me the gig is up. Now we bury it. R." Now he had something, he hoped, and his heart began to pound furiously, threatening to break through his rib cage and rip his shirt open. He knew that Richard, assuming the "R." in the message stood for Richard, referred to his father by the familial title of *"jefe,"* and that was enough to tell him that his theory regarding Richard's involvement wasn't as far-fetched as he might have initially thought, assuming that "the gig" referred to Jack's murder. Then his mind stuck on the fact that Richard seemed to have sent this memo to his own father.

His breathing rate increased still more as the information slowly percolated through his brain. He looked back down at the paper in his shaking hands. "Price is right, *jefe*." His eyes lingered over the lone sentence. His mind clicked back to the reality of the situation at hand, breaking the spell he was under, and he quickly folded the paper in half and stuck it in the breast pocket of his coveralls.

He looked at his watch. Four-fifty. Daylight would be approaching soon and he needed to get out. He looked around the room one last time for anything else that might be able to shed some light on this crime and Richard's involvement, but found nothing. He hurried back to the kitchen and again read the note Richard had left for the house sitter. He memorized the alarm code for the senator's house and then began to open cabinets. He knew it was in here somewhere. Every good son keeps an extra key to his parents' house. He opened a cabinet above the stove and hit pay dirt. There it was, complete with a nametag. He grabbed the key and put it in his pocket with the note he'd found. *Easy as pie,* he thought to himself.

He went back to the room where he'd left his bag and retrieved it, then returned to the front door. He set the burglar alarm again, unlocked the front door and let himself out slowly. He silently closed the door behind him. The house sitter would think he'd left the door unlocked. *In addition to having a horrible memory, you're not a terribly responsible house sitter,* Andy thought. He laughed silently to himself as he crept silently to the safety of the shadows along the side of the front yard. Once he made it back to the street, he began to hurry. The sky was getting lighter, and he needed to get back to the motel. He didn't want to be seen on the street, wearing dark coveralls streaked with dirt and sweat. Most of all he desperately needed sleep. Back at the car, he got in and quietly closed the door.

"Hot damn," he said to himself. "This is too easy." He stopped, remembering the last time he'd said that. "Well," he corrected himself, "almost too easy." He started the car and drove away, heading back to the motel. He still had a lot more work to do tomorrow. And that was just the beginning of things, as far as he was concerned. He hoped that the job tomorrow would provide him with more evidence of Richard's involvement, but he now suspected, though, that it wasn't just Cain that rose up and slew Abel. Now, it seemed, there might be another player in the game. But one more question kept nagging at him. It was the one question that dominated his thinking, the one question that seemed to have no answer. Why Jack? Why did these people, who clearly had so much to lose, want to kill Jack?

Answering that single question would be the real work. *Baby steps,* he reminded himself. *Take this slow and easy. One step at a time. Find your evidence and then find your killer.*

The voice in his head still told him he was on the wrong track.

CHAPTER TWENTY-SEVEN

Andy returned to the motel and went straight to his room. He was exhausted. He dropped the duffel bag on the floor and collapsed in the bed, and was immediately asleep. He awoke several hours later, ravishingly hungry. He had noticed a diner next door to the motel when he'd checked in. He stopped at the front of the motel and bought a newspaper, and walked over to the diner, where he ordered a chicken-fried steak. The menu said it was "Texas Tried and Texas True," so he figured he'd take a chance on it. He was the only customer in the small restaurant and he was able to read his paper without interruption while he waited for his meal to arrive. The paper carried continuing coverage of the murder investigation, quoting sources "on scene" that said the investigators were "close to wrapping up their work." *That's nice,* thought Andy. *They're close to finishing. I just wonder if that means they're close to finding the truth.*

When his meal arrived, O'Toole wolfed down the food. It was a behemoth piece of meat, deep fried in grease and slathered with thick cream gravy. Though he'd eaten at enough places like this to know not to expect much, this was, without doubt, a new low. The gravy tasted like flour and the steak tasted like cardboard. He didn't care, though; he was starving. When he'd finished, he ordered a beer to wash out the taste in his mouth. He drank it slowly, savoring the beer as a magical elixir healing him from the inside-out. He swallowed the last sip, paid his tab and then returned to his room at the motel to await darkness. He was full of nervous energy and he kept opening the curtain covering the one window in the room to see if night had yet fallen.

Outside on the highway, traffic roared by as commuters left their jobs and headed for home. Andy turned on the television set and watched the early news broadcast. The anchorman read the day's update on the Carlisle case, saying that a statement was expected any day now regarding the conclusion of the case. "Senator Carlisle is spearheading the organization and supervision of the investigation from Washington, while the rest of his family is staying at the Carlisle's vacation home on Nantucket Island. The senator has vowed that the person responsible for the murder of his son will pay dearly." The coverage changed to the senator, standing outside the United States Capitol, addressing the assembled reporters.

"I am confident that the investigators I've brought in will find the person or persons responsible for my son's murder. They assure me that they are close to finishing and I have faith that they will find the guilty party. I just thank God that He has delivered these people to me and that they are working around the clock to solve this case." The senator was dressed formally, in a dark colored pin-stripe suit and a white button-down shirt, a red necktie with a repeating pattern of blue diamonds tied around his neck. The shot then switched to the rest of the Carlisle family in Nantucket, standing outside their home in a group, as if attempting to show a sort of solidarity with one another in their time of tribulation. Andy noticed Richard standing to one side, next to his mother. He was dressed very casually in comparison to his father, but the resemblance was unmistakable. His face was set in a stern gaze, his eyes saying what his mouth wasn't regarding his anger and hatred for the person responsible. For a moment, O'Toole felt sorry for Richard. *Perhaps he's innocent and I'm just adding insult to injury here,* he thought. Then he visualized the note, the note he'd been thinking about from the moment he'd woken up. The note that said it was now time to "bury it." O'Toole had developed in his own mind a very good idea of what "it" was, and he had developed an equally good idea as to why the burying of "it" involved "we." The voice in his head continued to chant. *It's all circumstantial. Probably a rational explanation. You're chasing shadows, Andy.* He focused on the TV in an attempt at ignoring them.

"Hey, Richard, you old scoundrel," O'Toole said to the picture on the television screen. "Was over at the house last night. It looks good. You might want to get yourself a new house sitter, though. Just a thought. Kid can't remember his own name, for God's sake. And he left the door open. You never know who might be snooping around when you're out of town. Know what I mean?" He laughed aloud. "You bastard," he muttered. The cellular phone on the table between the beds rang and Andy answered it.

"Hello," he said, trying to sound unofficial.

"Andy? That you?" asked the voice of Peter Oswald.

"Hey, Peter," the sheriff said. "Yeah, it's me. How're you doing?"

"Andy where the hell are you?" Oswald asked. He sounded worried.

"I'm on vacation my friend. Tim Hawkins thought it would be good for me to get away for a while. And I have to say that I couldn't agree with him more."

"Andy," Peter continued urgently, "things around here are getting strange. Really strange."

Andy sat up in the bed. "How so, Peter?"

He could hear Peter's voice, low on the phone, and he knew that he was trying to be secretive. "There were some people here yesterday. I've been trying to call you ever since they left. Started asking me about finding the body. Told me that they'd found a bracelet on the body. Elephant hair, they told me it was. Said I must have missed it when we were recovering the body." There was a pause. "Do you have any idea what in the hell is going on?"

Andy's heart leapt into his throat. He was standing now, pacing the room. "Peter," he said, "listen to me. Don't tell them anything. Not a damn thing, you hear me? Something's up with that family. They're hiding something." He ran his hand nervously through his hair. "They must have found out I was asking around."

"Asking around about what?" Peter asked.

"Jesus, Peter. This is scaring me to death. I don't know how..." His voice trailed off. "Son of a bitch," he said into the phone in a voice now laced with anger combined with the beginnings of fear. "Those bastards tapped my phone. I guarantee you. They tapped my phone."

Peter's voice took on a tone of increasing fright. "Andy I don't know what you're talking about, but I'm not sure I want to know. Who tapped your phone?"

"Carlisle's guys. They must have. That's the only way they could have known. I asked Latkin if the kid had been wearing any jewelry. I asked him when I called him from my office. I specifically mentioned an elephant hair bracelet and asked if he'd found one on the body. Son of a bitch. They tapped my phone. Those bastards went into my private office and tapped my phone."

"Andy, stop. You're not making any sense."

Andy paused for a moment, then related the story to Peter, reminding him of the day he had come in and asked about whether or not he had noticed any jewelry on Jack's body on the morning when they'd brought it up from the ocean floor. It started to make sense to Peter all of a sudden. "You think the family was involved?" Peter asked finally.

"I don't know what to think, Peter. I've gotta go, though. I'm not supposed to be thinking about all of this. Hawkins' orders and all. I'll call you when I get back on-island," he said. He angrily pushed the button on his phone to end the call. He stewed in his own anger for a moment. Was it paranoia? Were there really men in black following his every move around Nantucket? He decided that he wouldn't be intimidated. Let them follow him. Let them listen in on his phone conversations. He was on a mission now, and they'd have to do a lot more than just tap his phone if they thought they were going to stop him.

But his determination was tempered by the fear of how far they might go to stop him. He took a deep breath and tried to relax. He concentrated only on organizing his thoughts into a logical, chronological order. Time was of the essence now. If they'd tapped his phone, they probably knew where he was, and it wasn't too big of a leap of logic to figure out what his intentions were by being there. He needed to get to the senator's house tonight, find what he needed to find, whatever that was, and get the hell out of town. His heart was pounding and he was sweating profusely. It was seven-thirty. He would have to wait a few hours before going to Carlisle's house.

He grabbed the phone book and looked up the local number for American Airlines reservations. He picked up his cellular phone and dialed the number, explaining to the agent that he needed a ticket from Waco to Boston for tomorrow.

"Sorry, sir," the woman replied. "Can't do it. I can get you on a redeye from Dallas to Boston tomorrow, leaves at seven o'clock in the morning. How's that work for you?"

He was beginning to think that there was never a flight into the Waco airport, as he'd been through this exact sequence of travel, only in reverse, a few days earlier. Andy calculated the time in his head. Two hours to get to the airport, then leave the rental car and catch the bus to the terminal. That would take at least half an hour. Then he'd have to get his ticket and get to the departure gate, another twenty minutes. Plus he'd need time to clear security and still have time to get to the gate an hour before his flight left. He needed four hours, and that was really pushing it. He needed to be leaving Waco by some time before three in the morning. But, he reminded himself, he had the key and the alarm code, which would save him time tonight. "That's fine," he heard himself say. "I'll pay for the ticket at the counter in Dallas. Thanks very much." He gave the agent his personal information and she told him to have a nice flight. He was getting tired of being told that, and he hoped it wouldn't be long before he'd heard it for the last time.

He hung up the phone and waited. As he waited, he recalled the conversation he'd had with Peter and thought more about his suspicion that they'd tapped his phone. They must have tapped it, he thought. That was the only explanation for how they apparently knew the things they knew. Then in a rush of fear, he realized that it had only occurred to him at the time that they'd tapped his office phone. But now he was concerned—scared, even— that they'd tapped his cellular phone, too. Paranoia was beginning to take control of his brain. There was no way to know for sure, but he felt, in his own mind, that they must have. He briefly cursed himself out loud for being so stupid as to have made his new travel reservations using it.

Night was slow in coming, as it seemed that time literally stood still while O'Toole waited, anxious to be out of the city. He packed his suitcase and called the motel's front desk to inform them that he'd be leaving tomorrow morning. He then put his luggage in the car, anticipating a speedy exit from Waco. Later he watched the evening news, just to see what new information the Carlisle team had uncovered. "Sources close to the investigation have said that Richard Carlisle will be returning to Waco this evening. His wife will be remaining behind on Nantucket. The sudden departure of the senator's son was blamed on work-related issues at home. Richard Carlisle is a well-known attorney here in Waco, and he told reporters that there was an issue at his office that required immediate attention. He did not elaborate further or offer any additional details about the investigation from this end. He left the island early this afternoon, bound for Waco. In other news..."

O'Toole turned off the television, his pulse banging away in his wrist. *Oh, God,* he thought to himself. *This is it. They know I'm here and they know what I'm doing. And now Richard is on his way here to deal with me in whatever way he sees fit.* At that moment, O'Toole was absolutely certain that his cellular phone had been tapped. He quickly called Davy Jones' Locker, being very careful to use the hotel phone on the bedside table. When Peter answered, O'Toole told him what he thought. "Peter, I'm sure they tapped my phones and I'm calling from the hotel right now. I don't want to sound overly dramatic here, but if you don't see me again, make sure that family pays for what they did."

"Andy," Peter began. "I don't know what you're up to, but you're scaring me to death here, and I want you to be careful, whatever it is you're doing."

"I'll be careful, Peter," Andy said. "I promise you that. I also promise you I'll be making the news one of these days." He hung up the phone. "I just hope it's not as an obituary," he said to the phone sitting on the table after he'd hung up. He leapt up and grabbed the duffel bag still sitting on the floor and emptied the tools. He then retrieved his coveralls and quickly stepped into them and ran out of the room to his car. He sped to the address he had for Senator Carlisle's house. He regretted not having time to look at the house a few times before going in, but he was now, for the first time since his arrival in Waco, being pressured into moving very quickly. And the penalty for moving too slowly, he reminded himself, was something he didn't want to consider. He simply had to hurry; there was no other option. There was no telling when Richard would come calling.

He parked his car down the street and walked quickly to the front door, carrying the empty duffel bag close to him. The house was bigger than Richard's, all white, and looked very majestic. Two large magnolia trees framed the house and rose bushes lined the front. He glanced around himself to make sure there were no eyes on him as he slid his key into the lock. He turned it and felt the bolt slide. He opened the door and immediately he heard the alarm's keypad beeping, giving him the time to turn it off with the code. He stepped inside and closed the door gently.

It took him a second to locate the control panel and when he found it, he pressed the numbers firmly and slowly, recalling from memory the code. When he had pressed the final number in the sequence, the beeping ceased and he sighed in relief. He climbed the stairs to the second floor of the house, sticking his head into the rooms that opened off the upstairs hallway. He found the room Jack had called his own when he was home from college. It was, Andy supposed, the way he'd left it. The large bed was made neatly, the desk in the corner was clean, the computer looked as if it had never been used. It reminded him of a military barracks, the way everything was rigidly perfect. *No doubt a result of the old man's drilling him.* A framed print of the Nantucket Rainbow Fleet hung on one wall and the bedside table had a small lamp that was made from clear glass with seashells filling the base. Three books were sitting on the table, stacked neatly. Andy glanced at the titles: *Beyond Good and Evil* by Friedrich Nietzsche, *The Communist Manifesto* by Karl Marx and the Revised Standard Version of the Holy Bible.

Andy opened the drawer of the table and found a small, leather-bound book. He opened it to the first page and discovered that it was the personal journal Jack had kept. He opened to the back pages, only to find them blank.

He turned the pages rapidly, working back towards the front of the book, until he found writing. He didn't have time to read it then, but he hoped that buried somewhere in all the writing was what he was looking for. He very much hoped that this discovery would somehow turn out to be the smoking gun that had eluded him to this point. He put the journal in his duffel bag and looked around the room quickly. He opened the drawers of the desk, and in one drawer found a stack of personal letters that Jack had received from various people. O'Toole grabbed the bundle of papers and put them in the duffel bag and then went out the bedroom door.

He walked slowly to the end of the hall to the bedroom Mr. and Mrs. Carlisle shared. He looked around the room and saw, next to the bed, a stack of file folders that he presumed belonged to Senator Carlisle. He reached down and grabbed the stack, thrusting them in his duffel bag. Outside he heard a car door slam. Dogs began to bark. Andy peered through the window that looked out over the front yard and saw Richard Carlisle making his way to the front door, key in hand.

O'Toole didn't have time to think. He didn't have time to notice the sweat pouring from his forehead. He didn't have time to notice his heart beating so hard it felt as if it would come out of his chest. He only knew he had to run, and he was painfully aware of that fact. He bolted down the stairs and headed for the back of the house. Anywhere was fine with him, just so long as it was somewhere away from the front door. He heard the key in the door, heard the door open, heard loud, deliberate footsteps entering the house. Richard didn't seem to be in any particular hurry, whatever his intended mission was.

O'Toole slipped into a room at the back of the house and went to the window. It was locked from the inside, but the locking mechanism was old and loose, and he was able to easily slide the catch open. He quietly lifted the window, only to find that there was a storm window on the outside that blocked his progress. *Goddamn rich people*, he cursed to himself. *They take so many goddamn precautions with their precious homes.* He found the catches on either side of the storm window, pulled them inward, and slid the window up. He could hear footsteps walking along the wood floor of the hallway, and he slipped out the window as quietly as he could.

He found himself standing in the middle of a rose bush, thorns sticking into his legs and arms. He ignored the pain of the thorns and ripped his coveralls free of their grasp, thankful, at least, that he'd worn them over his clothes. Once out of the confines of the bushes, he ran as hard as he could back towards where he had parked his car. Over his shoulder, he could hear

Richard yelling. He wasn't sure what he was yelling, but he was pretty confident it was something directed at him. He kept running across the lawn, made it to the street and darted to his car. He threw the bag in the back seat and started the engine. He turned the car around, so as not to have to drive by the Carlisle house again, and gunned the engine.

O'Toole had no idea where he was in relation to where he needed to be. All he knew was that people would be looking for him, and he didn't want to be found. He had a vague idea of which direction the highway was in, and he turned down side streets, hoping to find something that would lead him to the interstate. He finally hit upon a major road and turned left. He kept shooting glances into the rearview mirror to see if anyone was following him. The street behind him was dark. He pulled into a convenience store and ran in, leaving the car running. The clerk sat behind the counter reading an issue of *Penthouse*. When Andy entered, the clerk threw the magazine to the floor and looked up, his face beet-red from being caught red-handed.

"Which way to the interstate?" Andy asked between gasps. The clerk pointed him in the right direction and said it was hard to miss. Andy bolted out the door, got behind the wheel and threw the car into reverse. He turned around, put it in drive and accelerated back on to the street in the direction the clerk had indicated. Just then, his cellular phone rang again, sitting in the passenger seat next to him. He looked at the caller ID and saw that it was Davy Jones' Locker calling. Without thinking about the fact that his cellular phone was most likely being listened in on, he answered in a shaky voice.

"Andy, it's Peter again. I'm starting to think you're right. About your phone being tapped," he said, his voice quivering with fear.

"What happened now?" O'Toole asked, terrified of the potential answer.

"They came in here and talked to me. They asked me if you had called. Andy," he continued, sounding very serious. "This was literally ten minutes after you called today."

He couldn't believe it. He was sure that they must have tapped Peter's phone, too, because he remembered that he had been so careful to call from the hotel phone when he'd called him earlier that day. "Okay, Peter," he said, trying to sound calm in hopes of covering up the terror he was feeling, "what it sounds like happened was that they tapped your phone there, too. It's the only answer that makes any sense." Then he stopped, his heart skipping a beat. "You're calling me from the store, aren't you?"

"Yeah, but…" he began. Then said softly, "Oh, God."

"Hang up now, Peter," Andy said. "I'll talk to you when I get back to Nantucket." He ended the call, threw the phone angrily back in the passenger seat and slammed his hands on the steering wheel. He wanted to cry. That seemed like all there really was to do at this point. His life, as far as he knew, was going to be over at any moment, and he felt more scared than he'd ever felt in his life. He had promises to keep, though, to himself and to Jack Carlisle, and regardless of the difficulties he had to face, he wasn't going to let Jack down. With that thought, his resolve grew and he floored the accelerator, hurling the car through the darkness and closer, he hoped, to his ultimate safety.

CHAPTER TWENTY-EIGHT

Andy somehow made it to the interstate safely, though he had no idea how, and was headed north. He was still nervous and continued to check his mirrors often to look for anyone that might be following him. As he left the Waco city limits, he began to feel safer, and as he approached the downtown skyline of Fort Worth an hour-and-a-half later, he felt genuine relief. During his long drive through the early morning, he turned over in his mind the past forty-eight hours. The first part of this complex matrix of a plan had been a success. He'd gotten in and out, and though he'd gotten caught, he'd gotten away. *There is a reason that Richard suddenly came to Waco looking for me,* he told himself. That fact helped to silence the voice of doubt in his mind. He couldn't believe that Richard would have come all that way just to catch him in the act of what really didn't amount to much more than a juvenile prank; it was the same sort of thing a bunch of fraternity kids might do. No, he must have been trying to protect some piece of information. O'Toole hoped that he now had whatever it was he'd been so desperate to prevent becoming public.

In Fort Worth, Andy stopped and refueled the car and got a cup of coffee. It was very early in the morning and he hadn't slept in twenty-four hours, and he was physically and emotionally exhausted. But his nerves were still tense and taut from the near miss he'd had just a few hours earlier.

He exited the interstate at the highway that led to the airport and followed the signs. He exited the highway when he saw the sign for Dallas-Fort Worth International Airport and continued on what appeared to be just an extension of the highway itself. He saw the sign for rental car returns and pulled off. He checked his gas gauge. The tank was almost half-empty, but he decided he'd go ahead and pay to have them fill it up for him. He didn't want to think about it right now. He could only deal with so much and he'd long ago passed his limit. He pulled up to the small building in the middle of the parking lot. He felt a sense of urgency, a sense of being followed, a sense of fear. He figured it was just nerves. His watch said it was almost a quarter to five. He had time. He threw the keys on the desk and told the clerk to charge him whatever he was due, then signed the papers saying he'd returned the car. The bus was waiting outside the fenced-in parking lot and O'Toole grabbed his luggage from the back of the car and climbed on board. He was the only passenger on the bus and he told the driver he needed to go to the American Airlines terminal.

The driver looked sleepy; O'Toole could relate, but this was no time to delay. "Which terminal you want?" he mumbled. "International or domestic?"

It took a minute for O'Toole to realize that the driver was addressing him. "Domestic," he said.

The driver let out a long-winded sigh and grudgingly put the bus into gear, the gearbox grinding out its protests at being forced to move. Andy leaned back in the seat and closed his eyes. When the bus stopped and the driver announced their arrival, O'Toole opened one eye and was immediately confused. He'd dozed off during the trip and now didn't recognize his surroundings. He slowly grasped the idea, though, that the departure area was under the main terminal and that the escalators in front of him would take him up to where he needed to be.

He thanked the driver, retrieved his bags and climbed down. He paused outside the airport entrance to smoke a cigarette. He lit it and inhaled deeply. *God that's good,* he thought to himself. The bus rumbled off, leaving O'Toole standing alone. Despite the early time of day, the heat was already approaching unbearable levels for him. A digital thermometer above his head said it was eighty-two degrees. He wondered silently how people lived here in this intolerable summer heat. He smoked the cigarette down to the farthest point he could before he burned his fingers and dropped it on the ground. He stepped on to the moving stairs of the escalator and watched the terminal come into view as he ascended.

As he entered the main terminal, he found that there were noticeably fewer people than during his previous visit here. There were assorted harried looking businessmen, most of whom were carrying on conversations on cellular phones and pulling wheeled suitcases across the smooth floor. An

Asian woman sat with her child in a row of seats while her husband negotiated a ticket at the counter.

Andy saw the American Airlines ticket counter. But before he could put his feet in motion to approach the check-in podium, he noticed two men standing behind the counter. They weren't typical airport ticket agents. They were almost identical in their stature and build. Each was over six feet tall, hair cropped short, and both men were far too muscular to go unnoticed. But there was something else not quite right with the picture they cast. He couldn't put his finger on it. A uniformed pilot walked by, talking to a flight attendant. He looked back at the men behind the ticket counter. *Uniforms. They weren't wearing any kind of company uniforms.* He walked casually to the right, just enough to see the side of one of the men out of the corner of his eye. He couldn't be sure, but he thought he caught a glimpse of a wire coming from an earpiece trailing down the back of his head and into his shirt.

O'Toole's heart began to race and he tried to appear relaxed as he walked away from the ticket counter. He gauged the speed to walk by the people in front of him. He walked at the same pace as they did, keeping a constant distance between himself and them. He wanted to look like one of them, to blend into the crowd and become invisible. At the same time, though, he wanted to run as quickly as he could, but he knew that was out of the question. It occurred to him that he was now the one acting like a fugitive from justice. He had just broken the law, and now he was trying to run from his pursuers. He wanted to shoot a quick glance over his shoulder to see what was back there, just out of curiosity, but he was terrified of what he might see. He kept his head down and continued on his way, wherever that was.

He walked down a long and dimly lit hallway and then around a curve, and eventually came into another large area of the terminal, this one housing the ticket counters for several airlines, including US Airways. He strolled sheepishly up to the counter and inquired about a ticket to Boston. The clerk behind the counter yawned and entered the airport codes into the computer. "I've got nothing available into Boston today, sir. Busy time of year. I can put you on standby, if you'd like to do that." He looked bored standing there; he couldn't get motivated to find a way to get Andy to Boston.

"No," Andy replied. He thought. He needed to get out of here, and standby wouldn't guarantee him a place. This apparently wasn't going to be as easy as he'd hoped. He looked around. "Where can you get me anywhere in the northeast?" he asked. "Anywhere. Providence, Newark, New York, I don't care. Just somewhere in the northeast." The clerk entered more information into the computer, suddenly more interested in O'Toole's travel plans, and then scanned the monitor in front of him.

"Let's see. New York is all full. Let's try Providence." He typed in the information, only to discover that the day's flights to Providence were also booked.

"You guys fly to New Haven?" he asked hopefully.

The agent looked at O'Toole quizzically. "Know the airport abbreviation?"

O'Toole shook his head.

"Hang on a minute," the agent sighed. His interest was waning. He typed several keys on the keyboard, then announced, "It's HVN. Just for your information." O'Toole felt like he should be taking notes, just in case there was a test over this. He typed another entry. "I've got a flight leaving here in about an hour and a half. It goes to Philadelphia. From there you can connect to New Haven. How's that work?"

"That's fine," Andy said. "Get me on it." He exhaled heavily. "Please," he added in an attempt to seem less frantic.

"I'll warn you, sir," the agent said apologetically. "It's not going to be cheap. These walk-up fares are killers."

O'Toole nodded. "I'm sure. Everything's expensive these days. Go ahead and book it." He handed over his license and credit card.

The agent entered the information in the computer and the printer buzzed quietly. The agent reached down and produced a credit card receipt, which O'Toole signed. He then proceeded to check him in, giving him both boarding passes. "Your departure gate this morning is B-twenty. Through security, turn right, it's not too far down." He handed O'Toole the envelope containing his boarding passes. "Have a nice...."

"Don't say it," Andy said, cutting him off. "Thanks." He walked off with his ticket, clutching his duffel bag full of what he hoped would be evidence incriminating the Carlisle family in Jack's murder. He passed through the security screening area and found the departure gate. The electronic sign at the gate told travelers that the plane was scheduled to start boarding in an hour. He was still nervous and he wanted to at least appear relaxed, so he stopped off at a newsstand and bought the day's paper, and then walked across the way to a restaurant, where he ordered a cup of coffee.

As he sat drinking his coffee, he read over the day's news and he couldn't help but notice how dramatically different the paper in Dallas was from that of Waco. In Dallas, it seemed, the senator's situation was nothing more than a blip on the radar. He must not have the same social status here as he does down there, O'Toole mused. There was a brief story about the Carlisle investigation near the back of the first section of the paper, but it only said that nothing new had happened overnight, though it hinted that an announcement regarding the investigators' findings might be imminent. He perused the rest of the paper, not really reading anything beyond the headlines. He indulged himself the guilty pleasure of reading the comics, his favorite part of the morning's reading, and then left the paper on the table. He walked to the cashier and paid for his coffee, then proceeded on to the departure gate.

Just as he reached his gate and began to settle into a nearby seat, he heard a female voice announce over the airport intercom system, "Paging passenger O'Toole, passenger Andy O'Toole. Please pick up a white courtesy phone." Andy's heart stopped. He could feel the heat rising in his face. He wondered if he stuck out as badly and as obviously as he felt like he did. He glanced around him at the bleary-eyed passengers, still half-asleep, waiting to board the plane. Nobody seemed awake enough to notice that he looked like a deer paralyzed by headlights. The gate agent announced that the boarding of the flight would commence in just a few minutes. She called for those needing extra assistance and Andy wished she'd hurry. After what seemed an agonizingly long time, she announced that O'Toole's group could board the plane and he got in line quickly.

Again the announcement paging O'Toole came over the loudspeaker and he rushed to hand the flight attendant his boarding pass. She took it and ran it through the machine next to her.

"Mr. O'Toole, seat twenty-seven B," she said. Then she looked up. "Are you the person they're paging, sir?"

Andy nodded. "Yes, that's me. I already answered it. The office," he said, holding his hands up to add emphasis. "What can I do? They know where to find me," he said laughing.

She smiled and told him to have a nice flight. He laughed again and proceeded down the jet way to the plane. His good-natured appearance, though, soon faded. He was still nervous. People knew he was in the airport and the same people, presumably, knew that he had broken into Carlisle's house. He went directly to his seat and put his head back, closing his eyes. He gripped the armrests of the chair tightly, the knuckles in his hands going bone-white from the strain. After what seemed to him an eternity, he heard the plane's door shut and gradually released his grip on the armrests.

The captain came over the intercom, introduced himself and the remainder of the crew and gave a description of the flight plan for the trip to Philadelphia. The passengers were asked to direct their attention to the flight attendants, who would be demonstrating the safety features of the plane, but Andy wasn't listening. He was trying to focus on relaxing himself and trying to think about anything other than what he'd been through in the last couple of days. He closed his eyes and began to breath deeply, in through his nose and out through his mouth. It was a relaxation technique he'd learned during a brief stint in a Yoga class, a New Year's resolution that had lasted for about two days.

He felt the plane begin the pushback process and he opened his eyes to look out the window. The terminal was fading in the distance as the captain engaged the forward thrusters and moved the plane ahead towards the takeoff point. After a few minutes of taxiing, he heard the pilot's voice say, "Flight attendants prepare for take off," and he heard the sound of the plane's engines throttling up. At last he was really able to relax. The adrenaline built up inside of him began to dissipate and his body felt heavy and tired. He slipped off to sleep.

He awoke when he felt the jolt of the plane touching down in Philadelphia. The pilot welcomed the passengers to the City of Brotherly Love and requested that they stay seated with their seatbelts fastened until the plane had come to its final stop at the gate.

A flight attendant came over the intercom to announce connecting gate information. "For our customers going to New Haven, you'll be departing out of gate C-thirteen."

O'Toole smiled. *Lucky thirteen,* he thought to himself. But he'd made it this far; he'd make it all the way. He joined the throng of passengers exiting the plane, clutching his bag tightly. Paranoia still ruled his emotions and he was continually glancing around to see if any suspicious looking people were following. Everyone looked suspicious to him. He decided in the end that it was better to look straight ahead and just focus on putting one foot in front of the other until he was inside the airport.

His legs ached from sitting for so long. It was an effort to keep moving, but he managed to make his way to the correct gate. The flight was in the preliminary stages of boarding, so Andy bypassed the bank of chairs and approached the open door of the jet way. He scanned his boarding pass to find his row number, which was in the back of the plane. They called his section and he relinquished his boarding pass to the agent, glad to be getting near the end of this lengthy journey.

Tension was seeping out of his pores, it seemed. He'd put enough distance between himself and the goons in Texas to allow him some breathing room, literally. He dozed off as soon as he was in his seat.

The flight to New Haven was just over an hour long, and O'Toole slept fitfully. He kept having visions of being chased and caught, and awoke with a jump that seemed to amuse the person next to him. Fearing further humiliation, he vowed to stay awake. He watched the plane's shadow as it bolted across cloud banks below them. He managed to lose himself temporarily in the peaceful vision of what he thought were fluffy cotton balls as a child. But on final approach, Andy's nerves began to tense again as he thought about what was ahead. He wasn't home free yet. Far from it. He still had to get to Boston and then to Nantucket. He was afraid that Carlisle would have people waiting for him in Boston. Given recent events, he was pretty sure of it. He thought about how best to avoid them. He would have to present identification at the Cape Air ticket counter in order to board the plane, so flying out of Boston as he'd originally planned wasn't even worth considering. *There has got to be a way,* he thought to himself.

As the plane touched down, he thought of the ferry from Hyannis. That would work. He could rent a car, drive it to the boat dock in Hyannis and go from there. But he was sure that Carlisle would have staked out the ferry, too. That was a no-brainer. *After all,* he told himself, *he's obviously crazy enough to put some people at the airport. What's to say he won't cover all his bases?* He'd been thinking about what these people might do to him if they caught him somewhere, and his mind had created for him all sorts of various tortures and pains they might be willing to inflict. He knew, though, that if he could make it to Nantucket he'd be safe. Nobody would dare come after him on the island. Or at least that was his hope. It was out here in the "real world," away from the safe confines of the island, that he was being hunted and stalked. It was here that he was in danger.

His mind kept jumping from idea to idea and he couldn't concentrate on any single thought. When the plane finally stopped at the gate and the passengers were allowed to exit, he stood and made his way out with the rest of the passengers. He went to the baggage claim area and retrieved his suitcase. He still had no idea of how he was going to get back to Nantucket safely. He was a wanted man. It felt strange being on this side of the legal equation.

Clearly his cellular phone was bugged. He'd made his original travel plans out of Waco using it, and they'd been there to serve as his welcoming committee. So calling anybody for help was out. Then he thought of whom he might get to help him, even if he could call anybody. He was a man without a country, a man without a home. He was wanted. Desperation began to wreak havoc on his thinking. It seemed that he was stuck where he was, and that was all there was to it.

Then he struck on an idea. *I'll call Peter from a pay phone,* he said to himself. *He can get his boat to and from Hyannis on a tank of gas. I've heard him talk about it before. He takes divers to a couple of wrecks over there off the Cape.* That'll work. But this revised plan, he quickly realized, couldn't work, because he was positive that Peter's phone was also tapped by Carlisle's team, so he had no safe or private way of calling him. Again he wanted to cry.

He walked outside, unsure of what his next move should be. He was out of options and he needed to take a minute to regain his composure. He sat on a bench outside the terminal, took a cigarette from his shirt pocket and put it in his mouth. He fumbled around in his coat pockets looking for a lighter, when his fingers encountered something. He pulled it out and examined the treasure he'd discovered, a look of surprise coupled with relief coming across his face. There, in black numbers on a red background, was the answer to all of his problems. *Bingo,* he thought to himself. He had frequently joked with people that quitting smoking would have been hazardous to his health, but he had never thought that statement to be more true than he did right now. He said a brief prayer of thanks to whatever marketing guru had convinced the Jib and Jenny management to put their phone number on the matchbooks they gave out at the bar.

He ran back inside without smoking the cigarette he'd planned on and quickly located a bank of pay phones against the far wall. He pumped quarters into the coin slot on the phone and dialed the number, his fingers shaking, praying in the back of his mind that somebody would be there to help him. The phone on the other end of the line rang.

"Jib and Jenny." It was Steph. He wanted to sing, dance, jump, anything to express his excitement and happiness at having safely connected with somebody who could help him out in this time of extreme crisis.

He took a deep breath and said quietly into the phone, "Steph, it's Andy O'Toole. Don't say anything. Don't say my name. Just listen." Steph could tell from the sound of his voice that he was in grave danger and she listened intently. Andy said to her, "Steph, I need you to go next door to Davy Jones' Locker. Don't send somebody else. I need you to do it and make sure nobody watches you go in there and don't tell anybody where you're going. I need you to get Peter Oswald and bring him to the phone. I'll wait. Please, hurry." He heard Steph set the phone down and tell the restaurant manager that she'd be right back. A few minutes later, Peter Oswald's voice came over the line.

"Hello?" he said.

"Peter, it's Andy O'Toole. Listen. Don't say a word. I'm calling from a pay phone, so don't worry about anything. I need a huge favor from you. I'll explain it all later." He went on to ask Peter to meet him in Hyannis, somewhere out of the way of the ferry dock. He told him that he was in New Haven and that he could be in Hyannis in a few hours. He'd meet Peter wherever he said, just so long as it was nowhere near the ferry dock.

Peter knew the situation and wanted to do anything he could to help O'Toole, but the tone of Andy's voice had him scared. He wasn't sure why the sheriff kept stressing that he couldn't meet him near the ferry dock, but Andy had promised to explain it to him. He thought for a moment. "You got a car?" Peter asked finally.

"I'll get one. Tell me where you need me to be," he said.

"Harwich Port," he said. "There's a restaurant up there. Sandycove Clam Shack. They're right there on the water. It's a huge place that's really easy to find. I'll meet you there in three hours. That's about how long it should take you to get there from where you are."

Andy was breathing rapidly, trying to remember everything Peter had said. "Okay, Peter. I'll be there. Sandycove Clam Shack. See you there. And Peter," he added, "I promise you I'll explain all this later—you've got no idea what I've been through since I talked to you last—but you're really a life saver here." He hung up the phone.

As he gathered his bag from the ground in front of him, a soft voice came from behind him. "Excuse me, sir."

O'Toole froze. Could they have been following him all along and tracked him to this point? Slowly he turned to face the speaker, expecting to see a gun pointed at his face. A wave of relief covered him when he saw a diminutive woman wearing a plain gingham dress. "Hi. What can I do for you?" he asked in a shaky voice, his nerves still wound up tight.

"We'd like you to have this as our gift to you, sir," she said as she handed him a small Bible. "Would you care to make a donation to our church?"

His pulse still rapid, O'Toole replied, "Thanks. I'll be happy to give you something." He reached into his pocket, removed his wallet and gave the woman a five dollar bill.

The woman took the bill in her hands and clutched it like it was a Heaven-sent miracle, some tangible evidence of the existence of God. She thanked O'Toole for his generosity and continued on to find her next potential convert. O'Toole, meanwhile, put the Bible in his duffel bag, as he was more interested in saving his life right now than in finding out how religious teachings might suggest he best live it.

Though O'Toole had been to Harwich Port many times in his life, he had never been to the Sandycove Clam Shack. But he knew of the restaurant. They had used the same radio jingle for the last twenty or so years and once you'd heard it, you couldn't forget it, even if you wanted to.

He walked down the corridor and stopped at the first rental car agency he came to. There he arranged to rent a car, which he said he would drop off at the agency's local office in Hyannis, Massachusetts. He was directed out to the curb where he would be picked up by the courtesy bus. He felt like he was becoming an old pro at this whole travel thing, between renting cars and buying last-minute tickets. He just hoped he could afford to pay the bills when they all came in at once. It would be like Christmas, he figured, only worse. But he was beginning to feel empowered with his own abilities. He felt like he'd circumnavigated the Earth single-handedly. The courtesy bus arrived and he climbed aboard. When he was dropped off at the parking area a few minutes later, he presented his paperwork and was given the keys. He asked for directions to I-95, and the young woman working behind the desk told him to just follow the signs out the airport, that he'd be there in no time flat. He smiled, thanked her and walked to the car. He threw his bags in the backseat, started the car and rolled down the window. It felt good to be back in the northeast, back in what he deemed much more civilized and enjoyable temperatures.

He lit a cigarette, blowing smoke out the window, letting the cool breeze blow through the car. *Almost there,* he thought to himself. *It sure as hell hasn't been easy, but I'm almost there.* Then it occurred to him that perhaps it was a good thing that it hadn't been easy. *After all,* he told himself, *everything that used to see so easy has so far turned out to be more difficult than I'd ever imagined possible in the end. So maybe now difficulty will bring good luck in the end, and maybe the more extreme the difficulty, the more glorious the end result would be.* Only time would tell. And that precious commodity, he feared, was running short.

CHAPTER TWENTY-NINE

Andy knew, in the back of his mind, that this plan was crazy, but he kept telling himself that everything else in his life had gone completely insane, so it didn't matter how crazy the plan might seem. It was the only one he had, so it had to work. Like so many other situations he'd had to deal with on this journey, there was no option in the matter. It just had to work. The traffic on the interstate wasn't terribly heavy, and O'Toole made good time towards his destination. As he crossed into Massachusetts, he tapped lightly on the roof of the car as a way of saying thanks to whatever guardian angel had guided him there. It was a gorgeous day, with plenty of bright sunshine and blue skies. He was excited by the prospect of being back in the salt air of his home state, relishing the fact that he could again smell the ocean. He breathed in deeply, thankful to be back.

O'Toole exited I-95 when he saw the sign for Harwich and headed east. He was about to stop and ask directions to Sandycove when he saw a huge billboard advertising the restaurant: "That's where the best tasting clams are, Harwich Port," promised the advertisement. The sign said that he should keep going straight, continue ahead for three more miles and the restaurant would be on his right. Gulls flapped lazily in the light breeze and the sun was high in the afternoon sky. White clouds floated above and Andy was overcome with a sense of absolute tranquility. Out of nowhere, he said out loud as if compelled by some force beyond his own control, "God's in his Heaven, and all is right with the world." He couldn't help but smile as he said the words.

His mother had taught him to love poetry and it always struck his fellow officers as funny that he, a rough and tough kind of sheriff, was able to quote poetry at will. He used to tell his friends, when they expressed their shock that he was a connoisseur of poetry, that he was full of surprises. He thought of his parents; his mother had taught him to love art, while his father had taught him to love drink. His father had died first, and the obligation of dealing with the funeral had fallen to Andy, as he'd been the only child, and his mother had been in no shape emotionally to handle it.

He remembered feeling an almost duty-like sense of loss at the death of his father, like he was supposed to be sorry just because it was his father who had died. But he also realized that death was an inevitable part of life and he accepted that. Burying his father—and subsequently mourning his passing— were routine practices, actions performed by a machine masquerading as Andy. But when his mother had died, he felt as if a piece of his soul had been ripped out. He wasn't entirely sure he'd recovered from her death to this very day. He'd always been closer to his mother than to his father, and her death had scarred him deeply and permanently. The only pain he could recall as being greater was the death of his wife, after which he'd felt, for the first time in his life, absolutely alone in the world. He was sure he would go to his own grave mourning her death.

Returning his attention to his trip, O'Toole focused on the road, trying to banish from his mind all thoughts of the past, especially those relating to death. Ahead he could see a large sign signaling to him that he had reached his destination. He pulled into the crowded parking lot and stopped the car. He left the keys in the ignition, figuring that he'd call the rental car company from Nantucket to let them know where it was. He didn't want them to think he'd stolen it. He didn't need that right now.

The restaurant was built to resemble an old wharf cottage, though it was at least ten times larger than even the biggest house along any wharf he knew of. O'Toole walked in the front door. The place was full of people, mostly middle aged folks, eating at plain wooden tables. Against one side was the counter where customers ordered their food, and behind that was the kitchen. Andy walked up to the counter and asked for an order of fried clams to go. He presented his credit card to pay for the order. The woman behind the counter took it and said, "We've been having trouble with our computer today. I'll have to do it manually, but it'll still work. Don't worry." She reached down and placed on the counter in front of him an old credit card imprinter. She placed the card flat on the imprinter and covered it with a carbon form. She slid the black roller to the right then back to the left, took the carbon off and gave O'Toole back his credit card. She took a pen from behind her ear and wrote in the total. She looked up at Andy and asked him, "Do you happen to know the date today?"

O'Toole looked at the date on his watch. He paused momentarily, as if in distracted thought, then smiled at the clerk and said, "June ninth."

"Thanks," replied the clerk. "Summer's already here," she sighed longingly. She finished the transaction, had the sheriff sign the slip and handed O'Toole his receipt, which he put in his coat pocket. He stepped to the side to wait for his food. A few minutes later, the clerk handed him a paper container filled with small, crinkly bits of fried clam. He thanked her and walked out the back door.

Outside, on the water, the restaurant maintained a small pier where patrons could dock their own boats and come up for a quick bite to eat. Andy walked around the outside of the building towards the pier, figuring that was the most likely spot to find Peter. He walked part of the way out on the dock and saw Peter's boat, diver flags painted on the sides. Peter was standing in the bow, wearing a T-shirt that O'Toole thought he recognized as coming from Davy Jones' Locker, a pair of blue jeans, sunglasses and a baseball cap. Andy walked up to the boat and said to Peter, "You're lucky I'm too tired to do it, 'cause I'd just about kiss you on the mouth right now. God, am I glad to see you."

Peter laughed and said in his best pirate voice, "Ahoy, matey. Step aboard me pirate ship, if ye dare." He always referred to himself as a pirate, given his penchant for working around the water. He liked to refer to friends, too, as pirates; it was, in Peter's mind, a compliment, a token of how highly he thought of the person he was addressing. His store had even contemplated fielding a hockey team in the local recreational ice hockey league. He wanted to call his team the Davy Jones' Locker Pirates. As O'Toole walked towards the boat, Steph popped up from behind the console, smiling.

"Hey there, Sheriff," she yelled to O'Toole.

"Hey there yourself," he said with a tone of pleasant surprise. "It sure is nice to see such a vision of beauty this fine afternoon."

Steph blushed briefly, the first time Andy could remember seeing her even remotely embarrassed. "You sweet talker, Andy." Her mouth broke into a broad smile. "It's my day off, and I hope you didn't think for a minute I was going to leave you alone."

"Whacha got there, cutie?" he asked, pointing to a brown paper bag she held in her left hand.

"Something to help you on the ride over," she said grinning. She pulled a bottle of Jameson's Irish whiskey out of the bag just far enough for O'Toole to see what it was. "Thought you might need it."

He stepped lightly onto the boat and threw his bags onto the deck, placing his order of clams on top of the boat's console. "You're amazing, Steph," he said with heartfelt gratitude. Then he looked at Peter. "You people are a bad influence on me, you know that?" he asked. "But I sure do appreciate it," he finished with a wink.

"Arrgh," Peter muttered with a smile as he untied the boat from the restaurant's pier and started the engines. He pulled the throttle backwards, reversing slowly away from the dock, and turned the bow of the boat so that it pointed out of the harbor. Slowly he throttled forward, the engines moaning loudly. When they'd cleared the mouth of the harbor, Peter set the return course on his GPS plotter and looked up at his new passenger.

"Now, Andy. What say you tell me what in the world is going on?" Peter began in a more serious tone. "That whole island feels like a bad spy movie, and I feel like I'm an actor playing a major role in it." Andy moved back to the shelter of the console, bent down, and lit a cigarette.

"You remember what I told you that night at the Jib and Jenny, Peter? About telling you a story that you wouldn't believe?"

Peter nodded.

"Well, sir. I got a whopper to tell you now," he said. He looked at the clams sitting on the console and then looked at the cigarette still burning in his hand. He threw the half-smoked butt over the side of the boat and took his container of fried clams from the console. He began to eat them without really tasting anything as he spoke. He told them the story of his trip to Waco and of how he had broken in to both the houses of Richard and Leonard Carlisle. He told them about being chased out of the senator's house by Richard and about the men he saw at the ticket counter in the airport in Dallas, as well as about being paged repeatedly in the airport. He explained to Steph that somebody had been bugging their phones, and that's why he had had to call her at the bar. When he'd finished, he threw the remains of his food and the container they'd been served on into a compartment below the steering wheel.

"Good Lord," Steph said. "If I hadn't been living it, I wouldn't believe you."

"I know what you mean, honey," Andy replied. "I told you it was a whopper. But let's don't think about that right now," he said. "Onward and upward, so to speak. Let's see about that bottle of Ireland's finest," he said, pulling the bottle from the bag and twisting the cap off. The bag fluttered in the air briefly before it rocketed off into the water off the stern of the boat. After he'd removed the cap, O'Toole looked at the bottle's opening. "They put a pourer in the top of the bottle. What self-respecting Irishman in his right mind is going to want a pourer in the top of a bottle of whiskey?" he asked laughing. Peter produced a rusty knife from inside the console and handed it to O'Toole. Andy looked at the knife and then looked at Peter.

"That's to cut it out with," Peter said.

"I know that, smartass," said the sheriff as he looked closely at the knife. "I was just noticing that this thing's double-edged. Two blades, fixed handle." He laughed and shook his head. "You really are a pirate, Oswald," he said. "You and your goddamn illegal knives. Don't you ever learn your lesson?"

Peter laughed. "Arrrgh, matey," he said. "A pirate's got to have the proper tools, doesn't he?" Then, dropping the pirate voice, "You know me, Andy. Anything I can't sell in that store, I'll use it somehow." He smiled at the sheriff, who just laughed at Peter.

Andy returned his attention to getting the pourer out of the top of the bottle. He carefully cut the plastic spout from the top of the whiskey bottle, letting it fall to the bottom of the boat. He tilted the bottle up to his mouth and took a long sip. As he swallowed, the initial shock on his tongue was exhilarating, and the liquor burned satisfyingly all the way down. He looked at Peter and then looked again at the knife in his hand. He threw it into the compartment where Peter had gotten it from. "I didn't see anything," he said winking. "Nothing here but you, me, her, and my good friend Mr. Jameson," he said. He took another long drink from the bottle. "And I think I missed you most of all, Scarecrow," he said to the bottle. He stood up, facing the wind and mist of ocean spray coming over the bow of the boat, and yelled at the top of his lungs, "Yee-haw, boys and girls!"

Steph and Peter both looked at him, astonished at the sudden outburst.

"Hey. Cut me some slack, you two. I've been in Texas," he said apologetically, and then the three of them broke into loud laughter. O'Toole began to feel like this plan, which he'd thought earlier was so crazy, wasn't quite so ridiculous after all. He was silently grateful for the good friends he had, the good friends that were willing to go along with these crazy schemes and make them seem almost sane. He knew in his heart that they'd help him see this thing through to the end. And finishing it, he was sure, would require even more crazy schemes. But Peter and Steph would help. He was also sure of that.

CHAPTER THIRTY

After almost an hour-and-a-half in the boat, they neared the entrance to Nantucket harbor, and Peter guided the boat past the fog horn, keeping the boat between the red and green channel markers. When he approached Brant Point, he pulled the throttle back and slowly made his way around the point. "Steph parked her car over at the dock at Children's Beach," he said to Andy, pointing to the dock in front of them. "I'll let you guys off there."

Andy nodded. "That's fine," he said. He turned to Steph. "Can you take me out to the airport? I left my car out there."

"Be glad to, honey," she said smiling. As they neared the dock, Peter cut the engines and let the boat silently glide forward, gently nudging into the end of the dock. He walked quickly to the bow and tied a rope from a cleat on the boat to one of the dock's pilings.

"Ahoy, mateys, ye can all walk the plank now," he said laughing. Andy and Steph collected O'Toole's bags and stepped out of the boat. Andy turned back to Peter.

"Peter," he said, "I can't tell you how much I appreciate this. I promise you that I'll make it up to you." He embraced Peter in a bear hug, unable to verbally express how grateful he truly was.

Peter nodded and told him there was no need. He watched Steph and Andy walk to the car parked up the street, untied the boat from the dock, started the engines, and turned the boat around, heading back to his mooring. Andy and Steph got to her car and put the bags in the back seat. They got in and headed for the airport to retrieve Andy's car. O'Toole was looking around feverishly, sure that at any minute a group of men would jump from behind a bush and take him somewhere. He'd hoped for a feeling of sanctuary here on

Nantucket, but he still felt hunted. The island wasn't big enough for him to hide out. It was beginning to feel like the world wasn't big enough for him to escape their clutches.

As they were driving, Steph asked him, "So do you have any kind of theory on how the family was involved with the murder, Andy?" She kept looking straight ahead, with frequent glances into the rearview mirror. It was almost as if she had acquired O'Toole's paranoia about being followed.

Andy thought for a moment silently. "To tell you the truth, Steph, I'm not real sure yet. I'm still trying to figure it all out myself. But I do know for sure that they were involved somehow." Then he added in a tone of frustrated disbelief, "At least I think they were involved. Hell, at this point, I don't even know what it is that I think." When they got to the airport, Andy showed Steph where he had parked his car. As they neared it, Andy saw a circular piece of yellow metal attached to the right front wheel of his car and a renewed sense of intense fear of the unknown welled up inside his stomach. "I don't believe this," he said. "They put a boot on my car. These people are crazy," he said.

"Jesus, Andy," said Steph in an astonished tone. "What do they think you have?" Her voice, like Andy's, carried with it a sense of disbelief mixed with fear of what could potentially be happening.

"I have no idea, Steph," he said. "I don't even know what I have. I've been running around too much to read over any of the stuff I've got and I was too distracted on the flight to do anything. But judging from what I've seen and how these people are reacting, I'm guessing it's important. At least they sure as hell think it is." Andy looked out the windows of the car, scanning the parking lot for anyone that might be watching for him. Then he said to Steph, "Let's get out of here." They pulled out of the parking lot quickly and headed away from the airport.

"Where to?" asked Steph nervously, alternating glances from the road to O'Toole to the rearview mirror and back to the road in rapid succession.

The sheriff had no idea what to say to her in response. He was afraid to go home. He didn't know who or what was there waiting for him. He didn't dare go to town right now for fear of the senator's people seeing him. He turned to face her. "Would you mind if we went to your house?" he asked.

She laughed. "Andy, if you don't mind, I don't mind, honey." She turned left past the high school and headed towards Surfside Beach. She turned off abruptly at a dirt road, and the small car bumped its away along the rutted track. She veered into her driveway, marked by a white mailbox, and turned the car off. They went inside and Andy's feelings of paranoia returned immediately.

"It's like somebody's always watching me," he told her. "I can't shake this feeling."

"I know what you mean, honey," Steph said. "I feel the exact same way and they don't have any idea that I know anything at all." She paused for a moment, thinking. "They don't know, do they Andy?"

Andy was quick to reassure her. "There's no way they could know, Steph." He took her hand in his. "Don't worry, honey. You're safe." He gave her hand a quick squeeze.

She seemed to recover from her fear as she led the way to her front door. They went into the kitchen and Andy dropped his bags on the floor. The kitchen table was empty, save for a salt and pepper shaker, and he took the things he'd taken from the two Carlisle houses and set them on the table. He took out the legal pad containing the notes he'd taken at the library and put it next to the files on the table. "Steph," he asked, "did you say you were off from the bar all day today?"

She nodded.

"All day you have off?" he asked again, trying to make sure.

"Yeah, Andy. I'm free all day. Don't have to be in until tomorrow morning to set up."

"Good," he said. "I need you to do me a favor. Go to Davy Jones' Locker. Get Peter and ask him if he'll come out here to help me go through this stuff. I know the answer's in here somewhere, but I'm not sure where. I've got to figure it out and I could use all the help I can get. I'd call him, but," and he waved his hands to indicate that, because the phones were tapped, that wouldn't work. He was once again taking charge of the situation. It felt good to be calling the shots again.

She agreed and left to get Peter. Andy began to feel the effects of working on no sleep and he went to make coffee. He wanted to work; he needed to work. He had to get to the bottom of this, for his own sake. When the coffee had finished brewing, he poured a cup and then sat down at the table. He sorted through the papers he'd taken from the senator's house, placing those papers he felt had no bearing on what he was looking for in a pile on the floor, while leaving the ones that seemed relevant on the table. When he'd finished that, he looked at his pad of notes that he'd compiled at the library in Waco. He ripped off the pages he'd already written on, exposing a clean sheet, and began to jot down the things he felt were important. He was trying to construct for himself some sort of visual flowchart that would show him exactly what had happened in the life of Jack Carlisle that had led to his murder and, more importantly, the exact nature of his family members' involvement in that crime.

The senator, he had learned, had a reputation for being very conservative in his voting. He'd voted against any and all gun legislation restricting firearms sales. He'd been in favor of allowing prayer in the public schools. He felt that abortion was criminal, and was quoted as saying so. He was also a powerful leader in his church in Waco, holding one of the highest positions within the church that could be given to a layman. Andy suddenly stopped writing; it was like he'd been hit by lightning and had lost the ability to write. He rifled through the sheets of paper he'd taken notes on, remembering something he'd written down. When he found it, he immediately set it to one side and opened Jack Carlisle's journal.

He began to read the young man's writing, words which seemed to carry increasingly more resonance the more he read. Jack's writing was so heartfelt and honest that O'Toole's emotions were mixed. On one hand, O'Toole felt guilty for reading the young man's private thoughts, while on the other hand, he felt horrified and deeply saddened by what was contained within his writing. It was clear that Jack had been struggling with his own feelings of being homosexual for some time and he wrote extensively about his fears of telling his friends and family. He wrote that he'd been carrying on as if he were "normal," as he put it, by keeping a girlfriend, even though he didn't care about her at all. "It's all about social appearances in this family," Jack wrote. O'Toole alternated back and forth between his own notepad, where he was scribbling furiously, and Jack's journal. Andy heard the door behind him open and saw Steph and Peter coming into the kitchen.

The three exchanged no words. Peter and Steph sat at the table and waited for Andy to tell them what to do.

As Peter and Steph sat, Andy reached into his duffel bag and removed the Bible he'd been given in the New Haven airport. He opened to the same chapter of Leviticus that he'd read in the motel room in Waco and read again the words, this time out loud, to Peter and Steph: "If a man also lie with mankind, as he lieth with a woman, both of them have committed an abomination: they shall surely be put to death; their blood shall be upon them."

They looked at him in a sort of awkward silence, unsure as to what it was that had come over the sheriff. "What's that all about?" Peter finally managed to ask.

"It's a verse from the book of Leviticus, Peter. I had to read all of this stuff back when I was a kid in Sunday school," the sheriff explained. "But more importantly to our meeting here, it's the reason young Jack Carlisle was murdered. That, folks, is the motive."

O'Toole looked at the two stunned faces sitting across from him and realized that he'd need to lead them through his entire chart. Andy pushed one of the sheets of paper he'd taken from his notes towards Peter. "Read that," he said. "It's from the notes I took from an article on the good senator. Got that information in Waco." Peter read silently. When he'd finished, he looked up.

"So what?" he asked. "The senator spoke at a conference at Freemont University."

O'Toole's eyes were wide open and bright. "You've never heard of Freemont University, right?" he asked.

Peter shook his head. "Nope," he said.

"Neither had I. But I figured if it caused such an issue with people, that there must be a reason, right? There had to be a reason it made headlines and pissed people off so much. It's just a college, after all. Politicians give talks at schools all the time. Why is this one so controversial?" He was gesticulating wildly with his hands and getting worked up as he spoke. "So I went and looked up some information on the place. There wasn't much, besides the articles on the senator speaking there, but they do have an interesting outlook, I guess you'd say. Here's what I found," he said, pushing a piece of computer printer paper towards Peter.

Peter took the sheet in his hands and read silently. When he'd finished, he looked up. "My God," he said. "So you think the senator believes this garbage?"

O'Toole nodded vigorously. "That and the thing I read you earlier about homosexuality being a deadly sin, yes."

"What's the deal?" Steph asked anxiously, without any idea as to why Freemont University was worthy of such a reaction.

Peter turned to her, reading from the college's own profile: "We at Freemont University feel that it is our duty as educators and administrators to serve God's will in the instruction of our students. To that end, we follow the teachings of Jesus Christ as our one and only savior." He continued to read, citing the university's prohibition against any type of "sinful behavior," including, but not limited to, "any form of alcohol or drug use, fornication or same-gender relationships of an intimate nature."

Steph's face went pale. The reality of the situation had begun to infiltrate her brain, but she still didn't understand the complete relevance of what she was being told. "So you think the senator was so opposed to homosexuality that he would have killed his own son?"

Again the sheriff nodded with enthusiasm.

"But Andy," she said, "that's ridiculous. It can't be that way. For one thing, Jack told me himself that he had never told anyone in his family that he was gay. He said that they'd never accept it."

Andy gave her a very serious look. "I know he told you that, Steph," he said in a low tone. "He told a lot of people that. But read this," he said as he pushed the open journal towards her. "Read the entry for April twenty-first."

Steph took the book and began to read. She looked up at Andy. "He told his parents?" she asked in a quiet voice filled with horrified shock.

Andy nodded slowly. "That's what it says," he replied. He turned to Peter. "He told them at dinner one night. Says they were eating with his brother Richard. He just all of a sudden came out of the closet. Says his mother started crying, father called him a 'goddamn faggot,' told him to get the hell out of the house. Says his brother just sat there. Nobody could believe it." Andy pulled out the piece of paper he'd taken from Richard Carlisle's dresser and passed it to Steph. "Now read that," he said to her.

Steph read the short memo quickly, unable to truly believe what she was thinking. After she'd read it, she passed it to Peter, who read it silently, shaking his head and sighing deeply as he read. "Oh my God," Peter whispered when he'd finished. "They all knew about this whole thing all along. They planned the damn thing, for God's sake. And then they tried to cover it up."

Andy leaned back in his chair. "That's what I'm thinking. I'm thinking these two emailed back and forth, trying to figure out how to cover up the murder." He took a deep breath and exhaled noisily. "It's so easy to see now," he said. "It's plain as day, hiding out there in the broad daylight."

"But wait, Andy," Steph interjected. "If his parents kicked him out of the house and his father reacted that way, why would they allow him to come up here and spend the summer in their house?"

In lieu of an answer, the sheriff opened the journal to the last entry, an entry written several weeks before, from May second, in which Jack wrote that it had been more his parents' idea that he go to Nantucket, as that way he'd be, as Jack wrote, "out of the public spotlight" so that he could "recover" from his "gay phase in life."

As Steph read, tears began to well up in her eyes. She kept thinking of the nice young man that had been Jack Carlisle and what a good friend he'd been to her. She couldn't keep herself from crying as she read about the personal hell that he had endured every day of his life. When she'd finished, she said through the tears, "It's almost like he knew he was never coming back home. It's like he's saying goodbye to everyone." She turned to Peter. "He said he wasn't going to take his journal to Nantucket because he was afraid of what might happen if he did."

"I'm thinking this was all part of their grand plan," O'Toole said. "It's almost like the condemned man walking to the gas chamber. He knows what's coming, but he's forced to go anyway, right on to his death. His parents sent Jack up here to have him killed. And the really tragic thing is that he knew it was coming. He was a human sacrifice."

O'Toole took one of the letters he'd taken from Jack's desk drawer and read to the pair at the table: "You said that you were afraid of what your parents might be capable of. I'd tell you not to worry about it. Parents overreact to things, but I wouldn't worry too much about it." He put the letter down on the table. "This is from someone named Justin. Someone he apparently cared very deeply about."

Steph looked at O'Toole and said, "He mentions parents, as in both of them. Do you think the mother knew this murder plot?"

O'Toole cleared his throat, weighing the idea. "I've been thinking about that, Steph. The truth is, I can't say one way or another, but I can tell you that these files were in Waco, while Senator Carlisle was in Washington. So I can't be sure, but it looks like she might have known, yes."

The table was quiet. The three sat there, completely motionless, each waiting for someone else to say something. Finally Peter broke the silence. "So what do you plan to do now?" he asked in a shaky voice.

Andy looked at the two of them. "I don't know," he said. "I can't very well explain how I got this information." He paused for a moment. "But to tell you the truth, I'm glad you asked, Peter. I've got an idea." He turned to a fresh sheet of paper on the notepad and began to sketch out his newest idea for ensnaring the Carlisles. He mapped out for them what he wanted to do. When he'd finished explaining his plan, Peter let out a huge breath.

"You're crazy, Andy," he said. "You're going to get yourself killed."

Andy smiled grimly, recalling his own characterization of Peter's plan for getting him back to Nantucket as equally crazy. "Not a chance of my getting killed, Peter," he said. "I've got my own plans to keep that from happening. And they're almost as crazy as this one here," he said, indicating the notepad on which he'd just outlined his strategy. "The play's the thing wherein I'll catch the conscience of the king," he said dramatically. "But for the time being, I've got to get some sleep. I'm about to fall over right now." His exhaustion shone through his voice.

With that, Peter said goodbye to Steph and Andy, and headed outside. Steph gave Andy some blankets and a pillow and showed him where everything was. "If you need anything, honey," she said, "you let me know. Anything you want and it's yours."

Andy smiled. "Thanks, gorgeous," he said. "I never could have gotten this far without you." Steph just smiled at him and wished him pleasant dreams. He faded off immediately into the most restful sleep he could remember getting in a long time.

CHAPTER THIRTY-ONE

Andy spent the remainder of the afternoon sleeping on Steph's sofa. He awoke around five in the evening and had to think for a minute before he realized where he was. The house was empty; Steph had apparently gone to do something. He went to the kitchen and drank a glass of ice water. He was still exhausted; his body wasn't used to the abuse he'd been inflicting on it. Back in his twenties he could function quite well on little or no sleep. His sixties, he'd just discovered, were a different story. He shuffled groggily back to the sofa and resumed his position under the comforter. He clicked on the TV and briefly watched "This Week on Nantucket" on the local cable access channel. His eyelids began to drop, and the next thing he knew, it was eight o'clock the following morning.

When he woke up, he didn't want to make it known that he was on the island just yet. He wanted to give himself some time, time to catch Carlisle and his investigators in their own trap. He took his cellular phone and dialed the number for Davy Jones' Locker, and with that single call, the latest phase of his grand plan began to unfold. One of the salespeople at the store answered, and O'Toole asked, very clearly and distinctly, to speak to Peter Oswald. When Peter came on the line, Andy said to him in very deliberate words, "Peter, it's Andy O'Toole. I've been over on the Cape for a few days. Figured I'd take some time off. You know, the whole investigation thing and all. Anyway, I was hoping you'd meet me at the airport. I left my car out there, and I'm afraid I left the lights on, so the battery'll be dead by the time I get there."

Per the prearranged plan, Peter agreed to meet him at the airport, as Andy had instructed him to do the night before, and asked him what time he expected to arrive. Andy looked at his watch. It was now nine-thirty. A Cape Air flight was be due to leave Boston in twenty minutes. "I'm on the 9:50 Cape Air flight," he said. "I should be in Nantucket by about ten-forty-five, eleven at the latest."

Peter agreed to meet him at the airport and said that Andy should come out to meet him, as he didn't want to fight for a parking space. Andy hung up the phone. "See you there, you bastards," he said out loud. He rode with Steph to the Jib and Jenny and then walked across the street to the Town Building. His heartbeat was racing and he tried desperately to calm himself down. *Nothing to worry about,* he kept telling himself. Remember. *You were on the Cape, just for a few days, just to clear your head. Nothing else. Nothing to worry about. Act natural.*

He walked up the stairs to his office and opened the door with a trembling hand. Claudia was not at her desk, which he thought was strange, but nothing really surprised him at this point. He sat down at his desk, lit a cigarette and picked up the phone on his desk. He fingers were shaking uncontrollably as he dialed Tim Hawkins' office extension.

"Tim Hawkins," the voice said. O'Toole sensed a great deal of self-assurance in Hawkins' voice.

"Tim, it's Andy. I wanted to let you know I was back at the office. Totally refreshed. Went over to the Cape and took a little vacation. Feel much better," he said. "My taking some time off was the best idea you've had since I've known you," he added, trying to sound grateful to the selectman. "It was one of the most relaxing times I've had in my life," he lied. Relaxed was the absolute opposite of how he truly felt.

"Andy?" Hawkins asked in a shocked tone. "Where are you?"

Andy wanted to laugh. He bit his bottom lip so as not to, and said, "I'm up in my office, Tim." Then, in a tone of mock confusion, "Where'd you think I was?" He knew where Tim thought he was. Tim thought he was on a plane over the Atlantic headed back to Nantucket. No doubt to meet with an unfortunate accident upon finding his car booted for no apparent reason.

"Oh," Tim said, recovering his composure for the moment. "I just didn't realize you were downstairs. Listen," he said, "I've got great news." He sounded as if he were scrambling for words. "Why don't you come up to my office and talk to me."

"Be right there," the sheriff replied. Andy hung up the phone and crushed out the cigarette in the ashtray on his desk. He walked slowly to Hawkins' office, passing a surprised looking receptionist along the way. He smiled to her and told her to have a nice day.

He knocked on the door of Tim's office and Hawkins called for him to come in. As he walked in, he could tell that Hawkins had not been expecting this meeting. The look on his face told O'Toole that much. The two men shook hands. "You look great, Andy," said Hawkins in an unsure and quavering voice. "Where'd you end up going?"

Andy smiled. *Watch the little monkey dance.* "Went over to Boston first. Took a flight over there, figured I'd catch a Sox game. Couldn't get a ticket, though. You know how it is when your team's winning. Everybody's a fan all of a sudden." He laughed. "So I hopped on a bus down to Connecticut. I've got some friends live in New Haven." It wasn't a total lie; he did have friends in New Haven, the thought of whom had originallyprompted his idea of flying there. "Spent a night with them catching up and all. It was nice to see 'em. Haven't seen them since," he thought, "since I don't even remember when. Anyway, I rented a car in New Haven, figured I'd drive up the coast. Stopped off along the way in a few spots. Hit the Sandycove Clam place in Harwich Port." He tried to add some emphasis to the fact that he'd gone to Sandycove, and just for reinforcement added, "You know that place with the radio jingle? I'd been hearing about the place for so long, but I'd never been there, so I figured I'd give it a shot—damn good fried clams, if I do say so myself." He paused to look at Hawkins, who was staring straight at O'Toole in complete disbelief. "Finally got back to Hyannis this morning, caught the early boat over and here I am." He waited to see if the story was going to work.

Hawkins looked shaken and stunned. It was as if someone had just punched him very hard in the stomach. "Sounds like you had yourself a time," he finally managed to say.

"Absolutely," replied Andy, gaining confidence. His plan was working just like he'd written it down. Hawkins was on the ropes, ready to collapse. He was just waiting for his manager to throw in the towel and end this battle royal. "Best trip I've had in quite a while. Thanks again for the suggestion," he said.

"My pleasure," Hawkins replied meekly.

"Now what's this great news you've got for me?" he asked, trying to sound enthusiastic and interested. Truth be told, he really was interested in the news. He wanted to see what these monsters had created as the "real" truth. But more than anything, he wanted to move in for the kill. He wanted to expose the Carlisle family and Hawkins and whomever else had been in involved in this massive cover-up.

The selectman looked around the office, hoping for something, anything, to help him figure out this whole situation. O'Toole had supposedly gone to Waco. The senator had told him that. He'd told Hawkins that they'd tapped his phones and were monitoring his cellular calls. When Hawkins had suggested that might not be totally legal or ethical, the senator assured him it was for the sheriff's own protection, so Hawkins hadn't bothered with any other protests. He went along with the senator because he needed his support. He'd most definitely need public support from a major figure after this investigation in order to keep the tourists coming. But at this moment, he didn't know what was going on. He figured he'd try to call the sheriff's bluff. "So you had yourself some clams in Harwich Port?" he asked, trying to sound interested in the sheriff's vacation.

O'Toole's entire inside lit up. *Gotcha',* he thought to himself with a self-satisfaction he had never known before. "Yep," replied the sheriff nonchalantly, secretly glad Hawkins had taken the bait. "Real good ones, too." He fished into his pocket and brought out the receipt from the clams he'd purchased. Looking closely at the receipt, he remarked with a tone of humor in his voice, "A little expensive, though, I have to say. Seven bucks for a little order of clams." He shook his head. "What's this world coming to?" He thrust the receipt onto the selectman's desk, allowing Hawkins to see that, in fact, he had eaten at the Sandycove Clam Shack. "Look at how expensive they were," he said as he slid one finger towards the price written in at the bottom of the receipt, keeping another finger near the hand-written date.

Hawkins looked down at the receipt and noticed the date next to O'Toole's finger. June ninth was the date written on the receipt in the blank provided for that information. The senator had informed him that Andy was breaking into the Carlisle home in Waco, Texas, on June ninth, and Hawkins' eyes widened briefly. Andy noticed it and knew that he'd hit the mark. He mentally congratulated himself for having the foresight to tell the woman at Sandycove the wrong date. *Gotcha' again. You just fell for the oldest trick in the book. Like taking candy from a baby,* he told himself.

"That's nice," said the selectman in a stunned voice. "Real nice." He most definitely didn't think it was real nice. It was a huge problem, in fact. Now he was stuck. He didn't know why the senator had been so concerned about O'Toole and his whereabouts, but now it didn't matter. Andy had been in Harwich Port, not in Waco. Not even close to the state of Texas, for that matter. He tried to mentally shift gears. "So about that good news," he began, desperately trying to change the subject. "It seems that the senator's guys have figured out the mystery here." He tried to smile.

"That's great," Andy said, again with feigned enthusiasm. "Who did it?"

"It seems you were right all along, Andy," Hawkins said. "McKenzie thought it would be fun to go out and mess with one of the waiters from the Collins House. He thought they were all gay, so he sat across the street one night and watched Jack Carlisle come out with a few of his co-workers. They went down to the Jib and Jenny and McKenzie followed them there. The other guys in the group left after a while, but Jack stayed behind. McKenzie was sitting there with Bordham and he pointed to Jack standing at the end of the bar. Charlie knows the kid from working at the Collins House. So Bordham was a little drunk and he walked out the back door of the Jib and Jenny. Set up a little ambush back there. He grabbed the Carlisle kid, strangled him, then took him out and dumped him at the fog horn. Used one of his own weight belts to make him sink. That's what we figure, anyway." Then his tone suddenly changed to one of defiance. "Son of a bitch lost his guts and killed himself before we—I mean you—could arrest him. So we got McKenzie as an accessory and Bordham as the murderer, even though he's already dead."

Andy nodded as he noted the ferocity with which Hawkins both defended his version of the story and his verbal harangue of Bordham. "So Latkin decided it was a suicide after all? With Bordham, I mean."

"Yep," said the selectman nervously. "Found powder burns on his hand, fingerprints on the gun, the whole she-bang. Cut and dried suicide." He sat motionless in his chair, looking straight at Andy. "Oh, yeah," he added after a moment. "Latkin also found Jack's bracelet, I think he said it was elephant hair. Bordham must have left it on the kid's body when he cut off his hands. Latkin said something about giving it to one of Jack's brothers." He hadn't been told why that was important, but he had been told to be absolutely sure to tell O'Toole specifically about an elephant hair bracelet, and he was in the mindset to do exactly as he was told when one of the senator's people told him to do it.

O'Toole listened in silence as the selectman related the story of Jack Carlisle's murder and Bordham's suicide. He nodded occasionally, indicating that he was following the story. He didn't believe a word of it, with the exception of the fact that Bordham and McKenzie had been involved. His investigation wasn't finished yet; he knew that. Not quite finished, anyway.

He finally said to Hawkins, "That's great, Tim. I'm really glad we've finally gotten this whole mystery dealt with and solved. Now we can get on with the business of summer. By the way, how are the Carlisles doing?" He knew how they were doing. Hell, he'd just seen Richard a few nights ago. He knew the senator was out in Washington and that his wife was up on the cliff and that Richard was in Waco, all of them praying to God that the sheriff was lying dead somewhere, the victim of an apparent random shooting. Or perhaps a timely suicide. No note, of course. Just a medical examiner's report listing the cause of death as suicide. Or maybe killed by a deranged tow-truck driver called to help out a motorist at the airport whose car had mistakenly been disabled.

"They're doing as well as you'd expect, I guess," Hawkins replied.

Andy smiled. "That's good to hear, Tim." He looked at his watch. "I guess I better get going," he said. "Been away too long. Feels like it's been a month," he said. "I need to get back to work and start earning my paycheck." He winked and turned to leave. He walked back down to his office, closed the door behind him and sat at the desk. He lit a cigarette, thinking about what to do next.

So the bastards got to Latkin, he thought to himself. *I wonder what they threatened him with.* He hadn't fully expected the story about the confirmation of Bordham's suicide. Looking back on it, he should have known it was coming, but he hadn't planned for it. But it wasn't going to derail this train. He was going full-steam ahead, and in his mind there was no stopping him.

He didn't dare call the doctor. There was no telling what these people might do if he tried to contact anyone involved with the investigation. He felt like a prisoner. He needed to get into the doctor's office, though, somehow. He walked slowly down the stairs and out the door. He crossed the street to Davy Jones' Locker and entered the store. Peter was standing behind the counter, arguing with an angry customer who felt that the merchandise he had purchased was defective. Peter looked at the hat the customer had bought, threw it in the trash box next to the counter and told the man to get a new one. Andy walked up to the counter.

"Nice stuff you're pushing here, Oswald," he said smiling, glad to have a reason to show happiness.

Peter pulled the hat from the trash. "Nothing wrong with this," he said laughing. He put the hat on his head and part of the brim hung down where it had separated from the rest of the hat.

Andy looked around. "Peter," he said in a hushed tone, "you ever wanted to dress up and play cops and robbers?"

Peter removed the hat and returned it to the trash, then looked at the sheriff and raised his eyebrows. "What are you talking about now, Andy?"

Andy quietly explained his plan to Peter and asked him if he'd help. Peter laughed nervously and finally agreed to do it. "If I get caught, though, your ass is mine," he added. O'Toole assured him he wouldn't get caught, and if he did, he'd take the blame for it. He thanked Peter and walked next door to the Jib and Jenny. Steph was behind the bar, looking at a newspaper that was spread out in front of her.

When he walked in, she looked up and smiled. "Andy," she said. "Long time no see," and winked. "Little early to start on the Jameson's, but I guess it's as good a time as any."

Andy laughed softly. "No thanks, hon. Not just yet." He explained to her what he had planned and asked her if she would be willing to help. When he'd finished, she looked around at the bar.

"Andy, honey, if it'll help you out, I'll do it. And if it'll help you figure out who killed my friend, then you better believe I'll do it." She gave O'Toole a big smile, reached across the bar and hugged him.

"Thanks, Steph. You're one in a million, you sweet thing," he said. "One more thing," he added. "Would you call me a cab? I've got a feeling my car's probably drivable by now."

CHAPTER THIRTY-TWO

Andy got to the airport and found, to no surprise of his, that the boot had miraculously been removed from the wheel of his car. He went inside the terminal to the pay phones and dialed the number for the car rental agency from whom he'd rented the car in New Haven. A man's voice answered and O'Toole read the contract information to him. He explained that he'd been unexpectedly called away from lunch at the Sandycove Clam Shack in Harwich Port, Massachusetts, and that he'd left the car in the parking lot there, with the keys still in the ignition. He apologized for the inconvenience and told the clerk to charge him whatever fees were applicable. He hung up quickly before the young man had a chance to ask anything else.

He went back to his car and drove to his office. He needed to play the part of the sheriff for the rest of the day. He didn't need anybody thinking he knew anything. He wanted to seem as naïve as the average person on the street. He wanted everyone involved with his daily activities to think that he believed the story; to do that he would have to pretend that everything was as it should be. In his office, he shuffled papers around nervously, read and re-read reports that had sat on his desk for months and paced the floor. He tried to make the time pass, but it went by agonizingly slowly. Finally, the clock tower struck five o'clock and he felt like he should go home. He needed to keep up appearances. He drove to his house slowly, going over in his mind what he would be doing in a few hours. When he got home, he felt suspicious, his earlier paranoia returning in full force. He felt like someone was in the house, or had been recently. He walked through every room, opened every closet, looked everywhere, but found nothing out of the ordinary. It looked just as it had when he'd last been there. He opened the refrigerator, looking for something to eat, but found nothing. He figured he'd just eat later at Peter's house.

He went to his bedroom closet and opened the door. He took out his dress uniform from the Sheriff's Department and slowly changed into it. Official looking appearance was paramount to the success of the next part of his plan. The tan shirt was stiff against his collar and the pants felt somehow alien to his body. He pinned his service badge to his shirt over his left breast pocket. He looked in the mirror on the wall and said to his reflection, "O'Toole. Sheriff Andy O'Toole, Nantucket Sheriff's Department." He hoped it would work. *Just this one last time,* he prayed silently like a drunk suffering through a hangover. *Just let me get through this one, God, and we'll call it even.*

He sorted through the clothes hanging in front of him, pushing the hangers to one end of the rod running the length of the closet. There, in the far corner, were two of his old uniforms from his days as an officer of the Nantucket Police Department. He hadn't taken them out in years, but they looked clean, having spent the last several years wrapped in plastic from the dry cleaner's. *Thank God they didn't change these things,* he thought to himself. The officers of the day still wore the same light blue uniform shirts that they'd worn when Andy was on the force.

He took the shirts off their hangers and went back to his car outside. He put the shirts in the back seat, laying them gently on the seat to avoid putting any creases in them. Every detail was vital now. He needed all the details to be in perfect order for him to be able to pull off what he had to admit to himself was the weakest link in the plan's chain. He got in and drove through the early evening glow, down the road to Polpis to the house of Peter Oswald. When he pulled up the long driveway, he saw that Steph was already there. He grabbed the shirts from the back seat and approached the house. He walked up the steps to the front porch, opened the screen door and stuck his head in. "Peter?" he called.

"Yeah, Andy. Come on in," Peter's voice replied from inside. O'Toole walked in and found Steph and Peter, together with Peter's wife, in the living room watching the news. The lead story was on the investigation of the murder of Jack Carlisle, and the news agencies were announcing that the case had been solved. The story was verbatim the one he'd gotten from Tim Hawkins.

"Peter," Andy said, "you got any food in the kitchen? I haven't eaten all day." Peter pointed to the kitchen and told him to help himself. Peter, meanwhile, remained glued to the television, watching Senator Carlisle, who had flown in from Washington specifically for the occasion, together with his family, express their collective gratitude to the investigators and to Tim Hawkins, who had facilitated the capture of the guilty parties. Hawkins was standing next to the family, beaming with pride at his accomplishments. Andy found some deli meat wrapped in white paper in the refrigerator and made a sandwich. He ate it quickly, because he wanted to get on with the work of the evening. When he'd finished, he returned to the living room.

"Do you believe this, Andy?" asked Peter. "They're not giving you any credit for the work you did. You solved this case yourself and these people just used your evidence to prove it, but they're not giving you any credit at all." Then he added in a tone of growing anger, "And it's not even the whole truth."

Andy nodded grimly. "Don't worry, my boy. Like I told you before, I promise you I'll be in the news before too long. Not to worry. I'll have my day in the spotlight." He handed the shirts to Peter and Steph. "Put those on. Don't worry if they don't fit perfectly. Hopefully the guy at the hospital won't notice anything." Steph went to the bathroom to change, while Peter put the shirt on while he sat on the sofa. He looked up at Andy, standing above him.

"You think this'll work?" Peter asked doubtfully.

"Of course, Peter. I'm sure it'll work," O'Toole said. Steph returned wearing O'Toole's old shirt. It didn't even come close to fitting her, and she was shaking her head in disbelief that Andy thought this was even remotely possible.

"This looks ridiculous, Andy," she said.

"No, Steph, you look fine," the sheriff said, trying to sound confident. "It'll be fine. Bring another shirt with you, both of you, and you can change in the car after we're done. Nobody will find out, I promise. Besides, when you're changing, I'll close my eyes," he said to Steph.

"Makes one of us," Peter said coyly. His wife looked at him and groaned.

"I'm off to bed, you guys," she told the trio of would-be cops in her living room. "Be careful out there, whatever it is you're up to." She kissed Peter goodnight and made her way upstairs to bed.

Peter, Steph and Andy went out to O'Toole's car and drove in silence to the hospital. The tension in the car was thick, and all of the passengers could feel it. The radio weather report said to expect fog on the Cape and islands, especially on Nantucket. O'Toole pulled into the Cottage Hospital parking lot and parked the car. He turned off the ignition. Turning around so that he could face both Steph and Peter as he spoke, he said, "Now, everybody knows what we're doing, right? We know what we're looking for?" Steph and Peter both nodded. They'd gone over it and they knew. They just wanted to get on with it and get this whole operation done with.

The three walked together into the hospital, O'Toole in the lead. He carried a small leather briefcase with him. Andy presented his badge and identification. "I'm Sheriff Andy O'Toole. I'm with the Nantucket Sheriff's Department. This is officer Watson," he said, pointing at Peter, "and this is officer Brantley," motioning towards Steph. "We need to get into the morgue, if you don't mind. Official business." The young man at the desk seemed surprised to see the officers. Nobody had told him about any official business. "It's in relation to the Carlisle case," O'Toole added, trying to lend an air of authority to the request. Steph and Peter turned their backs to the young man in hopes of preventing him from studying their faces too closely.

The young man looked up at the assembled trio. They looked official enough. They were dressed like cops and the one who said he was the sheriff showed him a badge. Besides, he wasn't paid enough to screen visitors when he wasn't told they were coming, especially when they were cops. He asked them to sign in. O'Toole scratched a signature onto the paper. It could have been O'Toole, if you'd known what you were looking for, but it clearly wasn't his regular signature. Peter and Steph signed in as Mark Watson and Christine Brantley, respectively, which had been O'Toole's suggestion. No need, he'd said, to use your real names, just in case they come looking for us. The young man pointed down the hall in the direction of the morgue. "It's down there," he said casually, returning his gaze to the magazine that he'd been reading.

"Thanks, I know where it is," Andy said. He led Peter and Steph down the long corridor to the door of the morgue. "Right in here," he called over his shoulder, then silently turned to the left and entered the office of Doctor Tom Latkin, motioning for the other two to follow him. They left the lights turned off. Instead, O'Toole opened his briefcase and took out two flashlights, giving one to Oswald. He went immediately to the file cabinet in the corner while Peter scanned the desk and Steph stayed by the door, listening for anyone who might be curious to learn what they were doing. They worked methodically and the whole operation was going smoothly. In the file cabinet, Andy found the files for Jack Carlisle and Charlie Bordham. He opened them both and removed all the papers inside. He rolled them up and slid them into the briefcase and fastened it shut, then signaled for Peter to come with him.

Five minutes, in and out. The operation had gone far better than any of them had dared to hope. It went just like they'd planned. But they still had to get out and get back to Peter's house. And, assuming they got that far, they still had to figure out if there was any information in the reports that would be worth the risk they'd just taken.

Steph slowly opened the office door and peered out. The hallway was empty. They slid out the door, carefully shutting it behind them, and walked slowly back down the hallway. O'Toole expressed his thanks to the young man at the front desk and told him that he appreciated his cooperation. The young man nodded without looking up at them. They slowly walked out the door of the hospital and, when they heard the door close behind them, they simultaneously broke into a sprint to O'Toole's car. They got in and Andy started the engine, accelerating out of the parking lot quickly. On the way back to Polpis, Steph and Peter changed back into the shirts they'd brought with them and crumpled up the police uniforms they'd borrowed from Andy.

Andy tried to remain calm as he drove, but his heart was pounding furiously in his chest. He just hoped that the information he needed was somewhere in those files. The fog had rolled in thick and blanket-like, and Andy drove slowly through the thick mist. He continually looked back, but saw only the grey cloud they'd traveled through. Back at Peter's house, the trio hurried inside and went to the kitchen. O'Toole threw his briefcase on the table and unloaded the files he'd taken. He laid the medical examiner's reports out on the kitchen table and they began the laborious process of scouring over them.

The report on top, the one stamped "official" across it in big black letters, listed the cause of death of Jack Carlisle as a murder by strangulation. It listed a black elephant hair bracelet as being the only personal effect found on the body. "Bullshit," he said out loud to the report. He read over the other "official" report on the death of Charlie Bordham, which listed the cause of death as suicide, single gunshot to the head. Powder burns and GSR were indicated as having been on the deceased's hands. No mention was made of the red marks that Latkin had initially seen when he'd been there with O'Toole. Andy noticed that the signatures on both reports looked different, but beyond that, there was nothing to suggest any sort of tampering with the evidence. After all, both reports had the official seal of approval. The rest of the papers in the files made no sense to the sheriff, as they consisted primarily of medical terms and jargon, none of which he understood.

O'Toole finally sighed in resignation. "I guess they covered it all up," he said. "The bastards got away with it."

His earlier exuberance deflated immediately and he slumped over the table in despair. There was nothing in any of these papers that proved anything. The cover-up was complete, and he'd asked his friends to risk so much for nothing. He was on the verge of apologizing to them for putting them in such a potentially dangerous situation for nothing, when he made eye contact with Peter, who grinned back at him, his eyes wide and bright.

"I don't think so," he said confidently. He pushed across the table some of the papers he'd taken from Latkin's office, papers that he had been silently reading over while O'Toole was checking out the examiner's reports.

They were memos to Latkin from some unnamed source, but O'Toole, as he read them, knew immediately who they were from. One said briefly, "You found an elephant hair bracelet on Jack Carlisle's body." Another gave Latkin the "corrected" information for the cause of death for Charlie Bordham: "You found evidence of powder burns and GSR on right hand. Investigators found deceased's fingerprints on the trigger of gun. Marks on wrist were caused by wetsuit cuffs, which is a common condition with frequent scuba divers. Perhaps marks were from latex gloves from dishwashing. Regardless of source, no need to mention in report. Please make appropriate changes and resubmit." O'Toole looked at Peter.

"This is good," he said. "Very good. But it's not going to be enough. This doesn't quite prove it."

Peter smiled again and produced another stack of papers. "This does, though." He passed the copies of Latkin's initial medical reports, the ones the doctor had originally submitted to the investigators, across the table to the sheriff. "Found 'em in the garbage," Peter said. "I guess the good doctor didn't realize who he was dealing with. He didn't know that we were all a bunch of pirates that would go looking through his trash to find what we wanted." He leaned back in his chair with a sigh of satisfaction. "He should have bought a paper-shredder. I think we sell them, too," he added with a haughty laugh.

Andy scanned the reports. There, in Tom Latkin's own handwriting, were his original and truthful findings regarding the examinations of both bodies. No personal effects found on Jack Carlisle's dead body and Bordham's death had been ruled a "possible homicide of questionable circumstances" by Latkin. Andy was glad to see that on these reports the signatures looked identical. These, together with the revised reports and the memos, combined to give him enough evidence to prove it. This was what he'd been looking for. This was the real smoking gun. The evidence all finally added up and the trail that the various facts created led right to the senator himself. The sheriff smiled, exposing his teeth. "We've got them," he said softly. "We've really, really got them."

The only question remaining was how to proceed. It would be impossible to present any of this as evidence. All of it had been obtained illegally, and Andy was risking a lot if he made any of it public. "What now, Andy?" asked Peter. "We know what happened, but there's no way to tell anybody else."

Andy sat back in his chair, temporarily lost in thought, and then he looked at Peter and smiled. "Like you said, Peter. They don't know who they're dealing with." He folded his hands behind his head and smiled. "They don't have the first clue as to who they're dealing with."

He pushed back from the table and found, sitting on the kitchen counter, a copy of a recent newspaper, a large black-and-white photograph of Carlisle's smiling face gracing the front page. He returned to the table and put the newspaper flat, Senator Carlisle's image looking up at them. He pulled his briefcase closer to him and removed his own Bible from the interior, the leather cover of the old book dried and creased. He flipped through the pages, intently scanning the words. He stopped on one page and looked straight at Peter and Steph. Casting a last glance towards the table and seeing again the photograph, he cackled an evil laugh laced with hatred for the visage.

"Vengeance is Mine, and recompense; their foot shall slip in due time; for the day of their calamity is at hand, and the things to come hasten upon them. For the Lord will judge his people and have compassion on his servants, when He sees that their power is gone, and there is no one remaining, bond or free," he read. "Deuteronomy, chapter thirty-two, verses thirty-two to thirty-six," he explained. He closed the Bible solemnly and softly placed it on the table in front of him. He let out another satisfied laugh. "Pirates were known for getting revenge, weren't they Peter?" he asked.

O'Toole looked up at him and smiled. "I think that's right, Andy," he said.

The sheriff nodded his head. "I think this whole pirate thing is growing on me, Peter," he said.

He turned his eyes to the picture on the front page of the paper. Focusing on those eyes that seemed so full of happiness, he felt the need for revenge, the need to be God for just a moment, growing inside. "Pucker up, you bastard, and get ready to start kissing," he muttered at the picture bitterly. He crumpled the paper noisily and threw it in to the trash basket. He turned again to Peter. "I think I'm going to like being a pirate," he said. "I'm going to like it a lot."

CHAPTER THIRTY-THREE

On January sixth, the United States Congress convened during the official opening ceremony following the Christmas recess, as prescribed by the United States Constitution. In the Senate chamber, there was much pomp and circumstance, and the galley of onlookers overflowed with friends and family on hand to see the swearing in of the new senators. The senators paraded in two-by-two, each wearing a small blue silk ribbon pinned into a loop in remembrance of Jack Carlisle. The senators wanted to show their support for Leonard Carlisle. Partisan affiliation aside, they knew he was going through an emotional and difficult time and they wanted to show their support in unison for their colleague. After the formal ceremony, a crowd of reporters gathered outside the Capitol building. A story was breaking and each network wanted to be the first to report it. Rumors were running rampant all over the country and everyone anxiously waited to hear how Senator Carlisle would respond to the allegations.

As Leonard Carlisle descended the stairs of the Senate building, he was mobbed. "Senator, how do you respond to the allegations that you arranged for the murder of your son?" one reporter shouted at him.

"I have no idea what you're talking about, sir," the senator replied gruffly. "My son was killed in a heinous act of criminal violence by a deranged monster, and I would appreciate it if you would let the topic rest."

"But Senator," the reporter shouted, "we've got evidence of a cover-up, sir. The evidence points the finger at you and your family. There's evidence that you planned it, sir."

Carlisle tried to ignore the reporters, though his face indicated that perhaps he was worried, or even frightened, by the reporter's questions. "That's patently ridiculous," he spat at the offending interrogator.

He finally managed to push his way through the crowds to the sanctuary of his private office. Once inside, he took a moment to gather himself together and tried to calm his nerves, which were suddenly very much on edge. His secretary buzzed him, telling him his wife was on the phone for him.

"Hello, honey," he said into the phone, relieved to be able to talk to someone not peppering him with accusations, but at the same time worried about why she would call him at the office, and on the first day of the new session of all times.

"Leonard," she screamed in to the phone. "I'm at the townhouse. Turn on the television. Oh my God, Leonard."

As soon as he'd heard her voice, the senator knew something was very wrong. And he had a feeling of dread, a feeling that he knew exactly what was so wrong. Worse, the information was apparently now public knowledge. His heart began to pound in his chest and he began to sweat. Carlisle's stomach was doing somersaults as he turned on the small television he kept tuned to the twenty-four hour world news channel. When the picture was illuminated on the small screen, it was as if he suddenly had tunnel vision that magnified whatever it was he looked at. The television set became the dominant figure in Carlisle's sight; the rest of the world instantly melted away to black.

He went pale when he heard the reporter reading his son's journal, describing Jack's emotional battle with coming to grips with his own homosexuality and the fear he had about telling his parents. The reporter went on to read about Jack's telling his family that he was gay, and of his father's less-than-civil response to the news. The anchor continued, saying that evidence of a cover-up had come to light, including evidence suggesting that Senator Carlisle had used his authority to bring in his own investigators, who had apparently changed official police and medical reports.

All of this information, the anchor said, had been mailed to the network in a package of documents, including copies of both the original and the forged reports, copies of entries from Jack's personal journal and memos exchanged between Richard and Leonard Carlisle, memos that discussed the murder and subsequent cover-up they'd planned. The package, the anchor continued, had been mailed by an anonymous source. The postmark on the package was from Chicago, but there was no other information that the network had gleaned as to the identity of the person or people who had mailed the parcel.

No individual or group had come forward claiming responsibility, which had led to much speculation regarding Carlisle's political enemies as potential culprits. The only lead in the attempt to discover the sender's identity, beyond the Chicago postmark, was a Biblical reference at the beginning of the letter included with the documents contained in the parcel.

The author of the letter had typed the following passage from the eighth chapter of the book of Psalms: "Out of the mouth of babes and sucklings hast thou ordained strength because of thine enemies, that thou mightest still the enemy and the avenger."

"Some experts are speculating," said the anchorman, "that the anonymous sender had a beef against Senator Carlisle and perhaps had some sort of Biblical teaching or an otherwise religious motivation. There are theories that it was a disgruntled constituent who felt that Senator Carlisle was a traitor, of sorts, for not practicing the very things his own voters supported."

"Oh God," Carlisle said into the phone, his brain seemingly incapable of completely processing all the disastrous information that he was being presented with at this very moment.

"Leonard, it's on every station," his wife cried into the phone. "Every channel is saying the same thing. They're saying that you and Richard planned Jack's murder. That you covered it up. They know things, Leonard. Things about the family," she sobbed hysterically. "They know you did it," she added with an air of finality.

Carlisle was silent as he watched his political future, his entire life for that matter, unravel before him on the television screen. Outside the office, he could hear his secretary answering the phone, which was ringing constantly. The news reporter on the television screen was talking about "social appearances," reading again from Jack's journal. Everything Carlisle had planned so carefully, every last detail, was unfolding before his eyes in a quagmire of personal disaster. He'd stopped paying attention to the voice on the television; he'd heard what he needed to hear. The rest of the words were just nails in the coffin.

He told his wife he'd call her back and immediately dialed Richard's cellular phone number. Richard picked it up. "You watching the news, sport?" Carlisle asked sullenly.

"Yes, sir, *jefe*," Richard replied in a quiet voice with a tone that mirrored his father's. "I am." Both men were silent.

"It's over," the senator said into the phone, his voice emotionless and laden with the dull aftereffects of an intense shock. "We're all finished."

Epilogue

It was April on Nantucket, a time of new beginnings. Stores and restaurants that had been closed for the winter began to reopen as business owners started to gear-up for the coming summer tourist season. The first flowers of the season were blooming and the winter chill, though still present in the air, wasn't nearly as bitter as it had been in February. The days were getting longer, and more and more people were venturing into town. The previous summer had been a record one for Peter Oswald, as Davy Jones' Locker had far exceeded any previous summer's sales totals. He was hoping for another record this summer, though in the back of his mind he still harbored thoughts about the previous year's events, thoughts which occasionally took over the forefront of his thinking, blocking out those visions of record-breaking sales figures. It had been the talk of the island for the duration of the winter, as stories were traded back and forth by people in bars and restaurants, and by people sitting at their kitchen tables. Peter had chosen, though, to remain silent, preferring to keep the information regarding his own involvement a mystery to anyone who didn't already know the extent of it.

Following the Carlisle fiasco, Andy O'Toole had resigned his office as sheriff in July, a few days after the town's annual Fourth of July celebration. He'd cited irreconcilable differences with the town officials as his reason for leaving. He'd cashed in his life savings, sold his house and car, and left the island. Nobody had heard from him, though he'd told Peter he was going to get himself a motor home and drive around the country. He and his wife had planned to do it when he'd retired, but he'd scrapped the plans after her death. He said now, though, that he thought it would be a nice change for him.

Tim Hawkins remained in his position as Chairman of the Board of Selectmen, though he was not so widely supported by the residents of Nantucket as he once had been. He was coming up for re-election at the local Town Meeting the following April, and he had begun to focus his attention on what he might do if he were not successful in his bid for the office, a proposition that seemed more and more realistic with every passing day and with every new revelation about his involvement in the cover-up. The fact that he wasn't facing criminal charges was nothing short of a favor from the DA's office. He'd promised full cooperation and disclosure of what had gone down behind closed doors in meetings with Carlisle.

The newspapers had reported the story of Leonard and Richard Carlisle, and told how they had worked together with two local Nantucketers to murder and dispose of Jack Carlisle. It was said that the senator had learned of his son's homosexuality and became worried that he would be unable to continue his political dealings with the religious conservatives that he had always counted on for votes if the news was made known.

Because of this intense fear of public exposure regarding his son's sexual orientation, the reports read, the senator had arranged for his son Richard to contact Jamie McKenzie, a sort of handyman on Nantucket, and solicit the murder. McKenzie, it was revealed, had worked for a time as the Carlisle family's off-season caretaker, performing basic repairs to their Nantucket summer house in the winter. Speculation was rampant that the senator's motives were not only political. Many a pundit opined that the murder was simply a matter of sweeping the dirt under the rug. One commentator referred to it as "hiding the insane uncle in the attic."

McKenzie, upon learning of the new evidence, confirmed the basics of the story, saying he had been offered a million dollars to murder Jack Carlisle. He'd been unwilling to do it himself, but he'd arranged to have it done by one of his drinking buddies, Charlie Bordham; he'd agreed to give Bordham half the money. Details were slow in coming from McKenzie, but gradually the full story of the crime emerged. Days after the murder, Bordham had been sitting in the Jib and Jenny when he'd heard someone mention that Will Paterna was a prime suspect in the early stages of the investigation. He had proceeded to take Jack's severed head to Paterna's house as a way of throwing investigators off his trail. He had driven with Jamie McKenzie to the house and waited while McKenzie had stayed hidden in the bushes, waiting for an opportunity to plant the evidence. Once that opportunity presented itself, McKenzie had placed Jack's head in a trash bag, covering it with several fish carcasses that were already in the bag, then tied it shut and fled the premises.

Additionally, McKenzie told authorities that he was sure that Bordham had not committed suicide; McKenzie was convinced that Senator Carlisle had ordered the killing after finding out that Bordham was being sought by the authorities. This accusation was corroborated by phone records taken from the Carlisle home on Nantucket, records which indicated that calls had been made to an unlisted cellular phone number belonging to one of the investigators on the Carlisle team just before and after the estimated time of death of Mr. Bordham. Investigations into the cellular records indicated that the person the senator had called had, in fact, been on Nantucket at the time of the calls. McKenzie also added that he had feared for his own life following his arrest, but had been assured by one of Senator Carlisle's investigators that he would be well paid in exchange for keeping his mouth shut regarding his link to the Carlisle family.

Doctor Tom Latkin, in his report to the prosecutor's office, admitted that he had been approached by men who were connected to the senator who told him that he would need to change his reports regarding the autopsy reports on both Jack Carlisle and Charlie Bordham. When he'd refused—citing his own professional qualifications as reason enough to believe his opinion—he was bypassed. He'd been oblivious to any new autopsy reports; he said they must have been inserted into the files without his knowledge. As for the report's findings, he was quite critical. He'd been quoted in one newspaper as saying that he found especially bizarre the contention regarding the source of the marks he'd found on Bordham's wrists. "Wetsuit cuffs? Latex gloves? If either of those were around that man's wrists tight enough to make those marks, he wouldn't have had hands for very long," he told a reporter. When pressed further he said, "It's the kind of thing that if I were to say it, they'd laugh me out the door. But when the Feds come up with it, it's brilliant. When you get right down to it, though, their theories about wetsuits and gloves are absolute hogwash." This time his opinion was accepted as gospel truth.

Authorities were interested in talking to the various members of Carlisle's personal investigators, but none came forward. The senator had been careful to conceal their respective identities, and by the time the story had broken about the cover-up, they had dispersed from Nantucket and gone to parts unknown. Several news sources called it one of the most extensive and well-executed cover-ups since the Watergate scandal.

Following the discovery of his involvement in the crime, Leonard Carlisle immediately resigned from the Senate and, together with his son Richard, was disbarred from the Texas Bar Association, of which both men had previously been upstanding members. The senator and his wife had sold their home on Nantucket for an undisclosed amount of money and resigned their membership from the Harbor Club. They initially sought a safe haven at their home in Waco, but life there was lived no less under the microscope than it had been in Nantucket. They put their house on the market for three-quarters of a million dollars; there were no takers. They left town and purchased a flat in Paris overlooking the Seine River. The Carlisles' presence didn't register as a blip on the radar with the French press; they ignored the family altogether.

Richard Carlisle hadn't found any outpouring of support upon the news of his involvement, either. His law practice had dissolved with his disbarment. He divorced his wife, leaving her with the house and the remains of the former life they'd led, and fled to a resort town on the Pacific Coast of Mexico with his former secretary. Following his departure from the country, a supermarket tabloid featured his photo on its cover; it showed Richard kissing another man while the pair sat on the beach in Acapulco. Though everyone who claimed to know him discounted the photo's validity, the tabloid stood by its photographer and maintained that it was authentic. As proof, they offered unfettered access to the negative. Few interested parties responded.

Once the island had been thrust so suddenly into the national spotlight, everyone on Nantucket was immediately—miraculously, perhaps— acquainted with the Carlisles in some way or another. This one had landscaped their lawn; another one had worked on their cars. Some claimed to have gone to cocktail parties at their house. One brave soul even recounted how he and Mrs. Carlisle had spent a passionate afternoon together in her bed. But no single person who claimed to know the family came forward to defend them. It seemed that all of the friendships the Carlisles had worked so hard to cultivate and deemed so important to their lives had evaporated overnight, and those friends—real and imaginary alike—were suddenly unavailable for support.

There had been no legal inquiry into the murder in terms of the family, as McKenzie's incrimination of the Carlisles was obtained, their lawyers had successfully argued, as a result of illegally obtained evidence. There would be no trial in the case of the Carlisle family. After the revocation of his immunity deal, however, Jamie McKenzie had pled guilty to facilitating the murder and been given a fifteen year sentence in the state penitentiary as part of a plea bargain he'd worked out with the prosecutor's office, a deal that had included, among other things, his full disclosure of his knowledge regarding the Carlisle family's involvement.

The Carlisles, it seemed, had gotten away with the crime from a legal standpoint, though their social and political standing, along with the perfect image they had valued so highly and worked so hard to protect, had been destroyed.

Those who traded stories often wondered amongst themselves if the family hadn't been punished more severely by the loss of their social status and pristine image than they would have been punished in a jail. There were many, though, who relished the thought of the senator doing prison time. But to their disgust, that day of ultimate justice would never come.

The mailman came into Davy Jones' Locker whistling softly and deposited the day's mail on the counter. "Anything to go out?" he asked Peter.

"No, not today, thanks," Peter said smiling. He gathered up the mail and began to sort through it. A few bills from wholesalers, catalogs and a bank statement. *Nothing exciting,* he thought to himself. Then he saw, mixed in with the mail, a small picture of a topless woman sitting on a beach. Across the top of the picture, in large red letters, was written, "IT'S REALLY BETTER IN BELIZE!" Peter laughed out loud and turned the card over.

"Peter," the message began, "I told you I'd make the news one day. I just never thought it would be as an anonymous source. Give Steph a big kiss for me. You guys get down here soon. I hear the diving's great. Yours—Andy."

Peter laughed again. "Holy shit," he said, shaking his head slightly. Above Peter's head was a wooden shelf, the bottom of which was decorated with pictures from various places. He took a piece of tape and secured the postcard to the shelf. "Good for you, you old pirate," he said to the postcard, a huge smile of approval growing larger and larger across his face. "Good for you."

Printed in the United States
34978LVS00006B/67-78